About the Author

Ashley A. Sorrell is an upcoming author of fantasy, though her interests spread out to all genres, which she hopes to explore. She was born in Ontario and has lived there her whole life. When not writing, she can be found reading, leaving bookstores with piles of books in her arms, or taking up her new hobby, playing bass.

The Fatal Prophecy Vol. 1

Ashley A. Sorrell

The Fatal Prophecy Vol. 1

Olympia Publishers
London

www.olympiapublishers.com
OLYMPIA PAPERBACK EDITION

A CIP catalogue record for this title is
available from the British Library.

ISBN: 978-1-80074-272-7

This is a work of fiction.
Names, characters, places and incidents originate from the writer's imagination.
Any resemblance to actual persons, living or dead, is purely coincidental.

First Published in 2022

Olympia Publishers
Tallis House
2 Tallis Street
London
EC4Y 0AB

Printed in Great Britain

Dedication

This book is dedicated to my Uncle Greg, who helped my imagination blossom, my mother, Lucy, my biggest supporter, and Dylan, who was the first to read my novel.

CHAPTER 1

A tiny, young woman with ashen skin and pale green eyes stared vacantly at the floor as she sat upon her throne next to the king's, which sat empty. The room's entrance doors creaked open, echoing throughout the spacious room. Her eyes remained on the stone tiles.

The windows along the left side of the black wall howled as thunder rolled outside. Water dripped in from one of the windows where a crack had formed earlier, after one of the princess's shrill cries.

Alongside the opposite wall was a choir of witches dressed in a mix of purple and black robes, singing sullen tunes all hours of the day, only taking a five-minute rest between each song. The knights and anyone who wasn't the king or Princess Bella found the choir quite eerie and disturbing.

Upon the knights' arrival, the choir stopped and began to whisper.

Bella shot the choir a glance, and immediately they knew to continue their song. The princess looked back down to the floor.

"Your Royal Highness," one of the three knights said as they bowed, eyeing the choir, whose music made today's events seem even more haunting.

"We searched the valleys, the caves, every home, and every store," the knight who stood to the right began. He let out a gulp. "The king was nowhere to be found."

The princess snapped her head up. She let out a scream filled with all the rage and pain that she had bottled up inside of her. "I want him found!" She struck her small fists against the black metal armrests on her seat.

The knight's eyes widened; they had seen Bella angry before, but with the king gone, it seemed like the seal that had helped contain her anger, had been lifted. She was now able to let it all out.

"We've looked," the same knight continued to speak.

Before he could continue talking, the girl's irises washed over with a purple glow. She lifted her hand, fingers opened, which she aimed straight at the knight beside him. As she balled her fingers into a fist, the man began to choke. She pulled back her hand, making her grip on his throat tighter. The third knight, who stood behind them, watched on with wide eyes. The knight who spoke had little to no emotion, as he was used to the Carter family's wrath. The choking man then fell forward.

"Find him." The princess's voice softened. She spoke as if her lips had gone numb because they had. Just hours before, the news about her father's disappearance had spread throughout the entire kingdom.

The two remaining knights bowed without saying a word, scared to even breathe in the wrong direction. They straightened themselves and headed towards the door to exit and continue to search for her father.

Bella lowered her hand. She turned to the choir. "Out, all of you; return tomorrow at dawn." Her eyes fell back to the floor. When she heard the door shut, she looked up. Seeing that no one was around, she relaxed her body. Bella smiled. She had to keep up this act if she did not want to be convicted as an accessory to murder.

Sweat spotted Ben's forehead as he worked. He had held his paintbrush for so long that the muscles in his left hand burned while his skinny shoulders and back ached. His stomach was rumbling. He had barely eaten this morning.

He stood in front of his canvas. To his right was a small wooden bench where his collection of brushes and tubes of paint sat. His studio was a private room in the back corner of one of London's art galleries.

He had first discovered his love of art when he had visited an art exhibition ten years ago. A specific painting had inspired him. The painting was called *Albion Rose*, a picture of a man with many colors emitting from him. The image contained a naked man standing on a rock, the sunrise shining behind him, welcoming the dawn.

Ben had immediately connected with it. Ben was from Galdorwide, a kingdom from another dimension. In Galdorwide, witches were divided based on their auras. Their auras affected the color of the magic that came from their wands, either making purple, blue, red, or green waves. The magic colors apportioned the witches; some felt superior to others, while bad reputations followed others. Ben wished that the witches of

Galdorwide could be like the man in the painting, emitting all colors, so that no one could be judged based on the myths trying to explain the colors.

When Ben graduated from Galdorwide's School of Magic nine years ago, he chose to devote all his extra time to work on his paintings. He got this free time once a week if he was lucky. Back home, he had to give all his attention to his girlfriend and prove himself worthy of becoming her king.

The studio was cramped. To the left, right, and behind Ben were three other artists. They each worked on their paintings in their little corners of the already small room. The room was usually cold, but the owner of the gallery had recently built a fireplace. The crackling of the fire enhanced their imaginative minds.

Oliver, one of the artists, always brought his radio. He would play the sound of ocean waves, which added to the creative atmosphere. Despite the packed room, Ben felt at home in this epicenter of creativity, surrounded by fellow artists. If he had to paint back home, he would never get any work done. Here, he could work with no distractions, at any time. Day or night.

His stomach grumbled once more, and his eyes yearned to close. He rarely ate or slept. After all, he lived the life of a painter and the life of the soon-to-be king of Galdorwide. His great grandfather, Ayman Black, was promoted to a royal member by King Carter. Ayman had brought schooling to the Kingdom of Galdorwide, where children and teenagers could practice magic in a safe, controlled environment. Because of this extraordinary idea, the king transferred Ayman's Viridi aura to the aura of royalty. Pure is the only aura to be handed down from generation to generation, paternally. Ayman would have been so proud to see his grandson grow up to be king. However, this could only be official after marrying Princess Bella Carter.

Despite having a life that one would kill for, Ben would rather spend his days at the studio than at the palace. He had lived at the castle ever since he was fourteen, when he became Bella's protector, a person designated to look out for her well-being. Now that Ben was to be king, people at the castle were trained to watch his every move. Here, in the land of the Heofsijs, he was free to do as he pleased — well, besides using magic, as the magic that existed in his dimension was not the kind of magic that was used in this world. If he were to use his type of magic, who knew how the Heofsijs would react? They would most likely imprison him in some laboratory to try and understand his more direct, fast-acting magic.

Ben was from another world, one where different magic existed. Galdorwide was surrounded by a supernatural force that, when manipulated correctly, could alter the fabric of reality at a basic level. Magic was a source of energy obtained by those born with the Four Auras of Divination: Pure, Alet, Caerul, and Viridi. These aurae showed a witch their strengths and were demonstrated through magic streams that left their wand.

Today, Ben was extraordinarily prolific as he painted. He was in a frenzy of inspiration. This process was always thrilling. All his paintings depicted real-life events that he had witnessed back at Galdorwide. However, the humans, known to witches as Heofsijs, believed that Ben was merely a young man with a wild imagination. His paintings often depicted men, women, children, and creatures with strange appearances and abilities. He was also known for including himself in some of the pictures.

While in the Heofsij land, he slipped out of his royal clothing and purple cloak and threw on a worn-down T-shirt and baggy jeans. By the end of each night, blotches of every color covered his garment.

He wore his long, dark hair back in a bun whenever he painted, so as to not let it get in the way. He always leaned in close to his canvas to ensure that he could include every detail.

His current artwork was that of a cruel-faced Ben. Instead of fingers, he had steely-grey claws. This painting had to be one of his most disturbing yet, as he stood over a bloodied man. He had been working on this painting with no break. He had to finish it. He had to get the image out of his head; today's picture was of an incident that had happened earlier this morning. He stared at it, his blood curdled and his anxiety rose. He could feel his face grow warmer as his blood rushed to his head. He felt sick. The image made him feel as if he were back at the castle, standing over the king. The painting had not eased his thoughts. They only proved that the situation was real and was not going away. He lowered his brush and stepped back as far as he could without bumping into anyone.

He tried to admire his work.

Back in Galdorwide, a wolf howled in the distance, reminding Ben that a full moon was on its way. The leaves rustled as the wind rushed them in circles on the forest floor up ahead.

The wind was taking the leaves and brushing them off the path, making way for the soon-to-be queen. The night creatures stirred, making their buzzing noises. Bella appeared in the middle of the trail with Maddox, her most trusted knight. Twigs snapped between her heels as she walked over to Ben; a tawny owl sounded in the sky as a crow let out a horrifying caw. Bella shuffled her feet, brushing the dirt out of the way. A quick smile formed on her face once her eyes met his. Maddox tapped his fingers along the handle of his sword. Being reminded of the knight's presence, she made sure to frown.

"I can't believe it," Bella spoke, her lips numb from the cold as she talked to her boyfriend as they then began to head towards the castle.

Bella's mood was always a flip of a coin. Today, it had undoubtedly landed on the opposing side.

Ben walked carefully next to his girlfriend. To Ben, "girlfriend" seemed like the wrong word to describe her. To him, she was his soulmate.

They had been friends ever since he was hired to be Bella's protector. His initial job was to keep her safe as she attended Galdorwide High years back. He never let anyone get too close to him. Bella was the only exception.

King Carter had initially assigned Zein Scaasi to Bella, whom she refused to have as her protector. Because of this, she went to school with no one looking out for her safety. That was, until the annual Purification ceremony for the new, successful trainees. At this event, an old witch tried attacking Bella. A young Ben had intervened. He had pushed Bella out of the spell's path, allowing a knight to tackle the witch. The king then rewarded Ben by offering him the opportunity of becoming his eldest daughter's protector. Ben was attractive, protective, and had royal blood in him. He was perfect.

As they grew up, Ben noticed just how alike they were becoming. His hair grew darker and hers lighter until they were of the identical shade. For as long as Bella could remember, she had a scar across her forehead. After five years of dating, Ben had gotten into a broom accident that left him with a mark in the same spot.

Despite their outward similarities, they could not contrast more in personalities. Bella had a quick temper, and many prayed not to encounter her wrath of harsh words and insults. Despite this, Ben had fallen in love with her kind heart — no matter how deeply buried it was — and Bella had fallen in love with his deep care that he was always eager to lend.

"Can you give us a moment?" Bella turned to Maddox. "I'll meet you at the castle."

The guard bowed and took a seat on a nearby rock, giving them space, knowing not to head towards the castle until they were far out of sight. The king and the princess had made it clear that if any guard ever overheard a conversation meant to be private, the punishment would be death.

"If things keep going like this, we'll be thrown in prison," Bella said, looking over her shoulder to make sure her guard was keeping his distance and not looking over.

The couple continued walking. Tonight, was chillier than usual, as a soft wind blew around the duo. It was around this time of year that the weather usually took a turn for the worse.

Ben wore a purple cloak over a white dress shirt. His nightly walks had finally worn out his shiny black shoes. He could tell, as he felt the cold air and mud filter through the many holes.

Bella's wardrobe, on the other hand, was in much better shape. She wore her purple cloak over a blue corset-dress. The fabric was thin, and she wished that she had chosen warmer attire. Ben, who saw her shivering, wrapped his arm around her.

Galdorwide's forest was a collection of thin trees with thick, green leaves, no matter the season. At night, the woods were lit up by thousands of brightly shining fairies. The forest was a place for werewolves to roam, witches to camp, and home to Galdorwide's Phoenix Owls, the owls with fiery, red-feathered wings and orange-feathered bellies. You could always tell when one was nearby from the sound of the crackling sparks emitting from their sides. Like a phoenix, they were immortal and regenerated from their ashes when death met them.

"Tomorrow is a full moon. We will have to meet up at the Sleeping Sprite after you're done spending time in the Heofsij land," Bella reminded Ben.

When the full moon was out, witches knew to take their place elsewhere. The forest was where werewolves could take shelter and hunt for animals. However, some monsters, usually those who had chosen to become werewolves, found hunting witches to be much more fun. Wolves, specifically werewolves, had always been a fascinating interest in Galdorwide's history, as it was one of the few kingdoms with such a high concentration of them. It was not the witching hour yet, but the forest had already been cleared of its visitors. The people of Galdorwide tended to lock themselves in their homes at the stroke of the witching hour to avoid rebellious campers.

"So, about this morning," Ben began. They both had had a bone-chilling morning. "I wrapped your father in that old, stained carpet from the back entrance. I carried him out to the forest with no one seeing."

Suddenly, the couple's conversation had been interrupted. "I don't know!" a man shouted.

"You're the king's right-hand man! Don't tell me that you don't know!" another shouted. "Look what I can do!" The two men's voices were interrupted by that of a young boy. A mix of screams and cries rang throughout the forest.

Bella's heart began to beat rapidly. It felt as if her heart were going to pound out of her chest. They ran towards the chaos. In the distance, a fight was boiling between two men.

A raven flew above the couple, heading in the same direction. They ran to the edge of a large hill. They looked down at the scene from which the sounds were coming.

They could see Lewis Scaasi having a heated exchange with Alan Alderam, the late king's right-hand man. The two men cursed in front of Lewis's wife and son, Angel and Thomas, who stood off to the side.

Bella leaned over to Ben and whispered, "It seems like things haven't changed; all they did was fight back at Galdorwide High." The couple then headed down the side of the hill leading towards the heated fight.

"Your son is a spoiled little brat!" Alan shrieked as he kicked up dirt towards the young boy's face. He looked unlike himself, as he appeared to have been wearing a woman's dress and feather boa. "I should turn him into an insect for this!" Alan bent down towards his heeled boots and pulled out his wand, quickly aiming it at the young child. Turning the enemy into a bug and squishing them beneath his feet was a go-to of Alan's.

The two men had their wands drawn in the forest corner, still unaware of their peculiar audience. Lewis grabbed a lock of Alan's greasy black hair and began to jerk the man's head.

Angel gripped her son's dirty dress shirt tightly as if her hug would shield him from the view. She watched on with wide eyes. Her mouth drew down in disgust. She always hated seeing her husband so angry, and she wished that she had been numb to it by now.

When Angel looked up away from the horror, she saw her sister looking down at her and her family as they approached. She was surprised to see that Bella looked worried for them, a sight that she had never seen before. Angel blinked to make sure that Bella's apparition was not the moonlight playing a trick on her eyes. It had been four years since she had last seen her sister.

Lewis gave the man another shake. He restrained his violence, as he did not want his son to witness a brutal beating at such a young age. *That can be something he can see when he turns twelve*, Lewis thought to himself. The anger inside him did not cease. How could it, when someone as disturbing as Alan could assault him and his family?

Bella and Ben approached Angel and her family. Bella began to guide her sister and her nephew away from the two violent men with a gentle pat on Angel's shoulder. Usually, Angel would not have been so quick to follow her sister, but now she would rather be around her cruel sister than her husband for the time being.

Now that Angel and Thomas were not looking, Lewis could do whatever he wanted to Alan. Lewis struck the top of Alan's head once. Alan fell. Lewis bent down and repeatedly slammed his massive fist off the man's skull. Once Lewis grew bored, like a cat with a dead mouse, he turned his attention to the couple who had led his wife away.

He knew who they were. The thought of this only added fuel to the fire within him. The couple was wearing plum-colored robes, the Royal House Cloaks. They must have had some nerve, showing up around him and his wife after all this time of scorning their existence. Temper flaring up once again, he approached his family and the royals. He noticed that his wife was smiling. Then it struck him. His wife was happy to see her sister, the sister who had kicked her out of the royal family four years ago.

A conspiracy of ravens flew overhead. Thomas looked up at the blackbirds with gazing eyes and an open mouth. "Bird!" Thomas pointed to the sky and repeated the word as many times as there were ravens.

Shortly after the long walk, the broken family headed to the Galdorwide Café, where they would enjoy some hot tea and freshly baked bread.

Glasses clanged together as the café workers prepared drinks. The usually bustling café was nearly empty. The silence allowed their ears to hear the quietest drip from the Caffeine Quake maker into its pot. A man in a black hooded cloak stood in front of the counter, waiting to pay for the light meal given to him. He handed the cashier some coins with his thick, dirty hand. His heavy footsteps creaked on the wooden floor as he headed out of the café but not before bowing to the princesses.

"I am so sorry for your loss." His deep voice rippled throughout the quiet café.

The women curtsied before the group walked over to the extended table near the counter. A middle-aged woman with long, braided brown hair could be heard sipping her coffee.

Her swallows seemed boisterous in the deadened room. She began to stir her coffee; the spoon's clanging created an ear-ringing echo that sounded as if she wanted to make a toast. The woman flipped through the newspaper, not caring that the only sounds in the room were coming from her.

Soon, quiet chatter filled the room as eyes peered over to the two sisters. Everyone knew about their father's disappearance, as well as the sisters' strained relationship with one another. It had been so long since the two sisters had even been in the same room. Angel had no longer been allowed inside the castle, not even for public events, except for Bella's birthday, but even then, they rarely saw her, as the ballroom was always filled with an excessive number of guests.

Angel was willing to move on from the past and begin a new relationship with her sister. On the other hand, Lewis was not so ready, as he too was not spared from the Carter family's tyranny. He stared at the couple, his eyes filled with ferocity. The usually cold-hearted, rock-solid Lewis found himself uneasy around the royals. He had never been able to pass by a royal without being stared at or hearing cruel whispers. Angel was different from the rest of her royal family, as she treated everyone with sincere kindness. She was unlike the other royals, no matter how good they were at hiding it.

"Thomas," Angel sang as she placed her son on the high bar stool chair. "This is your Auntie Bella and her friend, Benjamin."

"Worthless worm food!"

Lewis stopped dead in his tracks as his son repeated something awful that he had once said to describe his sister-in-law and her boyfriend. No one expected such a cruel remark to come out of the young boy's mouth.

"Thomas!" Angel's singing turned to scorn. She was both embarrassed and enraged. She knew whom Thomas was parroting.

The child flinched and looked up from the cookie given to him by one of the waitresses.

To be hired as a waitress, one had to be a Reordian, a mind reader. As soon as the customers walked in, the waitress already knew what the customer craved.

Despite his mother being the one to shout, Thomas looked to his father, fearing that he was angry too. Instead of being angry, fear flooded through Lewis. He looked to his wife and opened his mouth to try and say something that would redeem him. Nothing came to mind. Angel snapped at her husband and seized him every time he tried to say a word.

"You know what, Angel?" Lewis had an opening. "After all this time, I bet that these two didn't know our son's name until today. Every time you heard the name, Bella, you would recoil, and now you want to enjoy a nice meal with her? I'm sorry, but if you ask me, that's quite stupid of you." Angel humbled herself, and tears began to filter over her eyes. "I mean, I understand why you hate your sister, heck I do too, but you're just going to sit here and act like everything is normal? After she and your father ridiculed you? Sorry," Lewis looked to the couple who had not left the table to allow the couple to dispute in private. "But," his rant was still not over. "Why are we even here, pretending that everything's okay? I mean, you made it clear that you two didn't want to have anything to do with us."

Bella and Ben looked to one another. Instead of looking offended, a smile ripped across their faces. "King Carter is gone. Today is a day of celebration." Bella beamed as she looked over to Lewis and Angel. Bella leaned over and hugged her sister, who flinched at first before returning a reluctant hug. Angel still resented what her sister had done to her, and she didn't want to forgive her so quickly, but she couldn't help but enjoy the flutter of happiness that this embrace gave her. Bella then stood and walked over to Lewis, sitting at the opposite end of the table. She embraced him. He did not return the gesture. Lewis was currently in the embrace of the most turbulent person he had ever met. That said a lot — coming from a man whose family was made up of well-known criminals. His father and his seven uncles and one aunt had all been arrested — twice. Lewis sat, rattled and rooted in his position. He wondered why Bella seemed so happy. Her father had just died earlier that morning.

"We should set for home. Who knows what freaks will be out tonight?" Angel looked at her son and husband. The two men she cared about most. "Father always had his loyal followers." Angel looked to her sister. "What happened to him? You must know more than the rest of us."

Bella looked at Ben, who, in turn, shifted uneasily. She then turned her attention back to her sister. "The last time I saw him was in the dining hall last night. There are no clues about his whereabouts or any suspects at the moment. Let us hope it stays that way." Bella murmured the last sentence to herself.

Lewis kept his eyes on Bella, who crossed her arms as if to hug herself. Bella cleared her throat, scratched her nose, and rubbed her chin. She was uncomfortable, and if his suspicions were correct, Bella was not to be trusted.

Lewis gave his wife a stern look and turned his attention back to the couple. He reached for Bella's hand; she furrowed her brow but accepted the gesture. Lewis could tune in and search through a person's memory with a single touch and enough focus. He was one of two Scaasis who could perform this magic. He was born with it, and so was his niece, Caressa. It was a power Lewis had never admitted to anyone except Caressa. He began to search through Bella's memories as he kept his hand on top of hers. Once he released her hand, a puzzle of images appeared in Lewis's mind, and he began to decipher a timeline.

The first image was of a teenaged Bella talking to their high school teacher, Mr Cabell. She told him of her dreams about what she believed to be her future. The futures she dreamt of always seemed to be dark and gloomy. She was either in prison or sent to her death, which was odd because those were not things she feared during waking life. Mr Cabell was the grade eleven Boda teacher. Mr Cabell taught students neuro/psychic magic such as telekinesis, memory restoration, precognition, and psychedelic powers. Before the image faded, he could hear Mr Cabell faintly whisper, *"You're a seer, Bella."* Lewis had already known about Bella being a seer; a seer was someone who could catch a glimpse of their future through their nightly dreams, though no precognitions were set in stone.

Lewis strained as he tried to search for some of her more recent memories. Alas, he had reached some of her more recent memories. She had woken up in her prison-like chamber, of which the windows were barred. Two guards stood outside of the doorway. She had had a nightmare. Last night she had dreamt of herself in a pale blue prisoner gown, laughing with hysteria. If she was a seer, was this her future? A stormy night sky hung above her and her rotten teeth. It was not Bella, or at least it was not present Bella.

This Bella had to be in her fifties. If it was Bella of the future, she still looked good despite the pale skin and protruding bones that came with the life of a prisoner. Next to her in her cell was who Lewis believed to be fifty-year-old Ben. He looked ragged, scarred, and he now sported a beard. After awakening, Bella and Ben went downstairs to dine with King Carter. That was all he could see; after that, her memories seemed to stop.

A young waitress brought over a tray with four cups of steaming tea. In her hand, she carried a mug of hot chocolate for the young boy. On top of the hot chocolate was a swirl of chocolate whipping cream, a dream come true for the young four-year-old.

Nervous, Lewis cleared his throat. "Er — Angel, sweetheart — we should get going." It had been the first time Lewis had been cut off from viewing someone's memory.

Not to his surprise, Angel scowled. "I know, darling," she snipped with a dangerously calm voice and bulging eyes. Her facial expression was supposed to go unnoticed by the other guests, but it did not. "Why the hurry?" she asked through gritted teeth. As much as she thought she would never want to see her sister again, she enjoyed the company. It had been months since Angel had talked to anyone besides Lewis or Thomas. Being out in public, enjoying tea was peaceful, peace, a feeling that her mind had forgotten long ago. She did not want to leave.

"The word of your father's death has already spread throughout all of Galdorwide. I can already hear fireworks or explosions or both. Also, don't you find it the tiniest bit odd that your sister, for some reason, wants to be your sister again on this night? Can't you see why we should be on edge?" Lewis crossed his arms.

Angel sipped her tea through pursed lips. Lewis wondered if he should dare say more, and he decided it was best not to. His heart began to sink low. He could trust their company as much as he could trust his mischievous son around their cat.

"Why don't you guys join us at the castle? Like old times." Bella beamed despite the tension in the room.

"Old times?" Lewis laughed. "My old times never included being invited to the castle. No, my old times consisted of being thrown out of the Royal Garden by two hefty guards. Old times for me included betrayal and isolation. You can relate to that, can't you, Angel? I mean, I never got to sleep on a king-sized bed or enjoy a feast."

Finally, Lewis's words struck something in his wife. She began to nod her head as she erased all the feelings of happiness that she had. She felt that the chance and hope of becoming a family were too far gone, never to be obtained again.

She scooped Thomas up into her arms as she stood up from her seat. In Thomas's tiny hand, his fingers latched onto his mug of hot chocolate.

"Thomas, put it down," Angel instructed sweetly.

21

The young waitress looked up from behind the counter with a sweet smile. "It's all yours, Mrs Scaasi."

Lewis and Angel left the café. Bella and Ben did not interfere, as they knew their place; Lewis had made it ruthlessly clear.

Just then, the café's bell chimed a second time as a tall, averagely built man with blue eyes and dark hair walked through the entrance. He shuffled in with an awkward gait. He was pale and shaky. He looked down at his feet as he walked with his hands stuffed into his cloak's pockets.

The soon-to-be queen furrowed her brow and looked to Ben, who shrugged. She turned her focus back on the man, who took a Solitaire seat by the window. He rubbed his leather-gloved hands nervously.

"Looks like a new freak has decided to plague Galdorwide with its presence," Bella sneered in disgust as she took a sip from her tea.

Lewis and Angel strolled past the blacksmith's workshop. The tinkering filled the silent night as they approached the tumbling creek near their home. Wings of ravens flapped in the sky. The couple unlocked the door to their two-storey cabin-like home where the fire was crackling.

The horses' feet pranced on the dirt road as the knights roamed the streets, anticipating the king's followers to emerge and start chaos.

After putting Thomas to bed, Lewis and Angel headed up the stairs of their small home. Angel finished her excruciatingly long night-time routine of removing her makeup and crawled into bed. The familiar sound of witches rushing through the air sounded outside their bedroom window.

Angel had already begun snoring softly and murmuring in her sleep. Lewis looked back at her, remembering how much in love he was with her. He closed the bedroom door behind him. Lewis headed towards the window, where a full array of crickets huddled. Lewis's heart almost skipped a beat as the piano on the ground floor began to play high notes to low. He shrugged it off, assuming it was one of the many rats that infested their home. Outside, he could see a flock of ravens fly across the grey sky, heading west towards the castle. The strange number of ravens was the least peculiar sight seen out of his bedroom window that night. Across the street was their unfortunate neighbor, Alan, standing outside in his green velvet cloak. He stared down at the corner of the road. It looked as if he were waiting for someone, but who or what?

The only thought in Lewis's mind was how he had never wanted this day to come. He did not want his son to live in a world filled with terror. The king's followers would surely bring chaos to Galdorwide, Alan included. He was the king's right-hand man, after all.

Lewis shivered before crawling into their queen-sized bed. Tossing and turning, it wasn't until a peaceful thought crossed his mind when Lewis was finally able to sleep. His last comforting thought was how he was proud of himself. Lewis had made it clear that he and his wife wanted nothing to do with the Carters. Seeing them again was a one in a billion chance. With this thought, he turned over to his wife, held her tight and finally fell asleep.

Alan, unlike Lewis, found himself wide awake. Fixed in position, he stared down at the end of the street from beneath his dim, flailing porch lantern. The witching hour struck, and he had no intention of leaving this spot.

The oak tree on his front lawn creaked as the wind blew around outside harshly. He could feel his face redden from the cold air's touch. A witch on a horse pranced down the street as insects buzzed around them. An owl hooted in the violent weather. Eventually, his ears grew so keen to the sounds around him that he could hear the tumbling creek that sat behind his home. A drizzle of rain fell onto the leaf-littered ground. The neighbors next to the Scaasis went outside to prepare a bonfire, most likely another set of witches celebrating the king's death.

Soon, a young lady with red hair appeared from the corner where Alan's dark brown eyes peered. He began to sweat and tremble.

The woman was tall and thin. She wore a cloak, red in color, a shade darker than her hair. The road was quiet. All he could hear was the clacking of her heels and the sweeping of her cloak through the leaves as she walked. She had hazel-colored eyes that hid behind a freckled nose. Her name was Adelaide Nillag.

Alan quickly straightened his posture and looked away from where she appeared. He tried to act as if he had not been waiting for her for over an hour. His heart quickened, and his hands began to sweat. He almost forgot how his body reacted to her presence. They had gone to Galdorwide High together, and his crush on her hadn't faded in the slightest.

Adelaide chuckled as she walked across his lawn and over to his wooden porch. She leaned in to give Alan a warm embrace. He wrapped his massive arms around her tiny body and quickly pulled back in fear that she would notice his sweaty body. "It's been too long, Alan." Her eyes admired the sight. She saw his bruised and bloody face. With his right hand in his pocket, he took her arm into his left. They headed down the street, where they would pace back and forth for the next hour. "You seem stiff. Are you okay?" Adelaide asked with concern.

Alan sniffed angrily. "You can't blame me for worrying." He grew defensive. "I'm not," Adelaide was taken back. "Wait — were you worried — about me?" He gave a sharp sideways glance. Adelaide did not flinch.

"It'd be okay, you know." Adelaide breathed a heavy sigh. "I mean, if you were worried about me. It'd be crazy not to worry. There have already been eight civilian disappearances. It won't be long before the whole kingdom goes rogue — Alan?" Her voice softened as she realized that Alan was now looking at the ground somberly.

"It does seem that way, and I'm glad you made it here tonight. I would've canceled, but I wanted to see you." Alan's voice grew coarse. He angled his head down to let his long strands of hair hide his face.

Adelaide sensed Alan's fear. "You're not worried about your safety, are you?" She suggested with a smile. "The town talks — and they all say that you, Alan Adelram, scare the king's guards and even the king himself!" Her playful tone turned into one of admiration.

"They glorify me," Alan replied monotonously. "The king had powers that no one else had, not even me. But no — I'm not worried — not about my safety."

"Well, you have one thing that he didn't: nobility." She leaned her head on her childhood friend's shoulder. Little did she know that this misunderstood man was not noble at all. Hours ago, he had attempted to turn a young boy into a bug so that he could crush him with ease.

Alan flinched. After all, she didn't know the real him, and she was showing him affection. The most angelic girl was showing a monster affection.

"Do you know what everyone's saying about what happened to the king?" Adelaide grew anxious, huddling closer to Alan as they walked. "Ben and Bella must be so distraught." She started to cry. Her heart was too big for a kingdom like this. She could always feel the pain of those closest to her.

"I haven't heard any rumors."

Arthur Williams, her boyfriend, whom she had been dating since her years at Galdorwide High, was a good friend of Ben's, and after a while, she got close with the soon-to-be king herself.

Alan reached into his cloak's pocket to retrieve his green handkerchief. He then proceeded to dab it beneath Adelaide's hazel-colored eyes. She sniffed then looked up at the moon's position.

"Arthur is late," she grimly stated as they approached Alan's property.

"Arthur is picking you up?" Alan nearly shouted. After all, he knew that they had been dating since high school, but he had hoped by now that they would have broken up. Arthur Williams's sister used to ridicule him throughout high school. He never understood how Adelaide could be with him.

Adelaide looked to the ground. Her face was becoming hot as all her blood rushed to her cheeks. She didn't know why, but she wanted to cry. "Arthur is a good guy, Alan, and you know that." Adelaide finally looked up to him. A wave of water remained in his eyes as he tried not to let it out.

"A good guy," Alan repeated, as if by restating it, he would believe it. "I should've been the most popular witch in our grade, and I would have been if the Williamses hadn't made my every living day at Galdorwide High miserable for me. I should have been a legend. I didn't deserve the life that the Williams family made for me."

"I know you didn't," Adelaide replied in a severe tone. "I can see the way that people look at me when I mention your name — all the heads in the room turn. Everyone looks down on you for reasons that he or she cannot even remember. It is not too late, and I truly believe that you can make a new name for yourself. You can become that legend that you were always meant to be."

Alan smiled to himself. He began to wonder why he never surrounded himself with Adelaide more. She always seemed to bring out the best in him. "Yeah, maybe you're right. So does Arthur know who you're with; the scum of Galdorwide?"

"Yes, he knows, and you're no scum. He'll be picking me up right here. He's coming on his motorcycle." Adelaide's face beamed with pride.

"You trust Arthur to drive you — on a motorcycle?"

"Of course," she laughed. "I trust Arthur with my life." She smiled to herself.

"Why? He's always been a careless soul, using the mechanics of Heofsijs. I mean, how can he trust motorcycles and cigarettes?" Alan replied grudgingly.

The two walked back over towards Alan's porch, and Adelaide changed the topic to their lives since Galdorwide High.

The low rumbling of Arthur's motorcycle broke the silence. The noise grew louder as he approached Alan's dark, wooden house.

Arthur had wild red hair that blew in the wind. The red hair on Adelaide's head looked magnificent to Alan; however, on Arthur, it angered him, sending his blood curdling. Arthur's large hands gripped the handles of his motorcycle with ease and control. On his feet, he wore leather boots. In his arms lay a bouquet, and that's when Alan was reminded of something he had long forgotten. Today marked the forty-seventh celebration of Nillags' day, to celebrate all that the Nillag family has contributed to the kingdom. Galdorians knew the Nillags for their charity work. They were always there when the kingdom needed them, especially when it came to helping children. They were most famous for the Nillag Orphanage, which they opened and continued to run.

"Arthur." A look of joy spread across her face. She approached her boyfriend. "What are you doing with those?" She eyed the bouquet in his arm that consisted of peach and orange roses along with daisies.

"It's for you." Arthur handed her the flowers. Delighted, she brought them closer to her chest. It looked as if she were giving the flowers a warm hug. "Hop on and hold on tight. Oh, and this is from Ben." He reached into his pocket and pulled out a basket the size of his fist. It had been shrunk to fit inside his leather coat. The basket had sweets of many kinds. She placed it into her pocket and got onto the motorcycle.

Arthur started his bike as he ignored Alan's presence.

"Goodbye," Alan said. He went to lean into hug Adelaide one last time, but before he could, Arthur took off. As he sped off, Adelaide looked back at Alan with a solemn face. She hoped that she would see him again soon.

When Adelaide walked through the doors of her home, she saw what looked like the wreckage from a tornado. Guests were swarming in and around the house. Fireworks and floating orange-colored flower petals surrounded the tiny apartment. In the corner of the room was a crib. Adelaide's four-month-old sister was sound asleep despite all the noises in and around the house. Her parents had enchanted the child's ears, so the only noise she heard was her mother singing a lullaby.

The guests bowed before Adelaide as she entered. Rather than returning the courtesy, she began to hug each one of her guests. After greeting the guests, she took a seat on the couch where she and Arthur sat firmly together. Arthur leaned over and gave his girlfriend a whiskery kiss.

The weather outside seemed to calm as owls began to hoot more gently. The couple sat together silently as they watched the fire within the fireplace crackle. When Arthur's eyes grew heavy, Adelaide reached over to the table and picked up the book she had been reading, *A Song of the New Generation*. A fictional novel that took place in future Galdorwide, about a war between aurae, ending when the auras came together to fight the emperor. Rumor had it that the unknown author was a seer and that the war was soon to come.

"Tea?" Adelaide's mother asked as she was stirring up a new pot. "Yes, please," Adelaide said with a smile.

Adelaide's orange, purring cat, Sunset, had begun to rub its body along her shins.

Lovetta Annettes, a young girl aged fourteen, let out a howl. She had successfully shot a firework out of her yellow wand outside of the Nillags' house as a bat flapped around her head.

"Calm down," her friendly, young teacher, Professor Gower Silwhet, whispered as he approached her. Gower Silwhet was not your typical Galdorian. Yes, he was a witch, but he was a wolf during a full moon. It was not something he had kept a secret, as those close to him had witnessed his first transformation.

"Ss-sorry," Lovetta said nervously. Embarrassed, she hid as hair fell in front of her face.

Gower patted Lovetta's shoulder as he passed by her to Adelaide's front steps. Once he arrived at the door, he pulled out an envelope from his red cloak pocket. He bent down and slipped the letter beneath the crack of the door. Gower then walked back over to Lovetta, who was still ecstatic.

"Amazing work," he said. For a full three minutes, he stood next to the young girl and admired the fireworks. Lovetta's body trembled as it always had in the presence of Mr Silwhet. He had green eyes and an orange mustache. He always wore cardigans and was there for anyone who needed him. She found herself attracted to him. Nervous, she blinked and sniffed, as she did not know how to act. When Gower looked down, he noticed how beautifully the purple fireworks reflected off her dark eyes. "Well," Professor Silwhet broke the silence. "I must be off. We have a long day tomorrow — back to school."

"Yeah." Lovetta's voice sounded like a mere muffle amongst the popping of colors above her head. "Goodnight, Professor Silwhet."

Gower swung his leg over his broomstick that he had parked mid-air along the curb of the Nillags' property. He flew off into the night.

Lovetta erased the fireworks with a flick of her wand and placed it inside her blue cloak.

She brought her attention to a group of male performers. They were a band called "Imaginary Kings", who were rising to fame. They often sang about triumphs. The lead singer, Elio, had an almost echoing type of vocal style. Rabbit, a man whose presence made her heart flutter, played an instrument known as haunted drums that once struck, made hollow, echoing sounds. "Saw some Black Voodoo women, saw some Black Voodoo women, I saw some Black Voodoo women, made me so very blind; I can't comprehend that she's a Black Voodoo woman," Elios sang.

Rabbit gave the young girl a wink. She blushed; she looked horrendous with her tousled hair that could never seem to untangle. She had dry lips and dark circles under her eyes; why would he wink at her? Probably just poking some fun, she thought.

The river behind them began to calm as the weather soothed. Lovetta walked over to her friends, John Jr Scaasi and Aldric Amell. The boys found themselves dancing, and Lovetta joined in. She could not help but laugh at Aldric's horrible dancing. It was so bad that while dancing, Aldric managed to twist his ankle as he tripped over his own feet.

Once the band had finished their song, titled "Black Voodoo Women", the howling shield player, Terry, came over to the group of friends. Terry was often considered "the dad" amongst his band as well as his many friends. He also spent his days working at Galdorwide High's hospital as Dr Terry August.

"Hey, saw you take a fall earlier. You okay, chap?" Terry approached Aldric.

"Bye, got to go." Lovetta ran to her horse. She was not ready to meet anyone remotely famous, even if their largest show was at a Nillags' day celebration.

Terry and John Jr helped Aldric limp over to a set of chairs arranged on the lawn for the day's earlier events.

"All right, put your leg up," Terry instructed, rolling up the sleeves of his black dress shirt.

Aldric winced as he brought his leg up to the chair.

"Roll up his pants," Terry instructed John Jr "How's the pain?" he asked Aldric.

"Severe," he grimaced.

Terry crouched. He pulled out his wand and summoned a light from out of its tip. He could see the swollen, bruised joint. "I'm just going to touch —" Terry feathered his fingertips along with the injury. Aldric recoiled in pain. It was apparent that his ankle was broken, as the bone was quite visibly out of place.

"Maybe you should take some dancing lessons," John Jr laughed.

"Hey!" Theodolphus, the basilisk marimba player and "mother" of the band and overall friend group, approached. "I happen to like his dancing. I use some of those moves myself."

"It's true," Terry confirmed with a cringe. "All right, you're going to feel a gentle tingly feeling." Terry aimed his wand. *"Inebrit et sana."* A pale, purple orb exited his rod; it circled Aldric's ankle and with a snap, Aldric's ankle was back in alignment. Aldric's ankle was coated, with two more spells, in a thin layer of ice, and a cast was placed over his ankle.

"Tingly? That garbage stung!"

"Well," Terry stood to his feet, "if I had told you the truth, you would've teleported out of here."

Soon, Rabbit joined the group. He looked at the two boys. "Hey, where's that girl that was dancing with you guys?"

"She left for home," John Jr replied.

"Why?" Aldric sneered.

Rabbit raised his hands in surrender. "Just wanted to say hello."

Lovetta was heading down the dark street, her horse clopping downhill. Coming from behind, a red wolf strolled down next to her. She was not frightened, as she had seen him before. The wolf had been following her for about a year now, ever since she first started school at Galdorwide High. She believed that the wolf followed her whenever there was a possibility of danger. The wolf only seemed to show at night when she was alone. She thought of the red wolf as her guardian.

When she arrived at her home, she went inside to grab a few blankets. She laid them out on the porch for her little friend, whom she had named Jack.

"Goodnight, Jack," she murmured, petting her wolf friend.

A breeze ruffled through the leaves of the apple tree that stood in the middle of Lovetta's yard. It was the only sound, along with crickets, that she could hear on this autumn night. The peaceful wolf rolled around on the fluffy blankets that the young girl had given him. He slept without waking; that was until soldiers ran down the road, their feet thrusting off the stone path, looking for someone or something. A small group of witches across the street whispered at the sight. The red wolf set off. He knew where he had to go.

CHAPTER 2

Ten days after King Carter's death, Galdorwide showed no signs of any of the expected outbursts. The sun rose and shone through Bella's open bedroom window. Despite it feeling like any other morning, today would be a day of significant change. Bella, on this day, would be crowned queen. Bella began to pace in front of the large fireplace that blazed within her bedroom. As she walked, she could not help but peer at the paintings that sat on top. She had never given these pictures much thought. The illustrations had eventually blended in with her ordinary furniture.

One picture caught her attention. It was a childhood painting of her in her father's arms with her mother at his side. They were all together, happy. In the image, Angel hadn't shared the same joy as the rest of her family had. She had been screaming at the top of her lungs. It was a hilarious yet cute memory that Bella held dear to her heart. Bella grimaced as she thought back to what she had made Ben do, as well as what she had done to Angel herself. Bella continued to stroll alongside the mantle. There were pictures of her brother, who had disappeared when they were all just kids. The more recent the photos became, the more it appeared as if her parents only ever had one child. The pictures were of her Coming-of-Age-Crowning to become the official princess of Galdorwide, sat among images of her mother kissing her cheek in the garden.

Angel, at the time those pictures were taken, still resided in the castle. However, she was a rebellious child, who rarely showed for family events. Everyone had thought that Angel was going to get together with Lewis's older brother, Krum, one of the worst Scaasis of his generation. At the age of seventeen, he had sailed off to sea to live the life of a pirate. Angel found herself captivated by his daring stories. However, Lewis had had his eyes on Angel for a while, for she was the prettiest girl he had ever seen. When he saw a desire between the two, he immediately moved in on her and took her for himself.

To the side of the painting was a frame that had been toppled over. When Bella picked it up, she stared at the image for a moment before it dropped to her feet as her hands began to quiver. The glass of the frame shattered, waking Ben up from his deep slumber. Not bothered, he rolled over onto his back as he tried to remember what he had dreamt. Ben was not a seer, thus he enjoyed dreams, unlike Bella, who feared them.

"Ben!" Bella shouted, unaware that the noise of the glass breaking into thousands of pieces had already woken him up. Ben, not caring about any drama that Bella wished to drag him into, remained silent. She ran over to him, unaware that he was merely ignoring her. "Look at this!" When she got to his bedside, she tossed him the photo that she had pulled out from between the shards of glass.

When Ben lifted the photo from off his stomach, he wiped his eyes and looked at it. The picture was of him, soaked in blood, clawing at the king.

"Someone knows what we did, and they have proof. What you did could get you a life sentence," Bella stated worriedly.

"Darling, today you become queen. Therefore, you will have to be the one to sentence me. Are you going to sentence me to life in prison?"

"No, of course not." She grew defensive.

"Great!" He jumped up to his feet. "Now we have nothing to worry about." He tapped her nose playfully and headed over towards his dresser. "Unless someone may want to take justice into their own hands, then, yes — we have a problem. But this is a warning," he waved the picture, "which is quite dull of them because now we'll be expecting them to strike."

Bella nodded before her worried expression returned. "What if someone sabotages my crowning?"

"Stop worrying. No one would dare mess with you, especially if whoever sent this knows what I did to your father." He gave her a cute smirk. He then pulled a white dress shirt over his bare chest and swapped his pajama pants for a pair of black slacks.

For a moment, what Ben had said comforted her. Bella was to be queen. Therefore, she need not worry. That was until she remembered the dream that she had had the night before her father's death. Her future with Ben showed them going insane on Galdorwide's private island prison. Its placement was meant to keep the prisoners from ever returning to civilization.

When the couple had finally dressed for breakfast, they headed down to the dining hall. Ben had his long hair combed back, giving his hair a fresh, flowy look. He wore a navy-colored suit with a matching tie, and he wore his white dress shirt with its collars standing upright. Bella, on the other hand, had yet to brush her hair. Her curly hair would only become frizzier, so she never bothered. She was wearing a ceremonial gold dress. Today, her purple cloak of royalty would become gold, the All-Powerful Cloak. She had danced in front of her mirror before heading down. She was awestruck by the gold dress with its see-through laced arms.

"I gave you an extra serving, Bella," said the sweet, plump chef. "I've known you all your life, and you've always been so small for your age. You are to be the queen, so you must look like one."

Bella was thin in her face and had knobbly knees. She had long black hair that seemed to consume the rest of her body. Despite these flaws, Bella also had a few flattering assets. She had emerald green eyes and a scar on her forehead that she believed made her look mysterious. Bella had gotten the injury at a young age. For the longest time, the scar filled her with shame, but she learned to embrace it. It reminded her of what she has been through and to never let it happen again. Ben never did ask her about the scar. He knew that if he were to ask her, her answer would most likely be a lie.

The chef placed two plates in front of the couple. Ben had his usual portion, while Bella's had a little extra food, making her plate look similar to Ben's. Bella sat at the head of the table while Ben sat immediately to her right.

"Won't you finally comb your hair? For today at least." The chef had one more criticism.

Luckily, Bella considered him like an uncle, so she didn't mind the odd tease. "I think messy hair gives me character, don't you?" She smiled.

"Well, it may, but you should consider a haircut, Rapunzel." The chef nudged her with his elbow.

No matter how many haircuts she got, her hair would rapidly grow back. It was a trait that was unique to her. When she was younger, her parents believed that this was a sign of lycanthropy. Since she was in her late twenties and had yet to transform, lycanthropy was out of the question.

The large, pink-faced man left the room with a cheerful smile. Alan walked solemnly into the kitchen as the chef exited. Alan's dark eyes seemed damp. Not from being reminded of the king's disappearance ten days before, but because Adelaide and Arthur were to be married.

After Bella finished her meal, she ran over to the pile of her crowning celebration gifts that were taunting her. Someone with weak eyes would have mistaken the collection of presents for a holiday tree. Bella kneeled before her presents and began to count them as if she were a child on Saturnalia morning. Ben knelt beside her. If Alan did not know any better, he would've mistaken the young couple for a pair of angels. They appeared innocent around the presents.

Presents that she was receiving far too soon.

"I got you this," Ben pulled out a tiny box from his coat pocket with a charming smile.

Bella lifted her brow and gave him a broad smile. "You didn't have to." She kissed him then proceeded to open the gift.

Once her hands began to pull the ribbon from off the lid, it expanded, showing its actual size. When she opened it, she saw a gold headdress. Its beads would fall to about the length of her hair. It reminded her of something that a goddess would wear. It was perfect.

Bella chuckled with excitement. She placed the headdress atop of her excessively curly hair.

"Oh. My. Avalon! How much did this cost?" She looked adorable in the headdress-turned-hair-dress.

"As much as you," Ben gave a wink.

A servant, by the name of Eldoris, approached Alan and whispered into his ear. The servant was new, yet he stood out from the rest. He was tall and slim with dark brown hair and blue eyes. He had protruding ears, thick lips, and high cheekbones.

After hearing Eldoris's whisper, Alan looked over to the couple and marched over to Ben to deliver the message.

"There's a letter for you, Ben." Alan interrupted Ben and Bella's exciting morning.

"Oh — okay." Ben was concerned, but he tried to pull it off as confused. He stood up and immediately ran over to Eldoris, who handed him the envelope.

Bella continued to open her gifts. Alan, also concerned by the letter, stayed by Bella. Most of her presents were either riding gear, dresses, or gold jewelry. Bella must have opened at least seventeen purple dresses, all beautiful and distinctive.

When Ben returned, he looked both grieved and angry.

"Who is it from?" Bella asked as her face still beamed with joy.

"Just a stupid prank."

At first, this did not strike Bella as odd, until it did, and when it did, her jaw dropped in horror. Since Alan was in their presence, Bella took their conversation to their minds.

"What did they say?"

"They threatened you, Bella. I am worried. I will let Alan know. He can be on guard as you stand before Galdorwide," Ben responded through his thoughts.

Bella looked at Ben, fury in her eyes. She did not want to spend the whole morning with her father's disturbing right-hand man. Ben felt sorry for her, but he knew that she would need to have a powerful witch by her side — just for precaution.

"We can have my brother-in-law stand at my side. I'd rather him than Alan!" She always talked poorly about the two men.

A racist father had raised her, and she talked like him. She always referred to those who wore green cloaks as if they were literal street rats.

"Lewis hates us, don't be silly," Ben replied. There was no way Lewis would ever be caught dead standing at her guard. Ben knew this. "What about — what is her name, your cousin — Anahita? She's strong and scary enough to be your bodyguard."

"She's on her vacation with Aspen Snowball," Bella snapped as if this were something Ben should have known. "I can stand by myself in front of the crowd. I'm powerful enough to protect myself."

Ben made a face like the one he had made as a young boy when he had bit into a sour lemon. "That's not an option, and I will stand by your side."

Alan stood watching the couple. They were making facial expressions and moving their hands wildly. They were not concerned about hiding the fact that they were conversing. Alan was not bothered by this, as it was a regular occurrence.

The castle's doorbell rang. Ben, frantic, ran towards the main door. Bella ran after, while Alan followed at his usual pace. When Ben opened the door, the joy that had been present on his face earlier had returned. The man who stood at the door was Oleander "Olly" Bell. Olly Bell was one of Ben's most fabulous friends during their time spent at Galdorwide High. Olly was quite skinny with a mouse-like face. Despite Olly's gentle demeanor, he was quite rebellious. He was well known back in high school as a misfit who later became normal after befriending Ben and Gower.

When Ben saw who stood behind the door, a broad smile grew on his face, and he embraced his longtime friend. Behind the hugging men, Bella rolled her eyes. Even though her father supplied Olly with a red cloak based on his Alet aura, the aura of the grounded, realistic, active, strong-willed and survival-oriented witches, she had always considered him to be of rodent species. Bella thought him to be like Lewis and Alan. She had felt her father had read his aura wrong and that he was indeed a Viridi, one of green color, for those who lived full of hate and jealousy, all the while believing the world revolved around them.

Twenty minutes later, Bella found herself sitting alone on the castle's steps. Her crowning was now only a few minutes away, and all she could picture was what her father would say.

"I'm warning you," he would say with a purple face that was right up close to hers. "Becoming a queen isn't something that is all fun and games. Any screw up, and you can bet that this kingdom will try to overthrow you, and I bet they will; you're still just a little girl."

Her father never did have any faith in her.

Bella became distraught as she imagined. Her rambling thoughts and wild delusions were driving her mad.

She ran into the kitchen in a rage of defiance, grabbed a pair of scissors in one hand, and the other she balled into a fist of anger and hatred towards her father, because he never did have confidence in her to become a powerful queen. "I'll show him," she cried, cutting the first handful of her long hair as it fell into the sink below. "I'll show all of them. I am Queen Bella Carter. Nobody messes with me!" she screamed out in pain and heartbreak. She even cut the parts of her hair that covered her scar, a mark she now wanted to show to the world.

She was no longer ashamed of her scar, that one or any other. She did not need any protection, the furious soon-to-be queen thought to herself as she walked into the bathroom to look at her new hair. Admiring herself in the mirror for what felt like ages, Queen Bella thought to herself, *Fierce, powerful, confident; how a queen should feel.*

Ben and Olly decided that they would walk beside their soon-to-be queen as she now stepped onto the castle's balcony before the crowd. The two men seemed to like her new appearance. She held herself with more confidence, and that was something that Ben found very attractive. However, Olly respected Ben and would never look at Bella in such a way.

To keep her confidence from wavering, Bella began to repeat in her head that nothing would go wrong. As soon as Bella was about to open her mouth to speak to the crowd, motorcycles began to approach. At first, she thought it was just a bunch of street scum, until the bikers flew up off their bikes, giving her a better view of the riders. The bikers began to surround her, baring their three rows of dagger-shaped teeth.

Vampires.

Bella's face turned a dark red. Half because of embarrassment and half because of the anger that was boiling within her. She began to summon her powers.

Bella was born with a purple aura, known as a Pure aura. This aura color was a usual sign that the child would grow up to be a good witch. However, being of royal blood, purple was the typical default color. It also suggested that she would have psychic abilities. Pure magic often required a wand and a cauldron to reach its full potential. Without these materials, her skills were weakened. Bella had always been fond of Caerul's air magic, where all you needed was a wand and oxygen to reach your maximum potential.

Purple smoke rose around her, and she pulled out her wand that lay on the inside of her sleeve. In the purple smoke, Ben could see black specks, suggesting that her aura was becoming tainted.

For a moment, Ben forgot about the vampires. He grew more concerned about his girlfriend's rotting aura. The crowd saw the specks of black. Their hearts grew heavy, knowing that they weren't completely free from the evil that ran in the Carter blood.

The purple wind that surrounded her wanted to ravage everything in sight. Bella, in control, did not let her powers take over her. Ben's cloud of purple wind and Olly's red flames merged.

The vampires charged. Bella lifted her wand and pushed her arm forward. Purple smog sent out of her wand and through the creatures, leaving them gasping for air and turning to ashes. A few of the vampires were able to avoid her attacks. She felt them behind her. She then swung her wand around to face them. Purple smog and red flames raced after the monsters.

"*Grama bomban*!" A dim, purple, glowing spike exited Ben's wand, striking Bella. It cast a skin-like barrier of demonic energy around her. He had done so, seeing she seemed to be their only target.

A vampire dropped out of a tree onto the balcony. The three of them looked up, alert. "I thought I smelled rotting corpses," Olly commented.

"Go inside!" Ben ordered, despite the protective shield he had placed around his girlfriend.

"I'm not going inside."

"Don't quarrel with me. Go inside."

"No."

Pushing Bella back into the castle's safety, Ben was immediately pounced on by a vampire. They crashed through a window, landing right in front of his soon-to-be crowned queen. The two were rolling back and forth on the ground, exchanging punches and words. This vampire had noticed Queen Bella's prominent scar and snickered, "Nice scar on your woman. How about I give her another?" This comment hit close to Ben's heart, as he had a feeling that Bella's scar was something that she was always self-conscious of and for a good reason.

Ben reached for a large piece of wood from the broken windowpane. Taking it firmly in his hand, he said back, "I don't know, but let me know how you like your new scar," as he stabbed the vampire clean through his head as the vampire dissolved into dust.

Ben lay there for only a brief second. He let out a blood-curdling scream as another one of the gang's vampires entered the castle walls and sunk his teeth deep into Ben's leg. The vampire responsible for biting Ben was one that Queen Bella had known all too well. Tassos Rudd. The two immediately began fighting. Ben started to panic at the thought of vampire venom coursing through his veins. Fighting back and forth, as Ben not only had to worry about being in the fight of his life against the strongest vampire he had ever encountered, he also had to worry about protecting his love. The girl whose safety he had pledged to make his number one priority from a very young age.

However, Rudd was too powerful for the weakened Ben, striking him hard on the head and leaving the soon-to-be king unconscious. Rudd was turning his attention to the queen as he unfurled a magical sac. "You! My sweet packet of lifeblood. You're coming with me," he ominously said as he scooped up the tiny queen, who was no match for the supernatural strength Tassos possessed.

Tassos rushed out of the castle door, jumped off the balcony to the ground, and sprinted towards a motorcycle to make a safe getaway, the crowd was helpless as their newfound queen let out heartbreaking cries. However, Ben slowly regained consciousness just in time to let out one last spell in a desperate attempt to save his queen. "Dunnian!" Ben chanted as he waved his wand. Luckily Rudd was just in the effective range of the spell, as he was immediately cast away to the castle's dungeon.

Groggy and frightened but committed to proving her strength and will power, Queen Bella had ordered Alan to proceed with the crowning ceremonies. She did not want the kingdom to have to wait any longer to have its new queen! Despite the attack, Bella considered this to be one of the best mornings that she had had.

Most of the witches that stood below chanted with joy. Only a few threw tantrums. It was a sunny Saturday morning, and a crowd of witch families, stood on her property, looking up at Bella.

Alan approached Bella with a purple-beaded crown that rested on a silk pillow of the same color. The last time that Bella had seen that tiara was when it was upon her mother's head.

Alan, being her father's right-hand man, was given the duty of crowning Bella. On this occasion, he was forced to wear a color that was not black. He wore the traditional Right-Hand red robe lined with white lynx fur.

A bald man approached Bella with the Golden Robe of Righteousness.

"Do you, Bella, daughter of King Carter, swear to bring justice based on the God and Goddess's morals to the kingdom of Galdorwide?" the man asked.

"I do," Bella replied as the bald man that she had barely ever spoken to draped the cloak around her shoulders.

The man wore a robe like Alan's. He reached into his pocket and pulled out a Red Beryl ring with diamonds. He placed it on her finger. In a way, this coronation was a symbol of her marriage and loyalty to the kingdom.

"Today, you are given the kingly power of justice. With this ring, I grant you the ability to govern mercy and execution. With this power, you must bring a long-lost justice back to Galdorwide."

The bald man turned to Alan and lifted the jeweled crown from off the silk pillow. The man raised it above Bella's head as she kneeled.

Once he placed the crown on her head, the people began to shout, "Long live the queen! Long live the queen!"

"Your faith and loyalty will bring everlasting life to your kingdom, forever and ever."

The crowd saluted the queen as she rose to her feet to face her people. What came next caught everyone off guard. One second the queen was waving to the crowd. The next, she was gone. Ben howled with horror.

The crowd gasped. Bella had vanished. The crowd began to go wild with confused chatter, as they thought that this vanishing act had been part of some performance to show the new crowned queen's power. Spectators were amazed by the vanishing finale's power but also scared, because it could have been how her father had disappeared. This mystery left the crowd concerned, terrified, and scrambling yet again. It seemed as if the crowning ceremony were showing how unpredictable the future of the kingdom would be. People began to scream as a black cloud-like mass rolled out from behind the castle. Everyone ran back toward the village. The bald man escaped on his broom which appeared out of thin air.

The cloud swarmed around Alan, Olly, and Ben, and they could swear that they heard a low hissing voice, "I will become king again." The cloud ate them up, swirling them around so fast that they thought that their heads would explode. The black mass then spat them out in the middle of the forest. When Ben took in his surroundings, he ran over to Bella, who lay unconscious with a rock beneath her bleeding head.

"Bella!" He began to shake his girlfriend vigorously.

"Where are we?" Olly could only gibber. He rubbed the back of his head. Disorientated, he could not tell whether his body was lying down or standing up straight.

Ben looked down at Bella's leg, which bent in such a way that it looked as if her knee had broken off. Ben lifted her dress enough to reveal her dislocated knee. He brought his hand down to squeeze the knee back together. He was no doctor, but he knew some necessary healing powers. His hands' pale purple glow surrounded his hands. Her knee returned to its proper place. Ben then ripped off the right sleeve of his white dress shirt. He wrapped it around Bella's head where blood oozed due to the rock's impact that had split her skin.

Ben grabbed his wand from out of his suit pocket and aimed it at her head. "*Inebriate et Sana.*" A pale purple orb exited his rod, and the spell seemed to work, as the blood that had stained the sleeve began to disappear. The three men sat around her.

They sat in the dark forest, wishing that they had eaten something before they were drifted off to an unknown location. The men decided that they would wait for Bella to awake before they teleported back home. Alan had gone out to catch some food, as he was no stranger to hunting.

Growing up, Alan spent most of his teenage years alone in the forest. He would sit beneath a tree and sit in silence with his thoughts. His parents had died when he was just thirteen years old. With no family members to take him in, he would spend his nights in the forest or the castle's barn. Alan never did find out how his parents died. All he could remember was walking home from school to see the windows of his house glaring a bright green. Alan did not like to discuss the event. His friends felt as if they were not allowed to ask him about that night or even ask if he was all right. Not even Adelaide dared to ask.

In school, Alan considered Adelaide to be his best friend. Adelaide would have maybe even dated Alan if he had been more kind and had developed better moral integrity. They used to spend all their time together, with the odd interruption from Arthur. Arthur would often sit with them and boast about his new inventions to win her over.

Arthur was jealous of Alan, more so than he would've liked to admit. From the first moment that he saw them sitting outside together, Arthur knew that he would have to make Alan's life a living abyss, and he did. He made his hatred of Alan public, and nobody liked to disagree with Arthur and his pack, which consisted of Gower, Ben, and Olly.

Ben would have joined Alan on his hunt, but he did not want to risk Bella waking up without him by her side.

Ben and Olly sat in silence for what felt like ten years.

CHAPTER 3

The Queen's disappearance led the kingdom to believe that was what had happened to the king as well. It had only been a single day, and people were already beginning to celebrate. If Bella had indeed disappeared, Angel would be next in line for the crown. Angel, along with those close to the Carter and Black families, did not want to celebrate. Instead, they were too concerned about the whereabouts of the couple.

Mary Black-Scaasi, Ben's older sister, sat in her living room. She was looking out of the bright, luxurious window that led to her balcony. She was looking out over her golf course-sized yard as she awaited her family's arrival. She sat, feeling as though the world around her was crumbling. Despite her despair, she had a talent for wearing a smile. On her lap was her youngest child, aged four, Harriet. She twirled the young girl's short brown curls, letting the soft strands slip through her fingers.

It was nearing three thirty, her children and husband's usual arrival time as they returned home from school and work. Mary and her husband, John Scaasi, were unlike the rest of the Scaasi family members. They were one of the most well-kept and happiest families of Galdorwide.

John had been born with a blue aura, unlike the usual Viridi that his family was accustomed to receiving. Being a Caerul gave him qualities such as creativity, intelligence, and peacemaking. Despite the differences between him and his brothers, he never felt like an outcast.

Walking up the long driveway towards the fountain, her husband and children approached. Her first pregnancy gave her the gift of twins. One was a boy whom they named John Jr and the other a girl whom they called Spencer. They were fourteen now. It felt like just yesterday was their eighth birthday. After their twins' birth, they had three girls —Lulia, aged thirteen, Olivia, aged ten, and four-year-old Harriet.

Like his father, John Jr was the only one of his siblings to be born with a different aura. Instead of being Caerul like his sisters, he was an

Alet. An Alet aura suggested that John Jr was born to be a leader. He was well versed in sports but had an undying oath to put his family first — always.

On the other hand, Spencer wanted to spend as much time as possible out of the house. This was her and her twin brother's first year at Galdorwide High. Spencer saw a ray of hope, as she only had four more years left of school. John Jr, however, did not want his school days to end. He enjoyed them too much. He had plenty of friends and always made school less about work and more about time together. In a way, his friends became his siblings.

On the first day of school, Spencer feared getting attacked in the girls' washroom. She was stressed, worrying that the "popular kids" would ridicule her for her nerdy behavior. With this fear, she asked her brother if she could hang out with him and his friends at school. Luckily, it didn't take long for Spencer to find some friends of her own. Her spending time with her friends gave John Jr some freedom, even though he never did see her company as a burden.

Mary thought that her children looked so delightful in their uniforms. The students at Galdorwide High were to wear attire that matched their given auras. It was a tradition of Galdorwide to wear their colors with pride. However, this led to a four-way split between most of the kingdom.

John Jr wore the uniform's red suit jacket with matching pants, which only made his brown hair seem darker. Spencer wore her white dress shirt with a baby blue kilt and a matching headband. The headband, along with other accessories, complemented her coffee-colored hair quite nicely.

Mary furrowed her brow as she saw the unusual sight of John Jr carrying Olivia in his arms. Little did Mary know that the fragile Olivia had broken her leg. She had tripped over John Jr's feline familiar during their trek home.

Both Lulia and Olivia, being under the age of fourteen, went to Galdorwide's Training School that sat across the street from Galdorwide High. The girls often waited outside for Spencer and John Jr, who would meet with them and walk them home. As John Jr approached his house, he knew that his mother would not be happy. He predicted the outcome quite accurately. He was now grounded from watching the show on the video box and eating cake. He saw this coming, considering that any inconvenience that happened was on him. After all, he was the one in charge when their parents were not around.

That evening, Lulia paraded around eating her chocolate cake. She wore her red curly pigtails high on top of her head. She reached across her brother to grab the video box's controller. "Looks like tonight's feature presentation won't be *Jocks and Nerds*. Instead, it's—" She flipped the channel. "*Gossip Witch*!" John Jr groaned and looked to his father. All John could do was give his son a sympathetic look.

"Just think about it." Spencer took a seat next to her brother. "This show will teach you about what not to do when you eventually get a girlfriend." She brought a chunk of her small slice of cake to her mouth.

Lulia sat on the ground while Harriet played with her toys next to her on the white carpet. Olivia was resting in her father's usual spot on the sofa with her leg up in the air with the help of a spell, since Olivia would complain her leg was too tired to hold up longer. Her parents planned that she would be brought over to Dr Notleaf in the morning. Both John and Mary felt incapable of healing her leg themselves. Healing magic was not easy, and any wrongdoings could be fatal.

Lulia spun her head around in such a way that John Jr could only describe as "A young girl possessed by Mania herself."

"This has to be my happiest moment." Lulia brought her hand to her chest. "I'll forever remember this day."

John Jr felt the urge to strangle his sister. He kept his breath in for so long that he thought two of his ribs had cracked.

"What even is this?" John Jr asked through his tight lips. His lips always grew tense when he feared that his words would get him in deeper trouble.

"Your new favorite show." Lulia widened her smile. John Jr looked at the screen.

"If you don't want to watch the show," his mother began, "I'd be more than happy to let you do some laundry."

"Gladly." John Jr stood up.

"Don't use magic!" Mary called after him. "You know what happened last time!"

Last time, John Jr thought that he could cheat his way through his chores. He had used sorcery, a cleaning spell that he had heard his mother cast often. As a result, he had turned Mary's white clothes, furniture, walls and even tiles bright pink. It took two hours' worth of spells to get it all back to normal.

John Jr doubted that that would happen again. However, he thought it would be best to listen, as he had already gotten himself into enough hot water for the day. Plus, he didn't want to walk into school wearing a pink suit like his mother had forced him to last time.

John followed his son.

"What? You don't want to watch 'This week's HOT gossip on Gossip Witch'?" John Jr asked his father, imitating the show's opening line.

John wrinkled his nose, making his answer visible.

Suddenly, there was a quiet yet threatening tap on the laundry room door that John had just closed. When John opened the door, Lulia stood behind it with her hands on her hips.

"Mom wants to see you, Junior." Her pitch was high, and she spoke in a sing-song tone, suggesting that John Jr was, in fact, in trouble once again.

Junior let out a gulp and looked at his father, who shrugged but decided to follow his son into battle. When they re-entered the living room, they saw that Olivia's face had turned a deep red. She had been crying in pain. What else could it be?

Out of thin air, a wooden spoon appeared next to Mary. This sight brought on an automatic, in-sync movement from the two men of the household. They both ducked. The spoon was heading right towards John Jr Luckily, they both dodged in time, sending the spoon smacking off the wall behind them.

John Jr's heart began to twang, as he knew that the night would end with at least one successful spoon hit. He stared up at his mother and raised his body slowly with his hands in the air. John made the smart move of stepping away from the target zone — his son.

John Jr's hands trembled as he tried to think of something quick to get him out of his predicament. Tantrum, his cat, rubbed up against his legs, unaware that he was now in the danger zone.

"How in Galdorwide could you let something this terrible happen to your sister!" Mary shouted in frustration as she worried about her daughter's health.

Lulia chuckled. It was inappropriate, but did she get scolded? No. John Jr seemed to be the only one receiving consequences for his wrong actions.

Still staring at his mother, he brought his arms down, as he realized how silly and scared he must have looked. Mary snorted with disgust. Olivia began to wail some more. A wooden spoon smacked John Jr's forehead, and his mother didn't give warning fire. The smack was unexpected and sharper than one would expect a spoon to feel. John Jr grabbed his forehead with one hand and snatched the spoon in the other. The spoon began to fight against his fingers. His hand began to shake vigorously as the spoon struggled against his grip. John Jr's face turned red then white, and he was about to pass out from fear. He was no stranger to his body shutting down when things became too hectic. There was no way he was going to let all his little sisters mock him for that — again.

"M-M-MOM!" he pleaded.

John went to help his son. Mary looked on with curiosity as her husband approached their son. As soon as she realized what was going on, she sent a spoon, smacking his forehead. Luckily, this spoon had the order of only hitting him once. After it struck his face, the spoon fell to the ground, followed by her husband's glasses.

Olivia, weak from crying, looked as if she too were about to faint. She made a choking noise.

"Olivia! Oh, my goodness! Olivia!" Mary's attention turned to her daughter.

John Jr's designated spoon became inanimate. With relief, he threw it onto the couch. "Lulia, take Harriet to your room — now," John ordered as he placed his round glasses back over his nose.

Lulia did not move.

"OUT!" John Scaasi, who was usually calm, roared. He gently pulled Lulia up from off the couch, picked up Harriet, and then placed their hands together. He guided his two daughters down the hall to ensure that they got to their room and stayed there.

"John," Mary said in a quivering voice, "what do we do?"

John began to pace the room, still wearing shiny black shoes after returning home from working with the Ministry.

John, late that evening, would do something that he thought he'd never do. He wrapped Olivia in the warmest blanket that he could find and carried her outside.

Galdorwide only had one doctor's office because most witches could cure and heal themselves. The doctor's office was located at Galdorwide High for convenience, as some classes involved magical duels.

John was about to do something he had not done for a while; visit his family's black sheep, his oldest brother, Ace Scaasi. Ace was the eldest of the five brothers. He was born, like any other Scaasi, with a green aura. However, when Ace came of age, they realized that he was a Nullum, meaning that he was born from witches but unable to perform magic.

When John knocked at his brother's wooden door in the middle of the nearby forest, he could hear a male screaming. However, John was unalarmed, as he knew that his brother's favorite music genre included goblin-like screeches and woman-like cries. The screams lowered.

"Who's there?" John heard his brother's deep voice ask.

"It's me… John. I need your help."

Ace took a few deep breaths then opened the door. He forced a smile, but John noticed the pain behind his brother's dark brown eyes.

"What happened?" Ace asked as he looked down at his niece, who had only been two years old the last time he saw her. "Bring her inside."

The house was tiny compared to John's. Ace lived alone with his son, who had suffered a traumatic brain injury in the last year. Ever since the accident, Ace had worked relentlessly to find a way to bring his son back to normal.

Ace educated himself in the science field. He had gone to a Heofsij school in New York to avoid ridicule. There, he studied science and was now known as one of Galdorwide's most excellent doctors.

John placed his daughter on Ace's corduroy couch. He took this moment to take in his surroundings. The receiver was off the wall, the clock seemed to have stopped, and there were dents on practically every wall.

In the far corner was a video box that John remembered Ace getting from his father at eighteen — almost thirty years ago. Above the video box was a birdcage where a depressing-looking owl stared back at him.

On top of the bookshelf behind the couch was a banged-up rifle. Everyone in Galdorwide needed protection, and for Ace, that meant Heofsij forms of it. On the bookshelf were scientific textbooks as well as some magical ones.

Olivia began to bawl, as the new position she was in made her leg ache. Shortly, her crying turned into screams. John and Ace looked at each other darkly, as they both feared the same thing. Yes, both science and magic were robust, but everything had its limits.

Frequent banging noises came from the basement. It sounded as if someone was purposefully knocking stuff over.

"It's Eion. He must be sleepwalking again." Ace shrugged off the mysterious noise from his basement.

Olivia let out a strangling cry, which once again brought her father's attention back to her. Her body went into convulsions. Ace and John had to wrestle to hold her down. Despite being much older and more powerful than her, they struggled against Olivia's body. After a minute of confused and worrisome fighting, the convulsions stopped. Her tiny hand grabbed hold of her uncle's shirt as she gasped for air.

"Go to the bathroom, down the hall, the first door on the left. There should be a syringe. Grab it!" Ace ordered John, who immediately began to race off. "And grab the oxygen tank by the basement door on your way back!"

John returned with everything that Ace had ordered him to. He handed his brother the mask attached to the tank. Ace placed it over Olivia's mouth. Once her breathing calmed, he gently penetrated her soft arm with the needle of the syringe. It was a sedative mixture prescribed for his son, who would often have similar fits.

Once the sedative had done its work, Ace began to focus on her leg. He grabbed a brown wrap and began to wrap it around her shin, giving it a mummified look.

"I'll be bringing her to Dr Notleaf tomorrow to heal her." John attempted to start a conversation. However, his words only made Ace cringe, as someone with magic had once again replaced him.

The two brothers sat quietly. John held his daughter's weightless hand. He was seated on the rough carpet, admiring the reassuring sound of his daughter's small breaths.

"What happened to her? I mean, all that mess for a broken bone?" John asked, dumbfounded.

"Did she break her leg after a fall?" Ace asked. John nodded. "Then she could've fractured her skull on impact, which means that this was most likely a post-traumatic seizure. Mention it to Notleaf tomorrow, and I'm sure he will be able to cure her." There was some hostility in his voice.

"Fractured skull? Seizure?" John grew anxious.

"Don't worry, she won't end up like Eion." Ace's words were cold. "I don't have to have magic to know what you're thinking, little brother." His heart hammered with long-suppressed anger.

Meanwhile, back at John's home, John Jr was getting an hour-long lecture. Mary sipped her tea furiously as she and her son sat in the living room alone.

Mary's shouts had kept the girls awake as they struggled to sleep. Once her lecturing was over, John Jr finally shuffled over to his bedroom. He dreaded this upcoming week with the knowledge that he would have to be Olivia's slave. Mary decided that she was going to keep Olivia bedridden. She wanted to ensure that her daughter healed perfectly. One part of John Jr's punishment was that he would not have to go to school tomorrow.

At this point he was glad, as it was already the witching hour, and if he were to go to school, he'd have to be up in seven hours. John Jr, like most teenagers, would rather bask in maximum hours of sleep. However, the next day he would have to look after his sister and help his mother with some housework.

The next morning, John Jr woke up to a sweet smell that filled the house. He had smelt it before, and it was a sure sign that his mother was baking. John Jr immediately hopped out of bed and ran to the kitchen. When he arrived, he saw his mother, still in her blue night robe, standing over the kitchen counter with wild, messy hair.

"Oh good, I was going to call you. Bring this to your sister." Mary held a bed tray. It was a great big piece of fruitcake, a glass of milk, a side of cookies, and even a vase with a purple tulip. "I have to run over to the store; watch your sister."

John Jr's cheerful face turned dark.

When he brought it to his sister, she asked him to stay and sing her a lullaby. "You're ten. You don't need a lullaby."

"You're right. However, I still want to hear your horrible singing voice," Olivia replied with a cheeky, devilish smile.

She is turning into a mini Lulia.

"You want to hear a song?" John Jr asked. Olivia nodded. He began to hum. Olivia recognized the tune but could not quite put her finger on it until he began to sing the lyrics. His voice grew purposefully haunting. *"Go to sleep, little one. Go to sleep and be at peace. Let the shadows surround you and rock you to sleep. Say hello to the monsters that sleep in your closet and follow them to your peaceful destination. Go to sleep, little one, go to sleep, and be at peace. Become one with the shadows. Only to wake in the morning if the night permits thee."*

Olivia began to scream in fright as her brother conjured up the shadow of a young boy. The boy's red eyes stared through the window, and she started to cry in fear. She whipped the covers over her head. The vase shattered as it hit the floor, and milk began to soak through her sheets.

"Mom!" She cried for help. Unfortunately, she was home alone with her brother. "Junior! Stop it!"

Her bedroom window began to creak open. "STOP IT."

John Jr began to cackle. "All right, all right, he's gone."

Slowly appearing from behind her covers, Olivia had a terrified look on her face as she stared deep into her brother's eyes. "Who made you this evil?" she softly cried. It was at this moment Oliva noticed her mother's apparition appear behind her brother. So she let out a subtle smile, an expression that only seemed to anger John Jr as he began to clench his teeth in anger towards his younger sister.

"I will ship you off to a Heofsij boarding school if you don't smarten up, Johnathan Thomas Matthew Scaasi," their mother shouted at Junior as she lifted him high up in the air. "And your father is on his way home right now to deal with you. And if you ever do something like this again, it will be the last thing you ever do," she threatened as she threw John Jr out of his sister's room and locked the door behind him.

John arrived home with a severe and stern look on his face as he picked up his son, and without resisting or even saying a word, the two hopped on John's broomstick and took a trip to a rundown hostel on the outskirts of town. They shared a room with another couple that, to Junior's perception, could not afford a set up much better than the rundown hostel they were currently staying at for the night.

In the morning, they ate stale cereal that was provided to them by the hostel. Their lunch came out of a tin can. The brown, lumpy and lame excuse of food was unknown to John Jr

During their afternoon meal, John Jr did nothing but stare at his father until he finally spoke. "Wouldn't it be better to be at home now?"

It was as if his father had not heard him. They left the hostel and began to fly off into the middle of the forest and above a bridge that John Jr had never seen before.

It was beginning to storm, and they were flying fast. Each raindrop felt like a bullet from a pellet gun striking the father and son's faces.

"It's Wednesday. I missed school yesterday. Shouldn't I be getting an education, and shouldn't you be back at work?" he tried to remind his father.

"I am educating you," his father replied. "And I am working — working on my family."

"I don't need a lesson. Mom's the crazy one."

John did not respond to this. He respected his wife enough not to side against her. However, he knew his son was not entirely at fault.

"Tomorrow is Harriet's birthday. We will be stopping to grab her some gifts and a cake." As he spoke, a broad smile appeared on his face. His little girl was turning five, his favorite number. "And I know just the place to go."

There weren't many stores in Galdorwide. Most of those employed worked at the odd bakery, clothing market, bank, or school. John worked as a well-respected member of the Ministry and as a high school teacher during the week. He juggled both jobs so that Mary could stay home and care for the children and the house.

There was a small store on an island not far from the forest. The shop looked like a rock compared to the towering lighthouse that stood behind it. Inside the store was everything that a witch parent could dream up.

On the outside, the shack of a building looked miserable. However, as soon as they entered, they saw a room filled with toys and baby supplies. The store had four sections for each of the auras: Viridi, Caerul, Alet, and Pure. John walked over to the Caerul area. John Jr followed.

"Go on, find something for Harriet. Grab anything you like," John instructed his son.

The two men browsed.

Every morning, since Harriet's birth, a frog would come by the window. Every witch had a familiar. Some appeared like animals, and some as witches. Familiars were assigned to help their designated witch. A witch's connection with a familiar was unbreakable and sometimes obsessive.

John believed that the frog had to be Harriet's familiar, so he snatched it when he laid his eyes on a blue stuffed frog. John heard the rumbling outside. The ride back was not going to be easy.

A toothless man approached John Jr as he was still having a hard time figuring out what to get his youngest sister. "Can I help you find s-something?" The man's voice was buried, and it was tough to understand him.

"I'm looking for a birthday gift for my sister, and she's turning five."

The man nodded and motioned for John Jr to follow him. He led him to the back of the store.

"A young girl always-s likes-s a gift to remind her that one day s-she will become a powerful witch." The older man reached up to the very top of a dusty shelf, where he strained his arm. When he grabbed hold of what he was looking for, he brought it down and revealed a small black box. The man blew the dust off the lid. As he did this, a whistling noise came from the wide gaps of what little teeth he had. He opened the box to reveal what was inside. It was a necklace with a clear stone. "A *Beorht Homl.* When she wears this, her aura light will shine through. It will become a flashlight of sorts if she ever finds herself in a dark place. If she does not want the light on, all she has to do is take it off."

"I'll take it!" John Jr grabbed the box from the man's hand. The older man grinned.

At the register, John pointed to a baby blue cake with pink sprinkles.

The cake was sitting in the see-through icebox behind the elderly clerk. He also grabbed a five-pack of blue birthday candles. John made his payments, took out his wand, and shrunk the giant teddy bear and cake. Then he placed the items into his coat pocket. The father and son then prepared to set off into the freezing night sky.

Icy pellets smacked their necks and their faces. John's round glasses turned into safety goggles to protect his eyes. He then instructed his son to use his back as a shield.

John Jr buried his face in the back of his father's blue cloak. After what seemed, and probably was, many hours, they finally arrived back home. They had come right on time, as John's hands began to slip and slide, losing the grip of his broom.

The sweet-smelling wave of hot air washed over the boys as they entered their long-awaited home. Mary sat by the fireplace, throwing logs inside. Her hair, usually up, was now down, as she was ready to nestle by the fire and read a book. Mary was wearing her usual silk house robe. She and the house looked peaceful. She even looked cheerful to see her husband and son.

In such a joyous mood, Mary did not mind embracing the two muddy, wet men. She did not even care that around their feet were puddles of mud. She hugged them and seemed not to mind that some dirt had gotten onto her nightwear, hair, and face.

"The girls are sleeping," Mary whispered. She raised her wand. A purple wind surrounded the boys, as well as clothing-friendly cleaning supplies. Within seconds, they looked as good as new. John could now see out of his glasses with crystal clarity.

As the night fell, the storm blew around outside. A fierce wind rattled the windows as John Jr sat by the fire petting Tantrum. Mr and Mrs Scaasi sat in their nightwear, reading old, dusty books. John Jr curled himself up in a blanket.

Junior decided that he would sleep in the living room like he had done when he was younger. The only thing that was missing was Spencer lying beside him. However, he did not want to risk waking the beast. If he had, she would have been angry at first but then would have joined him. Growing up, Spencer and John Jr had been close. They often did everything together.

His parents' eyes grew heavy as they read, and they shortly fell asleep. Despite the calmness inside the home, the furious storm raged on throughout the night. The rumbling rolls of thunder drowned out their snores. One specific strike of thunder sent chills up John Jr's back, waking him up in a fright. His stomach seemed to have been making just as much noise as the storm outside. He got up and walked over to the kitchen. He looked up at the timepiece to see that the hands had stopped ticking and had stayed on the witching hour.

He was ready to return to the living room after he grabbed a slice of fruitcake, but before John Jr was able to leave the kitchen, he heard a creak. It had come from behind the patio door. The sound of multiple footsteps slapping off the deck's wet floorboards followed. He could hear the leaves crunch beneath dragging feet. John Jr began to shiver, and when the noises stopped, a final clap of thunder struck.

A bright spark of lightning lit up the deck, where he saw four disheveled-looking people stare back at him. They knocked on the glass.

CHAPTER 4

A booming thunder jerked Bella awake. "Where am I?"

Ben, who stood a few feet back talking to Olly, ran and skidded on his knees to her side. In his hands, he clutched his wand. It was a sure sign that danger must be lurking.

Her face was almost entirely hidden by the shirt that he had wrapped around her bleeding head. Her eyes glistened familiarly. Her pale, green, snake-like eyes were unmistakable.

Her boyfriend looked over her, wearing nothing but a white tank top. She reached for the back of her head.

"I think I healed you all right," Ben squeezed her hand. "Does it still hurt?"

She nodded before she slipped back into unconsciousness. Ben began to shake her. "Bella! Hey! Bella! Darling! Sweetheart! Wake up!"

When she didn't, he sat back in defeat. Olly and Alan walked over and sat beside him. "She needs to be awake to teleport back home. You guys can leave now, and I'll wait for her to wake up."

"I'm not going to leave you," Olly placed his hand on his buddy's shoulder. The two men looked at Alan.

"I have nothing better to do," he shrugged.

A noise and a flash of light in the distance suggested that a storm was on its way.

"This isn't going to be an easy journey. Who knows when Bella will be healthy enough to teleport back home? If you guys truly want to stay, we should find some shelter then," Ben stated.

The men strode off deeper into the forest. Bella laid in Ben's arms as he looked ahead, where he swore that he saw a wild, shadowy face peer from behind one of the many trees. The figure was crouched and looked as if it were smiling.

When Olly finally saw what Ben was describing, he made a funny rasping noise. "Who goes there?" Ben asked with all the absolute superiority that he could muster.

"Shut up, you prune! Are you trying to get us killed?" Olly whispered angrily to his overly confident friend. Olly went to reach for Ben's arm to jerk him back, but Ben took another step closer to the creature.

Bending over and taking the most massive stone he could immediately find, Alan hurled the large rock at the creature. The creature let out a quiet, yelping sound, as did Olly. He was reaching in his red cloak to pull out his wand, clutching it between his trembling fingers. Ben demanded that the creature reveal himself from the shadows, only to receive a sinister laugh as the beast rose from his crouched position, revealing two eerily glowing yellow eyes staring back at the men. The creature stared at the wizards but did not speak.

The wizard's eyes felt heavy. They were bored with the situation, and the creature did not seem to intend to harm them. A roaring thunder rolled, followed by a flicker of light. Rain began to pour down quickly.

Alan, Ben, and Olly pointed their wands at the creature as they hurriedly passed it. The forest lit up, and they could see that more shadow creatures stalked the forest. A wave of overwhelming heat took over Olly, as the sight had frightened him. He felt faint but continued to follow the men.

"To the cave!" Ben pointed. Ahead of them was a stone cave where they would be able to set camp for the night.

When they arrived, Alan began to take all sorts of things out of his cloak's pockets: a kettle, a string of sausages, a mug, and a bottle of amber-colored liquor. Soon the cave smelled of sizzling sausages and freshly brewed tea. Ben and Olly looked on as Alan began to prepare them a meal.

"What were those things?" Olly asked. His voice still trembled.

"They're Cwaltt Videns. They live on a whole other plane but appear on ours when death is near," Alan explained before passing the men some sausages. "We're untouchable to them."

They were all so hungry that they felt as if they had never tasted anything so delicious. However, both Ben and Olly stared at Alan suspiciously, and they never took their eyes off him. Olly worried about the safety of his food while Ben focused on the awkward situation at hand. Like Olly, Alan had also gone to school with him. They had never been friends, considering Alan's green cloak.

Both Ben and Olly had been exceptionally cruel towards him. The two boys had helped Arthur win Adelaide's heart, and that was something that Alan didn't know.

Alan had taken a bite of his food, proving that he hadn't hexed or poisoned the sausages. He then gulped the steaming tea and wiped his mouth with the back of his hand. The silence was deafening and thick. They all seemed to shrink into the shadows of the cave. The thunder, the crackling of the fire, and Bella's snores began to sound like music the more that they focused on it.

Suddenly, Olly leaped to his feet, sending Ben reeling against the cave's wall in fright. "Do you hear that?" the frightened man asked.

"Hear what!" Ben yelled in reaction to his fear. Alan took another bite of his sausage.

"GUYS!" Olly squealed. The noise he heard was one that they had listened to all night — the sound of snoring. However, what they believed was Bella couldn't have been. The snoring was constant and dense, while her chest was only moving ever so slightly. What they had heard all night was multiple snores coming from the back of the cave.

Olly turned a pale shade of green and began to quiver in his panic. Ben stared at him with confusion and concern. Olly didn't speak. He let the silence take over in hopes that they would understand why he was so frightened.

Ben strained his ears in concentration. He heard the snoring then looked at Bella. When he saw her breathe lightly, he realized what Olly had — they were not alone. Ben gasped. Olly stretched out his hand to help Ben up.

"What is it?" Olly asked, his eyes filled with terror. Alan clapped his forehead into his hand.

"Oh... Yeah." Grey in the face, they both looked to Alan.

"Oh. Yeah. What?" Ben asked angrily through gritted teeth.

"Cave," Alan circled his finger by his head to gesture their surroundings. "Forest — vampires."

Olly shrieked, grabbing hold of Ben's sleeveless, goosebumpcovered arm. "Vampires?" Ben asked. His tone remained the same.

"Vampires," said Alan. "You know, the witches that come back from the dead for their unfinished business. That we saw yesterday." Alan stood up to his feet. "Oh, and actually, they say that if you poke a vampire, it's good luck. We could use some of that." Alan bent down and picked up the most massive stick he could find within zero walking distance. Olly shrieked as Alan began to walk towards the snoring. Just like that, Alan disappeared into the darkness. The boys shook their heads.

"What a freak." They took the words right out of each other's mouth. They never could wrap their minds around Alan and his strange, abnormal behavior.

"Let's get moving before an army of vampires begins to chase us." Ben drew in a breath and then lifted Bella over his shoulder.

Olly was still white as they left the cave and went out into the rainy night.

"Bullocks!" Ben roared. He couldn't leave Alan to face the vampires alone. Who knows how many there could be? He bolted to a distance far enough from the cave, Olly rushed after. Ben laid Bella onto the grass. "Watch her — how could Alan be this stupid?" He was exasperated as he began to head back to the cave.

"What? Ben! What — where are you going?" Olly shouted after him.

"I'm going to stop Alan from getting himself killed!" Ben's anger turned into anxiousness as he approached the cave. "Never. Did I ever think that I, Ben Black, would be saving the life of Alan Alderam," he mumbled, under his breath. However, he thought back to the bite on his leg. If he got bitten again, it'd change nothing. Though he hoped that since he hadn't turned yet, the vampire hadn't infected him.

Ben had arrived just in time as Alan began to extend the stick to one of the dead-looking vampires. The vampires' snores echoed off the cave walls. There had to have been fifty, all hanging from their toes with their arms wrapped around their chests.

Ben threw Alan a dirty look. Ben looked on, his wand aimed and ready. These vampires were the biggest threat to witches. They could sprout bat wings and breathe fire. Hundreds of years ago, Galdorians once believed that these vampires were demons. However, it turned out that these vampires were once just like any other witch.

Alan reached for the vampire. Ben let out a gulp but stood his ground. The first vampire awoke and let out a blood-curdling scream that woke up the remaining vampires in the cave. "Look what you've done now, Alan," Ben complained.

Alan chuckled back as the two witches prepared to engage in battle with the group of vampires. Ben and Alan were at least lucky enough to catch most of the vampires, sleeping and half-awake, off guard with various offensive spells to take out the majority of the group before the vampires had even known what was happening.

Down to the last few vampires, the men had grown tired and decided to use their teleportation spells to cast the remainder of them to a random location, as far from them as possible. "Always have to test your luck, don't you, Alan." Ben was visibly annoyed by Alan's lack of concern for his safety and that of Olly and Queen Bella.

"Hush, Ben, clearly luck was on our side because we got out of that alive," he snickered back. "But for both our sakes, don't tell the queen when she awakens."

Bella wiggled awake from her sleep. Olly smiled down at her sheepishly. "Where is everyone?"

"Uhm —" Olly shrugged. "Alan is doing stuff."

"And…" Bella urged. Olly didn't take the bait. He just kept smiling. "Where's Ben?"

"He's — uh — trying to stop Alan from doing stuff." Olly seemed proud of the story he conjured up.

She sat up in fright. "You trust Ben alone with Alan? Alan is a terrible man, Olly! He was my father's henchman and one of the most powerful witches I know!" She shouted loud enough for the entire kingdom to hear. "And did Ben leave *me* alone with *you*?" Her tone was offensive.

Olly, however, was not offended and said the only thing that came to his mind. "Sorry?"

She groaned with frustration before she continued to ask more questions. "Where are they? Are they in danger? We all know how those men try to get themselves killed!" she shouted. A blinding flash of green light exited from the cave. Evil, cold laughter came from within the hollow. Sadly, Olly watched while Bella whipped off Ben's dress shirt and grabbed her wand before running towards the cave.

When she ran in, the boys jumped. They had thought she was another vampire. Her consciousness and courage were back. The boys seemed to be safe and sound, as eighteen or so vampire bodies lay around their feet. "You're lucky I don't beat you up! You better get your priorities straight, Ben Canis Black!"

At that moment, Olly leaped into the cave, in a stance ready for battle. He pointed his wand as if it were a sword. Once Olly saw that there was no need for courage, his body relaxed. He flattened himself against the cave wall. Both Ben and Alan were breathing heavily and decided to sit down to prepare for Bella's lecture.

"What happened here?"

"Great question," Ben began with a goofy smile. He always had a knack for making jokes about serious things. "We camped here for a few hours before we realized we weren't alone. Besides your snores, there were many more people snoring — vampires. Upon this discovery, Alan wanted to stay rather than leave. He heard that it's lucky if you poke a vampire. When Olly and I left with you, I couldn't leave Alan to die, so I ran back to help him. The vampires put up a good fight. We were lucky we caught them off guard," Ben explained.

"So? Did you get any luck?"

"I think so," Alan spoke up. "I mean, we lived after fighting a colony of vampires. That seems pretty lucky to me."

"How long does the luck last?" she asked, her temper cooling. "Well, it usually grants you just one lucky experience."

Bella charged for Alan. Olly held her back while Ben stood up to help.

"Okay! Okay! Get off of me!" The boys still held her, not trusting her. A purple wind, tinged with black, pushed the boys off her. "What Abyss happened? Why did we disappear, and why did we vanish, and why did we not go home yet? Has no one come for his or her queen, lord, knight and—" she looked to Olly, "janitor…"

"We were waiting for you to wake up to teleport," Ben explained. He began to rub the back of his head which had smacked against the cave wall.

Bella raised her wand, and a flash of violet sprung from the tip. It made a firecracker sound, followed by what sounded like a train screeching to a halt. The next thing they knew, they stood outside of the forest, someplace familiar. Her magic was too weak to bring them all home. Unusual for her, but her injuries were affecting her power.

They landed hard on a rocky path. Before Bella could stand up completely, she howled with pain. Ben looked on, terrified. He grabbed her before she could fall over. He looked down at her as she lay in his arms.

"You need to see a professional doctor. I've already done what I could. My sister, her brother-in-law is a doctor. I don't know where he lives, but Mary lives right around the corner," Ben explained.

CHAPTER 5

Bella awoke early the next morning. She kept her eyes closed as her surroundings felt unfamiliar. *It was all a dream. My father's alive, my hair is long, and I am not queen. We did not get lost in a forest, and Alan did not seriously try to poke a vampire with a stick.*

The hushed whispers of those looking over her soon turned into a thundering wave of laughter. She opened her eyes as the noise sent her jumping in fright.

"Are you all right?" Ben asked as he sat next to her on his sister's couch.

The sun beamed through the windows of the lovely home. The room was peaceful except for her boyfriend's strange family, which had bred with the Scaasis. She looked around and saw that Alan had passed out on John's lazy boy.

Her left side ached with a pain that she could only describe as her large intestine swelling up like a balloon. When she made it clear that she was still not all right, Ace crouched beside her, placing his hand on her waist.

"Don't touch me," Bella slapped his hand. She furiously waved the *Diseased Nullum Man* away from her.

"Bella," Ben began with a calming voice. "He's been tending to you all night."

"Why?" She gritted her teeth. "We have an excellent doctor at the castle."

"We required Ace's help. You were too tired to journey back home," Ben explained. Mary walked in with a tray of peppermint tea for her guests.

"Let him look at you, please," Ben wrapped his hand around hers.

Bella yawned, stood up, and stretched her arms. "I am healthy enough to travel back to the castle now." Before she could complete her stretch, she crouched in pain. Her side began to feel as if a needle had punctured her balloon-sized intestine. She fell backward onto the couch.

"Ace!" Ben called him back over. Ace placed the mug that he had just taken off his sister-in-law's tray onto the coffee table and began to inspect her side. "What is it?" Ben asked when Ace made a face that suggested that his sweet Bella was far from being healthy.

"You will be paying me for this, right? She will require a lot of my supplies."

"Yes, you needn't worry about money, just help her."

Ace looked at Bella, whose eyes shut with pain. "Have you been feeling faint or dizzy?" She nodded. "Ben, take her to one of the bedrooms, take off her dress, cover her. I'll only need to be able to look at her abdomen."

Ben did as ordered, after putting Bella under a sleeping spell, as it was the only way that she would no longer fight her way out of Ace's care. After preparing her, Ben allowed the doctor to enter.

To his fright, Ace was correct. On Bella's lower left side, a large area of skin had turned a deep purple. She was bleeding internally. Her blood was beginning to sink into her soft skin tissues.

"She will need all the help she can get; any other powerful folk here good with healing magic?"

"I'll check."

Ben left the room and returned with his fourteen-year-old niece, Spencer. "You're good with healing magic?" Ace asked. Ben closed the door behind them.

"I have a ninety-eight in Healing Art of Magic at school."

That single sentence left Ace in awe. Healing magic was the hardest of all, hence the Heofsij ways of healing still took place in Galdorwide.

"All right, stand over on that side. I will have to make an incision and try to stop the bleeding. It's your job to make sure you keep Bella healthy, slow down her blood flow, and keep her hydrated."

Ben became in charge while Ace focused on saving Bella. "Spencer, go to Alan and tell him we need a leaf from one of his alder trees." Spencer nodded and ran out of the room. Ben looked at Ace. "A full moon would strengthen the magic."

"We don't have time to wait for a full moon, Ben," Ace grimaced. "What is up with you feeble-minded magic folk praising the full moon?"

Ben tensed his jaw and clenched his fist.

"I got it!" Spencer ran in with the leaf. She handed it to Ben, who placed it inside Bella's mouth.

"Does your mom still have her tiny cauldron?" Spencer nodded.

"Okay, grab it for me and grab any leaf you can find with morning dew. See if you can find any insects; a baby, or even a cocoon will do." Spencer ran off once more.

Ben closed the curtains of his sister's bedroom and switched the light off with a twitch. Ace groaned and took out a flashlight from his white coat pocket to see what he was doing. Shortly after, Spencer returned to the room out of breath, and she handed the objects to Ben.

"I found a baby moth. Will that work?"

Ben nodded.

He plucked a tiny hair from Bella's head and mixed it into the pot with the dewy leaf and sleeping moth. He grabbed out his wand that acted like a teaspoon for the little soup bowl-sized cauldron. Ben looked down at Bella. His heart ached. It felt like a creature from the underworld had seized his lungs and begun to pull them down. Ace had made an incision; Ace pulled her flesh apart for his scientific approach to healing Ben's only love.

When the tip of his wand turned into a blazing purple, he brought it out from the pot and over to Bella's heart. He then brought it down to her open stomach.

"Do you know The Hyrfing Sanitatem?"

"I think so," Spencer said with reluctance.

"Okay, I'll say it first, then you can repeat after me. Healing magic can be fatal if done incorrectly."

Spencer nodded and readied her wand next to Ben's. Her heart quickened. After all, she was excited. Spencer never thought that anyone would trust her doing such magic at a young age, let alone perform it on the queen.

"*Beorgan Eius Healsgebedda Anima Mea!*"

A thin stream of purple light exited his wand. Spencer repeated the spell. A small blue flow of water stemmed from hers. Ace continued to work, barely acknowledging the magic that took place around him. Spencer kept pouring the rain into Bella while Ben lifted his wand to the sky.

"*Bladesung!*" Ben shouted. Immediately, lightning struck outside. Ace jumped and luckily did not harm Bella in the process. He glared at Ben. "Well, if I can't have the moon, I'm gonna need some other strong, powerful force of the Universe."

Ace rolled his eyes and continued to work while Ben gave his niece a cheeky smile. Spencer held in a chuckle.

He held his wand over the cauldron. He looked at Spencer, who did the same. "*Beorgan Eius Healsgebedda Anima Mea!*"

One last stream of fire and water poured from their wands. The water turned the light into steam. Ben mixed the cauldron one last time before pouring it into Bella's stomach.

"Whatever you guys did, it's working." Ace looked at the two of his extended family members. "Her wound is crusting. I'll be fine from here." It was Ace's clear signal for them to leave the room.

Ben walked out of his sister's home and over to the nearby lake. Spencer followed. They took a seat on two bouldering rocks that looked over the small ditch that led to a turquoise lake. The lightning Ben had summoned had cleared from the sky. It was bright and held a sun that gleamed over the lake's waters.

"How've you been, Spence?" Ben asked.

"All right, I guess," she shrugged.

"Just all right?"

"Well, it's just — it's just mum who doesn't want us to use magic outside of school. I thought that once I went to high school that, you know, I'd get more freedom. However, I don't think mum ever heard that word before."

"Shame, you're a great witch, Spence. More powerful than I was at your age," said Ben. "Your mother means no harm, and she's always been a stubborn one. Proud of her, though. No man ever dared to cross her." He let out a chuckle.

"I believe it. I don't even want to cross my mom. Heck, John Jr practically walks on eggshells around her. One slip up, and he gets attacked by a wave of wooden spoons."

"Wooden spoons?" Ben laughed. "She's so much like our mother, except my ma would take off her clog of a shoe and enchant it with a boomerang spell. It never did miss its target. Your mom means well, though." He nudged her.

Spencer sat silently and thought about this. Ben sat, admiring a young elf who played her harp from across the lake. She had long, white-blond hair and enchanting blue eyes. Her white dress flowed beautifully in the wind. She began to sing, and when she did so, civilians came bearing gifts consisting of money, food, and jewelry.

"Wonderful talents the elves have," Ben muttered, snapping Spencer out of her daze.

"That is the first elf I've seen, Uncle Ben, and I didn't even know any roamed Galdorwide."

"They've always been here in Galdorwide. They're humble folk, though, don't like to be seen very often and prefer to stay among themselves."

At that moment, a boat bumped slightly against the harbor wall in front of them. Ben took his eyes off the elf to see his old friend, Gower Silwhet, and Adelaide Nillag climb up the stone steps.

Spencer avoided making eye contact with Gower, as he was her Terra Arts teacher, a class in which she learned spells related to the Earth element. Gower couldn't blame her, as he liked to keep a professional manner while at work.

"Gower," Adelaide panted as she reached the top, "what you wrote in your letter, is it true?"

"Yes, I'm afraid so." They approached Ben and his niece. "We have some unfortunate news, Ben. We would like to speak to you, Bella, John, and Olly as well. Adelaide, do you still have the letter?" Gower asked.

She nodded and took the envelope out of her red cloak pocket and handed it to Ben to read.

"Honey," Gower turned to Spencer sweetly, "do you know how to speak the ancient tongue of Galdorwide?"

"Of course she does!" Ben piped up. "She's my niece — and daughter of Professor John Scaasi, no less."

"Okay, just read the letter to yourself then, Ben." Gower had written the letter in the ancient tongue of Galdorwide, which translated to:

URGENT,

While looking into my crystal ball, I saw a horrific sight; a sound of howling wind and bells chimed in the background of the image. Beneath Doryu Edjer's church, at midnight on May 15th of this year, I could see two dragons growling. I suspect that Doryu's dragon eggs were not replicas but real dragon eggs. The crystal ball then showed me the dragons flying over Galdorwide High, where they attacked the school and everyone in it. It is of utmost importance that we, members of the Galdorwide Ministry, take action. Our goal is to protect our students and other faculty members before the vision comes to be.

Yours Truly,
Professor Gower Silwhet

"Can we believe what the crystal ball said?" Ben asked with concern. Gower nodded.

Ben had faced many beasts in his past, but a dragon was not one of them. It had been two thousand years since the last dragon had roamed Galdorwide. Doryu Edjer was a minister who was fond of dragons and their studies. He had opened his church that he treated as a shrine and museum, to view dragons' remains and artifacts. He had died May 15th in the year 918.

"What do you think we should do, my lord?" Adelaide addressed him formally.

"I'm not sure," he said as he sat up from the rock. They began to walk over to his sister's house to deliver the news to John, Olly, and Bella.

Witches playing and walking in the field behind the home parted way for Ben and his fellow Ministry members. Spencer kept close behind them, hoping to hear more of the matter.

Ben grew lost in thought. Could dragons be living beneath them? Could this be some nasty prank conjured up by his childhood friend, who always had a knack for laughter? He would've believed so if Gower hadn't come with Adelaide. There was no way Adelaide would allow Gower to lie about something like this.

They entered John's home. Mary and Bella sat in the corner. Bella took some scientific medicine that Ace handed to her as she held her aching belly. John and Olly sat on the couch while Alan was spread out along John's chair. The men's chatter came to a halt as soon as they saw that more guests had arrived. They wanted to wave, smile, and greet. However, the look on Gower and Adelaide's faces showed that this was not their typical visit.

"Everything all right?" John asked.

"We are here on Ministry business." Gower walked over to John and handed him the envelope.

"Good Merlin," said John after his intense read.

The house had gone completely still and quiet. John hurried out of the house, alarm in his eyes. The Ministry members followed, including Bella, who winced with each step. Spencer remained inside as they shut the door behind them.

John didn't know what to say. They all continued to stare at him as if they expected him to have a solution. Bella, on the other hand, had gleaming eyes as she read the letter.

"I can't believe it! Real live dragons," she beamed before crouching down as her pain humbled her.

Olly nervously made his way out the door. His left eye began to twitch. He gave them a questioning face.

"Dragons! Dragons, here in Galdorwide," Bella filled him in.

"D-D-Dragons?" Olly stammered as he grasped Ben's shoulder for support.

"Why did you join the Ministry if you're so weak-stomached?" Bella asked. Olly was just about to ask that himself. He let out a bothered laugh.

The Ministry members walked out into John's small courtyard. Bella grinned at Ben.

"Can you believe it? Actual dragons. Here. In Galdorwide."

"And I thought Ben and Alan were the ones that enjoyed near-death experiences," Olly spoke with a smile. His body still trembled at the thought of what was to come.

"Bella, I think it's best for us three to stay out of this. Just for now, I mean, considering everything that happened in the forest." He thought back to his pounding lower limb.

Bella gritted her teeth and clenched her fists. Just as she was about to explode, Gower interrupted. However, Bella was relieved, as she didn't feel that she had enough energy to give Ben the earful he deserved.

"I agree. I wasn't expecting to see you guys. I mean, you all disappeared two days ago. I'm glad all of you are okay."

Olly's head was spinning, and he took a seat on the bench that they stood around. He stared at his hands as he quivered. Beneath his hands, he saw a black dot appear in the cement.

"Guys!" Olly panicked. The hole was growing bigger.

Before they had any time to escape, they found themselves twisting and turning down the dark, tunnel-like hole. At the bottom of the new destination, the Ministry members heard a voice that greeted them.

"Welcome," a pale man with black hair approached them with a limp, "to Dwulong." The man bowed with a wicked smile.

They all looked up to see the hole they had fallen through was beginning to shrink in the ceiling. The six Ministry members took in their surroundings. Behind the well-dressed man was a desk. To its right was a stack of cauldrons, and to the left was a sign that read "DWULONG: THE PLACE YOU COME TO WHEN YOU NEED TO".

Typing on a keyboard, hums from green neon lights and disembodied whispers echoed in the room.

"I couldn't help but overhear your conversation." The man spoke with a high, girly-pitched tone. He lifted his shoulders and smiled bashfully. "I see that you fear the day when you will come face to face with a Weyr of dragons. However, worry not. You should look forward to defeating the dragons once you have everything you need!"

Despite the strange man's gentle demeanor, Olly couldn't help but look around him. "Stand up, all of you. I'm not just going to hand you what you need! Come, come." He motioned them over to his paper-littered desk. With a swish of his wand, pieces flew to the back of the room, piling on a pedestal. "Ben, darling, if you don't mind, can you go into the freezer. At the very far left — behind the swinging doors — grab me the box inside that reads 'Dragon Liver'."

Ben was hesitant at first but complied. He gripped his wand tightly in case this man was sending him into a trap. He had never heard of such a place before, and he was sure he would've needed it in the past.

As he made his way across the room, he took note of the cawing crows that flew around in a ceiling-length cage. They cried and flew, trying to break free desperately. Next to the crate was a silver telescope that sat next to a towering shelf. Its rows were filled with oddly labeled items: "Bat Wings", "Eel Skins", "Stag Antlers", "Cat Eyes", and even 2Swan Feathers". Spell books, quills, and vials with glowing potions also sat upon the shelf.

He had reached the freezer. Snowflakes danced around him. The freezer was towering, but luckily the boxes were in alphabetical order. "Dragon liver…" Ben mumbled as he browsed. He climbed up a wooden ladder to get a closer look at the items above. On the fourth row from the top, Ben spotted the box that was labeled "Dragon Liver". He grabbed it and rushed out of the frosty room.

The man brought his wand above the liver he had placed in the cauldron and began to cast a spell.

"*Wit doth ne ascian beinnan feohgyrnes. For wit, gewill be orlegweore sum denn.*" A green light mixed with shades of black stemmed from his wand. Once the stream of light faded, the man bowed before the cauldron and inserted his hand to retrieve a marble, stone-like ball. He handed it to Ben.

"On the dawn of May 15th, you must bring this," he held up the stone, "the Excogitatoris Draco stone, to the church and place it in the eldest dragon's mouth. Once you do, the dragon will turn to dust, as well as the rest of the dragons within forty-eight feet."

"Oh, well, won't that be easy, Ben?" Olly asked. "Just casually place a tiny marble into the eldest dragon's mouth and problem solved."

The man crinkled his nose. "With that tiny marble, your survival chances have increased by fifty percent."

"What do you want in return?" Ben asked, knowing from the man's green magic that he was not acting out of selflessness.

"A favor; I don't know when it'll be or why I'll need it. However, when I do, I will summon the six of you, and you must help me to the best of your abilities."

"Not sure I can agree to that." Ben grew suspicious.

"You can take the stone and owe me a favor, or you can leave it here and risk the fate of your kingdom. The choice is yours, Lord Benjamin Black."

Ben looked to his fellow Ministry members, who all seemed to have agreeing faces. All except for Olly, who shook his head with wild eyes.

"We'll take it."

"What?" Olly squeaked just before the hole reopened, sucking them back in. Their bodies flew upward through a series of twisting passageways. Their eyes stung as the air rushed past them. A burst of fire spat them back onto John's property.

"I think I'm going to be sick," Olly moaned as he gripped his stomach. His face turned a pale shade of green, and his knees still seemed to be trembling.

"Is it just me, or did anyone else find that quite mesmerizing?" Gower asked gleefully.

Ben helped Bella to her feet as Gower helped Adelaide to hers. John and Olly continued to sit on the cement floor. Bella rested her weak body on Bens.

"The task does seem easy, doesn't it?" Adelaide mentioned.

The air grew colder and colder. The ground began to rattle as another hole began to emerge from the field, this time more slowly. The majority of the Ministry members moved away, except Ben, who leaned over to see if he could better look at the bottom. Gower groaned and pulled Ben back to safety by his shirt's collar.

"Stand back," Gower ordered. He lifted his wand, allowing a fiery red stream of light to cover the hole.

"It wanted to suck us in. Shouldn't we have gone?" Adelaide asked.

"It's not very often that these holes lead to a fashionably dressed man wanting to help us out. These holes could easily lead us to someone who wishes us dead, Adelaide," said Gower.

Adelaide knew this to be true. She also knew that whatever was beneath the floor had to have been extraordinary. Portals like these could only be mastered by one with great skill. Before the hole could close completely, a box wrapped in brown paper emerged from it. Ben picked it up and began to unwrap it.

Inside was a red, male school uniform.

"Any of you attending school any time?" Olly asked, looking around.

"My son; he was born with the Alet aura. His school uniform is identical to that." John trailed into a horrible thought, as did the rest of the Ministry members. They ran back towards John's home.

They felt ill when they entered to see Mary being comforted by Spencer. They watched Alan, as he was on his knees, trying to find a soft spot in the floor.

John Jr did not have the luxury of ending up in Dwulong. Instead, he sat before a stout woman with grey hair in an old up-do. She wore a lilac-colored dress and sat behind her desk with a stern scowl. She wore a wide-brimmed royal blue hat with daisies sprouting from its side.

"Seems your father didn't take up the offer to be with you today; shame. Follow me." She stood up from her desk and began to walk to the back of the room. As he walked, he realized that he appeared to be in a store selling gowns, cloaks, and other attire.

A giant, animated pair of scissors hung from the ceiling. Robes of different styles, all in black, were displayed on mannequins. Further towards the back were black wedding gowns and brocade suits. On shelves lining the room were feathered hats. A specific black robe caught John Jr's eyes; next to it was a sweetheart-neck dress he knew Spencer would love. He passed by racks of more robes. The shop seemed to be never-ending. There were winter hats, scarves, and briefcases. The theme throughout the store remained constant: black and silver. He even noticed a sound blast necklace that, when triggered, would make those with unprotected ears go momentarily deaf. Next to it was a necklace that appeared to be made out of marbled stone.

Next, they passed a display case of watches, above which were ticking clocks in which gears could be seen moving within. Next up were coin purses, wristlets, patches, ties, jeweled T-shirts, sweaters, and tote bags.

"Lucius, dear," the elderly lady called.

A boy around the age of eighteen stood measuring the sleeves of a black gown. He looked at the lady, and his eyes didn't share the same anxiety John Jr had. The man had a beautiful, bored face and wore glasses similar to the lady.

"John Jr?" The boy asked.

John Jr nodded. The man waved the woman off and sat John Jr on a chair in front of a vanity.

"Do you know where you are?" John Jr shook his head. "All right, guess I have a bit of explaining to do." He took a seat in front of his guest. "This is Gescirpla, a clothing store run by my mother, Madam Helen Polly. My name is Lucius Polly. Here, we sell robes, cloaks, uniforms, and gowns along with other things as long as the witch is worthy. Moreover, John Jr Scaasi, we believe you to be very worthy of what we have to offer here."

"You summoned me here because I am worthy of clothes?" John Jr asked. The man ignored his question.

The more John Jr studied the young man, the more he remembered his uncle, Lewis.

They both had similar long, blond hair, and both seemed to talk with drawling voices. "Have you got your broom?" Lucius asked.

"No," said John Jr

"Such a crime that your parents and teachers treat you with such babyish care. You deserved your very own broom two years ago."

"A wizard must be sixteen or over before they can get a broom. I'm still only fourteen."

"Yes, but you have a talent and magical strength beyond your years. You have an Alet aura, correct?"

"Mmm." John Jr didn't have much to say.

"Here, in this kingdom, we select a few from all over the wizarding world. We look for little young witches who deserve more for their powers. Here, we do not single one another out with colored robes. Unlike Galdorwide, here we only have one color of robes: black."

"What about my sister, Spencer? She's powerful too, for her age." John Jr grew guilty.

"She's a pushover, though, wouldn't you say?"

"She's shy." John Jr was beginning to like Lucius less and less by the second.

"Her future is unclear, unlike yours. Who knows how she will turn out? Brilliant? A savage? A drunk? An arsonist?"

"Brilliant. Spencer will be brilliant," John Jr said coldly.

"You sure?" Lucius asked with a slight sneer.

John Jr no longer wished to be with Lucius any longer. Before he could get up and leave, Lucius continued to run his mouth.

"You come from the Scaasi family. You have the blood of your mother. On the other hand, Spencer shares the traits of those on your father's side, and you know how they all turned out. Creeps, murderers, thieves, kidnappers, and followers of the Evil King."

"My father became a great man."

"And so have you. We here turn witches into Gescpirian Knights. Only the pure-hearted can become a knight. We train so that we can help struggling kingdoms amidst a war."

Madam Polly returned. "Have you made your decision? Our next client is here." She looked at John Jr He shook his head. "Shame. When you do, flick your wand and say, 'take me to Madam Polly's Extravagant Gescirpla Store'." Her scowl turned into a smile of boisterous pride. She propped up her wand. A stream of purple-black smoke rose and reached the store's ceiling. A hole began to grow, and once it was large enough, it sucked John Jr back to Galdorwide.

"What happened?" Mary asked her son in a panic after she finished hugging him from his return.

"Nothing," he lied.

"Blimey, John Jr How dumb do you think I am!"

"Just leave me alone," John Jr said as he stood to his feet. He stomped off to his room.

John Jr did plan to tell them the truth about Madam Polly's Extravagant Gescirpla Store. However, right now, he just needed some time to think.

Once they heard the bedroom door slam shut, they knew that they now had the freedom to speak. "What do you think happened?" Mary stood up, looking at her husband, her face still wet with her tears. John shrugged.

"When I leaned over the second hole, I saw a shadow. It looked like a top hat," Ben chipped in.

"Well, doesn't that narrow down all the billions of dimensions he could've gone to." Gower rolled his eyes. Ben shrugged.

"Second hole?" Mary asked with concern.

"Yeah, we got suckered down into Dwulong, a magical lab place thing," John replied. "Then when we got back here, a second hole opened, but Gower was able to close it before we could fall in. This box popped out of it, which is how we knew to come here to see if John Jr was okay." John revealed the school uniform.

He handed it to her. She gasped. She raised her hand and smacked her husband across his face. "Our son was in danger, and you didn't think to go down the hole and find him!" Gower took a step forward, placing a protective arm in front of John.

"In our defense, ma'am, the package with the uniform sprung out of the hole after it closed. If we had known that it would've led to John Jr, then you know we would've done something." Gower tried to calm Mary. He then grabbed hold of John's arm and moved him away from the danger zone.

"Is there a way we can see where the opening took John Jr?" Mary tried to ask calmly.

"Ratio Foraminibus, more commonly known as Dimension Holes, are conjured up only by those witches who are powerful enough. Everyone can do it with a proper amount of practice. It's usually conjured up by witches who have a specialty in air magic. A specialty in air magic suggests that those with Caerul magic are more likely to achieve the skill. It'd be impossible to conjure a hole to a different dimension or location without knowing its name. John Jr is the only one who knows where he was, and we won't be able to go there unless he tells us where he had gone to."

When John Jr refused to leave his room, each house member had tried to talk to him. They eventually gave up and decided to move on for the day. Gower took Adelaide home to Arthur. Ben, Bella, and Alan made their way back to the castle, while Olly made his way back home. John chose to take a nap. Mary decided that she would spend the afternoon with Spencer. It had been a hectic day for the both of them. Also, there was nothing better than some girl bonding to escape their issues.

"Where would you like to go?" Mary asked Spencer as she waited for her daughter to hop onto the back of her broom.

"The library?" Spencer's replies always came out as questions.

"Lovely idea." Mary took off at a much softer speed than her husband would've. Eventually, they arrived at Prosperous Spot, Galdorwide's local library. They had it all: schoolbooks, stone age documents, as well as your everyday novels.

"Now, now." Mary approached her daughter. Spencer's small arm stretched for a book covered in various symbols under the Curses section. "Who on Earth could you possibly want to curse?"

Spencer shrugged. She didn't know the answer herself. She wouldn't mind if she could find a spell that would make her mother more lenient when it came to magic. Mary took the book from her daughter's hand and sent it back up to its rightful place on the towering shelf.

Spencer looked to a cauldron made of ice crystals. "You already have a perfect cauldron at home," Mary said.

However, there were a few things Mary did let Spencer buy; the school items that she needed. They bought the ingredients from a list her teacher had written down. Next week's Terra Arts class would require herbs, dried roots, a bundle of feathers, a vampire fang, and five werewolf claws.

"Do you need a new wand?" Mary asked. Spencer shook her head. "Guess we should head home then. We still need to celebrate Olivia's birthday. Have you got her a gift?" Spencer shook her head once more.

"I was thinking of maybe a little home for her toad friend," said Spencer.

They went to the Familiar Emporium. It had many items made for witches who wished to give their familiars a gift. The store had bat cages, cat toys, and food such as mice, for anyone whose familiar, was a hawk, or any other predatory familiars. At the back of the store, they found tanks for toads.

The store was narrow and shabby. In the distance, a bell chimed, which suggested that another customer had entered the shop. The back of Spencer's neck prickled. She could sense that a strong force of magic was near.

"Good afternoon," said a soft voice. Both Spencer and Mary jumped.

They turned to see an older man with pale eyes shining and as white as the moon. "Hello," they said awkwardly.

"Spencer, Mary." The man turned down an isle supplied with the screeching mice.

Their eyes widened with fear. They had never seen the man before. Mary grabbed the tank for the toad and brought it over to the counter in a very frantic manner. With her left hand, she pushed Spencer to keep moving.

The man crept from out of the aisle with a bag of mice; the tall man towered over them. They tried to pay him no attention. He stood so close to them that they could feel his shallow breaths on the back of their necks. They could even hear the sound of his swallows. The man extended a long, white finger and softly brushed back a strand of Mary's hair.

To her relief, the cashier cashed them out, and she grabbed hold of her daughter's hand. They ran out to the broom they had stationed nearby.

"Who was that?" Spencer shouted in panic after they arrived home.

"I don't know," said Mary. John walked into the living room, sipping his caffeine quake and reading the newspaper. "Go to your room." Her voice became stern. John looked up, unsure if his wife was talking to him or not.

"Er — okay," Spencer said as she shuffled her feet towards her bedroom.

"John, we need to talk." She looked at her husband.

John immediately placed his cup of caffeine quake and the newspaper down onto their marble coffee table. He took a seat on one side of the couch while Mary sat close to him. He wrapped his hands around hers.

Mary gripped her necklace tightly before she spoke. "Hmmm — well, okay, so — there was this elderly man that walked into the shop. He knew both of our names. I didn't recognize him, but something about him seemed familiar. He walked closely behind us in the store and stroked a piece of my hair." She motioned to her locks.

John suddenly realized that maybe all of these strange events were signs that the chaos was now upon them. "Right then, I don't want you two leaving the house without me, and the same goes for our daughters. I don't want them leaving the house without me or John Jr," he said. John took out his wand and waved it around his head, where a blue sea orbit of light grew. It expanded out to the exterior of his home. "You girls will not be able to exit the house unless you're holding hands with either John Jr or me."

A commotion came from their son's bedroom. Lulia was both laughing and screaming. The ear-piercing sounds grew closer as she turned the corner of the hall into the living room. In her hand, she held up John Jr's red sleep mask. "It's three p.m.! Why are you sleeping!" Lulia laughed as she ran past her parents, who were cuddling on the couch. They looked over to see their son in his red pajama shirt with matching plaid bottoms chasing his younger sister.

Lulia sprinted for the door. Her hands were outstretched to pull it open, only for the new forcefield to push her back at the same speed she had run into it. Her body flew back, smacking into John Jr and sending them both to the floor.

Lulia's fingers felt warm. The room blurred with red and gold colors. "What happened?" She moaned, rolling her head on John Jr's bony chest. Her brother let out a bout of uncontrollable laughter as soon as he took in the humor of the event.

"Oh! Lulia!" John cried, feeling guilty.

She began to mutter, not making any sense.

"I'm sorry." John grabbed his little girl and cradled her in his arms.

Lulia looked up with a pale stare. It was common for Lulia to exaggerate or lie about injuries for attention, but deep down, John knew that her pain was real. John Jr continued to roll on the floor, laughing.

"If you don't stop that right now, I'll make a unicorn tail sprout from your bottom!" John barked.

John Jr shivered and immediately stopped his laughter as he thought of arriving at school the next day with a unicorn tail.

The late afternoon sun hung in the sky. John and Mary were preparing their picnic table outside as fairies hovered above them.

The fall wind blew softly, and the couple could hear hooting faintly in the distance. The family gathered around to celebrate Harriet's special day.

Mary placed down seven plates with hamburgers, each made to his or her liking. John Jr kept looking around, saying nothing as his thoughts consumed his mind.

"You all right, Junior? You're very quiet," Mary asked quietly, hoping not to upset him. John Jr wasn't sure he could explain how he felt, and he sure wasn't ready to reveal Madame Polly's offer. John Jr continued to chew his burger, trying to think of some words to say.

"Bullocks," he began. Even though he wasn't ready, John Jr knew what he had to do. "Today, I was summoned by a woman named Madam

Polly. She introduced me to her son, who told me that they wished to have me in their kingdom. They said that I should move away from here because my powers are beyond my years, and here in Galdorwide, it'll go unnoticed and unappreciated."

John leaned across the table, and a kind smile appeared on his face.

"I was summoned by Madam Polly nineteen years ago," John explained.

CHAPTER 6

Adelaide had finally finished unpacking for her new home with Arthur. She no longer had to do anything that her parents told her to. There was less shouting at this new place, and Adelaide no longer had to sleep in the same room as her younger sister, Dahlia. She had been half-terrified and half-excited to be moving away from home. Her childhood house was something that she had known all her life. It was a little depressing, not waking up to her mom's breakfast or her dad's hugs. It was even harder not to fall asleep to Dahlia's soft breaths.

Arthur and Adelaide lay in bed, reading. Every night before bed, Adelaide would tick off another day on her calendar. She grew anxious, not knowing the future, especially with the dragons at hand. She wanted to remind herself that every day was a blessing. Every tick off the calendar motivated her to live her life more fully.

Arthur sighed softly, stretching his arms, causing the bed to creak. Besides the thunder rolling in the distance, the only other sound was the ticking of a clock. Arthur cleared his throat. Adelaide jumped at the sudden noise that came from beside her.

"Er — Adelaide?"

Adelaide sighed and closed her book. She hated being interrupted mid-chapter. "Er — I need to be at the castle tomorrow to meet with the queen."

Adelaide sighed again, this time more annoyed.

"Would it be all right if you joined me? I mean, I'm good with Ben, but you were close with Bella once. Well, close with Angel, at least. She scares me. Plus, you guys work together for the Ministry."

Adelaide waved her hand as if to say, say no more. "Thank you."

Adelaide pulled out the letter from her nightstand drawer. "They'll probably want to talk to you about this."

"I'm not part of the Ministry, though." Arthur looked at the letter his fiancée had had him read earlier in the morning.

Adelaide stared at him. "What?" he asked.

"I think that they want you to join the Ministry. Now that, you know — we're together, together."

"Don't be rubbish," said Arthur. "You seriously think that they want me to be a member of the Ministry?"

"Yes," she said quietly, despite her fiancé raising his tone.

"They must be barking mad — wanting me. I won't even bother agreeing. I mean, the process is strenuous enough."

Adelaide smiled, trying to continue the conversation in a friendly way. "I have to stop by Galdorwide High after we finish our visit. So if I have to go with you to see the queen, you have to go with me to see Dr Notleaf."

Amidst their sleep, Arthur awoke at two o'clock in the morning and found himself too nervous to fall back asleep. Arthur got up and put on fresh, appropriate clothing for a visit with the queen and lay back on top of the covers. Arthur would put on his Alet robe once he was prepared to leave, which wasn't for another eight hours. Arthur opened his nightstand drawer to take out the letter the queen had sent him. On it was a list of stuff he should bring, or at least have at hand. Arthur knew Adelaide had to be right about them wanting him to join the Ministry. There was no other possible reason for the queen to wish to meet with him. After an hour, Arthur began to pace the room, trying not to wake Adelaide but also hoping that she would. Two hours later, Adelaide awoke. Her red hair was a mess and her face most unpleasant, the face of a woman angry because she did not get enough hours of rest. She always complained of having a swollen face when she didn't get enough sleep, but Arthur never noticed.

They arrived at the castle earlier than expected. Bella and Ben had well rested and eager faces. They both found Bella to be strangely kind. Her words and actions showed love, but she wore a nasty grin on her face, as if she were buttering them up for a dark offering.

"Well, here is our living space. Sit, sit," Bella instructed her guests.

Arthur's heart flickered, his face grew hot, and his palms began to sweat. Being around the queen was like being around a ticking time bomb.

The room wasn't as big as you'd expect it to be. There were two cream-colored couches and wooden accented furniture. The room seemed cluttered with all the knick-knacks. If Bella had not been in the room, the place would have given off a relaxing vibe. They could hear birds, owls, cats, and dogs from beyond the opened window. Their many servants walked around as they went about their daily duties.

"You're probably wondering why we asked you here today," she said with an even nastier smile.

Arthur's mouth went dry. He realized that no matter how much he didn't want to be a Ministry member, no one would dare say no to Bella. What in Mania was he going to do?

Becoming desperate for support, he reached for Adelaide's hand.

"This is such a waste of time," Arthur muttered to Adelaide. Despite his seemingly calm manners, he was panicking. In the letter, Bella had said that they only wanted to speak to him for ten minutes. Just six more minutes were left. He felt alone even with Adelaide at his side.

"We would like you to join Galdorwide's Ministry."

"And what will I have to do to become a member? Find my way through a maze? Defeat a dragon? Make a human sacrifice?" Arthur brushed off the nonsense instinctively. "No, thanks."

At that moment, they all made a weird face, including Adelaide, as if his assumptions were correct.

"Well, with the dragon age soon to be upon us, yes, we were thinking of having your rite of passage be to help us kill the dragons. Up until that day, we will put you through training."

The Ministry was a constituted body of persons empowered by the ruling king or queen, intended to enforce the law to ensure citizens' safety, health, and possessions, while preventing crime and civil disorder. Their lawful powers included arrest and the use of force, legitimized by the king or queen.

Arthur swung his head to face Adelaide's. His face grew a fiery red that now matched his hair perfectly. His heart began to hammer.

"I don't think I can accept the offer."

"You must!" the small queen piped. "We need you, Arthur."

"You don't need me. You have enough members. Why not ask Alan or a Snowball?" Bella made a face that clearly showed that she had nothing to say to that.

"Sorry, but no." He had just the right amount of courage to get past ten minutes of saying no. He vanished.

Annoyed, Adelaide gave the royals an apology and assured them she'd try to convince Arthur to change his mind. She left and headed for the school's hospital ward to meet with Dr Notleaf, who had been treating her after a bizarre incident in Galdorwide's forest. After the accident, she had had no recollection of the night's events besides the fact that she must've hit her head, and her stomach felt sick.

"Excuse me?" She knocked at the doctor's office door, which resided at Galdorwide's school.

"Hello." Dr Notleaf swerved around on his wheeled office chair. He was tall and thin, making his movements look awkward. Besides his height, everything else about him seemed so small, and he often blended in with the students as he walked through the halls.

"Hi," she said awkwardly, still not in the office as she could only see him through the crack in the door.

"Don't be shy. Come on in," Dr Notleaf said with a smile as he brushed back his long blond hair.

"Okay." She crept in and shut the door behind her.

She looked to the back of the room, towards the hospital ward. The ward seemed occupied by many students with injuries and illnesses. The students chatted, admiring their time away from class. In the room, tiny, animated teddy bears roamed, comforting any patients sent from Galdorwide's Training School. Other bears were helping the nurses bring food and candy to the patients. Some bears were also telling jokes, as laughter was the best medicine. A bear walked over to Notleaf and handed him a file.

"Just gonna take these." The bear stepped onto the tip of its paws to reach into a colorful jar where Dr Notleaf displayed the lollipops for the patients. He pulled out a pawful. "For the students, of course."

Dr Notleaf smiled at the furry assistant before looking over to Adelaide. "What can I help you with today?" Dr Notleaf asked.

"I've lost my antidote, the one for common poisons."

"Oh, Adelaide, how long has it been missing?" He stood to his feet, taking out his wand.

The tip of his rod produced a bright light that shone in her eyes.

A teenage boy with dreadlocks walked in.

"What can I help you with today, Adam?" Dr Ace Scaasi asked, exiting his office in a closed-off room to the right of Notleaf's desk.

"Lawrence's spider bit me," the boy responded.

"Follow me." Dr Ace guided Adam over to the hospital wing.

"About two days," Adelaide answered.

"You have to take it every day, all right?" Dr Notleaf walked over to the shelf to his left and grabbed Adelaide a bottle of teal-colored liquid. "Just five more days of this, and you should no longer need it."

Adelaide reached into her cloak to retrieve some money. She held up eight feohs. "No, no, on me. Just take care of yourself, okay?" He smiled.

"Thanks." Adelaide brushed back her damp, sweaty hair. Before she exited, she turned to Dr Notleaf and smiled.

Adelaide entered her home to find Arthur pacing the living room. He had ruffled hair, and there was a mud stain on the side of his nose.

"Everythin' all right?" she asked as she took out a handkerchief from her cloak. She began to scrub the mud off of his nose. He squirmed away with a wriggled face.

"Ow, and yes, everything's all right. It's just, I went back to see Ben and Bella. I accepted their offer."

He picked up the black Ministry robe that they had supplied for him, a silver letter "A" stitched on the right of its chest.

"We will be able to tell ours apart, with the size and all. Mine's the small and yours the large," he laughed. That got him a well-deserved playful slap on his arm.

"Oh, shut up."

"Anyways, I'll have to be leaving soon. I have to do some training sessions with Ben and Gower."

"You should ask for a day off. You barely got any sleep. You look so tired." She brought her hand to his cheek.

She would never have guessed that Arthur would become a Galdorwide Ministry member, not after his initial reaction earlier that day. She would've asked him what had changed his mind, but she was sure she already knew the answer.

"Nope; as a Ministry member, I have to get used to never stopping."

She smiled. "Well, at least you've finally got a new robe. You could also tell ours apart with the caffeine quake stain that's along the chest of mine."

"Ah, yes. I almost forgot. You can't multitask. Y'know — walk and drink."

"Oh, shut up." She chuckled once more.

Arthur kissed Adelaide on the cheek as he threw his robe on. His nose was still pink from where Adelaide had tried and failed to rub the mud off.

"Behave yourself!" she called after him as he left.

Shortly after Arthur shut the door behind him, there was a knock, and she heard her younger sister, Dahlia, call.

"Adelaide!"

When Adelaide opened the door, her younger sister ran inside. Behind her were their parents, Zinnia and Antonio Nillag. In her mother's arm lay the newest member of the family, Rose.

"Can I look around the house? Mom? Eh? Please?" The eight-year-old, full of energy, pleaded.

"Ask your sister," Zinnia replied as she and her husband entered the home that was much bigger than their own.

"Yes, you can. However, remember, Dahlia, this isn't a playground," Adelaide allowed.

Dahlia jumped and ran off to the staircase at the back of the house. The parents walked in, admiring the crackling fireplace. On the table, three cups of tea were getting stirred by tiny silver spoons. Adelaide picked up her book from off the couch and placed it onto the coffee table to make room for her mother to sit.

"How do you like it here?" Zinnia asked as she heard an owl hoot in the distance.

"I like it very much, but I have to say I have to get used to the quietness. I was almost thinking of letting Abie in the house." Adelaide laughed.

Abie was Adelaide's familiar, a doe. Abie had been following Adelaide around since she had turned three. She came around whenever she felt that danger might be near her witch, or when Adelaide needed company. Her family was immensely proud to find out their daughter's familiar was a doe. Doe familiars usually appeared to the witches that were both wise and noble.

"Poor dear — it must be hard for you — to be home alone, considering that that was something so scarce for you."

"Don't worry, mum." She smiled.

"Has Arthur applied at Galdorwide High? I've heard that they've been looking for new teachers," Antonio asked.

"No, no, he hasn't, but he is currently going through his first day of training to become a member of the Ministry." Adelaide beamed proudly.

Multiple bangs and crashes came from upstairs. "Dahlia!" Zinnia shouted, waking up Rose, who began to cry. "You get down here this instant!"

Dahlia clambered down the stairs. She held in her tears, but Antonio pulled her in and kissed her on the forehead. "Don't cry."

Dahlia felt a great leap of relief, as she was expecting to be scolded. She cuddled into her father's arms.

Adelaide, Dahlia, and Rose all took after their mother. They had red hair, fair skin, rosy cheeks, and freckles. Antonio, on the other hand, had hair as black as crow feathers and olive-colored skin.

Antonio picked Dahlia up and placed her on his lap. Dahlia glanced at Adelaide, then looked away. She had been angry that her older sister had left home. Now, Dahlia would call for her mother in the middle of the night and sleep in Adelaide's old bed. She was too scared to be in her room all alone.

"Hello," Arthur said, returning home with the same mud stain he had on his face from earlier that day. "Wanna see something cool?" He pulled a tarantula from out of his cloak pocket.

Dahlia jumped out of her father's arms and ran towards the back of the room. Adelaide followed. Zinnia chuckled, and Antonio seemed unamused by his soon-to-be son-in-law.

"What spider is it?" Adelaide shouted.

"A tarantula," Arthur replied simply.

"Right— bring it outside — now." Adelaide's voice turned stern.

"All right, all right, don't get your panties in a twist." Arthur walked to the door and placed the spider on the porch before sliding the door shut.

When Arthur returned, he sat in an armchair opposite Antonio. The four girls now occupied the couch.

"Are you joining the Ministry?" Antonio blurted out. Arthur nodded.

"I am wearing a ministry cloak, aren't I?"

"Oh — well, I thought maybe Adelaide was pulling my leg or something." Antonio then turned to Adelaide. "And what's that on your forehead?" He pointed.

Adelaide removed her headband and allowed her bangs to cover her scar. "Remember I told you I got lost in the forest and bit by some poisonous insect? Well, I woke up in the forest, unconscious, and I'm guessing I must've fallen and scraped my head. Dr Ace found me on his morning walk and tended to me. I've been taking an antidote, and I have five more days left till the poison has completely left my body," she explained.

"So, you really can't remember anything from that night?" Antonio asked.

"All I remember is a green flash of light, then waking up in the school's hospital." Everyone sat and stared at her for a moment. With tilted heads, they studied her to see if they could find any other injuries. When Adelaide furrowed her brow, they all realized what they had been doing. They turned to study the window instead.

"How's everything been at home?" Adelaide asked her parents, taking their thoughts off of her.

"Just great." Zinnia smiled. Suddenly, her smile turned into a frown. "But your uncle Ren has decided to escape the witching life and move to Heofsij land to live amongst them."

"When does he leave?"

"He left last Tuesday." Zinnia shook her head, still boggled by her brother's actions.

"He already left? How come he didn't come to say goodbye to me?"

Zinnia ignored her daughter's question. "Such a shame. He truly was a great witch; the Heofsijs can be quite horrible. I hope he stays safe and keeps his magic under wraps. The last thing we need is another witch hunt to occur. I mean, all those poor witches and wizards who tried to escape our world for a better one, and all they got was hanged and burned."

A gloomy air filled the room. Arthur grew anxious and immediately acted out. He reached into his Ministry cloak pocket and pulled out a fat grey rat. The rat was asleep until the girls in the house began to scream.

"His name is Cluny. He's harmless."

"Arthur, can you please put that thing outside," Adelaide said through gritted teeth. "And where in Avalon do you keep finding these animals?"

"My first task was to learn how to take care of the animals that reside here in Galdorwide. So — as I was helping — I came across Widow and Cluny. I decided to take them home with me." Arthur smiled as he adoringly looked down at his new little rat friend.

"Widow?" Dahlia asked.

"The tarantula." Arthur continued to smile as he gave his reply. "Widow — a fitting name for a tarantula." Antonio spun his eyes.

"Yes, it is, for her, at least. She and her husband had gotten stuck beneath a fallen tree. I had to care of both of them, but her husband didn't make it. So, yeah, Widow."

"That had better be the only thing you brought home, Arthur Ruairidh Williams!" Adelaide warned. "Now put him and anything else you got in your cloak outside!"

Arthur's smile faded, and his cheeks turned red. He began to walk towards the door to place it outside. When he opened the door, Widow had still been waiting outside. He set Cluny down and started to pet him before saying his farewell.

"I'm sorry, buddy. I wish you could stay, but my fiancée won't allow it."

Arthur didn't see anything wrong with a few creatures in his house. After all, they needed food and a place to stay, just like them. Arthur let out a gasp. "Adelaide!" he called.

"What is it?" She ran over to him and looked out into the yard to see the king. A ghostly outline surrounded the king's mystical body, paralyzing the couple with both fear and disbelief. Giving off an eerie wave and a chilling smile that shocked the couple to their cores, the king's apparition disappeared as quickly as it showed. Arthur, petrified with fear for his wife's safety, immediately rushed her inside the house, slamming and locking the door in the process.

Laughing in both fear and surprise, the couple still couldn't believe what they had seen, and if it was real or not. "We have to tell the Ministry, Adelaide," Arthur said with a chill running down his spine. "Bella needs to know the truth about her father.

"We've got a lot to figure out." Adelaide rested against the door. Arthur joined.

After their breathing lowered, they sat back with her family. "Uhm…" the couple pondered in unison.

"Go ahead," Arthur gestured, not wanting the burden of telling everyone what he saw; he didn't know how to.

"Uhm — we all know that the king is powerful. He deserved the crown for his power, though his cruelty should've taken that from him. Outside, and I'm sure Arthur will agree with me when I say, we saw the king."

"He's alive?" Zinnia's eyes bulged.

"No, not exactly. King Delanie — looked like a ghost."

Everyone stared at the couple, not knowing how to process the news. Arthur stayed silent, nodding his head instead of talking whenever they would look at him. Around half past twelve, there was a clattering sound coming from beyond the window. A smiling, dimpled woman popped into view. She waved. It was Alizeh Nguyen, Olly's girlfriend, and one of Adelaide's best friends.

"Can I come in?" she shouted. Her silky black hair flowed frantically in the wind. Adelaide motioned her in.

The girl walked in, wearing her purple robe. She was a Lady of Galdorwide, which many tended to forget, as she had a fun, free spirit demeanor. They also forgot about her being born royalty, as she also had a boyfriend who worked as Galdorwide High's janitor. She took off her cloak and hung it on the coat rack to the left of the entrance. She wore a black dress with silver beads dotted all over it. Adelaide grew insecure as she took note of Alizeh's toned legs.

Alizeh, who hadn't had any breakfast, walked over to the kitchen. When she exited, she carried a Berry Candy bag, a slice of Crystal Ball Cake, Bat Brownies, and some Licorice Gems. Her face turned bright pink. Everyone had been staring at her oddly.

"I — uh — couldn't decide what I wanted, so I — uh — took a bit of everything, if you don't mind." They continued to stare.

"Hungry, are you?" Arthur asked. Zinnia shot him a glare, and Adelaide quietly kicked his shin.

"Uhm — yeah — starving, actually." She took her fork and dug it into her Crystal Ball Cake.

"Toss me a candy, will you?" Adelaide didn't want her to feel odd.

Alizeh tossed her a candy. She squeezed onto the couch beside Adelaide and her mother.

Dahlia took a seat on the floor to make room for her sister's friend. It was beautiful, sitting there with her friends and family. Alizeh decided to share the candies with the rest of Adelaide's guests.

"What are these?" Zinnia asked, holding up one of the Licorice Gems. They looked more like sparkly jewels rather than delicious candy. "They aren't real stones, are they?" Zinnia looked at the candy with reluctance.

"No, they are candies made in the kingdom of Gimmian. A kingdom where they adorn themselves with gems," Arthur explained. "I had picked some up during my travels."

Zinnia took a bite of the licorice. Its coating was durable. It almost felt as if she were biting into an actual stone, but soon she tasted its sweet flavor.

"So, anything new?" Alizeh asked. She too was a member of Galdorwide's Ministry.

Adelaide and Arthur both looked to one another; they both thought back to the grueling king with his crooked smile. They both looked into each other's eyes until they made a decision.

"I'm undergoing training to become a Ministry member," Arthur began.

"Oh, how wonderful! I knew you would take up the queen's offer. Also, how weird is this; Queen Bella? Our friend is now all grown up and queen. Never in a million years would I have expected the king to die. I thought he'd be immortal and rule for the centuries to come, with his stamina and stubbornness."

"About that, Alizeh. We should hold another Ministry meeting soon." Adelaide eased her into the conversation.

"Oh?" Alizeh asked, biting into one of the Berry Candies.

"The king; he appeared on our lawn just a half hour before you arrived. He didn't say anything. He just waved. However, we know it's him, there's no doubt about that — the thing is, he was a spirit."

"Are you positive it was him?" Alizeh challenged.

Arthur piped in. "Who could mistake his blue eyes, long, crooked nose, and flowing silver hair?"

Arthur sent a chill down all their spines, as his description described the king perfectly.

All kingdoms considered him to be the most powerful witch of modern times. He was best known for his defeat of the great wizard Aarv Actaeon in 1979. He was also known for his work in dark magic with his right-hand man, Alan Alderam.

Alizeh, astonished and frightened by the news, lifted her wand and summoned them to the Ministry's headquarters. Bella, Ben, Gower, Olly, John, and Gower's ex-girlfriend Dorothy Devarsh were present. They wore their Ministry robes. Gabriel Scaasi, John's cousin, soon followed them in. He was welcomed by all Ministry members, except for Bella. The last person to enter the Ministry's office was Ian Morgan, the castle's doctor.

Black, straight hair hung over Alizeh's pleasing, anguished face. Big brown eyes, set wickedly within their sockets, watched longingly over the Ministry members, of whom the majority she had attended Galdorwide High with, as they were told about the news of the king.

A scar stretched from the bottom of her left cheekbone, running towards the left side of her lip and ending on her chin, leaving an agonizing memory of her encounter with the king eight years ago when he had killed her father. The latter had deliberately set fire to royal property in protest. Arson was a crime the king took seriously. Buildings in Galdorwide were mostly made of wood, and when the building was lit, the flames spread quickly. Alizeh understood that what her father had done could have had the potential to affect the whole kingdom if it got out of control. However, Alizeh did not think that her father deserved the Judas Cradle, so she tried to fight her way to him, only for the king to catch her and swipe his sword's blade along her face, before making sure she kept her eyes on her father as he slowly died.

Ever since, Alizeh had stood as a true leader of the Ministry, bringing justice rather than consequences to the kingdom of Galdorwide. She stood tall and prominent with her slim, muscular frame.

Something was bewildering about her. Perhaps it was her disposition or particularly her attitude. Nonetheless, people tended to socialize with her while helping her out in any way that they could.

"If he's back, we can't let him rule. Galdorwide was becoming a little safer for us all." Alizeh wanted to cry but knew that she couldn't. She knew she'd have to keep her strong demeanor if she wanted to continue to have a prominent authority role within the Ministry.

Bella's dark hair which continued to proliferate, now sat at her shoulders. Her hair hung awkwardly on her fresh, tense face. Her expressive green eyes sat within their sockets, watching warmly over the Ministry, who had felt like a family for her for so long, but she was too cold ever to admit it. Several moles spread gracelessly on her neck and left a bitter memory of the bullying she had endured throughout her life. She wanted to be a utopian among Galdorians, even if her ideals weren't perfect to all. She stood awkwardly among the other members with her scrawny frame.

To Ben, there was something extraordinary about her. It was her composure. People tended to hopelessly try and seduce her, even royal knights trained with her whenever possible to be close with her.

She looked at her boyfriend, tense. She feared what truth might come out if her father was still walking around. Light brown hair, which seemed to grow darker with each day, hung over Ben's furrowed, gloomy face. Smart brown eyes, set gracefully within their sockets, watched emotionally over the Ministry that he had known for so long. A rapidly growing beard complemented his button nose.

He was a true hero of the Ministry. He stood average among the rest, despite his scraggy frame.

Bella found something mystifying about him. Perhaps it was their fortunate past that brought them together, or only a feeling of shame. She knew she didn't love him as much as he did her; she knew she should've let him go, but she couldn't. Bella had molded him into her perfect lover, yet the chemistry failed to blossom. Nonetheless, she took pride in being his girlfriend, even though she secretly despised him.

He eyed Bella, fearing the same as she did. What would the king reveal to the kingdom about his disappearance? What would they do when everyone found out the truth?

Red, wavy hair hung awkwardly over Gower's robust and friendly face. Wide amber eyes, set delicately in their sockets, watched vigorously over the Ministry as they discussed the emergency at hand.

A claw had left three marks from the top of his left cheek, ending above his right eye and left a lasting burden of the wolf war of 2004.

He became a genuine prodigy among secret werewolves by becoming public and embracing his curse and learning ways to manage the occurrences that would befall him on nights of full moons. He stood oddly among the rest with his slim frame.

Something was captivating about him. Perhaps it was Gower's odd friends Ben, Arthur, Olly, and John or particularly his character. Whatever it was, it had Dorothy feeling like this ex of hers was the one that got away. People who knew him tended to brag about it, all the while spreading rumors behind his back, trying to make him sound like less of an idol werewolf.

"If he's back, it won't matter. I'm sure there's something in the books about only the living can rule? If not, then we'd have a vampire monarchy, no?" he proposed.

Dirty, blond, well-groomed hair, tight in a ponytail, revealed Olly's full, gloomy face. Piercing blue eyes were set charmingly within their sockets, watching fearfully as the Ministry members spoke of the day's earlier events.

Scars reaching from the bottom of his right cheekbone, running towards his right nostril and ending above his right eye left an eternal punishment of liberated love when he fell for Alizeh, who at the time had been jailed for the interruption of her father's execution. He had purposefully gotten himself in there beside her after hunting angels, a species that were not allowed to be pursued due to their religious affiliations. Any such act would be a sign of a Mania worshipper. As a punishment, the king tortured him and castrated him. He stood seductively among others despite his fragile frame.

There was something seductive about him. Perhaps it was his company or particularly his sense of honesty. Nonetheless, people tended to ask him about his adventures while awkwardly avoiding the punishment the king had given him. However, he didn't feel like that brave man he once was. He'd rather hide from any danger than risk more pain.

"I don't think our ancestors thought they'd need to specify that only the living could rule," Olly pointed out.

After hearing the news, the room began to fill with a mumbled outrage of disbelief.

"I think they're telling the truth," Ben yelled over their voices as he referred to Arthur and Adelaide. "When we disappeared, I heard the king's voice as the smoke took hold of us. I can't quite remember what he said."

"I will become king again," Olly mumbled. "That's what I heard."

"I heard it too," Bella added.

John's eyes strayed to Ben and Bella. "Do you know anything about what happened to the king or anything about why he'd be back?" John asked the couple. They shook their heads.

"This is weird." Olly decided to take a seat at the table that everyone else had been standing around.

A breeze blew in the windowless room; the flames on the lanterns blew out. Exterminating the only light source.

Dragging feet walked along the edges of the room. The members lit up their wands and aimed at the site where the sound originated. In the glow of the multicolored rods, they saw the king lurking in the shadows, and a small smile grew on the older man's face. Another ghost joined him. It was a young woman with red, curly hair, wearing a black lace dress, who walked carefully behind him. She had an uncanny resemblance to Bella when she once had long hair. The woman was pale, skinny, and had wild locks.

Bella walked towards the ghost of her father and the woman. "Be careful," Ben called after her.

Bella grabbed her wand from beneath her black cloak. She looked at them carefully. "*Grama arodscipe.*" A rough, purple and black twisting coil shot out of her wand, sending a shockwave of demonic energy at the ghosts. The magic coiled the spirits, wrapping them before dragging them down through the floorboards and the soil, sending them to the underworld. She fell to her knees, shaking. The Ministry members ran to her side. "I expelled them — for now," she said numbly. "He's strong. If he escaped that plane before, he will again."

The majority of the Ministry members had attended Galdorwide High together, all except John, Ian, and Gabriel. However, John had the luxury of teaching them, and Ian had cared for them when he had worked at the school's hospital ward at the time.

They all agreed that they'd go out for dinner after the hectic day they had had and discuss a plan. They all attended, except Dorothy, who did not wish to spend any extra time around Gower. It pained her too much to see him. They had broken up just eleven months ago after a eight-year-long relationship.

They arrived at The Nightingale, Galdorwide's most famed restaurant. They all had a good time eating their Gooseberry Buns with Honey-Coated Boar. For dessert, they shared a platter of Gingerbread Cookies.

After dinner, they decided to enjoy more time together. The Ministry's members took a walk by the kingdom's countryside; the countryside was a mixture of neat fields, woods, dark rivers, and green hills. During their journey, they came across a round-faced, teary-eyed boy.

"Ben." Bella grabbed hold of her boyfriend's arm. "Is that Thomas?"

Ben looked to see where she had been pointing. The young, white-blond-haired boy sat in the grass. His silent tears soon turned to screams of angst. The nine adults all rushed to surround the young boy. Thomas wiped his eyes and looked up to them.

"Thomas, are you lost?" Bella asked, leaning down towards him. The boy nodded and began to wail once more.

"Do you remember me? I'm your Auntie Bella. Where's your mummy and daddy?"

"At the town square," the boy replied miserably.

"Okay, let's go find them," Bella said. She reached her arm to grab her nephew's hand.

"Noooo." The boy pulled his arm away before she could grab it. She tried again. This time, Thomas kicked the queen's shin.

Bella reached for her throbbing leg. With gritted teeth, she looked up at her boyfriend. She made a face similar to the one she had given him after the incident with her father the day she ordered Ben to kill him. Ben hid his smile well and leaned down.

"Thomas, it's me, your uncle, Ben. Now, don't you want to go find your mum and dad?" Ben asked. He went to nudge the boy's shoulder. Thomas quickly squirmed backward.

"Noooooo!"

"Why not?" Ben asked, annoyed.

"I don't have a mum or dad." The boy crossed his arms.

"Oh, I see." Ben sat back. "You ran away, didn't you?" The boy nodded. "How come?"

"Because my mum didn't want to buy me a pet rat."

"Oh, okay, but don't you miss your parents?"

The boy shook his head. Ben stood to his feet and looked at his fellow adults and shrugged. "That's all I got."

"If that were my son, I'd lose him as quickly as I could," said Bella as she continued to rub her leg.

The boy curled up in the grass as he prepared to fall asleep.

"Let's just go, pretend we didn't find him," Bella continued in disgust. Ben rolled his eyes and looked at John.

"You're his uncle, too, you know."

John knelt beside his nephew. "Your mum and dad must be worried sick; come on, let's go." John reached for the boy.

"Nooo!" Thomas kicked his uncle in the gut. John fell backwards.

"He's just like Bethdagon." Gabriel referred to his and John's youngest cousin, aged two. Soon, the boy found himself liking the attention. He gave the adults a wide smile.

"Look what I can do!" He grabbed his training wand and waved it around.

He waved the wand in full circles before directing his aim at Bella. A green wind exited the rod and surrounded his aunt, and her skin began to turn a bright yellow. The boy clapped, proud of himself.

Ben began to laugh. "You look like a Simpson!" He started to cackle. Olly, the only other witch of the group to have spent time in the Heofsij world, understood the reference. He began to laugh hysterically.

Bella rummaged through her cloak pockets and pulled out her crooked-shaped wand made of purified water and acacia wood, with its core being the heartstring of a vampire. Being used frequently, the rod's exterior was peeling, and its pale red interior showed.

She raised her wand right before Angel and Lewis approached frantically. Lewis looked as sad as Thomas, while Angel looked stern and ready to kill. The couple's long golden hair was in a bushy mess.

"Have you seen Thomas?" Angel looked at the Ministry members. Her tone was rather bossy. The adults stepped aside so that the pair could see their brat of a son. Thomas was sitting on the grass, clapping his hands in a frenzy as he looked at his aunt.

Angel looked at her son, then to Bella, taking note of her yellow skin. "Thomas, what did I tell you about doing unauthorized magic?"

The boy shook his head. "I don't want to say it."

"Thomas!" Angel persisted.

"You told me that every time I use unauthorized magic, a fairy dies." The adults were taken aback by the strange lie Angel had taught her son.

"Er — all right then." Ben scratched his head. "That's one way to teach your kids not to play around with magic."

Angel scowled at Ben before turning to her sister. Angel raised her wand. *"Normalem!"* She waved her wand until a stream of purple particles surrounded Bella and began to wipe her skin clean.

Bella looked at Ben; the look she gave made him aware that she did not like his previous laughter. "What, you don't find it funny any more?" Bella glared at her boyfriend. Angel and Lewis left, taking their badly behaved son with them.

"I hope never to see that child again." Ben tried to laugh the attention off of him. "Like, who taught him how to turn someone's skin yellow?"

"You, Mr Ben Black!" Bella ignored his question. "You are taking me to London tomorrow and showing me exactly what a Simpson is." She narrowed her gaze; Ben gulped. She then turned to Olly. "And Olly, I expect you will be joining us, as you found the situation quite hilarious yourself." Olly too. let out a gulp. Fear settled amongst the two men as they looked off into the distance with vacant stares. The Ministry continued their enchanting walk.

"The school needs a new teacher," Gower brought up. "We need a professor for the Art of Air Magic."

"I'll do it," Ben said eagerly. "I'll need something to do when Bella is busy being queen."

"Oh, no!" John laughed. "The whole brigade back at Galdorwide High," he continued as he referred to Gower, Ben, and Olly. John had just finished teaching them less than a decade ago. Bella continued to stare at Ben.

"Oh!" Ben shouted. "I didn't even think of that! The lads are back!" His jaw dropped into a wide smile as he looked at his friends from high school.

"It'll be all over the news," John laughed. Bella shook her head.

"Galdorwide must be pretty boring if the news has to report on new teachers." Her voice was cruel, and it sent a prickle of fear into Ben.

He knew better than to ask why she was upset. Mainly because he already knew; he knew better than to laugh at her, no matter what, and he had failed. The group stayed silent for a little while, as the air around them was too thick to speak.

"Tonight, the students are playing a game of Crash Ring. Maybe we can watch, like old times." Olly was strangely confident enough to be the first to break the ice that hung dreadfully in the air.

Crash Ring was the primary sport among the witches. It was quite a barbaric sport for children to play. However, it was a tradition. Each team got seven players. Each of the players got onto their broomsticks, or training sticks. They then entered a ring of colored lights, based on the team's aura. The two circles of groups had to use magic to knock an opposing team member off their broom — the team with the last witch standing won.

"Great idea," John beamed. "Tonight, my son John Jr will be playing against my nephews, Caden and Aldaricus Scaasi. Tonight, is the Viridi Vipers against Avalon's Alets."

John couldn't have been prouder of his son's aura; after all, Merlin himself was an Alet.

Caden, Aldaricus, and another boy from the Viridi Vipers walked into the Alets' changing room. John Jr recognized Caden the most, as he was one of his cousins closest to his age. Caden was his uncle Krum's son, while

Aldaricus was his uncle Roman's. Caden stared at John Jr with more interest than usual.

"Is it true?" he asked. "You're the new captain of Avalon's Alets?"

"Yes," John Jr said. He was always cautious around his cousins, as his father had warned him about them. He was much thinner than Caden and the rest of his family from a long history of freakishly strong and violent men.

Their great-great-grandfather, Westley Scaasi, had been thrown into prison. While working at Galdorwide's Black Magic Material Factory, he had been continuously teased there by one of his co-workers. So one day, he fought back, physically. He didn't need magic; he used his bare hands and squeezed the man's neck until his eyes began to bleed from their sockets.

Caden was only one year older than John Jr He had long, curly, dark brown hair with hauntingly blue eyes. He had an athletic build. He could usually be spotted wearing tight jeans and a leather jacket when he was not wearing his uniform.

Aldaricus was in his final year of school and held the role of Viridi Vipers' team captain. He had short blond hair but recently had begun to dye it black, making his blue eyes stand out more than usual. He had high cheekbones and a build similar to Caden's.

John Jr didn't know them well. They carried an atmosphere around them that would send a scrawny boy like him scattering away. Caden and the other boy stood on either side of Aldaricus, looking like his bodyguards.

"This is Jax Ambrose." Aldaricus motioned to the boy unrelated to them.

Jax was quite scrawny himself. However, he looked like a self-centered, spoiled, and arrogant kid.

"No need to feel defeated when you lose tonight. It's all in fun. Oh, and I saw you hanging out with Aldric Amell and Lovetta Annettes. Yo do know that just because you're an Alet, it doesn't mean you can't hang out with us. I mean, we'd rather that than have a family member hanging out with a drug abuser and a savage." Aldaricus made a face to prove his disgust in his cousin's choice of friends.

"I'll hang out with whom I want," John Jr tried to reply coolly.

"You're not falling in love with that wild girl, are you? She looks and acts as if wolves raised her, for Merlin's sake!"

A pale pink tinge appeared on John Jr's round cheeks.

"I'd be careful if I were you, Junior," he warned. "You hang around a crowd like that, and you might end up like your mother, or at the very least, attacked by that sadistic girl you call a friend."

"Who knows, she might rub off on him." Jax laughed.

Caden was leaning against one of the blue lockers, looking at John Jr solemnly. "Leave him alone, guys." He stood up protectively.

Both Aldaricus and Jax drew out their chests, as did Caden. John Jr walked to Caden's side. They looked like wild animals about to embark on a territorial brawl.

"Or what?" Aldaricus sneered.

Caden smirked as he cracked his neck.

The teams were equal — one scrawny boy paired with a seemingly genetically mutated one. Considering this, John Jr was oddly feeling brave.

Aldaricus switched spots with Jax. Now Aldaricus was in front of John Jr He leaned in close, his knuckles resting on the blue locker next to his cousin's head. Jax backed away from his angry partner. Footsteps approached the changing room. Aldaricus nodded to Jax, and they left. Caden remained by John Jr's side.

Aldric walked in. "What's going on?" he asked, staring at his pale-faced friend.

Aldric was strong but not as brawny as Caden and Aldaricus. He was more of the slim, muscular type. Many rumors had spread at the beginning of the year, stating that Aldric was addicted to bone dust. However, John Jr and Lovetta never had any reason to believe that these stories were true. Aldric always seemed clean to them; the odd time he'd have an Anvil cigarette, but that was about it.

His friend had blond hair and blue eyes. John Jr was always worried that Lovetta would like Aldric more than him.

Aldric took a closer look at his friend. He waved his hand in front of John Jr's eyes, which looked lost in thought.

"My cousin; what a dick." John Jr snapped out of his daze. Aldric looked up to Caden. "Not that cousin."

Caden smiled, patted John Jr on the shoulder and exited the changing room. "Boy, you sure do have many family members at the school — Spencer, your dad, Caden, Aldaricus, and Clancy. That's six of the Scaasi family members here. I've heard stories about your father's generation where there were only five of them, and all chaos broke loose. Let's hope there's no magic battle in the halls any time soon."

"Yeah, let's hope not."

John had warned John Jr about his cousins, but he never thought it'd be this bad. "Ready for the game?" Aldric changed the topic to get rid of the heaviness in the room.

"We need to hurry up and grab our Crash Ring uniforms. Coach Abbey just yelled at me in the hall for being late — again."

"Yeah." John Jr couldn't drop the familial subject too quickly. "I never thought that my cousins would be so childish, or at least Aldaricus. I mean, he sounds like a child making threats before playing a game of tag. By the way, you've got something on your cheek, Aldric, did you know?" It looked to be a speck of dirt.

Aldric shook his head and began to rub his cheek like a madman.

"Did I get it?" John Jr nodded.

The boys walked out of the changing room and headed to the school's back door leading to the Crash Ring court. Beyond the field they could see a thick, purple sky trekking over the sun and the mountains in the distance.

Once they arrived at the Alet team's bench, they took off their red varsity jackets with their team logo, a mountain. John Jr thought that the Alets' team name was lame and too traditional. He'd rather be a team of vipers or panthers or centaurs, like the other aura teams. However, no matter how much he disliked it, he was an Avalon's Alet.

They began to put on their gear: helmets, chest guard, gloves, elbow pads, and knee pads.

This was John Jr's second game of the season, and he was far from feeling confident. "The game will begin in five minutes," Abbey announced to her team.

John Jr's stomach lurched with nerves. His stomach made a funny sound that suggested he'd make a bowel movement soon if his nerves didn't cease. Aldric took note of his friend's paleness that hadn't faded since the locker room. He handed John Jr a candy, hoping it'd cheer him up.

The teams grabbed hold of their brooms and walked over to their circle. John Jr and Aldric were the first to stand over the field's glowing red mark. Once they were seated on their brooms, the ring lifted into the sky, taking the team up. John Jr shivered as the cold air rushed past him.

Slipping and sliding, they began to spin, their speed getting faster and faster. Oooohs and aahs came from the stadium of onlooking parents and students. John Jr was getting used to the pace and was now gliding smoothly in the current. The crowd grew silent, looking up at the teams' players.

It was time to begin.

"Heads down!" John Jr called. The captain of each team cast the first attack. He pointed his wand towards the opposing team. *"Bland!"* Red particles shaped like irregular corkscrews raced towards the group, hitting a target. The victim immediately became confused. The spell was a success.

"Videatur immortuos!" Aldaricus struck John Jr with a spell that would allow him to see the undead.

John Jr felt as if he were in a dark tunnel. Faces of horrifyingly deformed spirits began to reach for him. "Help," the ghosts moaned. Their voices were filled with sorrow and pain. John Jr was still in the ring, except the world around him appeared to look like they were all in some underground cave.

John Jr regained his strength and cast his next spell. *"Bland!"*

CHAPTER 7

Bella's short black hair carried a golden crown. She wore her favorite amethyst-colored gown as she swung open the castle doors. Her face was stern as she looked at Arthur. "The second day of training?" she asked.

Arthur nodded. A purple smoke surrounded them on the porch as she transported Arthur and herself to an abandoned mansion. The villa was large and propped up on a hill that looked over the forest's deadened trees. Bella walked up to the brown, rusted building and pushed the massive doors open.

Arthur took note of the mansion's large entrance hall. The entrance hall alone was three times bigger than his and Adelaide's home. The only light source came from the torches that hung along the stone walls. Besides that, it was total darkness. The dark of the night crawled in through the windows. It seemed fitting as Bella, the Queen of Darkness, guided him throughout the old home. He did not know this bone-chilling place they walked through. Arthur looked up to see nothing but duskiness. The ceiling seemed non-existent. That was until Arthur noticed the spiral staircase that reached up into the shade. He could have sworn that he could hear ghostly whispers masked behind the rain that splattered against the windows.

He followed Bella down the corridor, following her closely, closer than either of the two liked. He peered over her nervously.

"Welcome to your new home," said Bella. "Your task will begin shortly. Here, you will come to realize the love you have for your family back at home. This mansion is where you will stay over the next few months. Each day a Ministry member will come in to teach you. You will sleep and spend your days here, up until the day that we need your help with the dragons." Bella walked him into his temporary bedroom. He took a seat on the dusty bed. "Here, you'll learn about the noble history of our Ministry. Here, we expect you to become an even more outstanding witch. If you break any rule, I'll remove a finger of yours for a year."

Arthur's eyes gaped in horror.

"By May, you'll be awarded an official coronation ceremony. A great honor, if I do say so myself. I hope you will prove us right about you, Arthur. You do have some smartening up to do, but that will come with time. By joining this Ministry, you are sworn to protect and defend the people here in Galdorwide. After your training, you will be able to arrest and detain individuals accused of breaking the law. You will soon be involved in ensuring flyers follow broom laws, respond to emergencies when summoned, and patrol areas where crime may occur. You will have to document any action you take in detailed reports. First, you will need to start your research on the requirements to attend the Ministry. We will test you both mentally and physically. If all goes well, you just might be accepted full-time. Here we will train you on patrolling, broom control, fire spells, self-defense spells, healing magic, and your response to emergencies. There is a lot to learn. It takes time; I won't sugarcoat it. After your training is over, you will be officially a member of the Ministry. We will be coming in on weekdays, forty hours a week, and you needn't worry about finances, as you will be paid throughout your stay.

"After training, you will be categorized in a role as either an investigator or in wildlife protection, or you can choose to remain patrolling. You will be responsible for enforcing the law, looking out for any suspicious behavior, and investigating any complaints. You will be assigned a partner, and during shifts, you must wear your Ministry cloak; however, the job doesn't end when your shift is over. Anyway, I mustn't worry you about future stuff. You're not even close to that. Here you will learn communication skills and —" Her voice trailed. She noticed that his eye contact was too fixed, and his head was too still.

She smacked his knee, snapping him out of his trance. "Listening skills. However, you'll need to focus on your fitness. This job will require a lot of running and possibly battling suspects; it is a physically and mentally demanding job, with a high-stress level and is very dangerous."

Thunder rolled in the distance. Heavy gusts of wind slammed against the windows as the faded, brown, hardened and stained curtains rustled in front of barricaded windows. Footsteps walked on the creaky wooden floors and musty carpets of the hall.

"Who else is here?" Arthur asked.

"Just us." She gave a twisted smile.

Her eyes lingered on Arthur's Ministry cloak for a moment.

"I shall return when it is my turn to teach," said Bella. "Please don't do anything I wouldn't do." She vanished.

Arthur was finally able to let out a gulp. *Today's task better not hurt*, he said to himself. Arthur's heart gave a drop — he was all alone in the dark, where he would stay for the next seven months. He hadn't been expecting to be thrown into a place all alone, let alone go through trials nearly daily. Arthur anxiously went through a list of spells that he was confident using. He felt as if he were back at Galdorwide High. It was as if he were studying for his Final Examination Battle, a test in front of the entire school. His heart speedily pumped his blood throughout his body.

Arthur kept moving his eyes around the room, waiting for someone or something to appear and lead him to his downfall as a Ministry member.

Then, something he never imagined happened. It sent him reeling back towards the worn bed's headboard. Every move he made sent dust off the ground and into the air. He let out a scream. Eighteen ghosts gushed into the room from the walls.

The almost entirely transparent dead witches floated around — their attention on Arthur. They were wispy, translucent, and peculiarly fearsome. It was unexceptionally exceptional. He had never seen a ghost, but ever since he joined the Ministry, he had seen the king's and now this. One was enormous and looked reptilian-like. The thinnest and palest stood in the middle; a soft purple light surrounded her.

"Forgive or forget?" the ghost of a true-headless asked, his headless voice groggy and a bit scratchy.

"Forgive." Arthur spit out the answer that he thought they wanted to hear. He gripped onto the tiny sheeted bed that was spread to its limit. The sheet popped out of position and sent Arthur reeling forward in fear.

"He's already lying. Let's tell the queen to move on from this poor excuse of a witch," a shabby, weary ghost's voice screeched.

"W-What's going on?" Arthur decided to ask so that he could understand what he was to expect. He was speechless and sorrowful.

"We are here to ask and judge you. We must see behind your given aura and see if it is true to whom you've become today," the ghost in the middle explained. It looked as if the headless witch would be the one asking questions. The rest appeared to be members of a jury standing off to the side.

"Let's get on with it," the ghost that stood before him said with a sharp tone. "Stand up for us, will you? Geez, show some respect." The ghost glared.

Once he stood, he realized that he could barely stand. His legs were too busy shivering. Arthur always believed in ghosts and was quite happy to have not encountered them — until these past few days. He had to look up at them as they floated mid-air. The pale faces stared at him. The candles behind them flickered, making the ghosts look as if they were flames in a lantern. They shined a hazy grey color.

"Sky or sea?" the wizard asked in a whispered breath.

"Sea," Arthur replied.

Arthur stared back at all the ghosts, who whispered to one another. Then for a moment, there was complete silence.

"Brave or chivalrous?" the witch asked.

"Chivalrous," Arthur replied.

"Kind or cunning?" the witch asked.

"Kind." It was Arthur's most straightforward answer yet.

"Wrestle a troll or dehorn a unicorn?" the wizard asked.

"Wrestle a troll," Arthur replied. Trolls despised humans and deserved a little bit of wrestling. Unicorns, on the other hand, were harmless. However, their rainbow-colored horns' value put a target on the creatures' heads when hunting.

"We made a thorough study of you — quite the fascinating history, yet so tragic. A father lost, given up by your biological mother, and your uncle was, in fact, your father." The head ghost chuckled. "I've been inside that head of yours, Arthur. I've seen the web of lies you tell yourself and string together to keep that fragile psyche of yours intact. We are going to force you to confront who you are. Now, please, direct your eyes to the left, behind you. Meet Zelaji and Chipper."

A troll and a unicorn appeared in two cages.

"You have forty-seconds to unlock the cage of your choice. Be reminded. It was to wrestle a troll, no magic allowed."

Arthur stared.

Zelaji, the troll, was particularly large and hairy. It was beefed up. Arthur estimated that it was five times his size. It was almost hysterical how ugly the green beast was. It was murderously furious, striking and pulling at the cage's bars. The minimally-attired creature gave a powerful, frustrating jump as it gave a hungry growl. Trolls were ferocious and often used in battle. The miserable, stupid thing kept its eyes on Arthur. It's dumb eyes went crossed as it focused in on the red-haired man, who was much smaller than it was. It snapped it's broad, reptilian-like jaw.

"You have to make a choice. So, what's it going to be?"

Sorrowfully, Arthur reached for the key that hung from the unicorn's cage. He unlocked the door. Arthur reached his hand for the thin, pale horn and held his other hand on the unicorn's snout. He twisted, pulling the horn off. Arthur winced as the unicorn cried and began to kick wildly. He fell backward, and just as the unicorn extended to prance down its paw, it vanished.

"For your next test, Arthur, are you fearless or loyal?"

"Hmmph," Arthur replied confidently, despite feeling like a coward as he stood. "What a stupid question; both, of course!"

"Very well then," the ghost replied with a sinister grin on her face. Ben, along with three other people, a man, a woman, and a small child, suddenly appeared on the opposite side of the dark room. They were all bound to chairs with their mouths locked tight with some mute spell. "What kind of test is this?" Arthur inquired, insulted by how the ghost thought this was some challenge for his abilities. Suddenly, Arthur noticed the floors in the large, dark room beginning to shake, lightly at first, but becoming progressively more intense with each moment. He presumed a beast was coming his way. Arthur's anxiety rose with each second, as now he could hear what sounded like a large ax of some sort being dragged along by some creature that was coming after him, Ben, and the other captives. Arthur, brandishing his wand, prepared to defend himself from whatever the cursed ghost had summoned for his next test.

Taking one final gulp, hoping to swallow at least some of the fear that was building inside him, he whispered, "Fearless... You are fearless!" As soon as he finished this brief moment of self-motivation, Arthur's fears were confirmed. A massive minotaur emerged from the shadows with blood-soaked teeth and pure black, soulless eyes. "Oh, great, it's just a minotaur," Arthur chuckled to himself, hoping that his light-hearted veil would conceal the great internal fear he was experiencing.

Wand in hand, Arthur knew he had to do something to protect himself from the vicious beast before him. Internally knowing that he was by far not powerful enough to take the creature alone, he knew he had to find some other creative option to take the beast down. Each passing second Arthur was formulating a plan, the minotaur was getting closer to him. The panic was truly setting in. He did not know what to do. He knew he didn't have any offensive spells at his disposal to use, as he could see that the light green tinge on the outside of the minotaur's skin showed an active spell that would dispel all offensive spells cast on the creature.

The next thought that immediately came to his mind's surface was how royally fucked he and Ben and the captives were. Mostly, if he was incapable of freeing Ben, who was proven a far more powerful witch than Arthur. This was his next task; freeing his friend. "Strength in numbers," he whispered to himself. However, the next issue was the minotaur which now stood in the middle of the room, twenty feet from where Arthur stood, which was roughly half-way between him and the captives. "Simple," Arthur thought to himself, *I will just use a basic cutting spell to cut Ben free, then he will be free to help me slay this monster!*

Growing more confident with his game plan as time went on, Arthur felt ready to make his move and begin the fight. The minotaur seemed to be content with letting Arthur make the first move, as it hadn't moved in the last sixty seconds. Raising his wand and pointing it directly at Ben's chair, Arthur chanted "*Cyrf!*" with an arrogant grin on his face. An amateur spell like this was what it was going to take to end this battle. However, upon casting the spell, to Arthur's peril, the only thing that happened was a small puff of black smoke ejecting from the tip of his want as the wand went limp. Before Arthur even had time to process what had happened, the minotaur let out a blood-curdling roar as it threw its massive head back and began barreling towards the now defenseless Arthur. The monster was clearing distance at a supernatural speed. Before Arthur knew it, the creature was already half the distance to him. Being defenseless without any magic at his disposal, his last thoughts drifted to Ben and how he couldn't save him.

The minotaur stopped a mere three feet from Arthur, letting out one final massive bellow. It raised the large ax it had been carrying above its head. Closing his eyes and accepting his final fate, Arthur had time to shed a single tear as the ax came plummeting down towards his head.

WHOOSH. Arthur heard a loud wind sound coming from the room, which was not what he expected to hear. Upon opening his eyes, the room was back to normal. No Ben, no captives, no minotaur. Just the jury of ghosts. "You are right, Mister Williams, you are both fearless and loyal," the witch said in an approving-sounding tone. "The fact you chose not to wrestle the troll proves to us only that you do not put yourself in danger when it is not required of you."

The witch stepped away and walked over to the jury of ghosts before returning with a scroll in her hand. Arthur was starting to feel sick, and he began to think about whether or not his aura had changed. He didn't think so. He had always considered himself to be the same boy since birth.

Despite his confidence, Arthur began to worry. What if he was a Viridi? Adelaide was sure to break up with him then. Alan's Viridi aura was one reason she chose Arthur over him.

The ghosts' whispers sounded like hisses as they waited for the witch to read from the scroll. The spirits craned their heads to get a good look at Arthur.

"It's been a difficult decision," she read as she turned to face the red-haired man. "Based on your answers, you prove to have courage, talent, and the will to prove yourself. However, your kindness and your perseverance outweighed the rest of those traits. So, with this, we pronounce you to be a Caerul, truly."

Arthur began to shake just before he released the confusion within him. "So, you mean to tell me that half the people of Galdorwide are walking around with wrong auras?"

"Not wrong auras," the ghost wizard began. "People grow up and become new people based on their experiences. Sometimes experiences change a person. For example, you, you changed."

The ghosts cheered, as they were proud to have a third Caerul wizard in the Ministry. The wizard patted Arthur's shoulder in congratulation. "If I may say so myself, if you had any royal blood or became knighted, you'd prove yourself a great Pure wizard."

Caerul was an inviting aura, whereas the Alet aura was rumored as an aura that's possessors were creating a division in the kingdom. The Caeruls didn't see it like this. They saw everyone as the same, believing the auras only dignified the magic, not the personality. Many famous Caeruls taught Galdorians not to be biased when it came to auras. Arthur's patience, kindness, and reliability proved that his magic was humble and stable. Despite this, overall, auras didn't encompass the entirety of one's personality. Examples of Caerul's vast array of characters were Eddie Schneider, a charming psychopath who committed brutal crimes, which didn't compare remotely with Lovetta Annettes, who was protective and would defend anyone, even after knowing them for merely a few minutes.

The Caerul aura supplied Galdorwide with most of Angel's supporters, whom they all desperately still rooted for to be granted the throne. They felt a sense of duty for the most kind-hearted Carter they had seen in generations. They wanted the throne to belong to someone who was good and could be trusted to do the right thing. Angel's supporters were mature and wanted the jobs to get done. The spot where the ghost had placed his hand stung like ice. Arthur's face turned a pale green. "Will Adelaide be able to come by and visit? I want her to know that I'm not the person I said I was," he said bitterly.

The reptilian ghost vanished, as did the jury-like spirits. The main ghost, however, stayed. "She'll know soon enough. For now, you should go to the kitchen and make yourself some food." And with that, she vanished too.

After a half hour of walking down the long halls and making wrong turns, he found the kitchen. A tea kettle began to whistle, sending Arthur reeling back towards the kitchen wall. He grabbed his chest and calmed his breath. The kitchen was no prettier than the rest of the building. He was now sure that another stream of ghosts would make themselves present. A pot on the stove was boiling some water. In the far distance in the corner of the kitchen, he could hear a sinister chuckle followed by the clanging of cutlery.

As he approached, a shadow in the corner stood up. It was the king. He was beaming, almost happy to see Arthur. He held his arms wide open. The candle behind the king was as clear as day behind his pale purple embroidered vest buttons.

"Twrsal nietit." It sounded as if the king were trying to say a spell. Whatever it was, it wasn't working. If anything, the king just looked and sounded like a mad buffoon.

"Are you mad?" Arthur was going to speak his mind, as it was clear that ghosts were completely magicless.

The king glared at him. He knew he couldn't do anything, so he vanished. When he was gone, Arthur wasn't too sure about whether or not he should let out his laughter.

He shook his head with a proud smile. He walked over to the pantry and found nothing but a bag of potatoes. He placed them on the table's cutting board and took out his wand. "*Cyrf!*" A slight blue surge of waves exited his rod. For a moment, it took Arthur back. It was the first time that the color blue left his wand. He had almost forgotten. The waves sliced and diced the potatoes before carrying them over into the pot with the boiling water.

With nothing better to do with his time, he decided to conjure himself a feast of food.

Conjuring was hard. You had to envision every item you wanted down to a singular particle. Arthur wasn't superb at conjuring anything except for food. He could taste it all now.

He summoned two main courses: tea-smoked juniper yam and mustard tuna. For dessert, he made himself some peach fudge and rum snacks.

He piled a plate for himself with a little bit of everything that he had made. He took an empty seat at the large table draped with a browning white tablecloth. The food was delicious, but it was his first time in seven years of eating dinner without Adelaide. He was either always at her house or she at his before they had moved in together.

Left to his thoughts, he thought back to the king, who had tried to curse him or something. He had attempted a spell that Arthur had never heard before. He tried to picture the king, and he could've sworn that his royal garments were bloodied all around his abdomen. More questions filled his mind. Where was his body now? Somebody must've gone to great lengths to cover up the murder of the king.

He ate as much as he could and decided to wrap up and refrigerate all his leftovers to have for tomorrow.

Bella and Ben sat alone in their castle's kitchen, eating their plates of rum and wine pastries. "They know the king is dead, and soon they'll want to look for his body." Bella broke the silence once she was sure that no one was listening. "I mean, when my father pushed Angel into Snowbush Lake or when he held me by my ankles over the balcony edge, nobody batted a single goddamn eye."

"His body, we can deal with that — nothing a little magic can't solve. I'll go to the library wing and see if there are any spells we can use," Ben assured her.

She was beginning to feel warm and sleepy. She looked up to Ben; her eyes passed over him and over to Alan. He hadn't been there a moment ago; did he hear something? He stared directly into her eyes. She straightened herself up in her chair. She stared at Alan until he left the room. It was hard for her to shake off the feeling that Alan had heard something. Once he was gone, she broke her gaze and turned to Ben.

"How long was Alan there?"

"Not long. I saw him appear from the corner of my eye after I said 'solve'. However, maybe he could help us. I mean, he is no longer your father's right-hand man, he's yours."

"Not for long," Bella stated.

"Are you almost ready, love?" Ben wiped his mouth with a napkin, referring to her first ever meeting with Galdorians as their queen.

She gave a firm nod.

It was now time for Bella to announce her new rules to her kingdom. She stood on her balcony before the crowd of people. Bella tried to remember her father's training. She could hear her father's voice. "Shoulders back, chest out, chin up." Ben and Olly were on either side of her.

"I have new rules to share with you today. The forest from today on — is forbidden to all citizens of Galdorwide. Including Ministry members and Pures." Her eyes twinkled in the light as she looked down at the people who began to mutter. "It is also now of utmost importance that kids do not use any magic outside of school. If someone breaks these rules, the punishment will be death or imprisonment. The only way one can enter the forest or use unauthorized magic is if they get approval from me."

A man in the crowd laughed. The citizens saw her anger grow and decided to step away from the man to clear her target.

"You can't be serious? A little girl — is telling us what to do. Hysterical; last time I saw you on your balcony, your father was holding you by your ankles." The man found the whole situation quite amusing.

"I am quite serious." The queen frowned. "I have my reasoning for these rules that would be too ghastly for anyone to know. However, if you insist, a crystal ball revealed dragons, dragons here in Galdorwide. They are underneath Doryu Edjer's church. The matter is being dealt with by myself and the Ministry of Galdorwide. The forest has also been filled with more dangerous creatures, and as for unauthorized magic, the term 'unauthorized' stays unchanged, and considering that some children still tend to use it, a rule is now in place. I will have to punish those that use unauthorized magic off Galdorwide Training School's grounds. Thank you, have a good night, Galdorians!" She smirked and blew the crowd kisses as she skipped to the end.

The crowd looked to one another, murmuring in fear and confusion. Bella followed Ben and Olly down the marble staircase. Her leg had grown dense; she felt weak and hadn't had enough for breakfast. Bella yawned and dragged her feet. As they approached the ballroom, Bella closed her eyes to yawn, and when she opened them, she saw floating party horns that roared upon her arrival. The horns showered gold and purple confetti all around her. She smiled broader than Ben had ever seen before. She looked around the room, dumbfounded.

The ballroom was cozily decorated with furniture to allow guests to socialize without aching feet or being forced to dance. There was a small section in the middle of the room that was left bare for dancing. Olly took a seat on one of the purple squishy armchairs.

"This is the comfiest chair I've ever sat on!" he exclaimed.

"Auntie Bella!" A little boy ran towards her. Immediately, her grin faded as she moaned loudly.

"What's he doing here?" She turned to Ben, gritting her teeth.

"Look what I can do!"

There was a powerful popping sound that echoed throughout the room. Lewis, Angel, Ben, and Bella all looked to Thomas, who stood before the heavily locked door. The door's heavy chain had fallen to the floor. Before Bella had any time to react, Angel and Lewis vanished with their son.

"Finally, the Scaasis are afraid of me," she cackled. "I should probably punish Thomas. I don't need people to see that I continue to allow children to use their terrible magic as they please."

"Don't. Bella, I didn't invite them here so that we could take their son away from them." Ben grew protective of his soon-to-be nephew.

"That reminds me, why did you even invite them? They made it clear they wanted nothing to do with us." Bella crossed her arms. She looked stunning, as she wore a color not usual to her liking. She was wearing a long silk pink dress.

"Well, you wanted to try and be good with her, so I invited her and her family, and Bella, don't you know what day it is?" he asked.

She furrowed her brow.

"Bella, honey, it's your birthday."

Purple velvet curtains covered the ballroom's walls and windows. Since it was Bella's celebration and the sun wasn't entirely down, Ben knew to leave the drapes closed. She hated it when the sun seeped in through the windows like a wound.

Many guests were speaking to one another, wearing elegant clothing and sipping wine. Some danced, and some swarmed the buffet table.

Bella walked towards the forbidden door and pointed her wand at the lock. "*Insegal!*" Bright purple streams exited her wand. The streams intertwined into intricate designs and raised the chain back into its original locked position.

"I'm starving." She walked over to the long table that lined the left wall wholly. "Hmm, great food choices," she marveled. She made herself a plate that mainly consisted of Spicy Alligator.

Later that evening, when Bella returned to her room, exhausted, the king made another appearance. "It is not your destiny to rule the kingdom!" He scowled.

"It is my destiny, Father, and because of you, I'm queen."

"No, because of Ben, you are queen. Because of what you did to your brother, you are queen. Imagine what the kingdom and my followers will do when they find out you two were behind my death and the disappearance of your brother," he taunted.

The king's fingers gnarled into razor-sharp claws. He began to stab her repeatedly in all the same places where Ben had struck him. Her stomach stung with shock as she held onto her father's grey-lined arm. Looking into his eyes, she begged him to stop. Once he finished doing to her what Ben had done to him, he let her drop to the floor. Buckled forward, she held her bleeding stomach.

In the corner, behind the king, the red-haired ghost laughed as she watched Bella struggle. Suddenly, there was a spiky black blast of particles.

Bella awoke. She pushed her head deeper into her pillow.

CHAPTER 8

"Look! Over there!" Caden whispered to John Jr

"Where?"

"Do you not see that tall, red-head kid flirting with your sister?"

"Well... Yeah."

"She's uncomfortable." Caden continued to try to explain the situation in a hushed tone.

"Yeah... So?"

"You're the worst older brother ever. Did you know?"

"She's older than me — by three minutes."

Caden groaned and gripped his forehead in frustration. He then raised his wand and pointed it at himself once he was sure that no one could witness what he did next. *"Ahyrdincg mec in commuta habitum sum cyme be Spencer's brandhord."* An unstable green ray of sparks exited his wand and transformed his body into a new one.

The spell he cast turned him into a man of Spencer's desires. Caden's limbs lengthened. His blue eyes remained the same, but his long dark hair shortened and turned blond. He now sported a stubble beard.

He walked over to rescue Spencer. He slammed his still large arm between Spencer and the red-haired kid. "What are you doing talking to my girl?" he asked.

"Uh — I — I didn't know, I — I'm sorry." The red-haired kid sprinted in the opposite direction.

Caden turned to Spencer, whose face was both confused and relieved. He took note of her pale skin, which made her blue eyes appear a sickly grey. Caden had not seen her up close in a while. He had forgotten all about her hooked nose and the birthmark on her left cheek. Hair that broke off from her tight ponytail littered her baby blue polo shirt. Beneath her eyes were thick black circles. She looked as if she were dead. Nonetheless, Caden could still see Adam's attraction for his cousin.

"Your girl?" she asked.

He leaned towards her. Spencer jolted back, but he continued to lean in closer. He placed his lips beside her ear. "It's Caden." When he pulled away, he was back in his regular form.

"Merlin! Thank you. He's been creeping me out," she whispered as she always had whenever she spoke ill of anyone.

"Yeah, I could tell. If you ever need me, summon me. See you later, giggles." Caden winked and gave her a playful shove. His playful shove was hard enough to send her tiny body flying into the locker.

Whispers followed Spencer as she sat in her Terra Arts classroom. A few students were staring at her.

The class had not begun. The girls in her class were talking fast with their high-pitched voices. "Teenage girl", a language unknown to Spencer's old soul. The teacher, Mr Silwhet, had not yet turned off his beat-up tune box. Spencer never could put her finger on what type of music it was. That was, until today. She noticed that it sounded eerily similar to the elf's music in the forest behind her home. The music drowned out the dripping of the sink built into Mr Silwhet's desk. However, the music was not loud enough to drown out the sound of girls tittering. Spencer didn't bother to look around to see what had been so funny. She unzipped her backpack and grabbed out her agenda.

"*Plectrum.*" Spencer turned her wand into a quill and began to write down the date. "9/24/2018". When Mr Silwhet walked in, she could hear the rest of the students turning their wands into feathers. The transformation's noise was similar to the gliding of two metal tubes, followed by Spencer's, who described the sound like a chime of fairy bells.

It was the first time that Spencer hadn't arrived late to class. She was usually playfully attacked by Caden in the halls or stuck talking to Adam. Spencer was always too polite to turn him down. She couldn't even muster up the courage to end the conversation on her own. Adam didn't mind being late if it meant being with Spencer.

The janitor, Olly, walked into the classroom.

Earlier this morning, Spencer had managed to get on his wrong side. She had known him as her father's sweet and nerdy friend. Spencer had been wandering the halls and had taken a wrong turn. She began to pull at the door of her classroom. *Odd*, she thought as she pulled, and the door didn't open. Spencer knocked and knocked, and when there was no answer, she decided to use magic. *"Unlucan."* When the door unlocked, she pushed it open. Before she could get a good look inside, Olly's slender hands grasped the knob and drew it shut, pulling her with it.

"What're you doing?" he had asked.

"N-nothing, I thought it was my classroom."

Olly didn't believe this for one second. "I know you. You're a Scaasi. Your father's a great man, but blood as dark as the black void runs in your veins. Please don't lie to me. I know you were trying to break into my closet." He spoke through gritted teeth.

"I-I wasn't," she stuttered.

"I should lock you in the dungeon." Olly narrowed his eyes, his face growing more sinister by the second.

The dungeon he was referring to wasn't the one at the castle or in Skogen prison. He was referring to the one right here, beneath the school's grounds. The dungeons, in ancient times, were the detention rooms. Now it was a place for students to go when they deserved more severe punishment. Regular detentions took place in Mr Silwhet's room.

Mr Ben Black went to turn a corner before he noticed the situation at hand. Ben only had one class to teach, so he was to patrol the hallways when he was not teaching.

"Olly, is there a problem?" he asked his friend with a stern voice as he approached.

Ben looked at his niece, whom he had never seen so frightened. Her eyes were bulging like light bulbs out of her skull. Spencer grabbed her chest and began to wheeze. She was always tired and weak, and her body wasn't strong enough to handle this much panic. He glared at his friend, who he now felt betrayed him.

He began to guide Spencer down the hall towards the hospital wing. It may have been his fourth day teaching at the school, but he navigated through the many corridors with ease.

Ayman Black, Ben's great-grandfather, had built the school back in 1931. He had wanted to make a new school. He wanted to design a modern school that still matched Galdorwide's castle-like buildings.

Spencer finally relaxed when she took a seat in the school's hospital waiting room. She began to converse with Ben, who had never left her side.

"I hate him," she admitted. "Dad always talks about how sweet and caring Olly is. Does my dad not know how much of an as —," Spencer thought it was best not to finish that sentence. She was, after all, talking to her teacher as well as her mother's brother.

"Yes, that was odd behavior he displayed today, but don't worry, I'll talk with him," Ben assured her.

He handed her a book that sat on the wooden coffee table in front of them. The book was about interpreting and studying the stars. When he saw Spencer's disinterest, he reached for another. He placed a book about plants in her hands. She shook her head with a smile. Ben stretched for another, a magazine titled *The Current History of Galdorwide*. Spencer made a face of approval.

Olly spoke harshly to Mr Silwhet, his words inaudible from where Spencer sat. "Spencer?" Mr Gower repeated, unsure if he had heard his friend correctly. He turned to look at Spencer, his brow raised. "Spencer, Mr Bell would like to have a word with you."

Spencer gulped. She would've never thought that she would fear the scrawny janitor, but she did. She now saw how scary he could be. When Spencer stepped out into the hall with him, she didn't want to shut the door. Olly reached behind her and closed it, once again taking her with it.

"The halls here are complex, and I understand if today was an accident." It sounded as if Olly was leading up to an apology. "However, the halls in this school aren't safe. There are many ancient potions in my closet, spell books, and objects that are possibly cursed. The doctors and teachers here have been studying them. The janitor's closet is also a storage room," he explained. "However, if I catch you or any other of your family members trying to break into the closet again, so help me, Merlin, I will not hesitate to send any of you to the dungeons," his voice drawled.

By his words, she could tell that he also wouldn't hesitate to do something much worse than sending them to the dungeons. She pictured him turning her and her family into pigs. She entered the classroom like a lazy cat.

She took a seat at her desk and began to scribble the teacher's detailed notes. The teacher gave Spencer a small smile as his heart twanged as he saw her quake in her chair.

When the students began to leave the class after the bell rang, Mr Silwhet asked for her to stay. He sat at the small desk next to hers. Once the final classmate closed the door, Gower began to speak. "Don't take what Mr Bell has to say too seriously. Mr Black tells me he has been on edge ever since his encounter with a vampire last week. Well, it wasn't much of an encounter, as Mr Bell ran away." He began to laugh. "I had asked Mr Bell about the situation just for a laugh, and boy, did his face sure turn bright pink!"

Spencer smiled as she heard another story about Olly's cowardice. She had forgotten all of the ones her father had told her after this morning.

Spencer always heard of how her last name made her different from the rest — she hadn't believed that until today. She didn't understand how her family's past had anything to do with her.

At lunch, Spencer met up with her friends, Ellen Lefu, Regina Smith, and Lexi Snowball. Like Spencer, Lexi was a freshman. Ellen was in tenth grade while Regina was in the eleventh.

Ellen had always lived next door to Spencer, but they had never spoken until Ellen had waved her over to her table on John Jr's first sick day, the second Monday of the school year. He hadn't been ill. He simply didn't want to go. His parents were tired of fighting him as they had throughout his days back in training school. He was now old enough to make his own decisions, even though they were always wrong.

"What did the cafeteria have today?" Spencer asked, pulling out a paper lunch bag from her backpack.

"Fresh frog." Ellen pushed her tray away from her.

Spencer extended her hand, holding a plastic bag. "Want an onion boar sandwich?"

"No." Ellen shook her head, pulling her red cardigan sleeves over her hands.

"Take it. I'm not going to eat it," Spencer insisted.

Ellen shook her head once again. She almost looked as sickly as Spencer.

"I'll take it!" Lexi shouted while she chewed on a slice of her fresh frog. She raised her hand, bunching her white-blond curls on her shoulder.

Lexi was stunning. She had big hazel eyes that contrasted with her light hair. All the girls were jealous of her. Lexi seemed to be able to eat whatever she wanted without gaining a single pound. Everyone at school had wondered why the cute blond had decided to spend her time with three sickly-looking girls, especially Regina. She was a grade eleven student who had lost twice her weight within two years. She always had cracked lips, pale skin, patchy eyebrows, and never wore makeup. Worst of all, she didn't talk to anyone who wasn't in her friend group, and still, even with them, she barely spoke. Spencer tossed her the plastic bag with the sandwich.

"So, Spencer, how was your Terra Arts class?" Ellen asked. Ellen had agreed to tutor both Spencer and Lexi if they ever struggled in their classes.

"Not sure. I barely paid attention," Spencer groaned.

"What? How come? That's like, a major class that you need to focus on!" Ellen pulled back her brown hair up into a messy bun, a habit of hers whenever she became stressed.

"Regina, you've been here the longest. What can you tell me about Olly?"

"Not much, just that whenever he acts as a substitute teacher, he plies the students with tons of homework." She rolled her eyes.

Just then, Caden came into the cafeteria. He gave her friends a bit of a shock when he began to shake and push Spencer.

Lexi and Ellen's jaws dropped. Regina looked to her hands, as she feared to look into the Scaasi man's eyes and suffer his wrath. Spencer giggled in the crazed dizziness he was putting her in. With that, Caden carried on walking over to the table where Aldaricus and his other jock friends sat.

"O.M.M! Spencer, are you okay?" Lexi reached across the table to lend her a comforting hand.

"What? Oh, yeah, no, no, I'm fine. That's just my cousin."

"Oh, my Merlin! I felt sorry for you!" Lexi reached for her chest.

"Wait. You thought it was real, and you guys did nothing?" The girls, cowardly, put their heads down. "Nice." Spencer rolled her eyes.

Regina wondered why Spencer would think that they'd stick up for her. After all, Regina got bullied every day, and none of them ever stood up for her.

Spencer met up with John Jr at his locker after their last class came to an end. He always took his time packing his belongings. On the other hand, Spencer held her textbook from her previous study, Alchemy, in her arms. She had walked to her locker and pulled out her empty backpack. They met up with Lulia and Olivia, who sat outside of the school from across the street.

When they arrived home, Mary handed Spencer a letter. Spencer tore it open immediately.

Dear Spencer Scaasi,

I want to invite you out for a cup of coffee or tea, whichever you prefer. Would around five tomorrow work? I want to spend more time with you, you know, outside of school. Send an answer back.

Sincerely, Tris Smith.

Spencer blushed. Tristan "Tris" Smith was a friend from school. He was tall and athletically slim in stature. He had a chiseled face and short brown hair.

"*Plectrum.*" Her wand turned into a quill. "*Carte!*" A piece of paper appeared in front of Spencer. She took it, leaned over the kitchen table and began writing her letter of acceptance to his offer. "*Besendan!*" The paper folded and plopped inside an envelope that appeared out of thin air. Once sealed, the letter flew itself out of her kitchen window.

It was excellent, and Spencer now had something to look forward to after another day at Galdowide High. Ellen was always busy with homework, and Lexi was still busy helping her family set up for some extravagant event. The thought of seeing him would help her get through her classes.

The next day, Oleander Bell was her Terra Arts teacher replacement for the evening. Spencer scurried from her usual seat in the front of the class and sped to one at the back. She knew Olly disliked her, but after class, she realized he hated her.

The room was chillier than usual. A usual sign of a witch in distress due to great anger exceeding a burning sensation. A fit of rage that was so cold, with no hope of becoming warm. Before Olly had even begun his lesson, he sent Spencer into the hall to wait for him.

When he joined her, he began to lead her down to the dungeons. The hall leading to the caged rooms was lined with potions and other items.

"I bring with me a celebrity," Olly announced to someone whom Spencer could not see. She looked around, her heart thumping against her chest.

"Ah, Spencer Scaasi." A hunch-backed man approached. His fingers curled as he walked closer to get a better look. "What is she in for?" the man asked, walking over to his cluttered desk that acted as an entrance to the chambers.

"Delinquent behavior," Olly replied.

The two men began to lead Spencer to the last cell on the right. Unknown to Olly, Spencer, and the dungeon keeper, they were being followed. Caden, Aldaricus, Jax, and John Jr stalked behind. John Jr had been pulled out of his class by Caden, who disguised himself as his uncle, John. They had followed Olly and Spencer down the dark tunnel that led to the dungeon.

The boys were silent, and when they did speak, they whispered. Aldaricus, the most magically advanced of the boys, waved his wand. His lips curled into a sneer as he got a good view of his cousin's captors. "*Wyrtbedd und fungi.*" A gentle emerald blaze of sparks exited his wand. The flashes raced towards the two men before they could lock Spencer in the cell.

Herbs and vines emitted from the ground, holding the men's feet in place. Various species of fungus sprouted from their skin. They shrieked in pain as the foreign substances grew from within them and pushed their way out. Olly and the dungeon keeper tried to escape the vines' hold. Their veins grew green and spread across their skin. They shook, wearing a pained expression, groaning. They began to choke as vines grew from their mouths and ears. Bloody plants protruded from their bodies.

Spencer jumped back, frightened, and looked down at her skin to make sure she was not affected. To her relief, she wasn't, which was good. A fungus-filled face was not a good look for a date with Tris. Spencer whipped her head around to see Aldaricus wink. Spencer snickered, then Aldaricus waved her over.

Both Olly and the dungeon keeper did not look pleased. She would even say that they looked furious. Now, at least they knew that if they wanted to take her down, they'd have to go through her family first.

"*Normalem!*" Olly muttered a spell.

"Oh, shit! Spencer! Run!" Aldaricus shouted.

Spencer sprinted towards the boys. Olly and the dungeon keeper were close behind her.

The vines around their ankles began to release and the fungus on their skin shrank. "*Awefecung!*" A thin green stream of light exited Aldaricus's wand. Once it struck the two men, they immediately fell into a deep slumber.

Ben appeared to Arthur in the abandoned castle's office after he had finished teaching his final class. Today was Ben's day to train Arthur, who sat at a little desk while he sat atop a larger one. Disembodied footsteps walked around the room.

Scattered pieces of paper carpeted the floor. It was no one's permanent home, and no one felt the need to clean it, even if all he or she needed to do was flick their wand.

The creaky, old backyard gate swung in the wind. Every once in a while, it would bang as it clashed with the other side of the fence. Arthur's heavy breaths echoed off the table. He was both insecure and sweaty.

Outside, the sun was out, and the insects of the forest buzzed and clicked. The array of noises created an overpowering hum.

Ben reached into his pocket and pulled out the Excogitatoris Draco stone. "On May 15th, you will join the Ministry on your first official operation/mission/quest — whatever it is you wish to call it. We will head to Doryu Edjer's church, where we believe the dragons will be.

"Arthur, it will be your duty to place this stone inside the mouth of the eldest dragon. If successful, the eldest dragon and the dragons closest to it will turn to dust. If all goes well, we won't have a problem. Now, Arthur, if I told you that you were in charge of masking us from the dragons, what would you do?"

"I don't know," Arthur replied quietly. "Use Draca Bordrand?"

Draca Bordrand was a flowering plant. If rubbed all over a witch or wizard's body, their skin would become immune to the burn of a dragon's fire.

"You're not wrong, Arthur. Dragon shields are quite effective. We definitely should use that when we go to Doryu's church. However, Draca Bordrand, or Dragon Shield, despite its name, does not mask us from the dragons. Draca Bordrand only shields us from the powers that they inflict. We will need Draca Inuisibilitas. Once rubbed on the skin, we will become nearly invisible to the eyes of a dragon as well as any other serpent."

Arthur had been writing down everything that Ben said.

Back home, things didn't get better for Spencer. She walked in with her brother, two cousins, and their self-righteous friend, with Olivia following shortly after them.

Mr Bernard, the principal of Galdorwide High, had called Mary to inform her of the matter. He explained to her what had happened, or at least the only version of it he knew, Olly's.

Spencer had smuggled alcohol into class. He also told her about her son and nephew's magical outburst.

"I take full responsibility for the vines, fungus, and the slumber spell, Aunt Mary." Aldaricus took a step forward and placed a hand on his chest with sincerity.

Mary still scolded John and Spencer. However, she seemed to have accepted Aldaricus's apology. Mary yelled at her two eldest kids — shouting that they should be more like Lulia. Lulia was in the marble-furnished kitchen, brewing a potion assigned by her training school teacher, as she had stayed home, feeling ill. She was mixing kissing bugs in a concoction that turned dark green, filling the kitchen with blue smoke. The brew seemed to be working. Lulia, who stood on a stool, looked up from her cauldron and gave her older siblings a devilish smile.

"Spencer, is it true about the alcohol?" Mary asked. "My alarm didn't go off."

"Alarm?" Caden asked with a furrowed brow.

"Yes, alarm. When the children were born, I placed a set of alarms that would go off in our heads. For example, if Spencer truly did drink alcohol underaged, an alarm would sound in her mind. She would then see the hologram I registered of myself shouting, "PUT THAT ALCOHOL DOWN, YOUNG LADY!" Whereas my alarm would say, "Spencer: Alcohol. Spencer: Alcohol." She mimicked the alarm.

"No, mom, it's not true. That's why the alarm didn't go off. Olly is out to get me. Ask them." She pointed to her two cousins, who nodded. "He's been harassing me all week. You can even ask Uncle Ben."

"Why didn't you tell your father or me?" Mary asked. Her voice began to calm.

"I don't know. I didn't think Olly was that bad until today. He wanted me to spend the school day in the dungeon for no reason other than the fact that I am a Scaasi. I feel like every other teacher at the school feels the same way. They all hate me, all 'cause of my last name."

"I'll speak to your father. He'll deal with it," Mary assured her. "Now, you kids go into the homework room and study." She pointed to the door at the end of the hallway.

At five o'clock, Spencer left her home to meet Tris at Galdorwide's bakery, The Baking Devil. The building was small, wooden and was located at the edge of the forbidden forest.

Behind the cashier, Spencer could see the chef cooking on the open fire. In the corner of the room, she saw Tris, who looked as if he had been nervously watching her ever since she walked in.

He stood to his feet and greeted her with a hug. She blushed and took a seat across from him.

A waitress walked over with two mugs. "Green tea for the young lady and Twilight tea for the gentleman." The waitress smiled and walked away.

"Twilight tea? What does it taste like?" Spencer asked.

"It's refreshing. It's crisp and bitter. In a way, it kinda tastes like a winter's night." He noticed Spencer was looking at it longingly. "Try some." He pushed the mug closer to her. With a smile, she took the cup and sipped from it.

The waitress returned. This time, she placed a raspberry lemon tart in front of Tris and a slice of orange pie in front of Spencer.

"Oh, no, I shouldn't." Spencer pushed her plate away. The waitress furrowed her brow.

"Spence, the waitresses know what you want," Tris explained.

"I know, but I really shouldn't."

"If you want it, eat it." Tris pushed the plate back towards Spencer. She smiled and picked up her fork. The waitress smiled and left. "So, can you believe that we're no longer allowed into the forest?" Tris looked out of the window and over at the forest as the sun began to go down.

"Yeah, I know, it was kind of my quiet place, you know? Growing up, my brother and I would always go to the forest. There's a treehouse right smack dab in the middle where we would often spend our afternoons."

"Aw, nice, and yeah, it was my quiet place too." An awkward pause hung over the air. "I saw Olly take you down to the dungeons. What on earth did you do?" Tris laughed.

"Nothing!" she quarreled. "Olly has it in for me just because I'm a Scaasi."

"That's bollocks. I mean, the Scaasis aren't even that bad any more. Sure, one's a pirate, but the rest are pretty normal. I mean, your father is a well-respected teacher, and your uncle Ace is a doctor. The Scaasis were only bad, you know, back then." Tris seemed to know a lot about her family, but so did the rest of the kingdom. Tris didn't quite meet her eyes when he spoke. "It's rumored that it was your great-uncle Gabriel who robbed Galdorwide's bank back in 1949. No one ever did find any evidence, though."

Spencer grunted to herself and took a bite of her orange pie. "I've heard the stories. However, I wasn't there, so I don't know. So how have things been?" She changed the subject. She knew all too well about her family's past but didn't find it fit conversation for an occasion like this.

"Pretty good. I finally found out what my familiar is. It's uncommon in Galdorwide, hence it took me so long to figure out. It's a cheetah," Tris explained.

"A cheetah? No wonder it took you so long to figure it out. You should be proud! Cheetah familiars belong to unique witches and wizards created for a specific reason. Aren't you curious as to what your reason is?" Spencer's factual nerd came out.

"No, not really. That kind of stuff happens naturally. Who knows, maybe I've already filled my purpose." Tris shrugged.

The unofficial date was exciting and nerve-wracking for both of them. Before going in, Spencer couldn't help but wonder if they'd hit it off, have stuff in common, or be able to keep a conversation going — oh, how she dreaded awkward silences. She wondered how she should act, but she ended up just focusing on Tris while with him. By the time their hangout ended, she truly wanted to see him again. Before leaving, she wanted to make sure that Tris knew she was interested. Spencer expressed her gratitude. After all, he had paid for her, spent time with her and even walked her home.

"We should do this again," she smiled.

The next day, Spencer was walking down the hall when she heard Olly shout from behind her. "You — Spencer!" Spencer turned around to see him wearing his red janitorial uniform. It reminded her of a prison jumpsuit. He stomped over, and Spencer found herself cemented to the ground. *"You're pushing it, you know."* His face was an inch away from hers.

He grabbed hold of her arm and began to walk her down to the dungeons. Spencer's mind was racing. Her father should have already talked to him, so why did he continue to mistreat her? Also, why did he hate her so much?

"Cheer up," John Jr telepathically spoke to her from his classroom. *"Look forward to spending more time with Tris. I want to get to know him more, since I can tell you two like each other."* Both Spencer and John Jr smiled to themselves. He always knew how to comfort her.

Spencer was left alone with her thoughts for the whole day as she sat on the dungeon's stone floor. The dungeon keeper offered the students some nutmeg yogurt. He proposed it to everyone except Spencer, but she would have denied the food anyway. Her thoughts rambled on through her mind. Did her father speak to Olly? Did Olly know something about her family that she didn't? Wasn't he her father's friend?

CHAPTER 9

Growing up, Bella never thought that she'd hate someone as much as she hated Alan.

However, that was until she met Lewis. After she had successfully removed Angel from her life, she didn't have to put up with him either. In need of more Ministry members, Bella posted a notice at the kingdom's town square. Lewis groaned as Angel's eyes lit up as soon as her eyes spotted the purple flyer.

"Of course you'd be happy," Lewis said darkly. She turned, now holding the poster in her hands. Her eyes were still kindled. "You've got to be joking."

"I was friends with like, half of them, and they all like you. Not to mention you're related to two of the members." Angel had always wanted to be a part of the Ministry, mainly because of its history. When the department had first come into being, over sixty years ago, the members wore black cloaks and eye masks. They once held a very eery and heroic appearance. The eye masks were later considered unneeded. The Ministry was not a job where its members needed to hide their identities.

"Angel, Bella kicked you out of the castle and out of your entire family, for that matter. Why are you so eager to go back and make things good?" Lewis said rationally.

Angel, ever since she was a child, had always talked about the Ministry. Her voice would grow loud and excited whenever she spoke about her dream of becoming a member. She was still confident that the Ministry would accept her application. Only the strongest of witches and even Nullums could make it into the Ministry.

Once, a Heofsij bounty hunter had chased her during her visit to Rosemont, Pennsylvania. She had been the sole reason why she and her friends made it back to Galdorwide alive. She was also one of the top Crash Ring players at her school, a visible sign of a great witch.

Despite her exceptional skills, Lewis found it fit that she did not make it into the Ministry. As gifted as she was, she was quite an airhead. Half the time, she could barely talk without her words jumbling up.

"Lewis! She's my sister, okay? I miss her," Angel argued.

Angel was nervous, and she was going to try out for the Ministry one more time. She wished that she had had more time to mentally and physically prepare for this. Today was the deadline for the opening positions. To savor some more time, she decided to walk rather than fly. As she walked, she looked down at a book, straining her eyes until they began to hurt. The book was called *The History Of Galdorwide's Ministry*. She was hanging on to every word that she read. She was desperate to take in any tips and ideas to make this evening go smoothly. Her reading was interrupted when a letter appeared in front of her.

Mail wasn't typical for Angel, or any other Scaasi, for that matter. When she opened the envelope, she saw that there was a piece of Blasters Candy. She looked at the candy closely before stuffing the letter into the cloak's pocket. She didn't need any distractions. She was approaching her sister's castle, where she'd apply to live out her dream for the rest of her life. Before she could reach her hand for the castle's raven door knocker, someone stepped beside her. She looked; it was Lewis.

"I'm not letting you do this alone — it's dangerous," he replied to her excited and confused face. Though it was true he didn't want to see any harm come to his wife, he also didn't like the idea of her starting a job, one where there'd be other men around, so he decided to be there, just in case.

***

A small package appeared in front of Spencer as she sat in the cafeteria with her friends.

Her eyes lit up. She reached up for it and excitedly tore the packaging apart. "Aw, who's it from, Tris?" Lexi leaned forward.

"Come on, what is it?" Ellen shared her excitement.

Regina watched on silently but just as curiously as her friends. When Spencer saw what was inside, she didn't feel like answering. Her face fell and turned a bright scarlet. Inside the package was a photograph, a photograph of a blond girl. Spencer reached for her stomach as it began to shift. She stood up and took the box with her.

Breathing heavily, Spencer entered the girls' washroom and ran to the nearest stall. She lowered the toilet seat down and sat atop it. Spencer looked down at the picture: Omisha Tanda, a girl who had gone missing the night of Spencer's fourteenth birthday party. She was not missing, and Spencer reminded herself, she was dead. A week after the party, Omisha's body was found floating in the forest's lake.

Spencer's birthday party was a secret one, or at least a secret to her parents. Ben had convinced the king to allow the girls to use the castle's barn-turned-cabin for the night. That night, after begging her free spirit uncle, Ben was able to disarm her mother's alarm. It was a spell that he had learned as a teenager, when his mom had built signals into him as well. For the night, Spencer was able to drink as much as she pleased.

She hadn't ever gotten along with Omisha, a girl who had hung out with Spencer and her friends. She was bossy and always telling her what to do. In many ways, Spencer could even say that she hated Omisha — enough to kill. With no recollection of the night or what had happened, Spencer had always assumed the worse. The Ministry was on the case. The Ministry, of course, included her father and great-uncle. So it was easy for them to skip over her as a suspect.

Spencer, however, wasn't so sure that that was the right call. Despite her beliefs, the whole school believed that Regina was the cause of Omisha's death; after all, Regina was the strangest of them all.

Both Caden and Aldaricus quickly jumped to their feet in the cafeteria and headed towards Spencer's friends. "What's going on?" Caden asked with concern.

"Spencer got a package, and I'm assuming she didn't like what was in it." Lexi spoke more softly than usual. Her fair skin began to redden.

Caden scowled and looked to Aldaricus; they nodded, and with that, they headed over to the girls' washroom. When they knocked on the door, Spencer didn't answer. She kept herself quiet, holding in her breath, hoping they'd leave. The two boys then leaned against the wall on either side of the door.

"She can't stay in there forever." Aldaricus crossed his arms.

When the bell rang to commence the end of lunch, Spencer still hadn't left the washroom. The boys slid down the wall and sat on the cold, tiled floor. By three thirty, she hadn't exited. John Jr and Jax now joined Caden and Aldaricus; after many sweet calls and reassurances, Spencer fled from the room. Much to their dismay, she wore what seemed to be a permanent frown. The whites of her eyes had pooled red. Spencer pushed her way past them and began to walk out onto the courtyard.

It was a breezy, chilly day. Their feet crunched the snow-covered leaves that lay on the ground. To the left of the school was the road, straight ahead was the park, and to the left was the fenced-in forbidden forest. The trees swayed in the dark air that hung around them despite the shining sun in the sky. That's where Spencer was heading. The four boys looked to one another.

"What are you waiting for?" Caden barked as he turned to John Jr

John Jr glanced around, unsure if Caden was talking to him. He looked back to Caden, whose eyes may have even shown hints of fear. They were, after all, heading towards the forbidden forest because of his sister.

"Where are you going?" croaked John Jr as he called after his sister.

Spencer lifted her right arm. An old, tattered broom flew into her hands; its twigs were bunched and twisted oddly. Spencer raised her leg and hopped on. She headed towards the forest, traveling at the highest speed the old broom would allow.

"Where did you get a broom! You're not licensed!" John Jr strained his voice, hoping for her to hear him, but by the time he stopped his yelling, she had vanished.

Aldaricus summoned his worn-down broom that had been given to him by his father. It was once lovely, with long twigs and a green handle, or so his father Roman had explained.

"John, hop on." Aldaricus turned to him. John Jr made a face that made it clear that he did not want to get his feet off the ground, or even enter the forbidden forest for that matter. "Come on! She's most likely going to listen to you rather than us."

John Jr, with reluctance, sat behind Aldaricus. Caden and Jax summoned their brooms. The boys kicked off from the ground and into the air at the highest speed. John Jr gripped Aldaricus's green varsity jacket tightly. His father had always flown fast, but nothing like this. The boys leaned forward on their broomsticks. They spotted Spencer in the middle of the forest with her face buried into her knees.

When the boys landed, they were all too nervous and frightened to approach her. When she heard the sticks crack beneath their feet, her body juddered. When she saw that it wasn't a werewolf or any other dangerous creature, she relaxed. She then flung herself onto the ground and buried her face into the grass to hide her tears.

They had all stayed quiet as they sat around her. John Jr reached for her hand and clenched it. She looked up at her brother, her face covered with both old and new tear streaks. Pieces of dry grass stuck to her wet face. She sat up, and Aldaricus laid a supporting arm around her. Jax looked on as if he were holding in a laugh. He deserved his green aura, or maybe even a black one. He seemed to lack sympathy and a heart, for that matter.

"What's so funny, Jax?" Spencer scowled. The boys snapped their heads up and looked over at him.

"I think you should leave." Caden stood to his feet.

"You think so, eh?" Jax stood up. "I can't be the only one that finds it funny. You two barely ever spoke to this girl before she came to school, and now all of a sudden she's this child you need to protect?"

"Look." Caden grabbed Jax by his school uniform collar. "You don't get to pick whom or what we care about it. Got it?" Caden pushed Jax away from him. "She's family."

"Whatever," Jax said quietly with a nasty smile. He walked over to his broom. His blood pounded beneath his skin. He didn't like being told what to do. His feet kicked off of the ground much harder than needed. Air rushed through his hair. His green cloak whipped around wildly in the wind.

Once Caden was sure that Jax was gone, he took his seat back on the snowy grass beside Spencer.

"Thank you." Spencer wiped beneath her eyes once again with a sniffle. "I'm glad you now realize how much of a jerk he is."

"I've always known. I never cared, but that'd be the day I let him talk down to my family. Especially if it's you." Caden nudged her playfully. This time it was softer than usual.

The wind rippled through their hair. In the distance, the four relatives could hear the scream of an animal.

"We should get out of here." Aldaricus stood. He pulled Spencer up with him.

They stood, and as they were about to walk over to their brooms, a hand emerged from a hole in the ground beside Spencer. The gap widened. She had fallen as a second hand appeared and latched onto her ankle. The boys gripped her tightly, which had commenced a game of tug-of-war. They pulled her out just in time as the hole started to close up. They all toppled over onto their backs. Aldaricus looked around to make sure that they were all okay.

"Spencer..." a female voice whispered as they stood to their feet. "Spencer..." They all looked around — there was no one in sight. "SPENCER SCAASI!" The booming voice shook the ground. A female ghost rushed from out of the bushes and flew down — through her.

Spencer, who had lifted herself to her elbows, fell back onto the ground. She wasn't terrified. Instead, her heart sank with her body. The boys trembled, as the ghost had burst out of Spencer and began to run towards them. Aldaricus grabbed Spencer and raced them towards his broom.

"Johnny, get on with Caden." Aldaricus wrapped Spencer's numb arms around his waist as they hopped their legs over the broom.

Once they were off the ground, both Caden and Aldaricus flew at a steady pace beside one another.

"Never — in all my eighteen years — have I ever seen a ghost until today." Aldaricus turned his neck as far as it would allow and looked to Spencer. "How did she know your name?"

Spencer was pale, her lips blue and her eyes empty. She didn't answer him or meet his eyes.

"Spence?"

The wind that rushed past them drowned out her soft whimpers. She squeezed her eyes along with her grip on Aldaricus's jacket.

They headed for Spencer's home, and when they landed, they all walked numbly. However, Spencer was practically being carried by her two cousins as they headed inside, as the tips of her toes dragged against the patterned stone pathway. She was in trouble, but she also knew that that was the least of her concerns.

Luckily, after preparing to walk in and see Mary waiting at the door with an army of spoons, they realized that her parents were not home. "Can you guys stay with her?" John Jr turned to his cousins. "I need to pick up Lulia and Harriet at the park so that mom and dad aren't suspicious."

They nodded and proceeded to carry Spencer to her room. Her feet swept across the floor.

"What's my mom going to say?" Spencer asked as they laid her down on her blue, silk sheets.

"She won't find out." Aldaricus brushed back her hair as Caden fluffed her pillows. "But why don't you tell us what's going on with you."

Spencer, weak, was still able to clench her jaw tight. She looked miserable, confused and devastated all at once. Her stomach twisted as she thought about what she would say to them.

"Spence." Caden spoke up. "I want you to know that whatever you're going through, you don't have to do it alone. Heck, we're family. We all have problems, and we can be here for one another. For example, my dad's a fucking pirate! He got inspired by Blackbeard, some Heofsij pirate. As a child, every time I disobeyed him, he'd light his beard on fire. For the longest time, I believed my father was a demon."

"Yeah. As for me, my mother and father are like, devoted followers of the king. I swear that they're up to no good now that he's dead," Aldaricus added. "You got lucky, Spence. Your father is the best Scaasi known to our family."

Spencer was bewildered. Why were her cousins coming together for her, despite barely knowing her? She was confused and didn't know whether or not she could trust them. Something in their eyes told her that she could.

"I can trust you guys?" she asked. Aldaricus nodded. "Both of you?" She turned to Caden. He nodded. Spencer then sat up and took out the picture of Omisha from out of her blue cloak pocket. "It's Omisha." She handed the picture to Aldaricus, who then passed it over to Caden so that he could see. "I HATED her sometimes. She was a friend of my friends, and she had come to my fourteenth birthday party. It was at the castle's barn just outside the forbidden forest where they found her body. I don't remember anything from that night because I was drunk. Deep down,

136

I've always felt responsible."

"It's not your fault. The forest is dangerous. Everyone knows that." Caden handed her back the picture.

"I mean, deep down, I've felt that it was my fault. Like I killed Omisha."

The boys looked to one another, and they never would've expected this behavior from a girl born to John and Mary Scaasi.

"Someone mailed this picture to me. What if someone saw what happened?"

The boys were now entirely puzzled. When she saw that they were speechless, she reached for her pillow and buried her face. She grabbed out her wand. She was going to erase their memory.

"Don't, it's okay, Spencer, I promise." Aldaricus took her wand from out of her hand. She looked up at him. "You don't know who sent it. For all we know, it's her killer trying to make you feel guilty. I know you, Spencer, your parents are great people."

"I know! I know my parents are great!" She shot up into a seated position. "But I have your parents' blood in me too!"

Caden kept quiet, and he had no idea what to say. He did not expect this from Spencer.

"Don't worry. If you get another package, we will dig into it, but right now, enjoy life. Ever play Crash Ring?" He tried to sound excited.

She stared at him for a moment. She wasn't ready for their heated conversation to end, but then again, she didn't want to continue it either.

"Have you seen me? I'm way too tiny." Spencer wiped away her tears as she began to smile.

"Yes, I've seen your size. The same as your brother."

Spencer began to laugh, maybe a little too hard, but she needed it.

"But seriously, I saw you today, and you're great on a broom. Meet me in the yard after school tomorrow, and we can train you." Spencer's smile didn't fade.

It was almost dinner time. Spencer was finally able to convince herself to tell her brother what she had told their cousins. John Jr was somewhat shocked initially but found himself more concerned about running to the dinner table. By the time the food entered his mouth, he had completely forgotten what his sister had told him. He was starving. After all, today had been draining.

"So, how was your day?" John asked Spencer.

That's when John Jr's memory came back to the day's events. He looked over to Spencer; his mouth, full of food, dropped.

"Fine." Spencer faked a smile. "I'll be training with Aldaricus and Caden for Crash Ring."

"Crash Ring?" John almost choked on his food. "That's a dangerous game. Are you sure you want to play that?"

"I'm sure that I can handle it — after all, I do have the blood of the men who escaped from Skogen prison over forty years ago in me. Did it take them eight months to break out? The high-security prison."

"That'll be your last meal, Spencer Lynn Scaasi, if you speak of your father's family line like that one more time!" Mary waggled her fork wildly as if it were her finger.

"You're brave, Spencer, nobler than anyone this family has ever seen. Remember, you were not born with the Viridi aura like the rest of your family. You were born a Caerul, the aura of peace." John smiled.

"Yeah, so start acting like it!" Mary stabbed her fork into the table.

"I'm surprised you guys are even letting me talk to Aldaricus and Caden." Spencer couldn't help but fuel her mother's anger.

"The boys will make great trainers for you." John continued to make use of his peaceful aura. "My family, though not the highest of morals, have great loyalty. Aldaricus and Caden are great friends to have."

"I'll take you down any time, you Caerul Centaur!" John Jr piped up, pointing his meat-filled fork at her. He spoke with his mouth filled with food. He was barely audible. Particles of rabbit meat flung from out of his mouth.

"Try me, you red island!"

"Don't call me red island!" He puffed his chest.

"Well, don't call me a blue half-horse woman!" Spencer sized him up.

The twins burst into laughter. Mary buried her forehead into the palm of her hand while John shared in on the laugh. Lulia and Olivia had been entertaining themselves with a conversation of their own.

At midnight, while Spencer and her sisters la asleep in their room, the window began to shake. Spencer jolted up, wielding her wand like a sword. She inched closer to the window beside her bed and was relieved to see that Aldaricus and Caden stood behind it. They were both squeezing to look into the small window, and she pried the window open. Aldaricus was wearing a dark green hoodie and black jeans. Caden sported his usual leather jacket with a green plaid shirt beneath.

"Wanna see what's got Olly's panties in a twist?" Aldaricus asked.

"Huh?" Lulia sat up. Her hair was in a tangled mess.

Spencer whipped around. "*Awefcung!*" Lulia's body slammed back down onto the bed, and she began to snore. Spencer looked back to her cousins. "I can't leave — my mom registered this alarm in my brain if I ever sneak out."

"*Detrahere Arma.*" Aldaricus aimed his wand at Spencer's forehead. A wild emerald corkscrew of particles exited the rod and swirled inside her forehead, disarming her alarm. "What? Did you not think that the worshippers of the king would put alarms on me? Coming?"

Spencer nodded.

"Just give me a second to get ready." She beamed. She ran to her closet and pulled out a pale blue polo shirt, a black denim overall dress and blue nylons. The boys turned around and gave her some privacy as she changed. She grabbed her winter jacket and slipped on her boots. Caden and Aldaricus lent her a hand and helped her hop out of the window.

"Are you sure we should be walking around the kingdom at night?" Spencer shivered.

"Who knows," Caden began. "But if we get caught, we need a good cover story. So here it is: we were in the schoolyard to train for Crash Ring, when a man wearing a black mask and hoodie tried to rob us. Before he could hurt us, we made our way to the school."

"What if we get caught in Olly's closet?" Spencer asked.

"We stick to the story. We say that we were trying to find a room that was unlocked and that this one was."

They crept across the school's courtyard. Aldaricus took out his wand and pointed it at the lock of the school's large blue back door. "*Unlucan!*"

He then waved his wand above his head in a flowing circular motion around them. *"Dunnian!"* A bright, green rush of ripples exited his rod and fell around them. They were now invisible to everyone except for those who were under an invisible spell. Torches on the school walls were lit, making their travels easier than anticipated.

"I can't believe we're doing this," Spencer whispered. The sides of her lips quivered as she tried to hide her frown.

"It'll be all right," Aldaricus assured her.

"So — did you tell your brother what you told us?" Caden asked.

"Yeah," Spencer replied quietly.

"What did Junior say?"

"Nothing. Junior was more concerned about dinner, to be honest." Spencer smiled.

"Come on." Aldaricus motioned them over as they began to trail behind. He was standing in front of Olly's closet and had already used the unlocking spell.

Spencer and Caden rushed forward to be by Aldaricus's side as he pushed the door open. They followed him in. Before Spencer could take in the room, she noticed something chilling as she looked behind them as the door closed.

"There's no handle," she mumbled.

"What?" The boys turned to look at her. They saw what she saw. They were locked in the closet.

"There's no handle, and we can't get out. Now what? Now we wait for Olly to come here tomorrow morning? What are we going to say?" Spencer began to freak. The Mary in her was coming out.

"We stick to the story." Aldaricus tried to calm her.

"Shh — did you hear that?" Spencer motioned for the boys to stop talking and listen.

"Unlucan!" a familiar voice called from the other side of the door. Olly? They wondered.

The door was quickly pulled open. It was Jax, who was with a blond girl. Before the Scaasi could try to keep the door open, Jax and the girl pushed themselves in as they were kissing.

"No!" they shouted as the door snapped shut.

Jax and the girl flinched. They held each other closer in fear as they couldn't see their company.

140

"*Normalem!*" Aldaricus returned himself and his cousins to their visible forms.

"What the dried-out sack butler are you doing here?" Jax asked.

"Have you guys done this before? Do you guys know how to get out?" Aldaricus bombarded the couple.

"No — we haven't done this before. What do you mean by how to get out? You use an unlocking —" His eyes trailed to the handle-less door. Jax threw himself at the door. He began to slam his body and fists against it, as if that was going to work. The Scaasis hissed at him to be quiet.

Spencer took in her surroundings. No matter how many odd and weird artifacts there were, she was only concerned about finding a way out. She noticed that the room wasn't pitch black. There was no light switch or torch. There had to be natural light soaking in somehow. She watched their shadows. She looked up to find a tiny window at the back of the room that stood against the far wall. She could see the moon shine in through the window that was half-covered by the large shelf.

"Help me, will you?" She turned to her cousins. With every second that passed, she feared that Olly would walk in at any moment, but they were lucky. The boys had successfully moved the shelf before there were any signs of Olly.

"*Gemanigfieldan!*" Aldaricus aimed his wand at the window. A rough, green, intertwining duo of streams covered the window. The window began to enlarge.

They boosted Spencer onto their hands to aid her out of the window. The boys then sped out of the window, but before Jax and his girl could leave, Aldaricus aimed his wand at the window. "*Normalem!*"

Jax had just begun to pull himself out of the window but was squeezed back into the closet as the window returned to its standardized size. Spencer cackled.

"That was pointless. Jax knows where the window is. He'll get out soon and try to kill you." Caden stood to his feet.

"No, he won't. That kid hasn't paid attention to any of his classes, and that girl he's with is a Nullum. I can't wait to see what Olly does to him tomorrow." Aldaricus smiled, proud of himself. "That's what he gets for how he treated you earlier, baby cousin." He nudged Spencer, who stood up.

She smiled, but it immediately faded. "I don't know what Olly's going to do, but I do know what Jax will do. He'll tell Olly that we were here too. Knowing how much Olly loves our family, I know he will take his word."

"Hmm — you're right." Aldaricus kneeled back down and peered through the window.

He took out his wand and pointed it at the couple, who sat against the door, defeated. "*Forgietan!*" An unstable green line rushed towards the couple. The spell would make them forget anything that had happened twenty minutes prior.

The moonlight glimmered in the sky. The three Scaasis walked close to one another.

They hugged themselves as chilly winds blew past them.

The pale moon was the only wink of light in the kingdom. They edged along the forest, not daring to re-enter after their earlier encounter. The boys held out their wands in case they came across any unwanted company.

The sound of a person mumbling came from within the forest. A giant of a man emerged from the bushes just a few feet away from where they were. They jumped back, startled. Over the man's face, he wore a mask made out of a white sheet. It was hard to make out precisely what he was wearing at this time of night, but it looked like a pale blue jumpsuit. The jumpsuit looked identical to the ones that the Skogen prisoners wore. The man waved; in his hand he carried a knife. The moon glistened off of the silver blade, revealing its bloodied tip. They quickly scurried back towards the school. The man continued to mumble darkly to himself as he pursued them. Spencer soon became short of breath. Caden and Aldaricus latched on to each of her hands to help her with her speed.

Aldaricus re-unlocked the back door to the school. They hurried up the stairs. When they got to the second floor, they heard a spine-chilling sound.

"I know you're in here," the man said in a sing-song voice.

"This way!" Aldaricus was about to shout but decided to mouth his words instead. He pointed to Olly's closet. "*Unlucan!*" Once they were all safely in the closet, he shut its door quietly. They could hear the man growing nearer. In the shock of the sudden intruders, Jax and the blond girl had let out a frightened shriek.

"Shh!" Aldaricus hissed before getting into Jax's face. Jax scrunched his nose and looked as if he were about to go off. "I know you don't like it when I tell you what to do, but right now, I need you just to shut the fuck up."

They all began to look around the closet to see if any of the so-called dangerous stuff could be useful to them. The students didn't find anything that could help them.

Aldaricus turned to a red tapestry that had been hanging beside the back shelf. When Aldaricus tore it down, he saw that there was a hidden passageway. They ran through it, not caring that they had no idea where it was leading. When the passage ended, they found themselves in Spencer's Terra Arts classroom.

"Do you think we lost him?" Spencer asked.

"Lost who?" Jax squealed.

"Shh!" the Scaasis hissed.

Spencer was panting much harder than the rest. She bent over and began to wheeze and cough up blocks of spit. She began to gasp and reach for her chest. A prominent vein formed on the left side of her forehead.

Aldaricus and Caden leaned down beside her. "We need to get her to the hospital wing." Caden's heart began to beat faster than it had during their chase. "As quickly as possible." He looked up to his older cousin.

"Is this all some joke?" Jax asked. "You're not giving us any detail, and it seems like you guys are just trying to give us a good scare."

"Want details?" Caden asked. Jax and the blond girl nodded. "A tall, scary man wearing a mask, wielding a knife, chased us into the school. Now, because of all of this, Spencer seems to be having a panic attack. Shall we go to the hospital wing now?"

Their eyes widened, but they nodded and followed the Scaasis out into the hall. "Let's go." Aldaricus took the lead as Caden took hold of Spencer.

It wasn't going to be as simple as they wanted. The students hadn't taken more than twenty steps before they could hear footsteps in the far distance. They turned to see that the noise was coming from Olly's office. Something shot out of the closet. It was a purple magical spark that had been produced by the scary man. He seemed to have found a wand and knew precisely how to use it.

Aldaricus reached into his pocket. "Try me, you rotting anus! Come out!" Aldaricus nodded to everyone. They seemed more frightened by him than the man. Once they realized what he had said, they wielded their wands.

The man began to cackle from inside the closet.

"Wandering around at night, wandering around the school at night, tsk-tsk." The man exited the closet. "I think I should let Mr Bell know. I'm sure he'd love to hear what you kids have been up to." His voice was oddly soothing, and he sounded like some preacher or saint. However, his eyes glistened wickedly behind his mask. "I'll tell him — for your good, of course." The man took an intimidatingly slow step forward. "Kids these days aren't punished enough."

"Get away from us," snapped Aldaricus as he waved his wand. "*Crypel Aldor!*" An intricate green wave of fragments rushed towards the man. This spell was a mistake. He had just used an instant killing spell, one that would drain the life from the man. The man had ducked just in time, and he was now angrier than before.

The man aimed his wand at Aldaricus. "*Ad!*" Several bolts of purple fire charged towards Aldaricus.

He dodged the fire flashes. The five of them began to run for their lives as they ran towards the school's exit. As soon as they pushed it opened, it was slammed rearward, forcing them back into the school.

"This is it!" Jax squealed like a wounded pig. "We're all going to die!" They could hear the man rushing towards them.

"Get behind me." Aldaricus pushed them behind him as he turned to face the man. He raised his wand. "*Hearm!*" A fluid green blast of particles rushed towards the man.

The spell struck him, and the man was soon in a rageful fit of pain. He fell to the floor. His screams were nearly deafening.

"Let's get you to Uncle Ace's instead." Aldaricus turned to her. They all left the school in a scurry.

"Let go!" the Scaasis heard the blond girl say from behind them. When they turned, they saw that Jax was tightly gripping on to her green long-sleeved shirt. "You're such a pansy. You know that." She pulled her arm down and out of his grip. She looked up to see Aldaricus looking at her and Jax. When her eyes met him, she winked. With that, she stomped off.

The Scaasis turned back around to head over to their uncle's house. They didn't see the open field. Instead, they saw a scaly landscape. They saw a winged reptile that stood on four legs with a long tail thorned like a rose stem when they looked up.

"You've got to be fucking kidding me." Aldaricus's strength wavered.

The dragon was large enough to fill the school's Crash Ring field. The creature revealed its yellow fangs. It was standing tall and had its eyes fixed on the four kids. The dragon looked on curiously. It looked even more surprised to be looking at humans than they were to be looking at a dragon. The creature, after its intense studying, began to growl deep from within his belly.

"Okay, now we're dead!" Jax screeched.

"Yep, Jax, I think you're right." Caden nodded.

They then hurried back inside the school. They'd rather risk the possibility of getting attacked by the wounded man than the dragon. They ran through the halls so fast that any onlookers would've thought that they were flying. They expected the man to appear at any minute, but he never did. He must've hurried off somewhere else to find help with the curse that Aldaricus had placed on him. However, the man was hardly on any of their minds. All they cared about was getting to the opposite side of the school. Once outside, Jax summoned his broom and headed towards his home. The boys summoned heirs. Aldaricus placed Spencer behind him, and he made sure to keep one hand on her at all times.

Later that night, by the time they arrived back at Spencer's, the grey clouds became darker and fuller, grumbling above them, mirroring the three kids' mood as they saw the door swing open, revealing a disheveled, red-faced Mary.

"Where in Galdowide have you been?" Mary squealed. She surveyed their dirty clothing and hair as well as their hot and heavy breaths.

"Never mind that — we will tell you later — Spencer needs to see Uncle Ace immediately! However, it's not safe outside." Aldaricus, the bravest of the two, decided that he would be the one to try and speak to Mary. He took a while to talk as he tried to catch his breath.

John sprung forward and grabbed hold of his daughter and rushed outside with her. The boys followed despite Mary's howls for them to come back that instant. The boys were trembling and found it hard to keep their legs from collapsing.

They stayed silent for most of the journey. When John looked over at the boys, he saw their fear. They were looking around at their surroundings like paranoid people. They appeared to be traumatized, and he began to wonder if they would ever speak again.

"What were you boys thinking, sneaking your cousin out of the house this late at night?" John finally asked. "You three are in such trouble. I hope you know that!"

The boys were still trying to catch their breath. "I-I know you're upset, but trust me, us sneaking out in the middle of the night should be the least of your concerns." Aldaricus tried to hide his quick temper.

"What is this big picture that I'm not seeing?"

"Bluntly? Olly's an unexpected dick. An escapee of Skogen prison was wearing a sheet mask and chasing us. Oh, and yeah, there was a freaking dragon outside of the school!"

John glared at Aldaricus. "Dragons? Already?" John stopped in his tracks. His nephews looked on curiously. "I'll speak with the Ministry, but do you boys realize how you guys almost got yourselves and my baby girl killed?" He inched forward. "If, for whatever reason, my daughter's cause of death is you two, whether it is tonight or twenty years from now, I will not hesitate to kill you two myself. Your fathers would probably help me in the process, for that matter."

"What do you mean, 'already'?" Caden's question went unnoticed.

"We understand. We didn't intend to bring Spence into any danger tonight," Aldaricus apologized.

They arrived at Ace's house. John could hear a male's screams coming from inside.

Probably his dark music again, John thought to himself. John relaxed as the music lowered. He knew that Ace would be of great help to Spencer, just as he was to Olivia.

CHAPTER 10

Lewis couldn't believe his eyes when he read both his and Angel's letters of acceptance to Galdorwide's Ministry. Angel was tired yet cheerful. She had been up all night tossing and turning as she wondered whether or not she would be accepted. As expected, Angel pictured this as a moment of success and an opportunity for a great adventure. She knew of Lewis's disapproval but was pleased to have him by her side nonetheless. He wouldn't let her join the Ministry alone. After all, she would need protection. Being a member of the Ministry was going to be a dangerous job.

"It's going to be dangerous, Angel," said Lewis.

"Speaking of danger," Angel looked down to her feet. She refused to speak until Lewis urged her to continue. "I got a letter. I don't know who sent it. I ripped it up, though. It spoke about the village of Erith. They said they know what I did, what *we* did."

Lewis didn't show the slightest concern. He had always been the strong, silent type. That's what had attracted Angel to him in the first place, but now, she had to admit it was getting pretty annoying.

"Lewis! Hello!" She let out a groan. "This letter is an issue! Can't you see that?"

"We will figure it out, okay? We will find out who sent it to you, and we will make sure that whoever sent it never speaks of Erith or us again. When they send something again, which they probably will, we can put a tracking spell on it. Simple."

A letter flew in from the small crack at the bottom of their bedroom window. It was a thin envelope. It flew in and hovered in front of Lewis's face. When he opened it, he saw a single paragraph written on it:

You are a clone of your father, Tony, Lewis. I know what happens behind your closed doors. It's funny, considering he's not your birth father. I guess that has to do with all that nature vs. nurture.

Angel looked on as her husband's eyes widened. She gnawed at the nail of her thumb.

She was startled that Lewis had gotten a letter too. Lewis slowly backed up until he reached the wall covered in pale pink wallpaper. Once his back knocked against it, he dropped down into a seated position. Angel trembled as another letter swarmed in from the window and hit her head. She caught it before it could fall to the ground; she immediately ripped it open.

Inside was a picture that contained eight burnt bodies —the bodies lay on top of nicely patterned stones. Behind them was a building that appeared just as crisp as the corpses.

Angel gasped. She cupped her mouth with her hand as she held back her tears. She looked down at Lewis. "Is there anything we can do, now that we're Ministry members? I mean, these are threats, aren't they?"

"If we go to the Ministry with stuff like this, we will no longer be a part of the Ministry." Lewis threw his letter against the ground and placed his head in his hands. He looked up at Angel, his face stern. "These are threats to expose us. If we do anything about this, it's alone. No Bella and no Ben." Lewis had a hard time holding in his fear.

Angel moaned. She dragged her feet over to her husband, slumped down and rested her head on his shoulder.

Ace had ordered Caden and Aldaricus to head over to Spencer's house to fetch some of her belongings. She would be spending a few days at Ace's, in his basement, the part of his home where he kept in-patients.

Caden and Aldaricus entered their aunt's home. They headed upstairs to the bathroom to grab some of Spencer's belongings. Before they could reach the top of the stairs, Lulia popped out of thin air. She stood in their way.

"It's a terrible thing — what you two did." She crossed her arms. She made a face that made her dislike of them clear. "Maybe I should tell my parents exactly why you two wanted to break Spencer out of her room last night."

"It's not what you think, Lulia." Aldaricus gritted his teeth. "You're too young to understand."

Lulia grinned. "Yeah, what would I understand? I mean, I am just a little girl." Then her smile faded. She stepped down a step on the staircase. "But what I do know is that you were trying to break into Olly's closet. A member of the Ministry, but I suppose I must be missing something, since I'm too young to understand."

Before the boys could say anything, Mary appeared behind the young girl. "Lulia, that's enough."

"We're just here to grab some of Spencer's stuff, Aunt Mary. Uncle Ace wants her to spend a few nights there," Aldaricus explained. He cringed at the shaking of his voice. Why did he fear his aunt so much when his mother was the most powerful witch? Daeva Scaasi was a baroness working for the king under a following called Anbetl Globalno, who was tasked with making sure Aldaricus, unbeknownst to him, fulfilled his destiny as the Sword Crist. They existed in the shadows, manipulating things and protecting him.

"Yes, yes, John called me and told me all about the situation," Mary said with sorrow.

Lulia's face was filled with urgent horror. "Mom, did you hear what I said? About them breaking into Olly's closet at the school? Because it's true. If they hadn't broken Spencer out last night, she would be here — fine and healthy."

Caden and Aldaricus looked to one another, fearing what Mary would do next. "Lulia, don't you worry, these boys will not go unpunished." There was a compression of anger in her voice. After all, she was not their mother, and it was not her responsibility to punish them. Mary stomped down the stairs, trying to keep her composure and fake smile as she passed her nephews. Lulia smiled sadistically, lifting her nose into the air as she marched back up the stairs, proud of herself.

John Jr had a hard time focusing on his classes the following day. His mind kept wandering to Spencer's empty seat and to Ace's basement where she would be staying. According to Ace, her symptoms were much more deep-rooted than a panic attack. Ace said visitors were not allowed, but he would be able to write her letters. He skipped his meal at lunch.

When the final bell rang, he picked up his sisters and rushed home. Upon his arrival, he found Caden and Aldaricus packing Spencer's baby blue suitcase. Tossing his backpack by the door, he rolled onto Spencer's bed.

"I can't believe it," he sighed. "I never knew how sick Spencer was. I mean, I did, I felt it, but I didn't want to believe." He rolled onto his side and looked at his cousins. "Don't forget to pack her blue dress shirt, the one with the black tie. She loves it!" He reached into his red cloak pocket and pulled out his wand. "*Plectrum.*" His rod turned into a quill. "*Carte.*" He summoned a piece of paper in front of him. He began to write a letter to his sister, and the ink fell out in a lovely golden color.

After dinner, a dinner that Mary insisted the boys join, the boys set off towards Ace's house. With each of the boys carrying large suitcases, people gave them various hostile stares.

Some assumed that they were runaways. Meanwhile, some stared at their aura-colored bags that didn't look fitting for the teens.

It was a beautiful night. Children were playing outside, with some running around and shooting bubbles from the tips of their wands.

"Is that allowed?" Caden leaned over to John Jr "I thought children weren't allowed to use magic outside of school."

"I think so? It's not like the kids are doing anything unauthorized, like using teleportation spells."

They arrived at their uncle's home, with Ace greeting the boys at the door. Between his arm and waist, he carried a brown trunk as they walked in.

"That should be good." Ace eyed the three bags of luggage with glistening eyes. "Thank you, boys… I want to speak to you four about what will be going on here with Spencer. I want to make sure that you worry about nothing."

He closed the door behind them and placed the trunk on top of his wooden coffee table. Inside was a variety of food, drinks, and medicine. They all surrounded the chest while Spencer lay asleep on the sofa.

"The food and drinks here will help with her digestion as well as cleanse her digestive system. After evaluating her, it is clear that she is malnourished. The food and drinks here will help enhance her appetite. I am not just giving you the food to give her, because upon evaluation, it was clear that her health issues were not just physical but mental as well. I will counsel and support her during her recovery."

"Mental?" John asked numbly.

"No need to worry, brother, she's far from our ancestor's craziness.

150

She's just a teen girl going through a lot of stress and pressure," replied Ace. "Follow me."

Ace led them down into his basement as the poorly-shaped wood staircase creaked as they walked down it. Their shallow breaths hummed alongside the wind. Their feet patted against the floor, which looked and felt as if it were a sidewalk.

"That's Eion's room. He's sleeping." He pointed as they passed the first door to the right. "And that will be Spencer's room," he said to the second door on the right. There were a total of six rooms alongside the wall. At the end of the hall was a seating area for the patients.

When he opened the door, the first thing they took note of was the rusted water dripping from the ceiling. On the wall was a lit torch. Besides that, the room was empty.

"Ace, this looks like a dungeon in the castle. I won't allow my daughter to stay here in this condition," John refused.

Ace smiled. "The room will look exactly like Spencer's with a simple spell. She will feel as if she's at home, John — if you will do the honor." He stepped away.

John raised his wand. *"Spencer cubiculo!"* A jagged blue surge of ripples filled the room. Once the waves cleared, it was as if they were staring at Spencer's bedroom at home. Directly across from them sat a queen-sized bed with a white comforter with a baby blue forest's silhouette. Around the bed hung white transparent hangings that she would draw down while she slept. Above the ground was a picture of the ocean, and beside it, were two white night tables where lamps sat. To the left of the doorway, Lulia and Olivia's beds lay vacant, as they would for the remainder of Spencer's stay. John held in his tears as he looked around at the pink floral wallpaper that a young Spencer had picked out.

"I'll wake Spencer and show her to her room and let you say your farewells." Ace smiled and headed up the stairs.

He gently nudged Spencer awake. She was groggy, her eyes were too weak to open, and her stomach felt nauseated.

"I'm going to show you to your room now," Ace said, helping her stand up as she struggled.

***

A firebolt, high in the air, aimed right for the members of the Ministry as they surrounded the dragon on the school's Crash Ring field. It was heading for Alizeh, who was able to dodge it as she jumped forward. Before she could stand up and continue to fight, the beast turned, and its thorned and stiff tail pelted her head. The creature had turned to attack Gower. Ben swung his sword and slightly sliced off the first layer of the dragon's leg. The dragon howled in pain, and it looked up to the sky. Its belly rumbled as it prepared its next breath of fire. When it was ready to be released, it exhaled, sending the light up into the sky. The fire zigzagged above their heads. It then shot for Ben, who dived out of the way just in time. "See?" Dorothy panted. "A dragon's breath can rocket around."

"Yep — I see," Ben groaned.

"Is there any way we get out of this without dying?" Olly's panic was evident. He was still unaware that his girlfriend had been knocked unconscious.

"Yes, Olly, it's thirteen of us against one dragon," Bella snapped. "Don't worry, with Williams and Nillag, this birdbrain will be dead in no time."

Arthur, Angel, and Lewis had been called on to help with the situation. They were untrained Ministry members but very good sorcerers; nonetheless, they would need all the help they could to beat this foreign beast.

"*Cepan!*" A smooth dark purple wave of particles shot out of Bella's wand and reached for the dragon's head. The spell sent the dragon into a calm and almost meditative state.

"A dragon's weakness is ice," Dorothy spat out another one of her many facts. "*Forstig Bil!*" Soon, her wand turned into a double-edged sword. Frosty energy emitted from the blade. She struck the tail of the beast. The sword sliced through its tail as if it were a loaf of bread.

Ben understood what he had to do next. Before he could cast a spell, the dragon sent down its fiery claws and sliced them across Ben's chest. The pain was unlike any pain he had felt before. It was the mix of a cut's sting with the burn of hot lava.

Olly carefully aimed his wand at the beast while the rest zapped it with pain-inducing spells. Olly mustered up all his strength. *"Forlor!"* A robust green stream of corkscrew-shaped particles attacked the dragon, separating each atom in its body. The creature's divided body created a bloody mess that turned the entire school's Crash Ring field red. The Ministry members, drenched in blood, turned to look at Olly, as they had never seen such a spell cast before.

They turned when they heard Ben's agonizing screams. He was gripping his chest as he crawled over to Alizeh, who lay still. He feared the worst when he saw his loyal friend's blood-gushing forehead and pale lips.

Bella's doctor later treated Ben while Alizeh, unconscious, was taken to the school's hospital ward. "See? I told you joining the Ministry was a bad idea." Olly shook his head as he sat on her bedside.

Olly, not working for two months, never left Alizeh's side. The hospital ward was beginning to feel more like home than his actual residence.

Alizeh awoke on All Hallows Eve, the official transition from summer to fall. The night of Samhain meant that Galdorwide would grow colder and darker as the trees began to die. It was on this day that the living and dead worlds crossed. Ghosts of everyone's pasts were sure to return.

She looked on the nightstand beside her bed and saw that the calendar read October 31st, 2018.

Alizeh found herself alone in her solitary hospital room, with Olly nowhere in sight. She pulled herself up on the bed. Alizeh was now wearing a blue hospital gown. Her blue jacket, grey shirt, and black jeans that she had worn on the day she had fought the dragon were laid out on a chair in her isolated hospital room. Alizeh twirled to the side of the bed, where she found her black boots awaiting her.

When she stood, it took a moment for her to regain her balance. Alizeh had, after all, been laying down for almost two months straight. She headed towards the hospital's exit to find that outside the school was not the forest. It was now a damaged crop field.

In front of the field was a large woman who sat behind a wooden table. In front of her was nothing but a purple crystal ball. Alizeh approached the woman, taking note of her blue-starred head wrap and rosy cheeks. She wore a red dress and a green florally-patterned shawl, and many gold bangles, necklaces, and rings.

"I sense that you require some direction, young girl."

Before Alizeh could answer, her eyes traveled to a group of men in the distance. Some stood around a bonfire while others threw crops into the fire. A man, holding a lamb, approached the light. The lamb's cries echoed throughout the quiet night's air. Before Alizeh could even process what was happening, the man threw the animal into the fire.

"What are they doing?" Alizeh asked in horror.

"Sacrificing to Cerridwen, of course. The keeper of the cauldron, goddess of the moon, magic, and agriculture."

The men wore costumes made of animal skin. One, who Alizeh assumed was the leader, wore the head of a bear as a crown.

"Now tell me, child, would you like your fortune read? If so, this is the night to do it — when the answers could not be clearer." The lady spoke with a thick accent and wild enthusiasm. Alizeh nodded. The woman's smile faded as she looked down at the crystal ball with the ambiance of seriousness. "Dear girl, I see a feather. A spirit is here to help us read your fortune. You poor thing, I see you crying. I see a swarm of bats beneath grey clouds. Have you or someone you know encountered a vampire?"

"Yes, my boyfriend." Alizeh grew uncomfortable with the woman's accuracy. She always believed in fortune-tellers, or at least on All Hallows Eve, but she had never gone to one before.

"I see you again. You're terrified. You will be in great danger tonight, my dear Alizeh."

Alizeh could sense the sharp thrum of her heartbeat in her neck. Her heart was pounding quicker than she'd ever felt it. Her fists were tensed so tightly she could sense her nails drilling into her palms. Her belly fell into her boots as the feeling of dread rose. She stole a glance at the witches conducting their ceremony, still not believing what the fortune-teller had told her.

Instead of walking home for her frequent exercise, Alizeh thought it was best to summon her broom. When she arrived safely in her living room, it smelled delicious. The aroma of pumpkin and ginger filled the room.

"Ah, Alizeh, you're home." Olly appeared from around the corner. "I'm so glad you're all right." He wiped his red-stained hands on an orange washcloth. Once his hands were decent, he embraced his girlfriend.

A purple butterfly, Alizeh's familiar, flew down from the upstairs of their tiny home and over to Alizeh's face. She was excited to see her. "Annabelle!" Alizeh giggled. "You're tickling me!" The butterfly continued to dance along the girl's face.

The couple sat together on their brown sofa in the dimly lit room. Alizeh and Olly dug into their slices of pumpkin pie.

"So, how did it all work out with the dragon?" she asked.

"We were able to defeat it, and we're still trying to figure out where the dragon could've come from. It couldn't have been from Doryu Edjer's church. Those dragons are foretold to not attack until May." He seemed angry as he spoke.

"I'll order a meeting with the Ministry and let them know that I'm okay." Alizeh placed her empty plate onto the wooden coffee table and went to stand up.

"No!" Olly shouted. Alizeh jumped as he lashed forward. "No, not now, wait until tomorrow after you've rested." He lowered his voice. Olly had perched himself up onto the couch with his hand wrapped around her thin arm. "Dr Ace alerted me that you would have to take extra care after you came home."

Arthur kicked Olly's front door open. "We need help! There are like, seven freaking trolls that have exited the forest. Come on!" Arthur ran back outside.

Alizeh rushed after him, but to her dismay, the front yard was gone. The forest stood where Olly's garden once sat. Alizeh grabbed out her wand, as did Olly. She breathed a sigh of relief when she saw that the rest of the Ministry's members were there.

Dorothy lay on the forest floor, unconscious. One of the trolls lay dead beside her.

Alizeh had seen a troll once before when she was a young girl. She was forever haunted by its green reptilian-like skin that grew a thick layer of dark green fur. On the sides of its mouth were two short tusks. Trolls were quite repulsive but almost powerless without their weapons. However, they were quite tall.

A troll immediately approached her, and its long snake-like tongue fell out of its stupid mouth.

"*Bland!*" Particles shaped like irregular corkscrews the color of purple exited her wand. The magic headed towards the troll. It successfully temporarily confused the resigned beast.

An uproar from the forest shook the ground. "Stand behind me." Olly was unusually confident. He gently pulled Alizeh backward and placed her behind him.

"Where did the trolls come from, and how is the forest on your yard?"

"It was probably all them." Olly nodded towards Ben and Bella, who struck the trolls with spells. "A tactic of theirs to have us killed."

Different types of creatures exited from the forest. There was a wave of trolls, hoop snakes, and a species of small dragons called Jaculuses. All of the Ministry's members grew terrified and confused. However, Olly looked wholesomely calm.

Ben, Bella, Arthur, Adelaide, John, Gower, Gabriel, Ian, Angel and Lewis all attacked the creatures.

"Aren't you going to help?" Alizeh began to bite her lip. She was appreciating this uncommon manliness but yearned to help her friends.

Olly grabbed hold of Alizeh's hand and began to run away with her alongside the forest.

Soon, they heard the bush behind them rustle.

Alizeh jumped, fearing that a troll was behind her, but she saw her old friend Alan when she turned.

"What're you doing here?" Alizeh whispered. Olly wrapped his arm over her shoulder. She wanted to push it off her badly but kept it on to not anger him.

They quietly continued to walk away from the Ministry's members. "He's here because I called him here," Olly explained.

Before he continued speaking, Alizeh stopped in her tracks. "Can you smell that?" A burning stench reached her nostrils, and when she turned around, her eyes widened with fear. Olly's house had been burnt down, along with their neighbours' houses.

Alizeh pointed in horror as suddenly Olly and Alan pulled her into the shadows of the forest. Moonlight shone through small patches in the trees. Alizeh looked up to Olly to see a horrible sight as her slim, blue-eyed and blond boyfriend wore a sinister smile.

"W-what are you doing?" Alizeh muttered as the two men continued to hold on to each of her arms.

Her eyes began to feel foggy, her heart thumped, and her body sank. They tightened their grips on her arm. Just then, they threw her down on the forest floor as hard as they could. Their menacing eyes never left her. They leaned forward as they pointed their wands at her.

Alizeh began to think quickly and reached for a large branch that lay beside her, whacking Olly's shoulder. He yelped with pain, dropped his wand and clenched his hand around his shoulder. Alan, however, kept his rod pointed, but his eyes were now on Olly. She saw her opportunity to get up and run.

"Come on! She's getting away!" she heard Alan yell at Olly.

Her body grew numb, and it was a wonder how her body was still moving. Alan continued to shout. She could hear it echo throughout the forest, and they were approaching quickly. The forest seemed never-ending with no escape.

Trying to summon her broom that never came, she decided to pull out her wand. Tripping over a large log, screaming in pain, and with the discomfort she felt in her ankle, she was sure she had broken it. When Alizeh turned around, she saw Alan and Olly facing her once again. Their wands stared at her face. Alizeh sunk to the forest floor, half because of fright and half because she was beginning to give up.

"*Ad!*" Several bolts of red fire exited Olly's wand and charged towards her.

Alizeh swaggered out of her spot, turned onto her belly and thudded against the ground. She had been too late, and the fire bolts struck her. The flames engulfed her body whole. Her eyes began to water from the smoke. Her skin stung where the fire touched.

She scraped her fingers through the dirt, attempting to crawl. When she looked back, she saw that her movements went unnoticed by the men. When she looked back down at her hands, she realized that her nails didn't leave a marking in the dirt.

Alizeh, frightened and filled with rage, her vision began to fade to black. She cried for help. She looked at the two men, who continued their heated argument. She cried for aid, only to notice that the forest did not echo her calls, as the wind and trees couldn't hear her. She continued to scream and wail, and soon her words were muffled to her ears.

She looked down at the ground to see her skin melt into the dirt. Two Cwaltt Videns appeared. The shadow demons began to sing. Their shrill voices haunted her with what little her ears could hear. The world around her began to spin. The burns on her skin began to swell. It felt as if a sharp kitchen knife were cutting through the blisters. Her lungs ached as she struggled to inhale. An overwhelming smell of rotten eggs and burnt flesh choked her. She clenched her jaw tightly as she prepared for the final rush of pain. The pitch of the demons' singing heightened to sound like the ringing of bells.

However, there wasn't an ultimate pain, for she had already felt it. She now lay in a peaceful yet awakened slumber.

"Is she dead?" she heard Olly ask, his voice trembling.

"I think so." Alan bent down. He extended his hand to reach for her neck to feel a pulse. Once he touched her, he pulled his hand back, disgusted. "Urgh — her skin's all melted. There's no way she's alive."

He wiped her bloody and melted flesh off his hands and onto his black trousers.

A rumble through the woods approached. It sounded like all the creatures they had seen before were charging at them. Alizeh attempted to scream, but nothing came out. Olly whimpered and took a seat at the bottom of the tree that was closest to her. He clutched his heart.

Alan continued to bend over Alizeh's body, studying her. He looked over to Olly, whose lips had turned white.

"What in Galdorwide were you thinking?" Olly muttered to himself, his voice cold with fury. He smacked himself in the face.

Alan gave Olly a quick, piercing look. Olly looked down and threw his wand onto the ground in front of him.

"You've wanted this for how long now? Killing her was a necessary evil." Alan spoke flatly, trying to comfort his partner in crime.

Alizeh couldn't help but think of where she went wrong. She remembered the first time she met Olly. She and her friends, including

Alan, had often picked on Olly. He was both strange and nerdy. Then one day, her mom had told her to drop off a welcoming basket when Olly and his family had moved to a new home. He was a sheepish, young boy with blond hair and a gentle yet nervous smile. She had immediately regretted bullying him and had tried her best to make up for it. She did — or did she? If she hadn't fallen for Olly, she'd be alive right now. She couldn't help but feel that this couldn't be real. It had all happened so fast. *How could I be so foolish,* she thought to herself. She had been kind to everyone and especially Olly. She didn't deserve this.

"I'm very disappointed in you." Alan spoke in his familiar drawling voice. "I expected this to be hard for you, but you made your bed, and now you must lie in it. I thought you knew that?" With that, Alan left.

A troll approached, as did all the other creatures that had survived. An elf began to speak with its thick, groggy voice. "We were lucky. The Ministry is hard to take down, but we've done it. I will inform our master you have done your work. I will take her body, boss. You can go now."

Two trolls hurried over to Alizeh's body. Each of them grabbed hold of one of her ankles.

They didn't talk until they approached a small, shed-like building deep inside the forest. "We deserve a better reward than Olly — us creatures took down eleven Ministry members. All he did was tackle his birdbrain."

Once they arrived outside the shed's door, they muttered the password "Twisted".

They dragged her inside. The room was small yet filled with noisy witches and creatures. However, a ghost stood alone in the back, staring at a wall covered with monitored screens.

Just then, Alizeh grew ecstatic and relieved to find herself sitting up on her hospital bed, the date reading November 16th, 2018. She had awakened from her dream.

CHAPTER 11

"He wouldn't do that," Dorothy comforted Alizeh, who was still checked in at the school's hospital ward. "I know that lately, the school has been making complaints about Olly. However, he wouldn't try to kill you or anyone else for that matter."

"Everyone thinks that Olly is a saint. With what he went through, there's no way he is, and not to mention the stuff we did to him back in high school. What if he hasn't forgiven us?"

"Well ——- I wouldn't put it past him. Just be alert, and at the slightest bit of fear, summon the Ministry. We won't let him hurt you." Dorothy didn't know how to feel about Olly, but she did know that she didn't want her friend to get hurt.

Alizeh went over to Olly's home after being released from the hospital. She practically lived with him. When she arrived, she walked upstairs to the bedroom, where she could hear Olly snoring loudly. She lay in the bed beside him. Alizeh couldn't fall asleep. She tried her best to empty her mind. Her head, however, didn't forget the face of Alan and Olly as they stood over her. She tossed and turned.

The next morning, Alizeh sat up in her bed only to find that Olly was not in it. The smell of roasting potatoes seeped into the bedroom. Alizeh was nervous to see Olly, but he, however, was looking forward to seeing her.

"I'm making some breakfast." Olly had heard her creep down the stairs and enter the kitchen.

"I'm not hungry — thanks, though." Alizeh pulled her purple house robe closer together.

Olly looked over his shoulder, away from the stove. "At least have a piece of toast. You need all the nutrients you can get."

"No — I'm not hungry." Alizeh felt sick to her stomach.

"Alizeh." Olly turned off the stove, wiped his hand on a white washcloth, and approached her. "Honey, you're going to need some strength. Who knows what today might throw at us? We are Ministry members, after all. I made your favorite — potatoes." He summoned a plate. The potatoes from the pot flew over and filled it. He handed it to her.

She smiled dully. "Thanks."

As Galdorwide entered mid-November, the weather was beginning to turn colder. In September, it usually snowed, and from there, the temperature dropped dangerously. The forest became icy and white, and the lake had hardened like a steel floor. Frost coated the grass.

Coach Abbey was outside the school, preparing the field for the night's Crash Ring game.

With a simple flick of her wand, she defrosted the brooms. She then checked to make sure that the rings were unharmed due to the temperature. The last thing they needed was a ring full of students crashing down in the middle of a game. She wore a chunky brown scarf and a leather jacket.

Today was the Crash Ring's final game for the year, as the weather was becoming too dangerous for the sport. The two finalists were Avalon's Alets and the Viridi Vipers. If the Alet team won, it would end the Vipers' winning streak. The Viridi team had not lost the final game in eight years.

John Jr had been preparing for the finals ever since he had made the team. He had a list of arcane spells up his sleeve. John Jr had visited his great-uncle, Daemon Soleil, the twin brother of his grandmother, Aisley. Like many of those on his grandmother's side of the family, Daemon had stopped aging. He was now forever thirty-nine. John. Jr had visited Daemon, who ran the Python Seger School of the Arcane, with his two friends, Aaron and Michael. He was sure that the new spells his old relative taught him would be unexpected by the Viridi Vipers.

John Jr's parents were oddly interested in tonight's game. John reassured his son that he would do a brilliant job. Mary encouraged him by saying that she would have Dr Ace ready if he got injured.

Nonetheless, John Jr was excited to play, and he was sure glad to have a friend like Lovetta by his side. Over the past few weeks, John Jr had been too busy training with his uncle to do his homework. Lovetta had kindly offered to help.

"All right, students, it's time to hand in your essays on the type of magic you can harness during the Autumn Equinox," Mr Silwhet instructed his Terra Arts students.

In the second seat from the back of the class, John Jr hastily copied from Lovetta's essay, being sure to change a few words here and there. Students started to walk up and hand in their papers. However, John Jr and Lovetta remained seated. Mr Silwhet looked over, his brow furrowed. Lovetta could even say that their always gracious teacher looked quite angry.

"Mr Scaasi, whose paper are you copying from?"

In a panic, he looked to Lovetta and didn't have the heart to rat her out. After all, she was a good student, just trying to help him. "It's Aldric's, sir," he lied.

Lovetta looked up to Aldric, who held his hands open in questioning. Lovetta slumped back in her chair. She rested her head on the back of the seat and clapped her hands over her makeup-less face. Aldric, at the moment of John Jr's lie, had been handing in his paper.

The bell rang, and students began to rush out of class, especially John Jr and Lovetta. "Lovetta," Mr Silwhet called before she could exit. John Jr made a run for it.

Lovetta stepped back into the classroom, her hands wrapped around her books. Once the last student exited the room, she shut the door behind her and shyly looked up at him.

"Lovetta, honey, you're not in trouble, relax. I'm just wondering if Aldric and John have been making or forcing you to let them cheat off of you. I know what it's like to be the smart kid without having the courage to say no."

"Uhm… Sir? I copy off of them in the Art of Ignis class."

Mr Silwhet chuckled to himself. "Oh, okay, I was not expecting that." He motioned her out of the classroom as she reached for the doorknob.

"Oh, and by the way," he began. She turned to look at him as he spoke. "I had time to read your essay. You got a perfect score! You understand the ways of nature and how it connects with magic. Your work was so remarkable I gave you one hundred and one percent. Oh,

162

and Lovetta, there's a book I'd like you to read. It's a textbook for the Terra Arts class, but it's on a subject you won't learn until your third year. I think you might enjoy some extra learning on the side. I find the subject quite intriguing."

Mr Silwhet walked over to the bookshelf beside his desk. He reached to the top shelf and grabbed a book titled *The Encyclopedia of Werewolves*.

Always interested in creatures other than those with magic, Lovetta smiled. She began to read it as soon as she got to the lunch table.

She read the first section, "How Does One Become A Werewolf?" The first fifty-five pages explained the six ways in great detail. The first one was most obvious, getting bitten, and the second was a scratch. Even the slightest injury that a werewolf could induce could transform the victim into a beast.

The third was a curse in the mother's womb; this curse was one called Werewulf Arius. The evil came in the form of a potion. All one would need was a strand of the mother's hair, hair of a wolf or dog, soil, and lavender to mask the potion's foul taste. The mother of the cursed child would often not notice the affliction as it took its course.

The fourth way one could become a werewolf was by sleeping in the forest beneath a full moon. The fifth way was by drinking water from the footprint of a werewolf. The sixth way that one could become a werewolf was if one or more of a child's parents was a werewolf. It was common for Wolfism not to show in those who had not yet reached puberty. Those born with Wolfism often reached puberty at a later age than the average witch or wizard.

The exciting book her favorite teacher gave her had her hooked. When the bell had rung, she walked out onto the stands of the Crash Ring field to cheer on both John Jr and Aldric. It was freezing outside. She wore nothing except for her gray uniform pants and a baby blue buttoned shirt, so she wrapped her arms around her body as she shivered. The stand grew foggy with condensation. Professor Silwhet sat on the bench behind her. Being a werewolf, he didn't need his brown cardigan. He unbuttoned his sweater and draped it over the young girl's shoulders. She looked back, shocked when she saw who had placed it on her, and she smiled. He was now only wearing a white dress shirt and black tie; he smiled.

She blushed and quickly looked back to the field.

She buried herself in his cardigan, trying to warm herself. Olly limped up into the stands and took a seat next to her. Subconsciously, Lovetta leaned away from him and closer to the student beside her, despite not knowing him.

"What's that you've got there?" He eyed the book that she held in her hands. Lovetta didn't respond. She lifted the book so that he could get a better look.

"You can't be reading that! That's a teacher's copy! Give it to me." He stretched out his hand.

"I gave it to her." Gower stopped her from handing it over.

Olly, angry, looked behind him. Once he saw it was his friend, he tried to calm himself.

"Oh. All right." Olly gave a tense smile.

"What's wrong with your leg? I noticed that you've been limping all day," Gower said.

"It just hurts. I'll see Dr Scaasi about it tomorrow if the pain's still there."

The stands of the Alet fans were quite noisy this evening. It was still a few minutes before the game began, so Lovetta continued to read the book. She read the second section, "It's In The Name". This section described why these creatures were called werewolves. The word combined the Old English words "Were", "man", and "Wulf", "wolf." This section, however, also went into Lycanthropy, the ability to transform into a wolf.

Adelaide was restless. She had fought the dragon with Arthur but didn't have much time alone with him. During the battle, she had taken note of his new Caerul magic. Adelaide had to admit she was nervous. Arthur was not who he or she believed he was. *What if this changes how he sees the world and me?* Adelaide thought to herself.

Adelaide needed to talk to Arthur, so she volunteered to be the Ministry Trainer for the day. She made her way through the forest and over to the castle. Adelaide knocked on the door. When there was no answer, her heart began to beat, and her palms began to sweat. Adelaide tapped again — still nothing. Every second that she was not talking to him, the more she was starting to lose her strength.

Perhaps they were upstairs and could not hear her. Adelaide pushed the large, heavy doors open — her eyes fell on a horrible sight.

The three trainees stood in the mansion's main hallway. One of Arthur's legs was bloody and mangled. Angel was handing bandages to Lewis, and her lip was bleeding. Lewis was kneeling by Arthur's injured leg. A white bandage was wrapped around Lewis's head. Fresh blood seeped through it.

"I — I thought it was an angel," she was saying.

Adelaide left the doors open wide as she quickly ran over to them. "What on earth happened?" she asked in horror. Her voice shook with fear.

"A demon." Lewis stood to his feet.

"It was in my room," Angel began. "At first, it looked gentle. The demon had long, curly blond hair, a sweet smile, and a lovely white gown. A white light surrounded her, so I wasn't alarmed at first. Until I walked closer, and it changed. The bright light was overwhelming, and when it faded, she had goat horns and elvish ears. She was naked, her torso was like any other, but her legs were reptile-like and black. She had large bat-like wings with black feathers. After she changed, she began to attack me. Luckily, the boys had heard and had come running in. Unfortunately, they are worse off than me."

"It's a good thing I remembered all of those heavenly spells from back in the Art of Almighty Magic class." Arthur laughed to lighten the mood in the room.

"So, everything's all right now?" Adelaide asked. The trainees nodded. "Good. I'll alert the queen when I go to the castle, but Arthur, can I speak with you?" She couldn't help but care more about his Caerul aura over the health of her friends.

Adelaide helped her fiancé up the staircase and over into Arthur's temporary bedroom. "Everything all right?" Arthur asked as she closed the door behind them.

"Everything's all right — I'm just wondering if you are. You're a Caerul now." Adelaide tried to hide her nervousness.

"I'm still me. I've been Caerul for a while now. It just took a few ghosts to line up my magic with my aura." As he reassured her, his voice seemed out of breath. Adelaide smiled.

The Viridi Vipers and Avalon's Alets walked over to their team's circles. They hopped onto their brooms. They were immediately rushed into the air once all the players were secured. Today, John Jr was pleased not to get any threats from his two Viridi cousins. They were randomly beginning to get along. John Jr thought it best not to question it.

"Heads down!" both John Jr and Aldaricus shouted to their teammates.

The circle had begun spinning, and Aldaricus was waiting for his cousin to take his first shot; he didn't. John Jr just looked at him with a confident smirk.

"*Ad bord!*" Aldaricus cast. A straight, green, glowing corkscrew raised above his head. Soon, the corkscrew busted and green fiery energy surrounded him. He had given himself a temporary shield.

"*Blendan!*" John Jr aimed his wand. A transparent ruby surge of ripples raced towards the other team. It struck a girl, causing her to temporarily lose her eyesight; this caused her to topple over and fall off her broom. A smaller version of the Viridi ring appeared. It caught her and gently lowered her to the ground. Coach Abbey, Dr Notleaf, Dr Scaasi, and the Viridi team coach, Frederick Dodona, were ready to aid her. They carried her off into the school. Her parents quickly ran down from the stands and followed.

"*Levitate!*" Aldaricus cast. A light green surge of ripples raced towards John Jr The waves lifted him off his broom.

"*Anginn!*" John Jr used his second spell to lower himself back down onto his broom. "*Grama arodscipe!*" A wild, green, twisting wave of demonic energy exited Caden's wand and struck an Alet girl. The demonic power attacked her.

"*Anginn!*" Coach Abbey lowered the girl's broom to the ground so that she could seek medical attention.

At the end of the game, John Jr had used all the spells he had up his sleeve, including draining a target's energy and creating claws of shadow energy. After all the teammates had fallen due to demonic, blinding, and weaponry spells, it was just John Jr and Aldaricus left.

"*Cradocil!*" John Jr cast.

"*Lanuae Magicae!*" Aldaricus cast.

When the spells hit, Aldaricus turned into an infant. He tumbled off his broom. John Jr, however, was nowhere to be found, and the crowd gasped. Aldaricus had cast a teleportation spell. When conducting the attack, this would send John Jr to a location selected by random choice.

CHAPTER 12

Mary and John pulled up their brooms toward the curb outside the high school. Lulia and Olivia were strapped onto Mary's three-seated broom.

"Go bring the girls to school. I'm going to find Aldaricus and get to the bottom of this. Okay? All right."

"Okay." Mary nodded. "Wait, John, he's there!"

"What? Come on, I'm getting him," John said as he hopped off his broom. Mary followed.

"You! Shriveling worm! Hey! Hey! Hey! Excuse me."

"What's up, man?" John asked. "Think it's okay, huh? Sending John Jr off to a random land? You're lucky I don't end your life right now, fish-eyes."

"That's assault. It's disgusting," Mary scolded.

Aldaricus whimpered. John imitated his cries. "Not such a big man now, huh? Come on, duel me, show everyone how powerful you are! Taking on a freshman!" John scoffed.

"We're going to call your mom," Mary added. "And we may even alert the Ministry. What do you think of that, Aldaricus?"

"Oh, my Merlin." John turned to see Roman walking into the school. "Come on, let's get his dad. Mary, come on! Come on, Mary. Hurry up!"

"I think we're going to be late for school," Olivia said to Lulia. Lulia nodded.

John jogged down past corridor lockers, followed closely by Mary. Doubling back, he peered down a hallway. "Mary." Roman was walking down a hall. "Come on!"

Roman listened to music through earphones as Mary and John approached him from behind. "Hey! Hey, you! Excuse me. I'm talking to you."

John slugged Roman, knocking his brother to the ground. John shook his hand, and he felt his knuckle break.

"I'm going to sue you, man!" Roman looked up at his younger

brother.

"If we were worried about getting sued, would we do this?" Mary booted him in the crotch. He groaned.

Faculty members arrived. "Whoa. Whoa. What's happening here?" Mr Black asked.

"His son sent Junior to a random land!" Mary told her brother.

"You're going to the dungeon today!" John pointed.

"You mind summoning the Ministry?" Mary commanded Ben. "Hurry up!" John added.

"Absolutely." Ben nodded.

"Dust farmer!" She grunted as she kicked her brother-in-law again.

Outside, a crowd watched as Roman and Aldaricus were taken away in cuffs.

"It wasn't in the forbidden spell book list."

Krum placed Aldaricus on the back of his broom, and Gabriel put Roman on the back of his. "He's of age. Why am I being arrested?" Roman protested.

"Bye-bye, bullspit," John taunted.

"Garbage." Mary crossed her arms.

"You're detaining us?" John asked Bella as she began to cuff Mary. "Our son could be dead because of him. Why are you arresting us?"

"Good. Good work, Queen," Mary spat.

As Bella marched the couple to the back of Gower's three-seated broom, Mary locked eyes with Lulia and Olivia, who were being helped off the broom by Alizeh and Dorothy.

"For what it's worth," Gower began, "I heard what you two did in there. You know, you're good parents, worried about your son." Gower began to fly them off.

Later that night, John and Mary entered their home.

"Hey. Hey, baby," Mary said as Tantrum met them at the door. "My Merlin, it's so clean."

"Well, there are my little bandits; posting bail for my sister, again. Merlin, it's been what? Since high school?" Jadon Black chuckled. "Took me back to the good ol' days."

"Thank you, by the way," John said.

"Where are the girls?" Jadon asked as he held Harriet in his arms.

"Dorothy had to take them to a temporary placement for the night," Mary explained. "I love you, Jade." Mary draped her arms around her brother and gave him a tight hug.

Jadon's eyes welled up. "I love you both. Get some sleep." Jadon took his leave, handing his sister Harriet and closing the door behind him.

Mary plopped down on the couch beside John. She rested her face on her hand. "It's so clean and quiet in here." John looked around.

"I know. I hate it."

"Me too."

Thunder began to rumble.

The next morning, the rain still pouring, Lulia and Olivia sat looking out of the rain-specked window of Dr Terrance August's home, each holding a teddy bear.

"Hey," their parents greeted as Terrance let them in. "We are so sorry. Are you okay?" The girls nodded.

"Did you guys go to Skogen?" Lulia asked eagerly.

"No. We were just in the dungeon," Mary explained.

The Scaasis returned to their home. John sighed as he lingered near the door, watching on as Olivia and Lulia entered. Olivia held onto her and Lulia's teddy bear while Lulia smoothed her hair.

"Everybody, get ready for dinner," John said softly. The words barely came out.

Later, as Olivia sat before a plate of Sautéed Lesser Centipede Spaghetti, John topped it off with some shredded cheese before tossing it with a serving fork and spoon. "Here you go."

Olivia stared downward. "What if we never see Spencer or John again?"

"Don't worry." John looked at her. "People bound by blood always find each other. Besides, Spencer will be home as soon as she's healthy enough. Sure as eggs." Mary nodded.

"Okay," Olivia sniffled.

"It's okay, guys, right now, the five of us are all here together, and for that, we should be thankful," John added.

Lulia got up, headed off and began crying. She closed her bedroom door behind her. Mary set her napkin down, stepping away.

"Come on, princess, you haven't touched your food." John looked to Olivia. "You want me to reheat it for you?" John pulled out his wand.

Olivia rose from her seat, embracing her father and sobbing on his shoulder as Harriet looked on.

"It's okay, princess." John rubbed her back as he blinked back tears.

Later, he and Mary put the girls to bed, wishing them goodnight and putting strength into their "I love yous. They blew the blue lantern out in the bedroom.

In the living room, Mary began to fold laundry. John sat beside her and held up a pair of John Jr's pants.

Once he had arrived, he instantly knew where he was. John Jr had appeared in the stands of an arena made of sand. He was sitting amongst a crowd of roaring spectators. On the other side of the theater, a grey-haired man who wore a purple cloak sat on a golden throne, looking down at two men and a woman who were mid-brawl. They were only allowed to fight with rusted weapons as well as their bare hands. He had appeared next to a young girl by the name of Rian. She had bright blue eyes and white-blond hair, making her eyebrows nearly non-existent. Her face was freckled, and her body was lean. At first, she was frightened, but she smiled after seeing the young man's delicate nature.

After the brawl ended with the bearded man winning, the crowd roared. Though, by the looks of it, one would suspect that the winner would soon die from infected wounds, as the weapons had been used for centuries without being cleaned. John Jr slipped out of the arena along with Rian. Despite appearing out of thin air after the event at Crash Ring, John Jr was relieved to find that no one had discovered his sudden appearance out of the ordinary. He had blended in without raising any suspicion.

It was now mid-December, and John Jr was still hiding away in Atraemmont. The once hot and sandy place was now cold, bitter, and full of snow. John Jr had been hiding deep inside of Atraemmont's forest. He was sitting beneath his usual tree as he stared at the lake that had not completely frozen over yet. For the majority of his time in Atraemmont, he had been staying with Rian. She had harbored him until one day, John Jr had accidentally struck a royal guard with a snowball.

John Jr had been able to run away before they could make an arrest. He ran off, buried in the woods, struggling to survive through the stormy weather. He would often use his mediocre healing spells to nurse himself back to health.

Typically, being mid-December, John Jr would've been eager for the holiday of Saturnalia. A time for feasting, goodwill, generosity, gifts, and decorated trees. If he were at home, he'd be sitting by the fire, eating some of his mother's homemade desserts. They would be bundled up in their housecoats as chilly drafts from outside seeped in. The windows of his house would rattle due to Galdorwide's intense winter winds. However, no one minded it, for it was Saturnalia.

John Jr tried to remember the spell his cousin had used on him. "League Magical!" He would repeat this as he thought about home. When he concluded that the magic was incorrect, he thought back to his potions class. He was almost sure he remembered the Teleportation concoction. He would need a sliver of bronze, silver, and the skin of a dragon. Luckily, Atraemmont was one of the few magical lands accustomed to dragons. He had scrapped bronze from an abandoned gate and silver from a blade given to him by Rian. However, he had no idea where he could find a dragon. He had written a letter to Rian, explaining that he was safe and just in need of finding a dragon. She had written back, stating that he was crazy, but the dragons did not reside on Atraemmont land. However, if he insisted, they could be found on Atraemmont's island just north of the forest.

John Jr knew that this was insane, but he also knew that he needed to go back home. He couldn't sit and wait for his family to come for him any longer.

His goal was to be home by the 23rd, the final day of the Saturnalia celebration. It was his favorite holiday, and he couldn't bear to think about having to wait a whole other year. To keep himself going, he tried to convince himself that this would be the best Saturnalia ever. After all, his family and friends would be extra generous because of his disappearance.

When he reached the end of the forest where the lake had met him, he could see the island. It wasn't too far off. John Jr looked beside him, where he took note of a redwood tree. John Jr followed its trunk and saw that its top was nowhere in sight. He estimated its height to be about three hundred feet tall.

He aimed his wand at the bottom of the tree's trunk. *"Cyrf!"* A constant red surge of waves struck near the base of the tree. It had sliced the tree evenly, letting it fall into the water. It was just the right length to get close enough to the island. John Jr began to walk along the tree's thin trunk.

"Hi." A beautiful young woman with blue hair appeared from beneath the lake's surface. "Do you need any help?"

"Nah, I'm all right, thanks, though." John Jr had heard the stories of Atraemmont's nymphs. They were kind-natured spirits and posde no threat. However, he still found himself alarmed by the woman's sudden appearance. He gave an awkward, polite smile and continued to walk.

"Do you mind that once you finish what you're doing — removing the tree? It's in my way." The nymph swam beside him as he walked along the log. "Are you going to try and fight a dragon? Hoping to find it's jewels?"

Born with excellent manners, John Jr tried his best to maintain his balance and eye contact with the woman. He didn't succeed at retaining either of the two tasks. After she had finished asking all of her questions, he fell into the lake, almost on top of her.

Shaken by the icy touch of the water and shock of the fall, he grabbed hold of the nymph's arm. Once he relaxed enough to realize what he was doing, he released her arm. "Sorry, it was an accident." He looked at her newly wet face after dragging her down with him.

"It's not a crime to touch a nymph," she said silkily. "I'm just worried if you're hurt."

"No, I'm fine," he replied sheepishly.

She smiled. "Be grateful. Nature can hurt you sometimes, so we should get going before nightfall. We can swim. It looks easier than walking along the tree, don't you think?"

They began to swim against the harsh current. Despite the rough conditions, John Jr had a smile on his face. It had been a while since he had spoken to another being.

"I'll wait here," she said as they reached the edge of the waters. "I'll wait for you here, no matter how long you take."

"Thanks," John Jr blushed as he lifted himself onto the island's shore.

"Cheer up, you've got this," she encouraged. "Tell you what, when you get back, I will start a fire so you can get warm."

With that, he ventured off farther into the island's forest. The island didn't seem to only belong to dragons. Most of its trees had fairy lights and ornaments on them for Saturnalia celebrations. The last three, at the corner of the island, stood before a gigantic cave.

The island was spectacular as well as empty when it came to creatures. The trees sparkled from their trunks up to their very tips. John Jr had his wand ready as he stepped his right foot into the cave. Along the sides of the cave's floor were lit candles. If he hadn't known any better, he would have thought someone had planned him a romantic evening.

He ventured deeper into the cave until he heard the sound of someone, or something, breathing heavily. He softened his steps and crept along the left side of the cave. His ankles burned as the candle flames flickered close behind him. At one point, he looked down just to make sure that his pants hadn't caught on fire. When he got to the edge of the cave's first floor, he looked down and saw nine dragons, all awake. They were walking protectively around piles of golden objects. The depth between him and the dragons was large enough for the creatures to look ant-sized. He bent down and aimed his wand.

John Jr decided it'd be best to distinguish the dragons before trying to slice off their skin. "*Shockwave grama arodscipe!*" A violent, ruby line struck the first dragon, attacking it with a shockwave of demonic energy. The dragon toppled over.

The remaining eight dragons looked up to where they saw the young boy. Angry, their stomachs began to rumble as they prepared their breaths of fire.

He quickly scooted away from the edge. He stood to his feet and aimed his wand downwards.

A firebolt flew up at him. Luckily, he had moved away just in time.

He squeezed his eyes shut and looked up to the heavens. "Merlin, if you're up there, looking down at me, please let the dumb thing I plan to do next go well." He turned and faced the dragons. He aimed his wand mid-air. *"Port!"* A gentle, ruby intertwining duo of waves exited his wand. The waves circled in front of him until they made an oval shape large enough for John Jr to fit in. He grabbed out his knife as a second portal appeared down behind the dragons. John Jr stepped through the doorway. He kept his left foot in the original entrance while he reached towards the closest dragon's tail. He successfully sliced the surface of the dragon's tail and grabbed the scab of its skin for himself. The dragon wailed in pain, but before it could move its massive body around, John Jr had re-entered the portal, returning to the top level.

Having what he needed, John Jr ran out of the cave, dragon skin in hand. He would've teleported to Galdorwide there and then, but the nymph was kindly awaiting him.

"Did you get what you came for?" the nymph asked as he approached. It was apparent that she never did doubt that he'd make it out alive. She was now sitting on the edge of the island. She was wearing a white dress, and since it was soaked, it didn't do a great job of being clothing.

"Yep, your kind offer of a fireside kept me going." He smiled. "Oh, and I do have to leave by tomorrow morning." The sun was beginning to set.

"That's all right." The girl tossed her long blue hair over her shoulders as she prepared to dive into the water. Bubbles danced around her feet as she stood. She threw herself into the water. John Jr, however, was reluctant. Earlier, he had noticed that the water was colder than the frosty air.

"Coming?" she asked. He nodded slowly before flinging himself into the water. When he emerged back up, he gasped in shock. The icy chill of the lake was worse than he imagined.

"Oh — Merlin — it's — s-so c-cold." He shivered.

The nymph looked over to him, shocked. She did not find the water cold. She found it to be just the right temperature, as it always was. She reached for John Jr's arm and pulled him closer so he could feel the warm water that surrounded her.

Too close for comfort, John Jr grew self-conscious and tried to make conversation. "So — what's your name?"

"Aqua; my mother gave it to me because of my blue-green eyes," Aqua casually replied, as she was not disturbed by their closeness. "What's yours?"

"John... Named after my father." He continuously grew uncomfortable.

Keeping close contact, they swam back to Atraemmont's mainland. Even though John Jr had everything he needed for the potion, he realized that he didn't know the spell that went along with it. However, who knew, maybe Aqua could help? Nymphs were mythological beings, usually beautiful. They often inhabited woods and rivers, as well as other locations. They were believed to be spirits of nature. That being the case, she must have something to offer. When they arrived on land, she pulled herself up from out of the water, revealing her tiny physique. She was both short and skinny.

Aqua raised her hands, and a blue ball of magic formed in the middle of her two palms. She aimed it towards the ground, where she sent the magic down, striking the snowy dirt. A floating blue ball of fire then shot out from beneath the soil. John Jr approached the light in an attempt to warm himself.

"Are you affected by Atraemmont's ruler, Adam Harris?" he asked.

"No, only because I don't do any wrongdoings. If I were to, then yes, I would be affected. Adam has no free passes for any creature on this land. If you do anything wrong, he'd surely enjoy watching you die a meaningless death. After all, the winner has to keep fighting new opponents until they die, if their wounds don't kill them first. Have you been affected?" she asked. Her sweet eyes looked into his.

"No." He shook his head. He didn't want to risk her thinking lowly of him.

"Maybe you should leave now." She backed away. "I know a liar when I see one. I wish you good luck, but I can't risk Harris finding me with you. Are you John Scaasi? The wizard they've been looking for?" She looked at him in horror.

He wished he could have come up with an excuse or say a convincing "No, I'm not", but he decided it was best to obey her wishes. He didn't want to risk angering her. He was not well educated in the nymph species and feared what powers they might have.

"Okay, okay. Do you know the teleportation spell that goes with this potion? I have all the materials I need, but I don't know what to say."

The nymph wasn't very helpful. John Jr assumed it was because of his "criminal" background, so he wasn't surprised.

After many failed attempts, John Jr took a seat on the grass as his legs grew sore. Aqua rested her back against the tree with her arms crossed, hoping he'd figure out the spell and leave soon. She glared at him intensely, and it was a wonder that he hadn't felt it pierce through the back of his head.

"Apuldrerind mec be home — that's what you say." Aqua cringed as she helped him.

She had to wince a few more times as he struggled with pronunciation. She kept repeating the spell until he mastered it. When he did, he raised his wand high into the air. A red glowing circle popped out from his wand and fell around him where he sat.

"*Apuldrerind mec be home!*" The circle around him extended high into the air. He felt as if he were in a large red bubble. Once it fell back down, John Jr was no longer in Atraemmont.

In the master bedroom Mary woke up, finding herself alone.

As John watched the girls sleep from the doorway, Mary joined him. She nuzzled his shoulder.

The next morning, Tantrum shared the couch with Olivia and Harriet. Clearing her throat, Lulia peered out of the window. Jadon pulled up on his broom. They would be going over to their uncle's for their usual Saturnalia traditions. "All right. Get up! Come on, let's go." Lulia turned to her sisters. "Olivia, come on, get your stuff."

"Bye, Tantrum." Olivia waved. Mary heaved a sigh.

Walking onto the porch, Lulia looked to her uncle. This year wouldn't be the same without Spencer and John Jr She began to cry.

"Lulia." John stepped forward. She took off, running.

"I'll go get her; watch the kids." John looked at Mary.

"Just wait there, okay?" Mary looked to Olivia, who held onto Harriet.

The couple shouted for their daughter as they pursued her down the quiet side street.

Lulia rounded a corner onto a sidewalk and cut across the front yard of a house. John and Mary headed along the side of the home.

"Lulia!" John shouted. They stopped by a fenced-in area as they continued to call for their daughter. They could hear her sobbing. Peering through the fence slats, he could see Lulia huddled on the ground. "Lulia."

"Please, just go away."

"We're here. We love you."

A woman looked down from the balcony. "Hey, what the abyss is going on here?" she asked.

"Could you just give us a few minutes?" John motioned to the fenced-in area. "Please?" The woman spotted Lulia below.

"Oh, okay, sorry." She paced off.

"We know the most important thing to you, to all of us, is family. We know that. We love you," John assured her.

"Stop saying that, please go away. Please." Lulia kept her eyes shut tight. "Please."

John hung his head and glanced at Mary. They straightened and reluctantly withdrew from the fence. John and Mary walked to the curb where they sat in front of the woman's house. Jadon, along with the two girls, approached.

"Is Lulia okay?" Olivia asked.

"She's a little upset." Mary frowned.

"Everything okay?" John asked Jadon, who nodded.

Wiping her eyes, Lulia emerged from the dirt walkway along the side of the house. John and Mary stood to their feet.

"So... you think, being bonded by blood will help us find him?" the red-headed girl asked.

"Yep," John said with no doubt in his voice. "We have a cosmic connection." Lulia sighed.

"You kids are stuck with us. We will go to all of Junior's Crash Ring games next year, we will be scolding him about his grades, and we're going to buy Spencer's end-of-the-year ball dress when she turns eighteen, and it's going to be pretty. But not too revealing. Super sweet. You know, not too provocative. Just like that gorgeous sweet spot," John rambled.

"Yeah, and the twins will graduate. The five of us will be in the front row embarrassing them. Then we will be in the front row again when you graduate high school."

"And someday, I'll give Spencer and all you girls away at your weddings."

"What?" Mary got annoyed with her husband's rambling.

"Even if I don't like the guy and don't think he's good enough for my little girl."

"In the way, way future." Mary narrowed her eyes.

"Lulia, can we go to Uncle Jadon's now?" Olivia asked as Mary gently stroked her hair. John regarded Lulia with a lump in his throat.

She nodded with a chuckle. Arms spread, Mary looked her daughter in the eye as Lulia stayed put. She pulled her in for a hug. "I know you don't like this, but you're going to have to get used to this, okay?"

"Can I get one of those?" John piped up. "'Cause I haven't got one of those in two years from you. Please?"

Lulia embraced her father, laughing, then Olivia and Jadon, along with Harriet, made it a group hug.

As soon as the girls flew off with Jadon, John Scaasi marched into the trees without looking back at Mary. A cloth bandage covered the wound on his knuckles. He continued through the trees.

John stopped. He bowed his head. He turned and walked back in the direction he came. John paused and looked back over his shoulder. His eyes widened when he turned. He saw John Jr running toward him through the trees. John Jr stopped a few feet away and gazed up at his father before rushing forward and embracing him.

"People linked by blood will always find each other." John tightened his embrace.

The festivities in Galdorwide had started. John Jr was having too much of a good time to dwell on his time in Atraemmont. He didn't even brood about Spencer's absence. John Jr was home alone with his parents. His younger siblings had gone off to enjoy Saturnalia celebrations at the home of their uncle, Jadon Black. John Jr was finally able to enjoy a book by the fireside without Lulia throwing pieces of food at the back of his head.

He rested for an hour by the fire, reading and munching on the mango crispies that he usually had to fight his sisters to get. Now, John Jr also had time to scheme up some pranks for Lulia, for her natural welcome back home gift.

Mary and John babied their son, as one would expect. After all, they had believed that they would never see their eldest child again.

It was now the morning of the last day of Saturnalia. John Jr immediately looked forward to the joy, gifts, and food. The first thing he saw after he exited his room early that morning was a small package on his kitchen counter.

"Happy Saturnalia, Junior." John walked down the hallway wiping his sleepy eyes. Mary strode close behind him, wearing a plum-colored house robe.

"Happy Saturnalia." John Jr smiled. For once, he was up early and bright-eyed. "Thank you, guys. Honestly, I wasn't expecting any gifts, considering all the chaos over these past few weeks."

"Did you think we'd spend the last day of Saturnalia not opening presents?" John chuckled. He reached into his blue house robe and pulled out a small brown packaged box. John handed it to his wife.

Mary smiled and lifted her left hand. Purple smoke circled her palm, and a denser package appeared. She handed it to her husband.

"Shall we?" John asked.

The three of them began to open their presents. John Jr was the first to finish unwrapping his. He tore off the brown packaging, which then revealed a black box. He opened the box to find a necklace. Its pendant was a black feather with a silver tip.

"An onyx feather," Mary began as she looked on. John Jr held the necklace in his hand, studying it closely. "It empowers the soul and fuels the spirit of the wearer."

"Thank you." John Jr beamed. He draped the necklace over his head and around his neck. John Jr didn't plan on taking it off, ever. He gave each of his parents a hug before they could finish unwrapping their gifts.

Mary was the second to finish unwrapping her present. Beneath the brown packaging was another black box. When she opened it, she saw three pins: a witch, a werewolf, and a cauldron. These were the characters of a Galdorwide folklore story, "The Witch Without Hate". It was a story her mother would read to her and her two younger brothers. The story always remained close to her heart. She picked up the three black pins and held them close to her chest. She looked to her husband, who had been watching on with a big smile.

"Thank you." Tears welled in her eyes.

John placed his half-opened present on the kitchen counter to pull his wife in for a hug.

They stood in each other's arms for a few moments.

"Oh, go on." Mary wiped her tears as she pulled away from him. "Open your present, darling."

John's package was unlike theirs, as it was not boxy in shape. It was almost triangular. When he opened it, he saw a mini pyramid made out of moonstones.

"It can answer all the questions in the universe, my love," Mary began to explain. "When the moon is full, closely whisper your question, and the pyramid will grant you the answer."

"Thank you!" John beamed. He embraced her once more.

"Now you can ask your pyramid all the hundred questions you ask me. I don't know the answers to everything, you know."

The couple chuckled. The joyous feeling that John Jr had been waiting for had finally arrived. However, he didn't just intend to spend the evening with his family. It was a tradition for his parents and the elder siblings to visit Jadon and their younger siblings. There, they would eat garlic, winter greens, and cake. The night's evening hosts were Lulia, Olivia, and Harriet. Role reversal was a Saturnalia tradition, and the children would get to play the part of an adult. This year, John Jr had planned on visiting Lovetta. A few months ago, they had spoken of their shared love for Saturnalia. She had wanted John Jr to stop by, as her three younger brothers would be putting on a feast and light-hearted fun.

"What are you thinking about, Junior?" John asked once he noticed that his son was deep in thought.

John Jr's face turned pink. "I was wondering if I could spend the evening at Annette's. Lovetta had suggested that I come by for a visit on Saturnalia a few months ago."

"That was a few months ago." Mary's temper grew hot. "Your

invitation has expired. You will spend the evening enjoying your own family's festivities." Her tone ended the conversation, and he knew that her answer was final. "Now, go to your room and grab your sweater."

The sweater — the only downside about Saturnalia was the ugly sweaters Mary made her family wear. John Jr reluctantly walked to his room. When he returned, he was wearing a red knitted shirt with white reindeers. His parents wore the same sweater; Mary's was purple, and John's was blue.

"Isn't it nice of your mother to hand-knit us new sweaters each year?" John tried getting a "thank you" out of his son.

Every year they were always the same. "Yeah," John Jr mumbled.

The three of them exited their home. John held Mary's hand so that she could leave the barrier. They dashed onto their brooms and flew up into the snowy sky.

A flying letter came rushing towards John Jr It hit his face and began to tumble downwards. His heart sank as he reached for the falling object. He caught it just in time. He held on to it tightly for the remainder of his ride. He was scared that at any moment the harsh wind would blow the envelope right out of his frozen hand.

The family lowered their brooms as they headed down towards Jadon's home. He was a lord who lived alone in a distant yellow farmhouse with white trimming.

Before they entered the home, John Jr opened the envelope. In the letter was loopy handwriting that he had only ever seen before on Lovetta's homework sheets. The message read:

Dearest John Jr Scaasi, I have heard of your return to Galdorwide, which, by the way, I am so relieved to hear! I wondered if you wanted to come to my house later today to celebrate Saturnalia, as we discussed? If not, enjoy your festivities.

I look forward to seeing you when school returns. Sincerely, Lovetta Annettes.

John Jr felt strange. He did want to see Lovetta, and it had been so long since he had spent time with a real friend. Before John Jr could think of anything else or re-ask if he could visit the Annettes, Jadon's white door

182

flung open. Jadon stood behind it, sporting the usual long brown flowy hair of the Black family. John Jr was quite pleased to blend in with his mother's side. John Jr's hair was always perfectly luscious; he was tall and had a slim, athletic build.

Jadon wasn't your typical lord. He lived in a charming farmhouse and always sported flannel shirts.

"Happy Saturnalia!" Jadon beamed. "I'm glad to see you guys are wearing your traditional sweaters. The girls gave me quite a hard time this year." The towering man chuckled.

Jadon wore a purple sweater hand-knitted by Mary. Printed on its front were four ice-skating penguins.

"I have to say, sis, your sweaters get better and better every year." He smiled. His deep dimples appeared on his tanned, chiseled face.

His sweaters always took longer for Mary to knit. He had a more massive build than the rest of her family, and she took extra care when making it.

"Come on in, you guys." He stepped out of the way, allowing his family to enter. When he turned around, he saw that Lulia was still wearing her blue neon tank top and matching jeans. "Lulia! Put on your sweater this instant!" he roared.

John jumped. He yelled at his kids but never as aggressively as Jadon had. However, Jadon was a usually calm man, so John knew that Lulia must've been giving him a bit of trouble these past days.

Jadon noticed that the three little girls had frozen in position, staring up at him. He smiled to make up for his yell. "They're extra warm this year, Lulia."

Trying to act unalarmed by her uncle, she moaned and headed down the hall to the left, where the guest room was.

"So, John Jr, anything special you want this year for Saturnalia?" His uncle turned to him.

"A pet shark." John, Jr beamed.

"Well, that's not very realistic." Jadon chuckled. "Anything else?"

"Well, I did want to visit my friend Lovetta today and spend Saturnalia with her and her family," he admitted.

Jadon's eyes traveled to Mary then back to his nephew. He grabbed out his wand. "Which type of shark would you like?"

"Jade!" Mary scowled.

Jadon liked to give his family what they wanted for Saturnalia. He would ask and conjure up the gift on the spot. "Sorry, kiddo." Jadon began to twirl his wand as he pictured up a new gift for his nephew. A gym bag, workout clothes, energy potions, and chocolate bars appeared. The presents floated in front of John Jr, whose eyes lit up.

"Thanks!"

Lulia returned to the living room, biting into a peppermint chocolate bar. She continued to wear her tank top. Jadon rolled his eyes, stomped over to the guest room, and grabbed Lulia's blue sweater. When he returned, he began to shove it over her head, knocking her chocolate bar onto the floor.

"I don't want to!" She tried to fight off the bear-sized man. He proceeded to pull her arms through the sleeves.

"Saturnalia — is a time for family. So — when your mother puts effort into making you clothing to wear for eight hours, you will do so!" He grunted as he spoke during the struggle. His voice was loud but not as frightening as earlier.

Lulia attempted to rip off the sweater, but Jadon caught her arms just in time and pinned them to her sides. His teenage son Dallas joined them for the festivities. Jadon did his best caring for his son ever since his wife passed three years ago.

Once the festivities at the castle had come to an end, Ben and Bella arrived at Jadon's house just in time for dinner. The three girls had prepared the usual garlic winter greens and olive mammoth. Bella always made sure to eat all that she needed at the castle so that she wouldn't have to eat the food cooked by children. To set the mood for Saturnalia's dinner, Lulia had conjured up a mini prancing deer and some mini penguins. The animals danced above their heads as they ate. The adults were quite impressed by this. Seventy percent of the dinner's conversation was jokes told by Jadon.

Once everyone had finished their meals, each girl brought out a platter. Lulia carried the heaviest, being the gilded cake. Olivia brought out the cinnamon pudding, and Harriet carried out the almond wafers.

Everyone, to John Jr's amazement, seemed to be having fun, even Bella, whose face had gone pink from too much wine. Ben also shared the glee as he kept toasting to his girlfriend and politely kissing her hand — this made her cheeks turn a deep red. She was smiling so wide that her cheeks began to ache.

After dessert, Ben and Bella handed out their gifts. John Jr got a new red baseball hat and more candies than he could count. Lulia received a large box. Inside were coming-of-age items such as notebooks, makeup, and workout gear. Olivia got a new house robe and a pair of unicorn slippers, while Harriet had received a sweet and colorfully illustrated book about love.

Once all the gifts were open, the girls announced the evening's first activity — a snowball fight.

The snowball war immediately grew intense, girls against the boys. Despite being on opposing sides, John would shelter Mary from the snowballs' wrath thrown from Jadon, Junior, and Ben. After a half hour, the whole family was out of breath. Cold and wet, they were pleased to find out that the next activity was sitting by the warm fireplace. Lulia explained that John would read the classic Saturnalia storybook *The Owl of the Snow*.

After having much to eat, the girls found themselves too sleepy to do anything else for the evening. Harriet had fallen asleep on her brother's lap, while Olivia had fallen asleep on Mary's shoulder. Nonetheless, everyone enjoyed hearing John's rendition of the story.

Despite not getting to see Lovetta this Saturnalia, John Jr had to admit that this had been one of the best ones yet. Maybe it was because he didn't expect to spend it in Galdorwide this year.

When the night was over, John Jr had changed out of his warm sweater and into thin pajamas. He crawled into bed, where he lay awake. His fingers traced his onyx feather necklace. It didn't feel like an ordinary necklace. It felt light, as if he weren't wearing it at all. Soon, his thoughts began to drift to Lovetta. Unable to sleep, he got out of bed and wrote to Caden, who gave him the spell to turn off his mother's alarm. He decided he would sneak out of the house and see her, even if it was only for a few minutes. The rest of his family fell asleep almost instantly after they had mailed all of Spencer's gifts.

Outside was chilly, yet he seemed to be untouched by the air's frost. He had slipped his bare feet into his new pair of running shoes and pulled a blue sweater over his pajama shirt. The moonlight was dim, and shadows haunted the streets. It was a funny feeling. It had been the first time he had ever done anything without his alarm system. He felt wide-awake and more excited than ever. The joyous feeling flooded through him as he walked down the darkened streets. He could do whatever he wanted.

Before he knew it, he was standing outside of Lovetta's bedroom window. A red wolf on the porch sat up but didn't seem to be too concerned with him. Lovetta's hair was messier than usual, and drool dripped down her chin. He could hear her snores through the glass. He didn't know whether or not he should wake her. It was pretty late, after all.

His body became conflicted. He took a step back while his hand reached for the window.

Ultimately, his arm won. He tapped on the window. Lovetta jolted up into a seated position, looked at the window, and began to rub her tired eyes.

"Who's there?" she squeaked.

"It's me, John," he whispered, to make sure that he didn't wake up the rest of her family.

Instead of chatting briefly, Lovetta decided to sneak out with him. He had to help her out of her bedroom window. She had changed out of her sleepwear. She was now wearing a white buttoned shirt, ripped jeans, and a beanie over her uncombed hair. The two kids decided to venture off to the local library. Both of them enjoyed reading and often swapped books during their library visits.

An eerie vibe filled the dimly lit library, as no one except for the elderly librarian was inside. The librarian gave each of them a lamp to make their reading at this time of night easier. Galdorwide, from midnight until four a.m., suffered from total darkness. They had to admit that this trip to the library was creepier than usual.

Their favorite section was at the back of the library — the part that had books about creatures. They held up their lamps to read the titles. The light didn't do much good, as the book spines were either peeled, faded or stained. The hairs on the back of Lovetta's neck prickled, as she could hear whispers coming from behind them.

She brushed it off, contributing it to the dead silence of the night-time library. After they didn't come across any new books, they knelt and searched the bottom shelf. A large black and silver book caught John Jr's eye. The bottom bracket was packed tightly, as no book from the stand had been taken out yet. He fought with the book for a few moments. After a firm tug, the book fell to the floor and opened.

The writing was in a language unknown to them. The book was both written and illustrated by hand. There were images of plants, charts, and naked people, all on a single page. Disembodied footsteps walked around them. A dark presence surrounded them, and John Jr felt that someone or something didn't want this book in their hands. He stood up and held the book against his chest. Lovetta looked to him, her face pale. She had a bad feeling about the book, and she was more frightened to see that John Jr felt the same. They exited the library quickly after they decided to check the book out. They would have asked the librarian if she knew anything about the book, but she was too grumpy about being bothered.

They began to walk home before coming to an abrupt stop outside of the building. A man wearing a purple-trimmed suit of armor had ridden out onto the road. The knight looked down at them from atop his black horse. When the knight did nothing but breathe heavily into his helmet, they began to tremble. John Jr pressed the book tightly to his chest and reached for Lovetta's hand. Together, they started to run. They could hear the horse's hooves gain on them. With the sky turning into complete blackness, John Jr lost his way. He had no idea where he was going, but that didn't stop him from running. Suddenly, Jack, Lovetta's familiar, appeared. When they grew close to it, the wolf began to run, leading them. Luckily, they eventually lost their pursuer.

"So — was I correct? Did someone take my book?"

"Yes, Your Majesty," the knight answered his queen, who stood on the throne.

"Who?"

"Two teenagers. A boy and a girl. They ran off before I could get to them, but I will find them." The man lifted off his helmet. His long brown hair fell to his shoulders. On his forehead was a deep scar that extended down above his left eye.

"You mean to tell me that — you — on your steed — lost two children? I told you that you could do whatever you needed to seize the book from the stealer."

"Technically," the man stood from his kneeling position, "they are not stealers. The book was in a library. Why would you keep an important book at a public library?"

Bella's eyes narrowed. "Do you dare question your queen?"

"No, Your Majesty, I'm sorry." He bowed his head.

"For your information, I didn't know where the book was until tonight. I had dreamt of it. In my dream, I saw two people take it, and their faces were unclear. Were you able to get a good look at them?"

"I did, my queen," he replied.

"Good. When school returns, you will put on a new face. A teacher, a student, or any other face that would go unquestioned. When you find them, bring them to me."

The blood had drained from their faces, and sweat dripped down their foreheads. They tried to keep quiet, despite their heavy breaths. They still held their clammy hands together as they followed Jack to Lovetta's home. The kingdom was becoming a horror show — there were portals, dragons, a prison escapee, and a pissed off royal knight.

Lovetta stayed rooted at the edge of her lawn. She didn't want to leave John Jr to walk home by himself.

"I learned a teleportation spell while in Atraemmont. I'll poof home." He smiled. "I'm just going to make sure you get inside safely."

John Jr waited until she closed the door behind her. Jack began to twirl until he found a comfy position on the low wooden porch. "*Apuldrerind mec be home!*" As he approached the entrance of his home, he noticed that the door was ajar. He was sure he hadn't been the one to leave it open. In case of an intruder, John Jr squeezed through the door's tiny crack and held in his breath. He walked past his sisters' and parents' bedrooms to see that they were all peacefully asleep, to his relief. He let out his breath and leaned against the wall as he heard his family's quiet snores. John Jr walked back to the front door to shut it and began to walk over to his room.

He turned into the first room on the left, only to find that his bedroom was not as it was. It appeared to be a forest. He could see the trees' dark shapes, and critters, as the moonlight soaked in through the leaves. When he turned on the light switch, he saw that he was staring at himself. He jumped, only to find that he was not looking into a mirror. The other "him" was statue-like. He examined the man from top to bottom, and the being was dressed exactly like him. The only difference was that the man had clawed feet. Gradually, words in Galdorian appeared on the man's forehead like scars. "Ic eyre apuldrerind unc be incer cwaltt", which translated to, "I will take you to your death." His heart began to pound even more than it had when the royal knight was chasing him. The creature approached him.

Suddenly, the alternate version of John Jr raised its hands. Its cold fingers latched onto his shoulders. A straight black rush of spikes surrounded them. When the pegs cleared, his room was now a funeral home. John Jr's heart pounded as he walked towards the casket. What looked to be slightly older versions of Lulia, Olivia, Harriet, Jadon, and Caden kneeled before it. It was he who lay in the casket. Behind him, a man rushed in and over to a second coffin that appeared. John Jr approached the man to find him sobbing over the body of a slightly older-looking Lovetta. When he looked up, the room had enlarged. Along the wall were hundreds of caskets with a few people crying over them.

Tears began to stream down his face. He looked in each of the coffins: Aldaricus, Eion, his uncles, Krum and Ben, and lastly, Spencer. He stumbled backward as he saw that his twin sister's corpse hadn't aged as much as the rest of them. He couldn't bear to look inside any more of them. He began to scream.

His room had returned to normal, but his alternate version was still there. John Jr continued to bellow — his heart had never raced so much in one day. His parents came rushing in; Lulia and Olivia followed. His alternate version faded.

He was breathing heavily. He tenderly turned to face them — they instantly took note of his pale and fear-filled face. He extended his hand. Mary reached for it and held it tightly. She looked into her son's big hazel eyes and saw that a fountain of tears had streamed out of them. His long wavy hair was untidy, a usual side effect of being in the middle of a dizzy spell.

Everyone in the room was speechless. John, Jr's family had never seen him this frightened before. He was always confident or joking around, even at the worst of times. Being quite a bit shorter than her teenaged son, Mary embraced him, her head buried in his chest. Tears began to stream down her face.

"Mom?" he whimpered. "Dad?" More tears broke out of his eyes.

After a few hours, he began to break out of his sadness. A small smile stretched onto his face. He knew that he was lucky to have his family. Maybe seeing his family members' deaths was a way of letting him know that he has the chance to change the future for the better. What if it was his job to protect his family and friends? If so, he knew that he would do so at all costs. He tightened his arms around his mother. Inside him was a mixture of joy, along with a terrible ache of sadness. He remained in his mother's arms for a while. The images of his and his family's dead bodies didn't fade from his mind, and he wasn't so sure that they ever would. He eventually backed away from his mother. He took note of all their tired eyes as they sat on the couch in his room. "We should all go back to bed."

"Honey, tell us what happened first," said Mary.

"I just had a nightmare, a terrible one. Everyone I loved was dead." The tears that had dried returned.

"Even me?" Lulia asked, frightened.

"No — no, you were alive," John Jr replied sincerely. Lulia took offense.

"Don't worry, Junior, you're not a seer," his father tried to comfort him. *I know I'm not a seer, but it wasn't a dream.* John Jr hated lying to them, but he didn't exactly know how to explain the truth.

"I know," he replied under his breath. His family began to exit his room.

"Dad?" John Jr called. "Do you think you can lie on the couch?" He motioned to the sofa.

John smiled and nodded. Despite the unfortunate event, his heart fluttered. He loved it whenever his children admitted that they wanted or needed him.

The next morning, John Jr woke up to the smell of bacon. His mother only ever cooked more than pancakes and toast on special occasions,

190

good or bad.

As much as he loved his mother's bacon, he couldn't eat. He had seen his and his family's dead bodies, and he feared that the creature would return. He did not want to witness it all over again.

Later that afternoon, Lovetta came over to discuss the mysterious book. John Jr had almost forgotten about the book. After all, it didn't seem nearly as important as the vision he had seen last night. As she spoke, all he could think about was how irrelevant the book was. Who cared what ancient magic people used to perform? It wasn't like anyone needed it now, with today's magical education.

"Are you all right?" she eventually asked. "I've never seen you like this before."

He ended up telling her what had happened and how he was afraid that it would happen again. They were slowly walking down the street, heading over to Gower's house. Lovetta decided that they should ask Professor Silwhet. She couldn't wait for school to return to ask him about the book. She needed to know now. The streets looked more familiar in the daylight and less frightening, for that matter.

"If you want, we can head back, because this is probably all too much for you," she suggested after hearing about his night.

"No!" h,e hissed. Lovetta jumped at his unusual temper. "Sorry, it's just I want to feel normal again. I don't want to brood in my house for the rest of my life because of one stupid vision."

"Okay." Lovetta understood. "My legs are dead from last night." She laughed, trying to change the topic.

The cold breeze blew past them, so they tightened their grips on their jackets. "Are you sure you know where Professor Silwhet lives?" John Jr had asked after they had been walking quite a bit longer than she said they would. "I mean, I could've just asked my father where he lives. He would know."

"There it is!" Lovetta pointed into the forest. She ran for the forest. Confused, John Jr began to chase after her.

"Isn't the forest like, forbidden now?" he called after her.

She had come up to Professor Silwhet's home — his house was a literal cabin, the kind made out of logs. It was one storey with no porch and a wooden shed where a garage should've been. The house was very fairytale-like in Lovetta's eyes. She had always imagined herself living in a place like this one.

Upon hearing the kids approach, the door pulled open. Gower was sporting a brown suit jacket and matching slacks. He looked as if he were waiting for their visit. Despite being well dressed, the man looked tired, as black circles had formed beneath his eyes.

"Hi, sir," Lovetta began nervously. "I'm sorry for just dropping by like this, but I was wondering if we could ask you a few questions?"

"About the homework, or the book I gave you?" he asked.

"Not exactly." She gripped the book closer to her chest.

The professor smiled at his students and motioned them inside. Lovetta's jaw dropped as soon as she entered.

"I love your house, sir!"

Thus far, they could only see the living room. In the center was a black area rug with white tribal patterns. On top was a wooden coffee table that looked to be handmade by Professor Silwhet himself. Against the far wall was a black cushioned couch. Facing the sofa were two black leather armchairs. To the left of the room was a floating fireplace.

"People either love it or hate it." He chuckled. "Have a seat. So what is it I can help you two with?" He approached the couch while each of his students took a seat on one of the armchairs.

"Well, I was wondering if you could tell us anything about this book?" She handed it over to him.

He took it into his hands. He tilted his head as he looked along with the book's black cover and silver spine. He looked at his students from out of the corner of his eyes. In a way, they took this glare as a demand for an explanation.

"We found it at the back of Galdorwide's library. We think it might be some ancient text. Have you heard or seen anything about this book?" she asked.

"I have, in my crystal ball. The book isn't from the past. The book has yet to exist. It will, however, come to be — ten years from now."

John Jr and Lovetta looked to one another. "How is that possible?"

"People, for centuries, have had visions of both this book and the author. Whoever has been hiding this in Galdorwide must be one powerful witch."

"Hiding it?" Lovetta asked. "Who would be stupid enough to hide a book in a public library?"

"Not many people are into old magic, or its history. It's quite clever, since this is what the book appears to be."

"So why is this book so important? Why have people been having visions of it?" Lovetta asked her professor another question.

"Because this — this book right here," he lifted it, beginning to wave it forward and back, "has everything a witch needs to become the most powerful sorcerer."

Their eyes trailed to the book, their gazes fixated on the ordinary-looking object. "I think you should return it. Whoever lost it will be looking for it."

Taking that into consideration, John Jr and Lovetta looked to one another. "Do you think?" John Jr's voice quaked.

"Maybe…" she replied.

"What?" Professor Silwhet asked. He couldn't contain his curiosity.

"Last night," Lovetta looked to her teacher, "a royal knight appeared out of nowhere after we exited the library. The knight chased us."

For some reason, Gower didn't look surprised to hear about their encounter. "As I said, bring it back. It wouldn't be safe to have this in your possession."

Lovetta tilted her head to the side in protest. She gave her teacher her classic puppy eyes and formed a pout.

Gower narrowed his gaze, all the while maintaining his constant smile.

"But like, what if the person who hid the book plans on bringing damnation to the kingdom? Am I just supposed to return it then?" she challenged.

"It's not your business. You don't want to get involved in this."

"You're right."

Both John Jr and Gower looked to one another. It wasn't like her to give in so easily. "It's none of my business, but — it's yours. You are a Ministry member, after all. This book is something that should concern you."

Gower chuckled at her stubbornness. "All right, all right. I'll bring it to my next meeting."

"Thank you." Lovetta beamed.

After a cup of tea and a game of chess, Gower showed them out of his lovely home. More snow patted down on the forest's floor.

John Jr let out a sigh after they exited their teacher's cabin. "I've got a bad feeling about that book — wait!" He stopped in his tracks. Lovetta, frightened by his shout, remained still. She turned to him in questioning. "What if that bloody book also has something to do with what happened last night, with the creature?"

They both only had one thought in mind: walking back up to Gower's door and asking him one more question. Their fast feet slid against the slushy snow. Gower opened the door before they arrived back at the welcome mat that acted as a porch. Professor Silwhet was smiling with amusement.

John Jr's insides felt as if they were turning into ice. Lovetta had done most of the talking earlier, but now it was his turn. It was his turn to talk, but this time it was something much deeper than the book. The three of them took a seat on the tribal rug around the coffee table where they had played their chess game. John Jr spoke while sharing pieces of Gower's chocolate bar.

"So, to what do I owe this lovely pleasure?" He smiled. His eyes glistened with his usual joy. John Jr explained the unfortunate event of last night. "I am so, so sorry. What you saw was death."

"Like, *The* Death?" Lovetta asked, leaning forward.

"Yes, precisely. Did you have possession of the book last night?" John Jr nodded.

"It's possible that that was the first step to becoming the most powerful wizard in the world. It gifted you with the realization that no matter how powerful you become, you can't escape death."

"So what I saw wasn't the future? It's not real?" There was a skip of joy in his voice.

"I can't say for sure but — unfortunately, I don't think death would make up such a funeral. I believe that what you saw is the path of reality you are heading on. I also believe that the most powerful witch would also want to see facts. What you saw is most likely the truth, but it's not the only truth."

"But why would everyone I love die, all at once? Or maybe it wasn't all at once — Spencer, she looked younger than me in the coffin."

"Hmm." Gower shrugged. "I don't know," he said softly. "However, if it was the truth, it is not written in stone. Every day we all make different choices, altering not just our paths but the path of those around us."

"Will Death come back if the path changes?"

"I'm not sure, but if it comes around again, looking for you, you will be ready, and you will remember that whatever you see can still change, but death, no matter what, is inevitable. However, the book is no longer in your possession, so you shouldn't need to worry. It is now up to you to take the information you have learned and use it to create a better outcome, not just for you but also for those you love. You two should go home. You look exhausted, and if you have any other concerns, please come to see me again. My door will always be open for you two."

When John Jr returned home, he crawled onto his bed, shoving Tantrum from his pillow. John waltzed in, carrying his cushion and blanket as he prepared to slumber for another night on his son's couch.

The next day at school, everyone else was laughing. Lovetta had run out of her chair and over to the sink that sat on Mr Silwhet's desk. She turned on the tap and began to drink from it. She hadn't realized what she was doing until the entire class started to laugh.

Gower pulled out his wand and aimed it at his students. *"Forsuwung!"* A fluid red line of particles exited his rod and hit each of the student's mouths. They would remain mute until Professor Silwhet decided to use the anti-silence spell.

Gower grabbed hold of Lovetta's arm and immediately rushed her out of the closest classroom door. He slammed the door shut behind him. She looked up at him, frightened, only to find that his face was still just as kind-looking as it always was. Water dripped down her chin.

Water had seeped down her white uniform shirt, making her blue bra visible. "I-I'm sorry, I-I don't know what came over me." She panicked.

"Shh — I'm not mad. I'm just concerned about your health. What you did today shows that you have excessive thirst. Have you recently been injured?"

"No." She shook her head.

"Hmm," he pondered. "I have not seen that behavior in someone for a long time. I want you to promise me that if things worsen, don't — I repeat — don't go to Dr Scaasi or Dr Notleaf. Come to me."

"Uhm — sure — so, what's wrong with me?"

Gower grabbed hold of her shoulders and looked into her eyes. "Nothing, Lovetta Annettes, is wrong with you. You are a bright and brilliant girl."

"Uhm — thanks?"

Gower released her and stood back. He fixed his brown cardigan that he had once let her borrow. "If you like, you can go home now, and I can stay after school and re-teach you the lesson. I don't think you want to hear the lecture that I'm about to give those students."

"Okay."

Tris took a seat at Spencer's usual table, taking her place across from Ellen and Lexi.

Regina looked shocked to have a male sit next to her without teasing her shortly after.

"I miss going out for tea with Spence. Have you guys heard from her? Do you know when she's going to go back home?" he asked solemnly.

"She's at Dr Scaasi's. It sounds pretty severe. Why don't you write to her?" Lexi asked.

"Yeah — I will." Tris nodded. However, he still wasn't done with his questions. "Do you know what's wrong with her?"

Ellen and Lexi looked at one another. both from shock at the care he had for their friend and wondering if they should tell him the truth.

"You don't know?" Lexi asked, making sure that he had meant what he had asked.

"No." He shook his head, frustrated.

"She's — anorexic."

His heart sank, his head felt numb, and his stomach became sick. "Are you sure?"

"Yeah — I know an anorexic when I see one." Ellen looked down at the untouched food on her lunch tray. "I knew it from the moment I met her."

"How come she didn't tell me?" Tris asked, filled with both rage and confusion. He grew angry, at Spencer for not telling him and at himself for not realizing it.

"It's not something that's easy to talk about, Tris." Ellen looked up at him.

"So, anorexic — she doesn't eat because she doesn't like her body? How can her uncle help her with that? She should be here with her friends and family." He slammed his fist against the cafeteria table. Concerned, Caden and Aldaricus quickly took note of the angry student. Tris lowered his temper and waited for the boys to lose interest. After noticing that the girls showed no sign of fear, they went back to their conversation.

"It's much more than that." Ellen tried to hide her frustration. "It's a psychiatric illness. Anorexics often don't see the body that they have. They always see a larger one, but it's not about weight sometimes, it's about control, and sometimes it can even be a form of self-harm. However, I do agree with you that we should surround Spencer, and now you — now that you know."

"Just write to her," Lexi added. "But don't mention that you know. Tell her how you feel about her and tell her how much you want her to get better. I feel like that may help, even just a little." She smiled.

"But keep in mind," Ellen began, ruining the feel-good moment, "anorexia is a mental illness with the highest mortality rate. You have to prepare yourself for the worst."

CHAPTER 13

As per usual, Alan awoke after having a nightmare. It was always the same: him, thirteen, walking home late at night. That image would be followed by a blinding green flash of light, consuming his parents, whole. He had had this nightmare every night since the day it happened. The dream's long-term impact on him had started to wear. However, while in his dream, it always felt like he was experiencing it for the first time.

"You see? You have nothing to worry about," Dorothy encouraged Alizeh as they passed by Alan's home. He was sitting on his porch doing his usual brooding. "He still looks at you the way he did back in high school."

"What do you mean? The only one of us he ever looked at as more than a toy was Adelaide."

"No, he looked at you, me, and Angel as friends, and he still does. Yes, he may have worked for the king, but he is still and will always be our friend. Alan would never hurt us."

Alizeh, who had fully recovered from her coma, decided to head back to work as a Ministry member. She was still torn by the dream she had had of both Olly and Alan killing her. To keep her mind off things, she kept busy with research for current Ministry cases. Alizeh had spent many nights at the library, reading up on the history of dragons. She had tried to find books about Doryu Edjer and The Excogitatoris Draco stone but found nothing.

Despite struggling to find information, Alizeh didn't stress. They were always able to do well with what they had. It was also very possible that other members knew more than she did. The girls headed towards the library to skim through more history books. Dorothy and Alizeh often lived uneventful lives and had more time than the rest to do bookwork. They were often the researchers of the group. Ben, Bella, and Gabriel were the muscle; John, Gower, and Ian were the logical ones; Adelaide was the interviewer, while Olly was usually irrelevant. It was still unclear what the newcomers' roles would be.

Ben was pushing the team harder than usual for this case. No matter what their lives threw at them, this case had to come first, for all the Ministry members. Olly was sure that Ben was going crazy, as the usually calm, soon-to-be king was quite erratic. However, Alizeh seemed to agree with Ben's take on things. Dragons were to come in May, but one had already arrived, and who knew what else this case might have in store? If they succeeded in this case with no casualties, it would be the Ministry's most significant success yet. Plus, the more Alizeh tired herself doing research, the more she dreamt about dragons, which was good, considering that she would rather dream about that than her murder.

After finding nothing once again, the girls went to the night's Ministry meeting. The meeting mainly consisted of Ben giving the group a bit of bad news. He had gotten frustrated with this case and decided that they would need a new member on the team — Alan Alderam.

"Alan Alderam?" Bella gritted her teeth. Ben's plan was news to her as well. "When has he ever shown signs of wanting to be a member — let alone help us? He's a grave stalker! If anything, he'll probably literally try to feed us to the dragons!"

The rest of the room began to complain, all except for Adelaide, Alizeh, Dorothy, and Angel.

"Don't get mad at me! We all have to do what's best for the kingdom! The kingdom comes first! So put aside your hate and prejudice. Alan will be joining us for this case! So — if proven worthy, he can become a full-time member if he so wishes. I have chosen him for the case because he is powerful, chosen by the king for the highest non-royal position in this kingdom," Ben said as he lowered his tone and gripped the sides of his head before pressing his palms on the edge of the black-glassed tabletop as he struggled to stand on his feet.

"I don't want Alan near me," Bella stated. "Ever."

"He's your right-hand man, Bella." Ben rolled his eyes. They stayed at the back of his head for a few moments.

"No, he was my father's. I fired Alan and replaced him with Maddox." Bella's anger didn't lessen.

"Gee! I couldn't imagine why?" Ben's tone was suggestive. Bella eyed him.

At the end of the meeting, everyone stayed around to talk. Alizeh decided to head back to her house and enjoy some time to herself before Olly came home. Olly didn't mind, and he agreed that alone time for both of them was healthy. He stayed back with the rest of the Ministry.

"Don't talk to me." Bella shoved Ben away from her. He gritted his teeth. Bella's eyes widened as she noticed his transparent skin. She could see the veins that traveled beneath the surface of Ben's face.

"Ben — you look sick." Despite the hostile feelings she had towards Ben at the moment, she couldn't help but be concerned. She had never seen anything like it before.

"That's because I am sick — first Lewis and now Alan. I am physically sick because of you! You dislike all the Viridis and the Scaasis, only to like them after a week of truly knowing them! I mean, you made the same fuss when it came to John and Gabriel! You know what! You're off this case. If something happens to this kingdom, it is you I will throw in prison." Bella's jaw fell; those who remained in the room wore a similar expression.

She vanished. Ben followed.

"Bella, talk to me, please. I'm sorry. In my eyes, you're overreacting, but prove to me that you aren't." He approached Bella, who was now sitting at the side of her bed.

"Whether I am overreacting or not, you should respect my wishes. I am your queen." She was failing to keep from crying, but she couldn't help it. It took a bit more convincing from Ben, but he eventually got her to open up about her hatred for Alan.

"Do you remember when I broke my leg? A year ago?" Ben sat down beside her as he nodded.

"Lewis — and Alan," she said shakily. "I was on a walk to the library. They were arguing, and you know me, I'm — blunt. I said, 'move out of the way, moldy rogues', and they reacted. They channeled their hatred from each other on to me. Alan disarmed my wand; being my father's right hand, he knew where I kept it." Bella's arm trailed to the back of her right shin, and her voice cracked. "They didn't use magic to break my leg. They used their feet. They took turns stomping on me."

"How come you didn't tell your father or me?" Ben grew angry as

200

tears settled in his own eyes. A prominent vein on his temple throbbed.

"My father liked Alan more than me. He would say that I had done it to myself for attention or something just as false. I didn't tell you because I knew that you would have had them both killed. If that were to have happened, my father would have locked you up immediately. As much as I would've loved to see you torture them, I didn't want any more trouble. So I kept quiet, crawled home and replaced my wand. I lied and said I had fallen off my horse in the forest."

"I'll cancel the plans with both Alan and Lewis. Your safety and comfort mean more to me. I can find someone else in the kingdom just as powerful."

"Thank you," she stifled out.

Ben reached into his pocket and pulled out a chocolate stick he had purchased for her earlier. He handed it to his girlfriend, and this made her cry even more. He had been so distant lately, but the true him was starting to peek back through.

"You're more powerful than both Lewis and Alan combined. I'd rather you help with the case."

A weak smile formed on her face as she began to unwrap the chocolate.

"Thank you, Ben. I think I'm ready for bed." She lay back. She tossed her legs on top of his lap. He began to pull off her favorite pair of heels. They had metallic-plated heel pieces decorated with spinning gears, making them look like machines. Black laces and four buckles held each shoe together. Her favorite detail of the shoe was the bugbear fur that lay beneath its laces.

Alizeh gasped as she sat up in her bed. She hadn't dreamt of anything horrific. Instead, she dreamt of a book based on Doryu Edjer. The book, in her dream, resided in Doryu's museum, the church. After his death, the museum became a place to admire his artifacts and appreciate him and his work.

Alizeh raced out of her bed, threw on her denim jacket coated with fur and summoned her broom. She headed straight for the church, lowering herself to the ground. She started to walk up the snowy hill that the church sat on. Her nose was already dripping from the cold, and her toes were desperate for a warm fire. Alizeh had always avoided flying in the winter, but this was important, and she was determined to find answers.

Dead trees surrounded the building made of stone. The wooden sign on the yard was tipping to the side, as it was beginning to rot. Inside the abandoned church, rubble from the peeling walls and pointed roof covered the floor. The museum had become prone to robbers. There were only a few artifacts left. A red tableclothed altar sat at the front of the church. On top of it were a few wooden chests and the book that she had seen in her dreams. The book was simply titled *The Many Discoveries of Doryu Edjer*.

Alizeh banged on Dorothy's door, hoping that her friend was no longer at the Ministry's office. She was soon greeted by her friend's tired, pale face. Dorothy had her dark brown hair pulled back into a short braid. She wore her favorite comfy grey sweatshirt, of which the backing was held together with black lace.

"I found it! I found a book based on Doryu Edjer!"

The severe and calm Dorothy lit up like a child on Saturnalia morning. "Come in!" Dorothy ran upstairs to grab two pens and two notebooks. Alizeh barely had enough time to shut the door behind her before Dorothy returned.

"Where did you find it?"

"The church!"

"How come we never thought to look there before?" she asked excitedly.

The two girls took a seat at Dorothy's kitchen table. They sat upon two of the four large brown cushioned chairs that were much larger than needed. They sat at their edges; the backing of the chairs was far from their bodies. They each opened to a fresh page in their notebooks. Once ready, they frantically flipped through the pages of the long-awaited book.

"That stone that that guy gave Ben is mentioned!" Dorothy shouted excitedly. "It says here that Doryu made it."

"He made it? The stone to kill dragons? I thought he loved dragons," said Alizeh.

Dorothy had pulled the book closer to her, only for her jaw to drop.

"No way," Dorothy said in dismay.

"What?"

"Read this." She pushed it back over to Alizeh, who began to read the page.

Doryu Edjer was determined to make what is now known as The Excogitatoris Draco stone. He had become successful at creating an object with extraordinary powers. Once thrown into the mouth of a creature, the specimen would multiply. It is commonly called the Cloning Stone. There have been multiple sightings of the stone, but after Doryu's death, the rock seemed to have disappeared into thin air. Many presume that the stone no longer resides in the kingdom of Galdorwide. Instead, it is in the hands of someone in another land. Galdorwide will forever mourn the death of this great entrepreneur and anthropologist. Galdorians believed Doryu Edjer was immortal. However, this was proven false when Doryu fell gravely ill at the age of eighty-nine.

"Uhm… So, the stone is not a killing stone — it's a cloning one! I bet that's why that man gave it to us! He wasn't trying to help us. He was trying to ruin Galdorwide. Who gave it to Ben again?" Alizeh asked.

"Some guy in a land called Dwulong."

"Was he Ben's friend?"

Dorothy shook her head. "A stranger, I think."

"This man wanted Galdorwide to fall! We can't let Ben use this stone, or Galdorwide will burn to a crisp."

"No wonder no one else had heard of Dwulong: the place you go to when you need to. Dwulong and that man were all lies," Dorothy growled.

The following day, after Lovetta's incident in class, she sat alone in the cafeteria. She was now reading the chapter in the textbook titled "Treating Werewolf Bites". Soon, John Jr, who couldn't stop thinking about the book they had given to Professor Silwhet, joined her. They began dreaming up what they would do if they had the book's power.

"I'd try and make the world a better place. I'd want to help the people around me as well as everyone in the world. I'd want to feel satisfied with what I did with the power," John Jr mused.

"I'd become a master of Terra Arts. I love nature, and I'd want to educate others on the topic," Lovetta pondered.

The conversation began to fade as soon as Caden and Aldaricus entered the cafeteria. It was the first day back to school since the holidays. His two cousins stiffly walked by as Caden gave his younger cousin a small smile.

"You should confront him," Lovetta suggested once the boys were out of earshot. "Don't be afraid, do it. You need to."

"I'm not scared to face him." John, Jr's jaw tightened.

"Hmph — be that as it may, that's not what the whole school will think." Lovetta lifted her travel mug filled with Earl Grey tea and took a sip. She looked at her friend from the corner of her eye and then circled them around the room.

John Jr followed the movement. He saw that all the students in the cafeteria were either staring at him or at Aldaricus. A few boys who were looking at John Jr nudged one another with sneers. Those boys alone angered John Jr enough to stand up. He paused but knew he couldn't back down now. He began to walk over to his cousins. He began to shake, and his body moved to the beat of his aggressive heart's pumps. His arms felt numb, his stomach sick, and it was a wonder how he was even walking. His legs felt like they were taken from beneath him as he grew closer.

Lovetta immediately regretted encouraging him. Yes, she wanted him to stand up for himself, but the last thing she wanted was something terrible happening to her friend. After all, his cousins were the two most feared boys besides Clancy Scaasi and his misfit group.

The closer he got to his cousins, the more nervous he grew. No one who was watching on was calm either. They all expected the worst: the Scaasi boys going at it, right in front of them.

It all felt surreal, and John Jr even had to question if this was all just a dream. Despite his desire to run, he knew that he would have to face them eventually. Gower, Ben, John, and Olly entered the cafeteria. They had been enjoying their lunch two doors down the hall and had grown suspicious, as the cafeteria was much quieter than usual. The fact that his dad was going to witness this felt like pure torture. He always had a horrible feeling that all the adults in Galdorwide were skilled enough to read minds, even though they denied it. If they could read his mind, John

Jr would be embarrassed.

Lovetta got out of her seat. She was relieved to see that some responsible adults were in the room. Therefore, she didn't fear getting killed if she were to get involved in this predicament. She felt guilty. She wished that she was strong enough to stand up for a friend, even when her life was at risk. Lovetta pulled out her wand and subtly held it in her hand.

John Jr stood before his cousins, with Lovetta at his side. He turned to smile at her, only for it to fade, when he saw just how grim and worried she looked. He also took note of her yellow wand that she held in her hand. She began to repeat a spell, that would break Aldaricus's leg, in her head, to make sure that she wouldn't screw it up. She pushed the wand further up her sleeve once she noticed that John Jr had seen it.

Aldaricus stood up from the bench, but to his irritation, Caden did the same.

"Let's take this somewhere else." He lifted his hands in surrender. "We can leave our henchmen behind." He looked to Caden and then over to Lovetta.

John Jr agreed. They met up in the Alet locker room. Aldaricus had suggested the Viridi changing room, but John Jr's gut told him to refuse his offer.

"I'm sure you have lots to say to me," Aldaricus began, and his hands returned to surrender mode. "I don't want to pressure you or anything, but if we do not leave this room within ten minutes, every professor in this school will break down the door. Take a look into the hall."

John Jr raised his brow, his wand aimed at Aldaricus for precaution. When he cracked the door open, he saw curious students and concerned professors staring eagerly at the pale red door. John Jr closed the door and focused his attention back on his cousin. His heart somersaulted when he noticed that Aldaricus had his wand drawn, aiming it directly at his forehead.

"John!" a familiar voice yelled. The yeller crashed through the door, almost hitting John Jr, who had moved out of the way just in time. It was Aldric, his wand drawn. As per usual, Aldric must've been late to school, only to hear that his best friend was in the locker room getting destroyed.

John Jr would've laughed at the situation if he hadn't feared that his cousin would harm his friend. John Jr looked to Aldaricus to see that he was seething. He had never seen his cousin look so wicked.

In the hallway, Lovetta grew increasingly uncomfortable as the bored students turned their attention on her. They were looking at her not just because of John Jr but because of yesterday's incident. She could also feel someone rudely tugging on her long, bushy hair. She did her best to pretend that she didn't notice, but tears were already starting to rise in her eyes.

Eventually, the tugs became too painful to pretend not to feel. Lovetta whipped her head around to find Caden looking down at her. She glared at him with her teary eyes. Despite her grimace, he didn't flinch. She fixed her eyes on his, and she wasn't going to hesitate if any trouble arose. Caden noticed her hawk-like behavior.

"You know, Lovetta, you've got some nerve. You, looking down at us Scaasi men — except for Juni, of course. I'm guessing that's because you got the hots for him." Caden spoke loudly. The entire crowd's attention was now on them. Lovetta turned a bright red. She turned to face the door, only to meet the gawking eyes of her classmates. "But remember, Lovetta, the blood that runs in my veins is the exact blood that runs through his."

"I don't care about your blood type, Caden. I care about how you treat other people. You're the one who's got the nerve." Lovetta's words were valid and brave, but she could only mutter them while her back still faced him.

"You tell him, Lovetta." Lexi grabbed hold of the girl's arm in support. She glared at the attractive boy. Lexi shot him a rugged look that most girls were great at giving men. After getting her stern yet simple message across, she turned to face the door.

"Pfft," was the only response Caden had.

Ellen and Regina pushed their way through the crowd to get to their friend. The two sickly-looking girls approached as they bit into their apples nervously.

Inside the locker room, John Jr's courage had lessened. Not only did he have to worry about himself, but he also had to worry about Aldric.

"Aldric, there's no problem here, but if you don't leave, there will be a problem — for you." Aldaricus's eyes widened with a warning.

"Don't threaten him." John Jr hated how his cousins always thought that they were better than everyone else.

Aldaricus was growing frustrated, but he knew that he had to create peace between him and John Jr — it was dire. "Leave us. To talk," Aldaricus said once more. This time he spoke to Aldric with a bit more timidness in his voice. Aldric obeyed.

The boys barely had enough time to get out a few words of an apology before Aldric returned. This time, his wand aimed at John Jr "*Nestan!*" A cluster of bright purple glowing particles exited his rod and raced towards his friend. Once the spell had reached John Jr, his body lifted into the air and began to spin around.

John Jr couldn't see anything besides the flash of colors as the world around him blended. Based on the little he could make out, John Jr guessed that he was seeing the two boys wrestling. He saw a green blur on top of a red one.

John Jr began to yell as an intense pressure grew in his head. The pain made him question whether or not it was possible to die from spinning.

Aldaricus huffed in frustration as he realized that Aldric was almost as strong as him. The two boys were in a fit of switching between being on top of one another.

"What is wrong with you?" Aldaricus puffed. Aldric responded with a severe fit of laughter.

Tired, Aldaricus didn't hold back. He began to whirl his fists against the younger student's face.

When Aldric had grown too weak to fight, Aldaricus turned to face his cousin. John Jr was starting to spin even faster. "*Heg!*" A cluster of thin green glowing particles exited Aldaricus's wand. It aimed for John Jr Once it struck, the spinning stopped, but he was still in mid-air.

"*Anginn!*" John Jr lowered himself to the ground. His body rocked as he struggled to regain his balance.

Suddenly, clear purple streams surrounded the bloodied Aldric. Once the waves had disappeared, a bear-sized man lay in his place. The man stood up. He was much taller than the two boys. Blood still dripped from the man's face after his brawl with the teen. However, his face carried many other scars from past duels.

The two boys shrieked — this was something that they were not expecting. John Jr recognized the man, not by his face but by the armor he wore, the knight's silver and purple armor. John Jr, in fear, grabbed hold of his cousin's arm. Once they both realized John Jr had been holding his arm, they grew uncomfortable. John Jr released his cousin's bicep.

The two boys raised their wands, and aimed them at the knight.

"Aldaricus, go. It's me he wants." John Jr motioned to the door with a nod of his head.

"What? No," Aldaricus said with a firm nod of reassurance. The two boys looked away from one another and focused their attention back on the burly man.

Within five seconds, the boys were no longer in the locker room. The knight had successfully whipped them off school property.

Time was up, and the teachers entered the locker room to check in on the boys. Students followed closely behind. Olly pushed the door open, his wand aimed and ready. He looked around and saw no one. The room was empty. The teachers' eyes trailed to the ground by the entrance where fresh blood lay. Olly and the teachers who stood behind him turned to face John, who fell to his knees. His face was pale, and his lips began to quiver. He felt a comforting hand on his shoulder. It was Gower's.

"We will find him," Professor Silwhet whispered to his friend.

John left school shortly after. Ben offered to be his stand-in. He hopped onto his broom and set off for home. John had never felt so sorrowful and pained in his life. He didn't know what to tell Mary because he already knew what she would say. She'd ask John why he left their son alone with the same boy who had cast him away in the first place. He thought about the worst-case scenario — Mary would finally neglect him. The afternoon air had never smelled and felt so bitter. John walked over the damp grass as he began reliving this past year's events. He thought back to the man who approached Mary and Spencer in the store, Spencer sneaking out with her cousins, a prisoner and a dragon chasing Spencer, Spencer leaving home to live with his brother, John Jr being cast off to Atraemmont, and now the bloodstain on the locker room floor.

John reached the front steps of his home. He rested his hand on the door frame, bowed his head, and thought about what his best opening line would be. John wanted to find the best possible way to save himself from Mary's wrath. He looked up at the house. The house he and Mary had worked so hard to get. It was a home they felt would give them and their children their best lives. The sun shone through the windows. The house looked peaceful.

Once he was somewhat confident in the thoughts he had collected, he entered his home. As he shut the door behind him, Lulia was hurriedly walking up the stairs. She walked past him with her head down and headed straight for her room.

"Oh, do I have loads to tell you about your daughter!" Mary growled from the top of the staircase. She carelessly threw a white washcloth over her shoulder, her hair a mess. With her hands on her hips, she wielded a wooden spoon in her right hand.

Aldaricus and John Jr walked through the forest with their hands tied to a rope. The rope acted as a leash as the fearsome knight held on to its end. They had no choice but to follow him, wherever he planned on taking them.

They walked through the thick of the trees. Branches scratched at their skin. They began to scan through the leaves to see where they were heading but saw nothing. Soon, someone else joined their travels. It was a tall man who wore a red cloak draped over his body. On his face, he wore a burgundy wool mask. The only thing visible was his blue eyes. The mysterious man didn't seem to be interested in the boys. He didn't even acknowledge their presence. The two men walked ahead of them. The two of them looked like great pals.

"So, why are you taking them through the forbidden forest of all places?" the man asked while he looked back at the boys before looking back at the path ahead of them.

"Well — if some wild creature decides to make an appearance, the kids will suffer. So — why not?" the knight responded. His voice was just as deep and as heavy as they had expected. His voice was icy as he made his lack of care for the boys clear. "Any news on The Excogitatoris Draco stone?"

The mysterious man took his response to a whisper in the knight's ear. The boys looked to one another, nodded and quickened their paces to see if they could get closer. However, when they got too close, the man turned to face them. His eyes flickered a bright purple before sending them flying as far as the rope would allow. Their backs smacked off the firm ground. A small pointed stick penetrated Aldaricus's tailbone, though he barely noticed. Once the boys were back on their feet, the four men continued their trek.

"Have you figured out how to control the beasts yet?" the knight asked the much shorter and thinner man. He slowly shook his head. "Well, you better figure it out. If you don't, you won't just have the queen as an enemy. You will have me." The knight stood still in his tracks and faced him, making his message clear.

"What's that supposed to mean?" the mysterious man asked. He seemed confident despite the odds of him ever winning in a physical fight against the man.

"You know what that means," the knight said through gritted teeth. They continued to walk, and so did the boys, who earlier had frozen in position as if they had been the ones threatened by the knight.

An owl hooted loudly in the distance, making it impossible to hear what the knight had begun to whisper to the man. They entered a clearing in the forest. It was almost dark, as the sun was beginning to set. The mysterious man's voice remained confident throughout the walk despite his trembling body. Once in the clear, they knew where they were — the queen's backyard. She was standing beside a golden rose bush. She wore a dark purple dress with a gold embroidered bodice.

Once she laid eyes on the boys, the man in red took off his mask, revealing long golden locks. His back was towards them, but John Jr could swear that he recognized the man. He couldn't put his finger entirely on whom. After all, that man was the least of his problems. She promptly began to approach them.

"What is this?" She took note of Aldaricus's bloodied nose and her boyfriend's nephew. "One of them is responsible for stealing your book; the other," he motioned to Aldaricus, "got in the way."

"Did you hurt him?" Her attention turned to John Jr

"Yeah, he did. Look at my nose," Aldaricus answered, as if the queen cared about his well-being. "But it's okay. Did you see the black eye I gave him?"

The knight raised his hand that bore a silver gauntlet, striking the boy. The sharp metal blades left four deep cuts along the side of his face. Aldaricus brought his head back up, gritted his teeth and held back his tears. He did an excellent job at it, as John Jr didn't notice. Instead, all he saw was his cousin standing his ground.

Bella looked on, not with concern but with admiration. "You're a strong one." She eyed the eighteen-year-old. She looked back to the knight whom she addressed as Maddox, her right hand. "Take them before my throne, where we will discuss the matter further."

"Discuss what?" John Jr stayed rooted.

"Discuss how you stole my book."

When they got to her throne, she made sure that Maddox locked all the doors. She then ordered him to stand guard at the front entrance to ensure Ben wouldn't interrupt the meeting.

"So you mean to tell me the man in Dwulong lied?" Ben asked the girls, who had run into him at a local coffee shop. The girls nodded. "How do you know this?"

"It's all here in this book." Dorothy pulled Doryu's biography out of her brown knapsack.

"Why would the man lie?"

"Because he isn't a friend of Galdorwide," Alizeh stated. "And Dwulong isn't a place you go to when you need to, or whatever their dumb slogan was."

"So now we have to come up with a new plan?" He sat back onto his barstool, defeated.

CHAPTER 14

Aldaricus was even braver than John Jr had expected. He looked pale but showed no other signs of fear.

Ben was walking down the corridors when he noticed that Bella had Maddox standing in front of the throne room's entrance. Assuming Bella locked the doors, he settled for pressing his ear against one of the thinnest doors. He could only hear muffled voices, so he walked to the room's entrance around the corner. The knight was wearing his usual sullen demeanor. As long as Maddox wore this face, Ben knew that he did not stand a chance of being granted passage. Ben gave a small wave and smile and pretended to tend to something across the hall. After a few moments, he walked back over to the thin door. For once, Ben had something else to focus on that wasn't dragons or his pounding headache.

"I don't know what book you're freaking talking about, lady. I didn't steal shit."

"I'm not asking you — you irritating wee rascal." The young queen sat upon her throne. She turned to John Jr

"Well, then I don't know why we're here. Johnny boy over there would never even dream of killing a fly, let alone steal something."

To John Jr's relief, it didn't sound like he would have to say much. He had a great advocate on his case.

"That doesn't matter. The person who stole my book wouldn't have known that they were stealing."

"How does that make any sense? How can someone steal a book without knowing they're stealing a book? It's not like your book was in a library."

She glared, this time more discourteous than usual.

"Wait — your book was actually in the library?" He began to laugh and turned to John Jr

John Jr stepped away from his cousin and made sure that it was clear that he was not laughing along with him. Aldaricus began to laugh so hard that he was making loud snorting noises. He leaned back, holding his stomach from the pain that the laughter was causing him. Aldaricus gasped for air as he continued his laughing.

"*Forsuwung!*" A fluid purple line of particles exited her wand and hit the eighteen-year-old's mouth. All the noises emitting from his mouth ceased. Aldaricus now looked silly. Despite being mute, his mouth was wide open as he continued his silent laugh. He was pink-faced, and bent over. His knees were almost collapsing beneath him. "Congratulations, Mr Scaasi, you've just earned yourself a night in the castle's dungeon." She turned to John Jr "ow, Junior, do you have anything to say for yourself?"

"I — I — uh…" He trembled as the queen stood up from her throne. John Jr began to walk back as the fiery girl approached him.

Aldaricus's laughing manners faded. He stood up straight and managed to muffle out a few angry sounds despite her powerful spell.

She aimed her wand at the problematic boy. "*Dimbus!*" An irregular violet wave of particles exited the tip of her rod. The waves surrounded the boy, and once the ripples faded, he was gone.

"I will only ask one more time — where is my book?" For the first time, she raised her voice at him.

The right door of the room plunged open. John Jr's Uncle Ben stood beneath the door frame.

"Bella!" he shouted angrily. "Are you insane?"

"He stole my book! I don't care if he's your nephew. I need my book!"

Ben, stern, calmly approached. He looked to John Jr, taking note of his dirty and blood-speckled face. "Did you steal her book?"

"Not on purpose, I swear it! However, I don't have it."

"Does the girl who stole it with you have it?" she asked, pleased to hear him say what she had known all along.

"No." He shook his head. He wanted to say how, being a part of the Ministry, she must've known. Maybe Gower knew that the book would only lead to danger in the hands of the queen.

Perhaps he didn't tell her. "When your freakish knight was chasing us, we ditched it. We threw it somewhere. If I knew where it was, I'd tell you."

"You better find it for me." When she saw that John Jr wasn't leaving at once, she began to scream at the top of her lungs. "NOW!" Instead of appearing intimidating, she sounded like an immature girl who had spilled wine on her dress at a gala.

"Bella. Stop it. He doesn't know where it is." With that, Ben rested his hand on his nephew's trembling back and began to guide him out of the castle.

It had been one of the first days of beautiful weather that Galdorwide had seen in a while.

The sky was clear, and there was a feeling of spring in the air.

"Mary? What are you doing here?" Ben asked as he stepped out onto the castle's porch. His elder sister was approaching. Her hair and clothes were in a frantic mess — she looked out of place here in the castle's courtyard. Ben grew concerned. She resembled someone who had just been mauled by a wild bugbear.

"Looking for him!" She pointed with relief. "My baby boy!" she cried aloud as she took her son into an embrace. John Jr was half glad and half embarrassed.

"What happened?" Mary pulled away from her son and looked to her brother. "Where did you find my boy?"

"He was uh —" He began to scratch his head nervously as he tried to find the right words to say.

John Jr's eyes widened and circled his surroundings as he tried to think of a cover-up story. He had to be cautious. He had to think of something that wouldn't enrage his mother. "In the forest, behind the castle," John Jr began. "Aldaricus and I were having a great chat, and we decided to visit Ben." The boy stifled a smile. He braced himself as he awaited his mother's response, as her face stayed statue-like.

"Where's Aldaricus? Roman and Daeva are worried sick about him."

"He pissed off the queen. He's going to spend the night in the dungeon as punishment," John Jr explained.

Both Ben and Mary looked shocked to hear what was the first truth out of his mouth. Ben looked angry while Mary brushed it off with an eye roll. Oh, Aldaricus, she thought to herself.

"Mary," Ben called after his sister, who had just taken one step off the castle's porch. "Tell your husband, that we need to scratch the whole dragon plan. Tell him that if he can come up with any solutions, it'd be greatly appreciated."

Mary nodded with a smile.

Once his sister and nephew were out of view, Ben went inside, where Bella was waiting with her arms crossed.

"You're mad. You know that?" Ben began as he shut the massive door behind him. "You locked a child up in the dungeon!" he shouted in a manner that was unlike himself.

"A child? He's eighteen and more powerful than most people his age." Bella rolled her eyes. "Can we talk about something important?" She grew impatient. "Like — what the hell are we going to do about the dragons? We've already encountered one dragon, and it's only February, so who knows what else the crystals didn't show us?"

"We'll talk about it later." He brushed off his girlfriend. It was unlike him to do so, especially when it came to a Ministry case. He began to shuffle up the staircase.

"Fine!" Bella called after him. She always needed the last word. When he was out of earshot, she let out a lavishly loud groan of frustration.

***

"Do you think it had to do with the book?" Lovetta asked.

"It most definitely did. That's why Bella had us brought to the castle, and it's a good thing the knight didn't come looking for you. He knew you were with me that night. The queen's ruthless. She locked Aldaricus up in her dungeon!"

"He probably deserved it, though, right?" she asked.

John Jr shrugged with a smile as he popped a cream chestnut into his mouth.

"Can someone please explain what the hell you two are talking about?" Aldric asked.

Lovetta and Aldric had been sitting outside of John Jr's home, awaiting his return. Aldric was tired of doing homework and decided to join the two friends on their crazy journeys. He had brought along his backpack just in case Lovetta was willing to let him copy her homework.

"That's not everything," John Jr began, ignoring Aldric's question. "This man was walking beside the knight. He was wearing a mask, but when the queen approached, he took it off, and I caught a quick glimpse of his face. I didn't concentrate on it much, as I was more worried about the queen's wrath, but — I think it was Olly. It was like he was like, friends with the knight. They were talking about an Excogitatoris Draco stone. The stone is something I've heard my dad mention to my mom before. The knight also asked if said person had learned how to control the beasts yet."

"I don't believe that that could've been Oleander Bell, our sweet janitor." Lovetta brushed it off.

"What do you mean? He harassed Spencer like, every day. All the stress he put on her made her sickness worse. Also, didn't he want to take that werewolf textbook away from you? Plus, didn't he give you a huge, disturbing vibe?" John Jr snipped.

"I don't know," she said quietly.

"Seriously? Maybe I can get your boyfriend to convince you that Olly is up to no good." John Jr grew hot.

"Wait," Aldric piped up. "I'm so lost. Doesn't everyone refer to you as her boyfriend?"

"Yeah, I don't know why though." His words cut through everyone present, including himself. He stood up on his porch. "Go talk to Gower, if that's what it'll take for you to understand how much of a dick Olly is."

Lovetta stood to her feet and grabbed hold of John Jr's arm before he could reach for his doorknob. "I'm sorry. All the signs against Olly are there, but we do need more information on Olly. We need to understand how to stop him from controlling the beasts — if that was him. Come with us to see — Professor Silwhet."

The three kids approached Professor Silwhet's door, and he graciously opened it. He welcomed them in. The four of them sat on the black tribal carpet around his wooden coffee table.

"If I begin to bore you, just let me know. Back in high school," Gower began, "Olly was the school freak, and everyone was trying to get him in trouble — to torture the poor guy. His detention file was larger than that of any of the Scaasi students. It was a terrible time for Olly.

216

People were always knocking his books out of his hands whenever they'd pass him. He was always getting threatened by a Scaasi or by the people he calls friends today: Alizeh, Alan, Adelaide, Dorothy, and Angel. Those five had given him the most trouble. However, shortly after, Alizeh befriended him, and they fell in love. Before Alizeh, he had Ben and me.

"The more high school went on, the more distant he became. That only seemed to make him weirder in the eyes of the Scaasis. Despite Alizeh's relationship with Olly, her friends were still creeped out by him. The rumors surrounding Olly began to get worse and worse. There was one rumor that hurt him the most. People began to say that he took pictures of girls in their locker rooms through a peephole. Sometimes it's hard to look past a rumor, especially when classmates dock it as 'truth'. Things between him and me weren't always that great either. We'd pick fights, mainly because he had a crush on my sister before he and Alizeh became a thing.

"There is one event that I recall. I believe it to be the worst thing that happened to him. Ben had invited Olly to his birthday party. The guests were unaware of this and ridiculed him for showing up. Unfortunately, celebrating at the castle made it impossible for Ben to know what was going on. I think, after, Alizeh saved him, just by being a friend and eventual girlfriend. I mean, they got into a few arguments at first, mainly because she was a bit embarrassed to let the school know. Olly then began to take arcane magic classes with your excellent uncle, Daemon." Gower looked to John Jr "He had somewhat turned into a new man, one that Alizeh was proud to show off." Gower trailed off, as he was beginning to run out of things to say.

"You have a sister?" Lovetta asked an overdue question.

Gower chuckled. "Yes, Haniel Silwhet. She dated Olly for a bit until he eventually fell in love with Alizeh. So, why did you want to know Olly's deep, dark secrets?" His eyes flared with exaggeration.

"Well — we were hoping for a bit more than just high school drama, to be honest, sir," John Jr stated.

"Well, I'm sure you all know about his time in the king's dungeon, years back."

The students nodded. "He harassed Spencer most days at school. He has this strong, disturbing vibe, and well," John Jr continued, "today,

217

Aldaricus and I got attacked by one of the queen's knights. The queen had found out about me taking 'her' book. When he was taking us to the castle, a man joined him. I think it was Olly. It was as if he and the knight were friends."

"Which knight?" Gower leaned forward.

"He had a weird name, uh — uh — Maddox, I think."

Gower leaned back. He looked shocked and as if he needed a moment to process this new information. "What did they discuss? Do you know?"

"They talked about that Excogitatoris Draco stone my father always whispers about to my mom. I also heard the knight ask the man I think is Olly if he had learned how to control the beasts. We feel like it could be Olly, and that he's up to no good, and neither is the queen. Don't worry. I didn't tell her that you had the book."

Gower gave a faint smile. He stood up and walked over to the small window on the right wall. He reached for the brown blind and pulled it down. The room grew increasingly dark as the tall lamp on the side table became the only light source.

"What is it?" Lovetta asked their professor, who began to bite at his long nails.

The hot room began to reach a boiling point as their anxiety merged with the heat from the blazing fireplace. Before Gower answered, he asked if any of them wanted tea. Even though they all did, they declined his offer, as they were much more curious about what he would say.

"What was your question again, Lovetta?" he asked, disorientated.

"I asked, what is it? Why did you close the blinds?"

"Galdorwide is a mess, and it's only going to get worse. We live in a kingdom, the nature of which will always be cloudy. From dragons to Bella, and now, possibly Olly, it's nearly impossible for this kingdom to have a happy ending." Gower paced around in front of the students, who sat staring up at him. "But — I may or may not have a tiny solution."

"What?" the kids asked.

"Well — okay — so, I spoke with your father." He looked to John Jr "He had been gloating about getting a moonstone pyramid for Saturnalia. A moonstone pyramid is an object you can ask any question and get the answers you need. Well — I trusted John and decided that

218

you three and us two are the only ones who should know about the book. Now — I wasn't planning on doing this before, but now that Olly may be in the picture, we have to take some precautions. I asked the pyramid about the book; it responded. The book is dangerous in the hands of one but a gift in many. Well — of course, this was little to go on, so we asked what it meant by 'the hands of many'. It told us that the book, shared between many, could give each holder a fragment of its unbinding powers. The unbinding powers are unclear for now, but we know the first power and to whom it was gifted: precognition. The book gave that gift to you, John Jr You can see the future; it gave you a fragment of its power, and now you must nurture it. The five of us will each spend nights with the book until our gifts are unlocked. Once achieved, we will pass it to someone else. For now, I will hold on to it."

Lovetta's mouth yanked into a smile. "You're going to give us powers?" Her voice was warm and flattered. "You trust us?"

John Jr and Aldric glared at her. They didn't want her questioning to make their professor second guess his plan.

"I don't suppose you kids getting a few extra powers will do any harm. You're all good kids; yes, even you, Aldric. After I have received my power with the book, it will go to John Sr., then to Lovetta, and lastly, Aldric. However, if more powers need unlocking, we will continue the circle. John and I will do our best to translate the book while it is in our possession."

As exciting as this news was, John Jr couldn't help but be worried. One night with the book left him scarred for the rest of his life. However, he prayed that he had the worse one. He didn't want his friends to suffer the way he did. He also hoped that by the time it reached Aldric, no other powers would be left to spare. Despite his worries, he was somewhat excited to learn how to nurture his new ability.

"Do you think that you two will be able to translate it?" Lovetta challenged.

"I hope so, and if not, don't worry, we will not tell another soul about this, and neither can you three, understood?" The three students nodded.

"Hopefully, you'll be able to translate it," Lovetta mumbled to herself. She began to fan herself in hopes of creating chilly drafts of air. It failed.

There was a knock at the door. Tensed, Gower walked over to the window and peeked out to see who was there. To his relief, it was John. With a smile, the teacher opened the door for his friend. Before he could shut the door behind them, a fly flew in and bit his neck. Gower's body began to rock and vibrate. John thought back to the convulsions Olivia had had when she had broken her leg.

Gower began to howl in pain. His body began to shift into a wolf, then a cat, a spider, a fox, a snake, a raccoon, an ant, and finally, back to his healthy body. The room went silent.

"Ah," he said nervously. He was soon embarrassed as his students had to witness him at such a weak moment. He began to fiddle with the ends of his cardigan's sleeves restlessly before bending over to help clear his airway. "That was a — uh — first."

Gower's legs weakened, and he lowered himself down to his knees. John crouched beside him. He rested his hand on Gower's shoulder.

"You just unlocked your power."

"It's not a good power." He frowned.

"I was able to translate the second section. I had written down the passages and stayed awake all night reading them. You have a power called mimicry. Once honed into your powers, you will be able to mimic the appearance and skills of those around you. You can be anything; an animal, sorcerer, vampire, or any other creature out there. Hint, hint — dragon!"

Gower turned to his friend and made a face that clearly said, too soon.

"Okay, well, tonight you and I will go to town and get a few drinks, all right? We can have a guys' night and play some cards."

Gower looked somewhat comforted by his friend's offer.

"What do we do after we get our powers, like, how do we learn how to harness them?" Lovetta asked.

"Well," John stood to his feet, "I've been reading, and each power has a section explaining how to govern your power to the fullest. It also gives you some spells to use, but the more you practice, the fewer spells you will need." He looked to Gower. "I'll take the book from you now."

"With pleasure." Gower then stood up and walked down the short hallway to retrieve the book hidden underneath his bed.

"I will read the first section about precognition. I will write down some notes for you, Junior. So tomorrow, I will work with you." He smiled. He looked to Gower, who handed him the vital book. "Then once Junior is well settled, I will read up on how to hone in on your mimicry powers." He looked pleased with himself, but the rest of the people in the room seemed afraid.

None of them wanted the curse of receiving these powers. None of the skills sounded fun, or at least not their initial giving. John began to nod to himself, as he understood why they felt this way.

"When any of you three have the book, you can stay here with Gower and me until you unlock your gift. You don't have to go through this alone."

The offer seemed to cheer up the kids slightly. Despite his confidence, John did worry for himself. Later that night, he asked Gower if he could stay there as he awaited his power.

"I truly wonder what it's like to have a peaceful life," John sighed as he took a sip out of his glass of Ancient Bliss. "Just today, John Jr went missing... again. Before I even had time to tell my wife, she told me that my daughter, Lulia, had been hurting her brother's cat. Like, isn't that a sign of a future serial killer or something? It's like all the badness in my bloodline skipped me and fell all on top of her. It's like every day of my life it gets worse and worse, you know?

"Also, Mary — well, she's gotten herself in this weird cleaning mode. She's cleaning the whole house with her — hands — I think it's some stress thing."

The boys were at a bar, The Echor Erlking's, a pub run by three of the five Echor siblings, Owen, Adam, and Ann. The bar, at first, was a place for people to go to have fun. It then became a place for people to think, vent, and overall mope. This change happened due to bartenders Owen and Adam. They were always calm and gave excellent advice. However, their sister Ann was unlike her brothers — if you went to her for answers, she'd snap and tell you how it was, no matter how much the truth would hurt. As you can guess, not many people went looking for advice from the tiny blond woman.

Around breakfast time the next morning, Gower sent letters to his students. He explained that the book unlocked John's power. Last night, it had never rained so much.

Enormous amounts of water began to flood the kingdom, or at least it did for John. Ferocious, grey water covered the windows. The rough waves' pressure began to crack the window panes, allowing the tide to rush into the house. The tiny home soon began to fill violently with water. The waves swept John up. He started to panic, only to realize that even beneath the water, he could still breathe.

The kids had hurriedly eaten their meals prepared by their parents. Once finished, Lovetta and Aldric met up at John Jr's home before venturing off to their teacher's cabin in the woods.

"How long do you think it'll take to harness our powers?" Aldric asked.

"Who knows? We are dealing with some powerful stuff, and I'm beginning to doubt that I even have a chance. How can I master a whole new power? Especially by May," Lovetta replied sorrowfully.

"Guys." John Jr stopped in his tracks.

Olly was a few feet away — he was burying his face in a newspaper outside of the Echor Barber Shop. He nodded in the man's direction —a barber shop owned by the rest of the Echor siblings, Stan and Anthony. The kids quieted themselves until they reached Gower's home.

"Do you think he heard anything?" John Jr asked as they approached their teacher's welcome mat. Aldric and Lovetta shrugged.

John, despite this morning's scare, decided to go through with training his son. Gower had taken Lovetta and Aldric out for lunch while John gave John Jr a rundown of his new power. They had stepped out to the back of Gower's home. John Jr's skin had flushed from both dread and excitement.

"It's dawn, so don't expect too much out of this lesson. Precognition works much better when done beneath the moon. Lay down on your back, palms down," he instructed.

John Jr was hesitant to lay down. He always felt vulnerable in this position.

John studied the book intensely. It rested on the length of his forearm. "Okay, I want you to close your eyes and press into the ground beneath you. Begin to describe how it feels. Describe it to yourself — in your head."

Rough and cracked. Something underneath the ground was beginning to move. "Draw in a breath and hold it until I instruct otherwise."

As soon as he had begun to hold in his breath, a scraping noise came from under the ground. A crack began to form, and it aligned with his spine. His body started to go into convulsions. He was still able to control his breathing, or lack thereof. The sight wasn't pretty, and John found it troublesome to watch. His son's skin was tinged an ashen color. Out of his control, his eyes opened, his breathing remained still. His irises began to glow a bright orange.

"It's beautiful," he murmured. His hand reached up to pet something invisible to his father's eyes. What John Jr saw above him was a red flamingo. The creature began to grow.

Suddenly, the little color he had in his face disappeared. He leaped up to his feet. "Breathe. Junior, what do you see?"

"There's — there's somebody — a young boy. He's approaching me — running," he explained. He squinted his eyes. The boy had white-blond hair, and there was no mistaking who he was; his cousin, Thomas.

John Jr stumbled back, and his jaw dropped, as the boy looked to be quite a few years older.

"It's — it's Thomas!" The boy didn't pay any concern to the flamingo. "He's — he's all right — he's smiling. However, it doesn't look genuine."

Suddenly, the day turned into night. The boy now stood still in his tracks. He began to stare at Thomas.

"Let him go!" A man emerged from the corner of his eye. It was his uncle, Lewis, who now sported short hair. "He deserves to be free!"

"I can't!" Angel appeared to his left. She sported a pixie haircut and wore a black dress with white crosses that replaced polka dots. "If I do, he'll be gone forever! He's too young to die!"

The two adults faded, which directed his attention back to his young cousin. The boy smiled, revealing the pointed fangs of a vampire.

"Thomas?" he called out, a lump in his throat. "Thomas, is it still you? Do you recognize me, buddy?"

"Junior?" John cried out as he saw his son's fear. John Jr was too caught up in this other world to hear him.

"Thomas!" John Jr yelled. The vampire boy licked his lips.

"I can't!" Angel reappeared. "Not yet!"

John Jr turned to Angel, who stood in the space his dad had been occupying. "Angel?" he asked.

John looked behind him to see that his sister-in-law was not behind him. He turned back to see that his son was looking directly at him. "No, it's me — John — your father."

John Jr snapped out of his trance.

"Were you able to strengthen your precognition?" Lovetta asked her friend when she had returned. He nodded, avoiding eye contact. "Brilliant!" He handed her the book.

The next week went by slowly as Lovetta waited for her power to unlock. On Wednesday night, Lovetta, Gower, and John were all sitting in the living room. They conversed as they took sips from their cups of hot chocolate. Each of them huddled beneath wool blankets as the cold night air seeped through the cracks of the log home. The three of them had planned on heading to bed shortly. Lovetta had almost completely forgotten about the book and how her power was next to unlock. The clock tolled midnight. A bird popped out from Gower's clock that hung above the fireplace.

A man appeared before Lovetta. She jolted, spilling hot chocolate all over herself, the white blanket, and the black couch. The men were almost as startled as she was, but they could not see the man. They placed their mugs down and rushed to her side.

The creature had a rat-like face; light brown fur coated its skin, and it had a thick black nose and whiskers. The beast stood on two legs, and it had long, light brown hair on top of its head that fell just above its shoulders. The man bared his bucked teeth. His mouth opened as wide as his head as he bent down and bit her shoulder. In a panic, she tried to fight him off. The rat-man had taken a small chunk of skin from her neck. Out of instinct, she kicked him in the gut. The kick sent the man flailing backward onto Gower's sturdy wooden table. The table broke from the impact as the man's body fell into it. The collapsed table was something that her two teachers could see. Lovetta, terrified, stood up from the couch and looked over at the man, who appeared to be dead. However, she hadn't hit him that hard, had she? He looked as if he had been hit by a truck. The body vanished before her eyes.

"He — bit me." She began to hover her fingers over the wound. She could feel the droplets of her warm blood against her shaking fingertips. "I'm sorry about all the blood." She brought her attention back to the coffee table, which was dripping with gore.

"Blood?" Gower asked. First, he looked at her and then followed her eyes to the table. He couldn't see any blood.

"That was the most horrible-looking man I have ever seen. I feel like I have seen him before, in a nightmare or something." She winced.

"I'm sorry, Lovetta," John began before placing his palm against her arm.

"We couldn't see him. What did he look like?" Gower asked, trying to hide his concern for his student.

"He looked like a man hybridized with a rat or some other rodent. I was frightened, and I uh — I uh — think I killed him."

There was a tap on the door. Lovetta, assuming that she needed to encounter more eerie events to obtain her gift, walked towards the door. Opening it, she looked back at the two men. "It's my dad!" She was half excited and half angry at him for disturbing her stay. Her father hurriedly rushed in. He was tall, averagely built, with dark brown hair and blue eyes. A blind person could see the resemblance between him and his daughter.

"Are you all right?" he asked. He rested both of his hands on her shoulders as he bent down to look into her eyes.

Avoiding eye contact, she nodded.

"Well, I thought I should stay here with you. It's been a week now, and I haven't stopped worrying about you."

"Dad, that's very sweet, but I'm fine. The boys need you home."

"The least you could've done was visit me." He stood up straight and began to talk with a stern voice. It was the harshest the charming man could be while looking at his child.

"I know, but as I said, the school experiment needs all of my focus. I couldn't leave."

"And what is this experiment again?" He looked over at the two gentlemen who had been watching over his daughter the past week. "I've never heard of such an assignment before."

The two men stuttered, as they didn't know what Lovetta had told him and didn't want to give him a wrong answer.

"It's an experiment," Lovetta began, annoyed. "To gain and practice a new power."

"New power?" her father asked, confused. There was only magic, no special powers.

"Yes, I know it sounds strange, and to be honest, we're not sure if it's possible, but that's why it is called an experiment."

"So, what will this new power be?"

"We don't know yet."

"You look terrible, Lovetta." Her father took note of her tired eyes and pale skin. "You should come home."

"I always look terrible." She laughed.

"Now, now, we both know that that's not true." Her father smiled and laid a hand of support back onto her shoulder. He looked above his daughter's head — his eyes trailed over to the broken coffee table. He furrowed his brow and stepped past his daughter to get a better look. He looked back to his daughter, who still had her hand on her neck in a way that seemed casual. She acted as if she were scratching an itch. She forced a smile when their eyes met.

His eyes widened as his mind raced to the worst. He stomped over to Lovetta and pulled back her hand to reveal the bite.

"What happened?" he asked his daughter sternly. When she couldn't find an answer, she looked to John and Gower to see if they could step in. However, David, her worried father, took it as a look of, "Them — they're the ones who did this to me".

Before John and Gower could even comprehend the matter, David slugged them both. "Dad! Stop!" she cried out.

To David's surprise, he found that John was putting up a much better fight than Gower. Finally, he knocked John to the ground, giving him a chance to wail on Gower, and that's when Lovetta had enough. She rushed to her father and pushed him in an attempt to get him off her favorite professor. She was successful but not in a way that she had hoped. Her father went flying, falling on top of John. The attention of the three men in the room was now on her. They even looked horrified by

226

her. She looked down at her hands.

"I reckon we found your new power," Gower said behind his bloodied and bruising face.

By the next morning, Lovetta's neck had swelled to twice its usual size. They decided it was best to wait for school to end before seeing Dr Scaasi. They knew that the odds of Dr Scaasi becoming suspicious were slim, but as for Dr Notleaf — not much slipped by him. For years, the Ministry had wanted him to join them. However, curing people was his priority. Around noon, the bite around her neck had begun to grow larger, and it was starting to turn a deep purple.

"What if that thing that bit her is poisonous?" David asked the two men as they stood outside Gower's bedroom door, where she lay asleep.

"He's right. We have to see Julian — damn the consequences." John nodded.

They entered Gower's bedroom. David carefully picked up his ill daughter. The three men teleported to the school's hospital wing. Dr Notleaf and Dr Scaasi treated them kindly, no questions asked. The men had come up with a lie as they sat in the waiting room. They decided that they would say that something from outside of Gower's home had bitten her. They knew that this wouldn't raise a brow since almost everyone knew that he resided in the now forbidden forest.

"Why weren't you two at work today?" Dr Notleaf pushed his glasses back up to their place. The man had asked a question that both John and Gower weren't prepared to answer.

They had notified Principal Bernard that they were both ill, but here they both were. "Sick," Gower replied reluctantly.

"Sick." John nodded a bit more casually to hide his guilt.

Dr Notleaf didn't buy their answer for a second — his face had made that clear. He furrowed his brow before giving his co-workers a forced smile. He took his seat back behind his desk. Now that Lovetta was in good hands, the men exited the doctor's office.

"Once she trains her new power, this will all be over," Gower reassured David.

Lovetta bolted up from her lying position. She had broken out in an ailing sweat. The sheets of the hospital bed beneath her soaked up as much perspiration as they could. However, some pockets of water still sat on the surface. She needed air, and she wanted to rip the clothes off her body. Her stomach twisted, her ears rang, and her vision began to fade.

"Dad!" she tried to scream, but the word never left her mouth.

The nurses immediately got the attention of the two doctors who sat in the office. Hearing the uproar, the three men rushed in.

"Go back to the waiting room," a nurse ordered, her voice panicked. "I can't let you see this… Don't worry. The doctors can handle this."

David attempted to push by her, but the boys held him back. His eyes began to swell with tears.

Back in the hospital ward, Lovetta's whole body was beginning to swell.

"Lovetta, honey, you have to lay down for me, okay?" Dr Scaasi instructed the terrified girl. He turned to an onlooking nurse. "Grab me a bucket of water and a cloth."

"*Frore!*" An intricate, red glowing cluster of fragments exited Dr Notleaf's wand. Once the magic reached her, a layer of thin ice blanketed her skin from head to toe.

"*Pressio!*" A rounded, red twisting stream exited his wand, and her body slowly began to compress back to its standard size.

"*Levitate!*" A simple, red glowing beam slightly lifted her body into the air.

The nurse had arrived with the items Dr Scaasi had ordered. He dipped the cloth into the water and began to wipe her wound. Dr Scaasi, once he finished cleaning the damage, nodded to Dr Notleaf, who lifted his wand and aimed it at the girl's bite mark.

"*Frore!*" A thicker patch of ice layered her wound. "*Anginn!*" The lower half of Lovetta's body sank back down to the bed. She now remained seated.

It was a dark, cloudy night. Both Ben and Bella were a bit late to the Ministry's meeting.

Ben had refused to leave the castle until their arguing had ceased. Bella grabbed a bottle of Almond Fury for the journey. It was common for her to take out glasses or even bottles of alcohol when she was in one of her fits. Bella muffled a complaint under her breath as they exited the castle. Ben didn't bother to ask what she had said; instead, he continued to walk down the porch. Ben clenched his fists tightly and tugged on his hair. His body was shaky, and he wanted to implode. He gritted his teeth as he held all of his anger inside. Ben felt that if he were to keep it in any longer, then his body would explode.

Midnight was just about to strike as they entered the Ministry's office. They began to walk up the long, shiny black reflective staircase. The Ministry's headquarters was one of the tallest buildings in Galdorwide.

They began to walk through the dark corridor that would lead to the office's massive doors. A sudden movement in the distance made the couple stop in their tracks. It was no ghost of Bella's father or the red-haired girl. Instead, the hair-raising sight was of Lewis, who had his hands on his wife's shoulder. He was shaking her body like a rag doll as he yelled. Angel's face was scrunched back as spit flew from out of his mouth.

Before they had any time to react, John exited the office's doors after hearing his brother's angry shouts. He reached for Lewis's ear and squeezed it tightly as he pulled his younger brother downward.

"*Dimbus!*" An irregular violet wave of particles exited the tip of Bella's wand and surrounded Lewis. He vanished, as her spell had cast him into a dungeon in her castle.

"Thank you," Angel turned to John first and then to her sister. Her body was trembling slightly.

"What was that all about?" Ben asked, his wand still drawn.

"It was just a misunderstanding." she smiled faintly. "You can take Lewis out of your dungeon, Bells, he's just been stressed about… the — uh — whole dragon case."

"Distasteful." A tall, averagely built man emerged from the shadows of the corridor behind Ben and Bella. He had dark brown hair and green eyes. His was a familiar yet unexpected face; Krum Scaasi, the third oldest of the five Scaasi brothers. He looked at his sister-in-law, whom he had not seen for three years. "If he ever does that again, you tell me, and I'll kill him. I don't care that he's my brother."

Angel felt as if she had taken a breath for the very first time. She tried her best to tame her smile. Krum had a similar expression; one corner of his mouth rose into a smile. It was an odd sight for the rest of the members in the room. Krum had always had a stern and even scary demeanor, even at a young age. Angel's heart fluttered when her eyes met his. The two of them let out their full smiles as soon as the attention was off them. Ben, Bella, and John had all decided that it was time to enter the meeting room.

Once Krum entered the office, he switched back to his usual sternness. "Well, well, well." He looked at the members seated. "Look who needs me now."

CHAPTER 15

Things couldn't have been worse for the Ministry.

Ben had taken the Ministry over to the training castle, where all members would have to reside until May, when Gower foretold the dragons were to rise. Ben, Olly, Gower, and John had alerted Principal Bernard on the matter. Mary stepped in as one of the substitute teachers for the time being.

The Ministry sat in the basement that looked like a mini classroom. Everyone had taken a seat, while Ben and Bella stood in front. Krum looked especially odd in the setting. He had not sat at a classroom desk since the tenth grade. Everyone stood still and quiet, and no one was happy with the new Ministry set up. Krum and his Aunt Selena and Uncle Teddy were added to the bureau. Ben had asked Selena and Teddy last night to join the Ministry; they were in their lower sixties but were both robust and fit for their age. Gabriel was happy to have his older brother and his wife on the team.

Angel sat trembling as Lewis walked in. She was sure it was from the cold. Krum sat up straight. Lewis took the seat next to his wife, in front of Krum.

"Lewis," Ben boomed as loud as a foghorn. "You have been dismissed from the Ministry."

The blond man looked up, infuriated. "For what?"

"On account of your violent tendencies. First with Bella and second with your wife." Ben stood his ground while secretly wondering why this wasn't obvious.

"What in the underworld did I do to Bella?" Lewis shouted as he remained seated. He leaned back in his chair. Krum clenched his fist as he restrained himself from grabbing the man's long locks and smashing his head off the desk.

"I told him." Bella stood up straight, her arms crossed and her voice calm. "I told him what you and Alan did to my leg. Teddy and Selena are

— your and Alan's replacements." She gave a sly smirk.

Lewis looked back at his older brother, his teeth clenched. He stood up and looked down at Angel. "Fine, let's go."

"She's not going anywhere," Ben said with a subtle tone of protectiveness and annoyance. He began to rub the side of his head and turned a sickly pale.

"You don't speak for my wife!" Lewis looked to the young lord. His body trembled with anger as a red hue washed over his vision.

"Neither do you," Bella snapped. "Angel, do you want to stay here and fulfill your lifelong dream of being a member of the Ministry or go back home with your failure of a husband?"

"I want to stay," she said under her breath as she hung her head, looking down at her folded arms.

"Okay, fine. I'll go home, pack my bags, and take Thomas with me," he threatened.

"No!" Angel bolted up from her chair.

"Then come with me!" he demanded.

"*Endebyrdnes mec Thomas!*" Krum cast. A dim green intertwining duo of waves appeared atop Krum's lap. Once the waves faded, his nephew Thomas sat in their place. "She stays... so does your son." He spoke with his usual drawling voice.

Lewis gave his wife a menacing stare before he stomped out of the room and up the stairs.

"Thank you," Angel said as her body quaked. Krum nodded and handed her her son. The room went back to being silent. The Ministry members continued to do what they were doing before the intrusion — thinking of a plan to defeat the dragons. Ben paced the room. His thoughts raced, as he didn't know whether he or the Ministry could handle this case. May was approaching, and they still had no sure way to protect the kingdom. How could he have been so stupid as to believe in the Dwulong man's lies? If he hadn't trusted him, they could have been scheming up a new plan months ago.

As most people in the room focused on the dragon case, a few had other things on their minds. John and Gower both thought about how they had left the kids alone at the mercy of the book. Angel concentrated her thoughts on her husband as she wondered what she would arrive home to in May. Adelaide was gazing at Krum with dreamy eyes, as her feelings led her back to when she was fourteen years old. Adelaide could still picture the then twenty-one-year-old Krum as if it were yesterday. Her main reminiscences focused on when she first met him. She was inside the late king's dungeon for trespassing. Krum, disgusted by the king's cruelty, had rescued her. However, Krum's thoughts focused on Angel, who looked lost in thought as she rocked the four-year-old boy in her arms.

In unison, the Ministry members thought about how things for the kingdom couldn't get worse. They were immediately proven wrong. Pure dread hung above their heads, a feeling that had been looming over them for quite some time now.

Ben's friends had brushed off his sick appearance as him being too stressed. However, this was not the case. The real reason now stood before them.

"Ben!" Bella cried out in fear.

Ben's body was shaking violently. A red and almost holy light outlined his figure. The Ministry members stood up from their chairs, drawing out their wands. Oh, how they wished it were a dragon standing before them.

He now stood still. His eyes shone a bright bronze color. His skin was snow-white, and his hair was tar-black — a vampire.

Ben sat up on one of the Ministry's dusty, king-sized beds as he rubbed the back of his head. He looked in front of him to see himself in the mirror. Ben wasn't undead. Instead, he was what was known as a Vivacious Vampire. He would relatively act and live the same life. The only difference being the torture of the scorching sun and his new appearance. He couldn't believe that it had happened; the bite had finally caught up to him. At this point he was beginning to think that he was off the hook from transforming. Bella stood in the corner of the room as she chomped on her thumbnail.

"It makes sense," Gower began. "You've been looking sick. We all assumed it was from the stress."

"And it also explains the mood swings," Bella added with the tip of her thumb in her mouth, looking out the window. "And your extra strength."

"How could we have missed this?" John asked.

"I'm stupid." Ben shook his head in disbelief. "I should've told you all sooner, when Bella's crowning ceremony commenced. One of the vampires bit me. I thought that, you know, since I didn't turn immediately that I might've been okay," Ben explained to his friends, who stood hovering above him. "Is there any way I can de-vamp myself? I don't think I can pull off this shade of hair." He tried to stifle a joke.

"There is a way," Dorothy spoke up. "You would have to catch the vampire who bit you." The people in the room groaned. "And — that's the easiest part."

Ben caught Bella's eyes, and she looked away hurriedly. He could tell that she was disturbed and bewildered by the discovery. He knew how much of a sacrifice she'd have to make by marrying a vampire.

"I can't deal with this," Olly burst. "Dragons, prisoners, AND vampires in FOUR months! We also now have a freaking pirate and a vampire on our team! No offense, Ben."

"None taken." Ben brushed his fingers through his hair with a cheesy smile.

"You've got a problem with pirates, miniature man?" Krum curled his fingers into a fist and dug his knuckles into the bed's feathered mattress. He leaned forward to intimidate Olly. He had succeeded — so much that even Ben, who sat between the two men, felt uncomfortable.

Ben could feel the large man's heavy puffs exit from his thick nose.

"Krum…" Angel called as if she were scolding Thomas.

"Leave him alone," Alizeh added. She had attempted to sound strong, and she did — until her sentence ended in a squeak.

"I can do whatever I damn well please." Krum stiffened his muscles, holding his ground. Olly's stomach sank, and his heart plummeted.

Olly didn't sleep much that night. He could hear Ben sobbing silently into his pillow after Bella had refused to share the bed with the "new" him. Olly couldn't think of anything to say that would cheer up his friend. Ben never needed comforting; he was always the one doing the uplifting speeches. Olly knew that Ben was just as stressed and panicked about the future as he was. Olly also wondered if Krum was engineering a plan to go into his room and slit his throat. These were just a few of the thousands of thoughts that raced through his mind during the night.

Restless, once he could hear Ben's snores, he softly snuck out of his bed. Usually sleepless at night, he often wandered his house until his eyes could barely stay open. So, tonight, he decided to roam the castle. Too scared to venture off anywhere new, he decided to head down to the classroom in the basement. He held up a lantern where red light energy bounced around inside of it. Just further behind the chalkboard was a solitaire kitchen. He walked to the dusty table, littered with piles and piles of papers and folders. Still feeling wide awake, he decided to read some of the documents, hoping that it would help make him tired. However, after stumbling over a particular piece of paper, he knew that he would not be getting any sleep any time soon. It was a document that appeared to be handwritten by a child with a green crayon.

See the running of Krum? I think he's mad at the Reptilium.

He finds it hard to see the man, overshadowed by the dreamy light. Who is that? They are frightened behind the trees.

He is but a worried man.

He is not alone as he brings along a dragon.

The dragon likes to chase, especially when he's by the fireplace. Krum points his flintlock at the undone.

Haven't you known all along that he's the chosen one?

Olly's stomach turned as he tried to wrap his head around all the new information.

Early the next morning, Krum was the only one still asleep. The rest of the Ministry members stood in the basement. From being one of the most hated and feared Scaasi men, he was suddenly the most desired. Even Alizeh and Arthur showed their admiration after reading the poem. They had finally found their new solution to the dragon case.

Throughout the day, the Ministry members stared at him. None of them had expected him to be the chosen one, despite the poem suggesting that they would.

"Thanks for joining the team." Angel smiled widely at the pirate as she bounced Thomas on her knee in the mansion's large living room decorated with old cherrywood furniture. On the walls hung swords and framed black eye masks that had been once worn by the Ministry members.

Bella was the only one not impressed. "We can't entrust our whole plan on the writings of a poorly-written child's poem. We definitely can't put our only defense on a weapon of a pirate. I'm a seer, and I've seen plenty of prophecies, and nearly none of them turn out to be correct. So why should we trust this one?"

"Bella's right," Krum agreed. "Well — besides the whole remark on my 'pirate weapon', dear Angelica is a beauty, and I trust her with all my heart." He lifted out his flintlock pistol. It was a stout gun that had three barrels. It was a handy weapon that he had grown fond of on his journeys.

"We don't have any better plans, though," Angel stated.

It was a bit too late for the rest of them not to get their hopes up. The room became divided between those who believed and those who did not. The Ministry's members were beginning to argue over the little piece of paper that Olly had found. Seeing the trouble he had caused, he decided that he would be done trying to find the Ministry solutions. Things could never go easy.

Krum sat in the middle of the room, wiping down Angelica with a white handkerchief. He couldn't help but feel embarrassed. Everyone was arguing about whether or not he had what it took to be the one to defeat the dragons. It was quite a relief to see that the majority did, all except for Bella and Alizeh. Bella had been most defensive in her position opposing him.

Whenever she spat out an insult, the members in the room would look to Krum in fear that he'd lash out. He never did. He just kept wiping Angelica, his face reddening.

"Guys, look at the weapon. What good would that thing do on a one-hundred-and-fifty-foot dragon?" Bella thundered as she ended her question.

The Ministry adventure hadn't turned out to be at all what Angel had expected. Any thoughts of excitement towards their mission were gone.

Bella and Alizeh spent the rest of the day ignoring the other Ministry members. Everyone else avoided meeting Krum's eyes, and for the rest of the day, he became referred to as "the pirate". Nobody had directly invited him to join the Ministry, but no one turned him away because, deep down, they knew they needed more help.

Angel, as the night went on, stopped speaking to Krum. Earlier, both Bella and Alizeh would stare at her and whisper to one another whenever she had spoken to him.

John and Gower sat in the corner of the Ministry's kitchen. They sat beside one another, becoming suffocated by their thoughts. The two of them weren't having as much of a bad day as Krum, but they couldn't help but feel sorry for themselves. They had left their students alone, and the two of them had never felt guiltier.

Ben, however, despite his newfound identity, was glad that the day of the dragons was nearing. He focused all of his attention on the mission rather than his new fangs and distant girlfriend. He, Arthur, and Adelaide had spent the evening in Ben and Olly's room. They sat reading through papers and books that they had found in the basement. They grabbed anything that even remotely looked like it could serve the case. Ben assigned Adelaide to find potions, and Ben ordered Arthur to recover spells. Ben decided to read books that dated back to the age of dragons.

A week later, Ben found himself walking down the long corridor of the third floor. Before he could head down the stairs, he stopped. Ben could hear the sounds of a woman's sobbing. As he drew closer, he matched the woman's voice to that of Angel's.

"Lewis — please — it's been long enough."

He strained his ear to see if he could hear what Lewis was saying, but he could not. Just this morning, they had allowed Lewis to visit his wife despite him being off the case. Ben inched closer to Angel's room.

"Fine — go ahead." She began to sob.

With no warning sign, Angel rushed out of the room, straightening her purple dress. It was a gown that she wore often. It was thick, purple with gold embroidery and a red ribbon wrapped around her right arm's sleeve. Her face was red, and it was clear that she had been crying for a while. A prominent vein on her forehead was throbbing. She strode past Ben. She hadn't even noticed that he was there. Once Angel was out of sight, Ben grabbed his wand from his navy double-breasted suit jacket. He turned the corner and entered her room, but Lewis had already vanished. He told himself that next time — Lewis wouldn't get off so quickly.

Distraught, Ben walked over to his room, where Bella already was. She had the unfortunate task of educating Krum on the Ministry's code. Ben shut the door behind him to tell the two people who cared about Angel the most what he had heard.

"That's it!" Krum roared as he stood to his feet. "I'm going to find that bloody bastard and rip out his intestines and hang them from the chandelier!"

"That'd break Angel. She loves him, it's stupid, but she does," Bella added. "If we do anything to Lewis without her knowing, it'd break her heart."

"Maybe we can talk to Angel," Ben suggested. "I bet there's something we can say to her to get it through her head. What do you think?" He looked to Bella, who would know Angel best.

Bella shrugged. They looked up to Krum, who huffed angrily with eyes that looked as if they were ready to set the building on fire. "We put him in prison. Something you guys should've done a long time ago. She can't get mad at us for giving him justice."

"The penalty for beating a spouse is a death sentence," Bella said as she crossed her arms for comfort.

"We've got no other choice. Angel is too scared to leave him," Krum said, his eyes still fixed on the musty green wallpaper.

"He's right," Ben agreed. "It's time we're done being friendly to Lewis just on behalf of Angel. If we throw him in prison, we won't give him the death penalty. We'd release him once the dragons come. Maybe by then, he will have a new outlook on his life. If not — we can focus on him, since the dragons would be out of the way."

Bella didn't look convinced. Krum lowered his head as he focused his attention on Bella after noting her disagreement. She took a step back, as she did not like the look he was giving her. "It's a good plan." His deep voice was surprisingly soft. It was a tone she had only ever heard him use when he conversed with Angel. "But if you don't like it, Your Highness — I'm still down to kill him." Krum reached into his black and gold brocade jacket and pulled out his wand. A smooth green blast of particles sparked from out of its tip. "A bolt of electric energy should do the trick." He admired the firework appearance and its crackling sounds.

Bella smirked. She had to admit that he was growing on her. Bella began to picture Krum standing opposite Maddox on either side of her throne. She then imagined them escorting her through the crowd at one of her gatherings.

"No — we can't kill him." Ben was finally frustrated by all of his friends with psychopathic tendencies. The excitement in Bella's heart diminished.

The following morning, everyone at the Ministry had received letters from their families. They opened the letters as they sipped from their mugs of caffeine quake. Most of the letters were the same. They were from their families, wishing them well. However, both John and Gower had received a different kind of message. They each received the same letter.

Dear Professor Scaasi/Professor Silwhet,

Aldric unlocked his power, the power to control the elements. This power should be natural for him to master. Galdorwide High has plenty of teachers who desire to teach us the use of elemental forces. Including you, Professor Silwhet. The book is now with John Jr, and we aren't sure whether or not there is another power. If something happens further, we will keep you updated.

With love, Lovetta, John Jr, and Aldric.

Ben had expected the Ministry members to mumble and groan as he announced that they needed to have another formal meeting. However, to his surprise, they were compliant. Their compliance made Ben sure that this mission was in good hands.

All fifteen Ministry members walked down to the basement. Angel had almost forgotten that Lewis would not be attending the meeting. However, his seat did not go empty. Krum sat in it. Angel looked up to him with a small smile as Thomas played with one of her long curls. Krum winked before focusing his attention on the front of the room where Ben and Bella stood. The only light source came from a purple lantern that Ben had lit before the meeting. He placed it on the long table in front of him.

"We have to think about the poem and what it means to us," Ben began. It was clear that he had been planning this speech for a while. He spoke clearly and with ease. "We also, however, cannot solely trust the poem as Bella had kindly mentioned. Not all divinations come true."

Kindly? the twelve seated Ministry members thought.

"It's a pity what Galdorwide will have to face in just a few more months. We will have to do our best to do what we can to save the kingdom from destruction. However, there is another pressing matter we — the Ministry members — must face. That is — the elephant in the room."

"Krum?" Olly answered. He was sure that he was correct. Krum, who had folded a piece of paper into an airplane, successfully threw it at the blond man's head.

"No." Ben pinched his nose in annoyance. "No, no." He looked up, his eyes directed to Angel. "I'm talking about Lewis, who, in front of our very eyes, committed a crime. Violence towards a spouse."

"Violence?" Angel asked. It was as if she was almost shocked by the soon-to-be king's statement.

"Yes, violence, Angel. I saw him thrashing you in his arms like a ragdoll," Ben explained sternly, hoping that she would not start a debate.

"Yeah, but it's not like you saw him hit me." To his disappointment, she began a debate. "Ange," Bella spoke up. "The law says violence towards a spouse is not limited to punches and hitting. What he did was, in fact, an act of violence." Bella spoke softer than usual.

A soft wave now covered Angel's eyes. "You don't need to punish him."

"Open your eyes!" Krum blurted out loud as he slammed his abnormally large fist against the small desk's surface.

Angel jumped. "He's stressed. It won't happen again." Angel tried to defend her husband. The tears in her eyes were getting harder and harder to hold in.

"I know my brother. Heck, I know every abusive man in this town and trust me, they don't change." Krum lowered his voice, but his temper was still hot.

"He's right, Angel," Ben added, the tip of his thumb resting on his bottom lip. "We don't want him near you."

"We will no longer sit by and watch him hurt you," Bella said. "You think we're stupid. The cut on your arm from a knife rack? The bruising on your chest? He's going to keep hurting you again and again."

"Merlin! Angel, why are you still with him?" Krum asked, shaking his head in disbelief. He hadn't known about the cut or the bruise.

Angel was now lamenting. Half because she knew that they were right and half because of their verbal attacks. They were looking at her like they had never looked at her before. There were no smiles, just sullen faces with stone-cold eyes. She buried her head into her tiny hands to shield them from her sight. Thomas looked up and reached up to pet his mom's hair.

"We know you wanted him to be a better guy," Bella said, now with a softened tone. "But it's time to wake up," Bella said with a stern yet uplifting voice.

Angel looked up out of her wet hands. She went to open her mouth.

"No more excuses." Bella narrowed her evil eyes but softened her look with a lift of the right corner of her mouth.

The moon was full and bright, but the clouds in the sky slowly passed over it, masking the kingdom with shadowed air. Angel stood outside. She held her purple cloak tightly against her chest as she looked out into the forest. Gower stepped outside to head over to the woods and to his home, where he could turn into his wolf form in peace. Before Gower could hop off the porch, they heard a woman's shout in the distance. The forest let out a ground-shaking moan as it settled into a new position.

"What was that?" Angel asked.

Gower raised his hand to silence her, and her heart began to rattle against her chest. He crept down the porch.

"It came from the forest, Gower. We shouldn't go in. It's forbidden," Angel said. "We'll surely come out of there in pieces."

"It's not forbidden for me. It's my home," he said as he further approached the darkened trees.

Angel gulped. Gower squinted his eyes and stood dead in his tracks. "It's the forest," he said. "This hasn't happened for centuries."

"The forest?" Angel asked, her voice shaken. "What does that mean?"

Gower took another step forward. Angel reached for Gower's red cloak's sleeve. "It's nothing we can't handle." He looked back at her and gave the princess a nod of assurance.

"Get everyone, and tell Krum to bring his ax," he ordered.

Angel ran inside and returned with Ben and the rest of the Ministry behind her a few moments later. Krum ran up to his bedroom, where he had all his weapons safely stored beneath his designated grimy bed.

"Craving blood yet, friend?" Gower asked with a cheeky smile as he looked at Ben. Ben cowered his head down. Gower knew the answer.

"No, it's a good thing. I'm going to need you." Gower gave his old friend a wink.

Krum exited the mansion with his ax in hand. He gripped it tightly as he carried a stern face. The Ministry members streamed off the porch, wands drawn.

"Angel, stay here with Thomas; the rest of you, let's go." Gower motioned towards the forest.

The Ministry followed on demand.

"Be careful!" Angel called after them before proceeding to bite her thumbnail.

"If things go smoothly, this shouldn't take too long. We will be back by midnight," Gower explained.

"*If* things go smoothly?" Ben asked. His brow furrowed as his long black hair flowed wildly in the night's wind.

"Things may not go smoothly, and as Angel had brought to my attention earlier, we might come out in — pieces."

Ben shivered as he looked back towards the mansion. Ben lifted his lantern and pointed his wand at it.

"*Ad!*" Several bolts of purple fire exited his wand. The flames entered the glass of his lantern and danced freely within it.

"You know what we should do? Move away from Galdorwide." Olly chuckled. "Maybe then I could finally get some sleep."

"Maybe another time," Gower replied. He stood still once they got to the center of an opening in the forest. "Okay, what we're doing today is dangerous. We can't take any risks." His eyes flickered to Krum. "All of you will have to follow me and do as I say."

Gower then proceeded to walk them further into the forest. He didn't stop until they reached the edge of the woods. He took the lamp from Ben's hand and aimed its light down a narrow, winding path lined with

242

deadened trees. The fire didn't do much good, as the trail appeared to vanish at its end. Ben, Olly, Gower, and Krum stood in front, staring down the path. The wild breeze blew their long strands of hair around.

"The forest is awake. It's something that only a powerful sorcerer can formulate. We need to find whoever did this or wherever the ritual took place. If not, Galdorwide might not be able to see the day of the dragons." Gower's voice darkened. "The forest won't be able to hurt us for another hour or so. So, if we find the person or place, we can stop this before things get out of hand. Unfortunately, if we find nothing by the end of this path, we will have to split up when it branches off."

Alas, the two branching paths approached. They had not come across anything peculiar on the darkened road.

"Ben, Bella, Dorothy, Alizeh, Adelaide, Olly, Arthur, Ian, and I will head down the left path. This path is the most likely path the conjurers took. John, Teddy, Selena, and Krum, I trust that you four can handle the unlikely but possible path on your own." Gower nodded, and so did the Scaasis. "Now, when either group comes across said sorcerer or place — send up sparks. If you see sparks, follow them. The counter-spell will need all of our strength."

The two groups walked down their designated paths. The night was black and soundless.

Everyone walked softly, keeping their ears open for any unusual sounds. Moonlight shone through an opening in trees. Gower's eyes widened after taking note of Ben and Olly's worried faces.

"You two head back." He stopped in his tracks, his voice stern.

It was too late. The three men burst out of their clothes like ticking time bombs. The hairs on their skin grew ten times their length, and their teeth grew into fangs. Ben's did not extend as much as they usually would have now that his teeth had elongated to that of a vampire's; only a few centimeters shorter than a wolf's. They fell to their hands and knees as their bones clicked into their new formations.

In front of the startled Ministry members now stood three wolves. Bella gripped her stomach, and her knees collapsed beneath her. Her face turned a pale green, and she bent over to her right by a bush where she vomited. Ben and Olly's wolfism was news to everyone who stood around them. The color of their fur quickly identified each of the wolves.

Olly had a yellow coat of fur, Gower red, and Ben was black, a new look now that he had a vampire's darker hair.

Bella crawled over to a mossy stump. The air was silent, and the only sound came from the running water from the nearby lake.

"Bella, are you all right?" Alizeh whispered as she knelt beside the queen. "This is news to me too." Her eyes trailed to the short yellow wolf.

Arthur hoisted the four girls off the path. Ian followed. The wolves howled with fierceness; Arthur and Ian wielded their wands. They stood quietly after the wolves had finished crying to see if they could hear anything. At first it was silent, but soon they could detect the sound of crunching leaves. They squinted their eyes — they couldn't see anything. The noises began to fade.

"Bullocks," Arthur muttered to himself. They all looked to where he was watching.

The wolves stalked further into the abyss. The fellow Ministry members reluctantly followed. They strained their ears to listen to their surroundings. They entered a section of the path where the moon was shedding no light. Suddenly, a bush further up the road to their right ruffled.

"Who's there?" Arthur asked. "Show yourself!"

A silver figure immediately emerged from out of the tiny trees. It was a tall, blue-eyed, grey-haired man that they all knew well — the king. The wolves growled as the rest of the Ministry members' jaws dropped. Arthur, however, was unbothered by the apparition.

"What a relief," Arthur said, straightening his posture. "And here I thought I'd have to face something — you know — dangerous."

The king walked closer, his eyes empty.

"Shut up," Adelaide whispered through gritted teeth as she patted her fiancé's shoulder. "He could be the one controlling the forest."

"I'll believe that Thomas is the one controlling the forest before I even think that a ghost is behind it."

Adelaide let out a soft whimper, as the king had heard him, loud and clear. "He's sorry, m'lord," Adelaide lied.

"Sorry?" Arthur chuckled. He threw his head back as if what she had said was hysterical.

When his fit ended, he looked back to the king, who had been standing eerily still. *"M'lord*, it was nice seeing you, but we're on a mission to find out who is turning the forest against itself."

A movement in the trees behind the king began to rustle. The Ministry members lifted their wands. An averagely-built man with hazel eyes and long light brown hair emerged from the dark.

"Roman," Bella hissed.

"Good evening, Your Majesty," Roman mocked with an exaggerated bow. He walked towards the king and stood by his side. He looked quite stout next to the tall ghost. The two men smirked before vanishing into thin air.

The wolves began to prance deeper into the forest. Their noses were sniffing the air above their heads. The Ministry members followed. They looked around, hoping that they would not fall victim to the king and his follower.

"Never insult the king again," Adelaide hissed.

"He's not the king, dear. We have a queen now." Arthur looked behind him towards Bella, who gave an unexpected smile. "And he's a ghost."

"And he's got a Roman — and probably thousands of other followers!" Adelaide was exasperated as she shouted at her husband with wild hand gestures.

"Bella, if you had to guess, how many followers do you think your dad has?" Alizeh asked.

"A fair amount, I presume. However, devoted to my father they are, they will probably come crawling if I call upon them. I wouldn't worry too much about them. They'd probably turn on one another before they could hurt anyone else."

"Do you think they're the ones who brought the forest to life?" Olly, in wolf form, asked. "Nooo," Bella exaggerated. "It was the other evil people in the forest that did this." Bella rolled her eyes.

The Ministry members continued to walk through the foggy, dense forest. Each of them looked over their shoulders as the trees creaked into new positions. The wolves felt another presence. Bella felt the company too, and she had to admit that she now felt safer with her friends in wolf form. They had just made a right turn at a splitting path when Adelaide grabbed hold of Arthur's arm.

"Look! Over there!" She pointed to the left of them. Green sparks sprung up from behind the trees. "The Scaasis."

"You guys stay here. I'll go check it out. Wait here, and I'll come back for you." Arthur turned to Ian and the Ministry girls, considering that the rest of their company were werewolves.

Arthur bolted further into the forest — they could hear him pushing past the tree branches. The crunching noises were getting further and further. The girls looked to one another, frightened. They crossed their arms, as the chill in the air seemed to have gotten colder.

"You don't think they're in danger, do you?" Dorothy asked.

"They better not be," Bella began. "Because if those four are in danger, then so are we."

The minutes they stood waiting felt like hours. They strained their ears to see what they could hear. The wind moaned, and the leaves rustled. Twigs on the ground began to crack. It sounded like someone was approaching. Who was it? They drew up their wands.

At last, Arthur emerged from the trees. Krum and a brown wolf stood beside him.

"We need to split up again. John's a werewolf too," Arthur announced. "So Krum's going to need more magic power on his side. Bella, can you join them?" Arthur then looked to Ian. "And Ian, you will also join them. They found a wounded girl. They will need your medical expertise. I will stay here with this group."

Bella didn't complain, which was a surprise to both Arthur and Krum. She set off with the pirate, the doctor, and the wolf into the heart of the forest. The four Scaasis had stumbled upon something terrifying, so much so that Krum said they'd need help. The thought of Krum being worried sent her heart into a frantic flurry. They walked for about half an hour before they came across the place where Krum had set off the sparks. The path seemed to end as they stood before thick trees that clumped together.

"The trees have gotten closer together," Krum noted.

Krum took the lead, John behind, and Ian walked beside Bella at the group's back. Bella looked down at the ground and saw a thick stream of blood that seemed to be going in their walking direction. She noticed that

246

blood lined the end of her purple and blue dress. She looked up and saw the moonlight reflect off specks of blood that had splattered on trees and bushes. Bella could see a clearing through the hanging leaves of a sacred willow tree. Her instincts wanted her to run, as she doubted her ability to help the Scaasi family.

"Look." Krum stood in his tracks and pointed his hand that held a green-lit lantern as they joined Teddy and Selena. Something was lying on the ground.

It was a girl. Ian had never seen anything so beautiful and so morbid at the same time. She was a small, voluptuous woman, who wore a teal blouse, and grey trousers. She had her brown hair cropped short, and it was a little bit longer than Bella's. Her legs were spread out at odd angles. She lay still upon dark, blood-soaked leaves.

Krum had taken one step towards the girl when a hooded figure emerged from the bushes beside her. The cloaked person looked to its frightened audience and gave a fangy smile; a vampire. The vampire casually approached the woman and knelt by her side. It leaned over and began to suck blood from the woman's neck.

"Uugh," The woman moved her head restlessly as the rest of her body lay motionless.

Krum raced towards the vampire. The vampire looked up from the girl, blood dripping from the corners of its mouth. It stood to its feet, challenging the pirate.

The vampire experienced a pain it had never felt. Krum had swiftly plummeted his ax into the vampire's skull. The monster lost its vision and staggered backward. The leaves behind the Ministry rustled.

The vampire fell to its knees. Steam began to exit the vampire's wound.

"What's happening?" Ian asked.

"Holy blade. A priest blessed it," Krum said as he looked on at his dying subject. He tilted his head as he enjoyed the view.

The vampire's skin began to bubble around its wound's edges. The smoke trailed down, sending the vampire's skin into boiling blisters. Eventually, the blisters burst with water. Nothing but a puddle of liquid remained where the monster once kneeled. Once their entertainment had vanished, they looked over to the bleeding girl. The silver king now stood beside her.

"Get away from her!" Ian shouted, his wand drawn. To their surprise, the ghost obeyed and vanished into thin air.

The four of them inched around the puddle and went over to the woman's side. "Are you all right?" Ian asked.

"As — good as — could be expected." The woman spoke as blood gushed from her mouth.

Ian lifted the woman into a seated position. She had big brown eyes that were fit for a puppy. Ian assessed the girl with his eyes, looking for any other injuries besides the obvious. He noticed that her forearms had plentiful old scars — self-inflicted, he presumed. Needle marks were prominent on the inside of her left arm.

"Can you tell me your name?" he asked

"Samantha Scott," she replied as she lifted a weak hand to support her forehead, as her head weighed down on her body.

"Well, Samantha, we better get you to the hospital. The forest is not safe right now." Ian spoke therapeutically.

"You do know that I've forbidden the forest, don't you?" Bella asked with a scowl as she folded her arms.

"Yes, Your Majesty," the woman said with little to no respect for her queen, "I do. I woke up in the forest. I have no idea how I got here."

"Do you mind if I carry you?" Ian asked.

"Lift away, my prince." Samantha smiled. She was not the damsel in distress that they had imagined. Ian slipped one arm beneath hers and his other arm beneath her deformed knees. Samantha winced in pain as she gripped on to his grey suit jacket.

"My name is Dr Ian Morgan. I am with the Ministry." He pointed behind him at the queen and a burly man with a stern face. "This is Mr Krum Scaasi and Queen Bella Carter, Selena, and Teddy Scassi."

"And this furry fella here is my brother, John Scaasi." Krum nodded towards the brown wolf. Samantha looked down at the wolf, who gave a graceful bow. She smiled at the kind creature. She reached down and petted him.

They heard sudden footsteps crunch leaves behind them. Three familiar wolves ran into the clearing, panting heavily.

"We have to get out now." Ben's voice came from behind the black wolf's mouth. Samantha gripped tighter on Ian's shoulder as her pain was becoming too painful to handle. "Who is that?" Ben asked, motioning to the girl in the doctor's arms.

"Samantha Scott, she's injured. I'm assuming by Roman and his followers," Ian replied.

"Roman?" Krum asked.

"Your brother, we saw him with the king." Ian looked to the ground as he gave the pirate the bad news. It was a task he had been trying so hard to avoid.

Krum stiffened his body, his jaw tight. He looked at Samantha. "Do you know who your captor was?"

She shook her head. Krum scowled at her as if the look in his eyes would make her confess the truth. She clutched Ian's shoulder once more.

"Krum, she doesn't know," Ian said after taking note of the man's furious glare. "And Ben, do you have any idea what's going on in this forest?"

"Yes — and that's why we have to leave. We need to come up with an organized plan," Ben said before bolting off with the other wolves in the direction from which they had emerged. The rest of them followed without question.

After a while, Ben slowed down into a prance. "Get down," he instructed the humans in the group. "You will have to crawl; Ian, teleport yourself and Samantha to the hospital."

Ian raised his wand high into the air. A green glowing circle popped out from his wand and fell around him where he sat. "*Apuldrerind mec be Galdorwide hospital!*" The ring around him extended high into the air. Once it dropped back down, Ian and Samantha were no longer in sight.

Bella, Krum, Teddy, and Selena crawled close behind the wolves. Bella couldn't tell if it was silent because of possible danger or because of the awkwardness. Ben, Olly, and John had been hiding the secret from their loved ones that they were werewolves. Krum was a pirate, whom the majority of the kingdom disliked. Gower, she assumed, was quiet because he was checking their surroundings as he took the lead. They were passing a cluster of dense trees when Gower came to a sudden halt.

"Krum? Bella? Do you have any idea why someone abducted Samantha?" the red wolf asked.

"No," Krum replied in his usual drawling voice. "I just assumed she got mixed up in the dangers of the forest."

"Or with your brother," Bella had to mention.

"Well — I think you're all wrong." Gower motioned ahead of them.

When they looked over the wolf's shoulder, they saw a hideous giant beast. It had the head of a lion, wings of a dragon, and a scorpion tail. A creature they all had heard of but had never seen; a manticore. The beast was lying so still and quiet; it almost looked dead. Bella stared at the back of Krum's head, where she could see black vampire blood spotted on his long brown hair.

"It couldn't have been a manticore that attacked Samantha. They eat their prey whole," Krum whispered. "It has triple rows of teeth — they leave no bones behind."

"Is anyone else suspicious why Krum knows everything about everything?" Olly asked a question that nobody else was thinking.

"My cousin, Scott, he's a hunter. He's told me all kinds of stories, and the ones he tells of manticores are chilling to the bone. However, he's not here right now. One thing I don't know is what the fuck to do."

Bella stood to her feet. She ironed the skirt of her dress with her hands as she stood. Krum smirked and obediently stood to his feet with a shake of his head.

Before a smile on Bella's face could form, a heart-crushing sound echoed throughout the forest. The beast had awakened; its growl outweighed the sound of the rustling leaves. The creature let out a second roar. Arthur and the rest of the Ministry came racing to their side.

"Are you guys all right?" Arthur asked through heavy puffs.

"As one could expect," Bella snapped.

"Where's Ian and the dead girl?" Arthur asked quickly as the beast began to stand. "Hospital with the dead girl, who turns out to not be dead," Krum informed him.

"Okay, great, let's go to the hospital before we die," Olly suggested as he looked over his shoulder nervously. The hairs of his yellow fur stood on end.

"No," Krum said simply. "We're the Ministry. It's our job to keep the kingdom safe, even if that means killing a large, hungry manticore."

Olly shivered as the rest of the Ministry stalked past him. The dark sky was beginning to lighten as dawn approached.

With no warning, the manticore leaped through the bushes. It stood high above the Ministry members.

"*Thee!*" A fluid green surge exited Krum's wand. The running lights swarmed the creature, freezing it in position. However, it did have the strength to lift its paw and plummet it down, nearly striking Adelaide's head. Krum lunged forward, pushing her out of the way. As a result, three deep scratches sliced through his beige brocade vest. Blood seeped through the openings of the fabric. He fell to his knees and exhaled in relief as he saw that his spell had worked. The manticore had shrunk into a plastic version of itself.

CHAPTER 16

In years to come, Aldric would look back, wondering how they could do so well in school and work on their new skills. The days crept by as they trained their magic, based on the quick translations John had left for them.

The air outside was becoming warm. It was usually a sign of summer break, which generally left everyone in the kingdom feeling comforted. However, this year, the warm air seemed threatening. The beautiful weather meant that soon — if the crystals were correct — the school would be surrounded by dragons.

Gower's classroom, now run by Professor Mary Scaasi, was sweltering hot. Sweat dripped from Lovetta's forehead as the rest of her classmates panted for fresh air. The room was to be spell-free for all the students to write the written test on Spirit Guides and Familiars.

The written tests were often considered harder for students. However, Lovetta zipped through the test. Unlike the rest of her peers, she dreaded the performance tests in her following classes. For alchemy, she would have to turn monkey bones into bananas. Students were unable to use the cheat version — a simple spell. She would have to use runes to add power to the more complicated formula.

The muscles in her arms pounded against her pale skin. For the past week, she had had to cover up her arms and legs to hide the repulsive sight. She had written to Gower and John in a panic, wondering if she was turning into a muscular mutated freak. They assured her that she would appear normal once her body adjusted to the new power.

John Jr arrived at school late. Last night, he had had a terrible dream. It was an image of a hooded figure with blood dripping from its chin. Besides that, he couldn't see any other facial features, as the scenery was dark and its hood shadowed its face. He hoped that it was not another precognition. The creature was in the thick of the forbidden forest. It was all that his dream had revealed to him. When he walked in, John Jr envied his friends, as they all looked wide awake and only fatigued by the room's oppressive heat. They had powers, but none of them were as haunting as seeing images of frightening creatures at night.

Lovetta and Aldric were finishing up the test's last few questions. Mary gave her son a warning glare, followed by a test paper and a pencil. With three more tests to go, no one felt as relieved as they would have liked. Lovetta and Aldric gave their friend a worried look as they noticed his pale skin. Dark circles lay prominent beneath his brown eyes.

"It was easier than I thought it'd be," Aldric whispered to his friend before proceeding to hand in the test to Professor Scaasi.

Aldric and Lovetta were sent outside to the school's sunny grounds as they awaited the second bell's ring. She had brought along her werewolf textbook but decided to spend time with Aldric.

"We have to turn monkey bones into bananas…" Aldric said, exasperated, in a tone that highlighted what they would be doing once ten o'clock rolled around. Lovetta laughed as the two of them headed down to the lake.

It was a large body of water that stretched between the school's grounds and the forbidden forest. It had become the three friends' new hangout. It was where they devoted their break time to training their new powers.

"After today, we won't have to do any more studying until next year." He lay down on the long neon grass. The creek was gorgeous around this time of year. A glow in both the water and the grass would omit neon rays as the sun's bright radiance beat down on them. "Aren't you excited?"

"Excited — yes. Relaxed as you are — no," Lovetta stated as she sat upright on the ground beside him. She rubbed her forehead.

"Are you still having headaches?" he asked, taking note of her face that was paler than usual. "Maybe you should go to the hospital ward."

"But what if it has to do with my super strength or something? We can't risk exposing this mission."

"Go see Dr Scaasi. He's the least likely to put two and two together. He's a nullum, remember?"

"Yeah, I guess, but what if he doesn't know what's wrong and gets help from Notleaf, August, or Morgan?" She shook her head, her mind made up. "It doesn't feel like a sick headache or a stress one — it's like a pain I've never felt before," she said.

"Don't worry, Lovetta." He sat up, as he realized she would not be joining him in the comfort of the grass. "It's probably just your body getting used to its new powers. Soon Mr Scaasi and Mr Silwhet will be back home."

Lovetta nodded as she rested her chin on top of her knees. She felt like she was missing something. With everything going on — new powers and school — she knew that there had to be at least one thing out of order. There always was. Across the lake, she noticed a red wolf stalking around.

"Aldric…" Lovetta began. "Do you think there's any way we can visit Gower while he's at the Ministry's mansion?"

"Are you kidding? No way! It'd be way too suspicious! Plus, the queen will be there, and both Gower and John don't trust her. She locked Aldaricus in the dungeon for talking back. Imagine what she would do if she knew we had her precious book and were stealing its powers," Aldric strongly objected with a firm shake of his head.

"Okay, okay, but I've just remembered something. Tonight's a full moon, right?"

Aldric nodded, not too sure where his friend was going with this.

"Okay, well, maybe we can tell him to meet us at his cabin. He can tell the Ministry that he wants to turn there in peace. Then we can see him." Lovetta was becoming drained the more her thoughts rambled on. *"Carte!"* she gathered a piece of paper before receiving Aldric's agreement. She began to write to Gower in hopes that he'd agree to meet with them later that night.

"What's so important that you have to see him tonight?"

Before she could answer, they were interrupted by a familiar voice.

"Yeah — what's so important?"

They whipped their heads behind them. It was Caden who appeared, rested beneath a large tree just a few feet behind them. He sat with his uniform sleeves rolled up, sucking on a chocolate ice lollipop. He gave his usual wide, cheeky smile before licking his lips wet.

"How long have you been there?" Aldric stood to his feet.

"Ignore him. He hasn't been there long," Lovetta said as she continued to write her letter to her teacher.

"Oh — is that so?" the Scaasi boy asked, amused.

"Yeah; there's no way you — Caden Scaasi — finished a test before this moment in time," Lovetta said monotonously.

"Hmm… You're right. I haven't been here long. All that I could hear was some stuff about new powers and meeting up with Gower tonight. Also — I even heard something about the queen's book that you guys are stealing power from." Before he had finished talking, Lovetta joined Aldric, getting up onto her feet.

Caden smiled as he looked at his audience. They had their eyebrows raised, jaws dropped, and noses scrunched.

"This wouldn't happen to have something to do with the book my cousins got interrogated for, would it?" He knew the answer already.

"Obviously," Lovetta answered, annoyed. "What do you want? What will it take for you to not tell anyone about this?"

"What do I want? — I want in," he replied quietly.

Lovetta and Aldric looked to one another in despair, as they knew that they had no other option. The air became cold and gloomy as the sun faded beneath a set of black clouds. John Jr approached, taking note of his friend's stiff posture. When he neared, he saw them staring down at his cousin. They then explained the incident with Caden. Caden listened to their explanation as he sucked on his lolly. John Jr rolled his eyes but knew that he could trust his cousin.

"Okay," he brushed it off, "but I agree with you, Lovetta, about meeting with Gower tonight. I had a horrible dream, and I think he should know about it. It was of a hooded figure. I don't know who it was, but during my walk to school, I was able to dwell on who or what it could be: one, a vampire; two, the king; three, a king's follower. Alternatively, four, the worst but likely option, something or someone unknown and dangerous to us. The figure was in the forest, so if we are going to see Gower, we're going to need to prepare." After talking about the dream, they all looked towards the brush of trees they weren't sitting far from.

"What's so important about a dream?" Caden laughed after he saw the fear in their eyes. "It's not like you're a seer."

"No, I'm not a seer. However — the queen's book gave me the power of precognition. Speaking of," John Jr whipped the book from his red cloak's pocket, "this is yours now."

John Jr threw the book over at his egotistic cousin, who had surprisingly caught it with his left hand. He looked at the gold medallion glued to its cover.

"Sweet."

The school bell rang. "We will meet back here after school," Lovetta instructed. "Oh, and Caden, I swear — if you tell anyone about this, Jax, or even Aldaricus — I will put my super strength to use." Her tone scared both of her two friends, who had seen her powers in use. Just the other day, she had beaten a thick tree down outside on one of their breaks after repeatedly kicking it. Aldric had then used his elemental powers to restore it to its original state.

Caden smirked. He almost admired the young girl's bravery but didn't seem to be too threatened by her or her statement. He lifted his right hand to his forehead and saluted her.

Mary Scaasi was approaching the students angrily. Her hair and clothing were messy, which had been typical lately, but it would have been rather unusual just a few months ago.

"Have you not heard the bell?" she asked with her hands on her hips. It was a free period for her, which meant that it was her turn to patrol the school grounds. "What can be more important than your mid-term tests?" Her nostrils flared.

"It's a secret."

Mary peered down to see her nephew peek from behind the large tree the three other students had looked so fixed on. "Go on inside. I have no time for your childish nonsense." Mary motioned the three students angrily. The three students passed her, their heads down. Caden remained seated in the shade of the mothering tree. "You too — I know you have a mysticism test with Professor Agnete right now."

Caden sighed, threw his lollipop to the ground and walked past his dear aunt with a smile. She aggravated him, but she was one of the most winsome girls in his family.

After six more hours of tests, the students met up where they had planned. Lovetta was the last to approach. This time, she was carrying a different book.

"Given up on werewolves, have you?" Caden smiled as he leaned

256

his back against the tree.

She rolled her eyes and ultimately ignored his comment as a whole. "I found this book at the back of the library last night. This book is why I want to speak to Gower. It's a book titled *Galdorwide's Book of Prophecies*. This book contains every prophecy that the seers of Galdorwide have recorded. There's one in here from a child, written in the form of a poem. It's not the best and not very clear on its meaning, but the author of the book tried to decode it to the best of their ability. The poem mentions dragons, an unnamed man, and a man named Krum."

"Krum." Caden's eyes widened. "My father?"

"Possibly — maybe this can answer it for us — do you know what a flintlock is?"

"Angelica," Caden answered numbly yet confident that his response meant something.

Lovetta furrowed her brow and slowly repeated the woman's name to see if she had heard him correctly. Caden nodded.

"It's the name my father gave his gun. A flintlock pistol — it's his prized possession."

She smiled and looked down at her book. "Now, for the unnamed man, I'm guessing it's Olly. The poem states the man brings forth dragons. It's either him or one of the king's rogue followers." She looked up from the poem. "We will show this to Gower and get his input. We can't get our hopes up too much. The poem was written forty-one years ago by a child. However, with all the similarities to the present-time Galdorwide, it's worth the mention. We will head to the forest tonight, just before the full moon. We can —"

"Good afternoon," a woman's smooth voice interrupted. She had short-cropped hair and dressed in cheap clothing in shades of blue. Her feet were bare. She was an unfamiliar face to all those who were present. "Nice day for a walk. Will you guys be venturing off in the forest tonight?" she asked with a twisted smile. When the kids looked at her with jaws agape, she continued to speak. "Best be careful if you do. Tonight's a full moon and — well — we all know that full moons can make us do some crazy things." The woman's big brown eyes widened as she spoke.

Officially creeped out, the gray students smiled at the woman. They brushed past her and began to walk back over to the school. When they looked over their shoulders, they saw the woman stride into the forest's arched opening.

Caden grabbed hold of Lovetta's arm as they walked, getting her attention. "Okay, when we're in the forest, we HAVE to look out for that bitch." Caden pointed behind them.

Lovetta chuckled. "We will. However, I think this was a good wake-up call. We might encounter some strange people in the forest. Someone might even question why we're wandering around in the forest. We should come up with a cover story."

"John Jr lost his cat," Caden replied almost instinctively. They looked at him with raised brows. "What? I'm a compulsive liar. What can I say?" Lovetta rolled her eyes.

"That works," said John Jr "And I'm down for this whole adventure thing but no sidetracks, okay? We go straight to Professor Silwhet's home and wait for him there." However, John Jr's single request went ignored. The four of them stumbled across a door that stood in the middle of the forest. John Jr and Aldric fell pale, while Lovetta and Caden's eyes glistened at the sight.

A white wooden-paneled door stood in the middle of an opening in the forest. A spotlight created by the moon shone on the door and its surroundings. It almost made the eerie sight seem peaceful. The bottom of the door had dirt smeared across it, as if an army of people had kicked it in with their muddy shoes.

"Let's go to Gower's, okay? Who knows what this is? After all, it could just be a normal door." John Jr spoke unusually fast as he pleaded.

"A normal door — in the middle of the forbidden forest? Yeah right. Nothing's normal in here." His cousin laughed.

Lovetta reached her thin arm towards the doorknob.

"Are you mad?" John Jr grabbed hold of her arm before she could open it.

"I wouldn't open it," Aldric agreed with his friend. "The queen did forbid us from the forest. Who knows what evil secrets are behind this door?"

Lovetta still looked at the door, yearning for its answers.

"Gower will be at the cabin soon," John Jr began. "We don't want to miss him. Think about the dragons, Olly, and Caden's father. That poem has to be more important than this door. Without this information, the Ministry might lose against the dragons. Is that something you want? Do you want to see the school burned to the ground?" John Jr was halfway through his persuasive speech.

"Yes." Caden gave his unwanted answer, interrupting the flow of his cousin's appeal. "That'd be the best day of my entire life — the school burning down."

"I know you wouldn't want to see that, Lovetta. Think about your friends and family who may die from the fiery breath of a dragon. So I don't know about you, but I'm going to Gower's home now." He glared at his friends before marching off into the darkness. He wanted to get as far away from the door as possible.

"He's right." Lovetta's voice was higher, softer, and quieter than usual. The three of them strolled off towards their friend.

They reached their teacher's cabin, where they waited anxiously for his arrival. Relief washed over them as they approached the familiar place. They considered themselves lucky. No one and nothing had interrupted their journey. However, the night was not over, and they still sat in the forest. Lovetta rested on the porch by the door's lantern so that she could read the poem. She read it over and over again to see if there was anything that she had missed. When this became too boring, and she was sure that she had read everything correctly, she began to read through other precognitions. The three boys didn't talk much as their thoughts rambled over any possible evil encounter. Lovetta closed her book as her eyes grew heavy. She rested her head against the wooden logs of the cabin. Aldric yawned and curled himself on the porch before wrapping himself in his red cloak.

"What are you kids doing here?" The ghost of the king appeared from behind the cabin.

Lovetta, Aldric, and John Jr all froze into position. The sight that none of them wanted to see was standing before them. Caden, however, took control of the situation.

"Nothing, Your Majesty." The pirate's son stood up straight.

The ghost made noises that resembled heavy breaths. "You're not causing any trouble, are you?"

"No, Your Majesty."

"Well, you better head on home. Tonight's not a good night to be out. It'd be a shame if something were to happen." The king continued to speak in his high-pitched, groggy voice.

"We will."

A woman in a black hooded cloak approached them. She halted beside the king. She gave the kids a smile that was both enchanting and sinister. The short, averagely-built woman, who looked older than her age, was familiar to the two Scaasi boys. It was their aunt, Daeva. She had dark brown eyes with just as dark long hair, and she wore red lipstick fit for the goddess of the underworld. She looked to Lovetta and tilted her head. "What's that you have there, dear?" she asked, looking at the book in Lovetta's arm.

With no hesitation, Lovetta stood up and ran off.

"What is she doing?" Daeva laughed to herself, shaking her head. "You can't run far from me, dearie!" She crossed her arms to form the letter X. "*Feng!*" A mixed black and grey glowing bundle of barbed wire morphed around her arms.

The wires thickened. Once the buildup was at its full strength, Daeva pushed out her arms. The magic wires chased after the young girl. It looked as if a mini-tornado were following her. As Daeva presumed, Lovetta didn't get far. The wires entrapped her and pulled her back towards her friend's aunt. It spun her around, making her face the wicked woman.

"I'm assuming you didn't understand my question. Now — listen closely." Daeva leaned close to Lovetta's ear. Lovetta wiggled around in fear as her friends watched on. "What's that little book you have there?" Lovetta didn't answer. Daeva slipped her hands through the magic wires and wrapped her wrinkled fingers around the large book. She pulled it out from Lovetta's hands that had frozen in position.

"I won't let you take it!" Caden raised his wand.

"Put your wand down, Caden — don't be an idiot." His aunt laughed.

"I'm not an idiot, you sphincter pig," he replied, his wand still drawn. "Aren't you a little too old to dwell on the evil side of things? I mean, isn't it time for retirement or something?"

Daeva's eyes flickered red as she took a step towards her nephew. The distraction caused her magic that held Lovetta in place to release.

"*Ad!*" Green firebolts exited his wand and aimed for his aunt. To Caden's relief, he missed. He didn't want to know what Aldaricus would do if he killed his mother.

"*Cunnan cunnan hemming til mec!*" A mix of grey and black glowing sparks exited Daeva's wand, summoning her familiar, a fox.

Lovetta crawled backwards as the black fox appeared in front of her. She had never met her friend's aunt before but based on her familiar, she could gather a bit of information about the woman. Witches whose familiar were foxes, had a keen sense of awareness. They were also cunning, swift, and lovers of the dark.

"*Electrica arodscipe!*" A transparent green blast of particles exited Caden's wand and struck his aunt's chest. The green particles zapped her. The green waves traveled throughout her body. She began to go into convulsions until the electrical energy had diminished.

Daeva fell to the ground, infuriating her fox, sending him into a fury of rage. It ran towards Caden, and before he had time to cast a spell, it had jumped onto him, biting his arm. He toppled over, struggling to get the animal off him.

Lovetta grabbed the book from Daeva's hand as she lay in and out of consciousness. John Jr and Aldric had run over to help their friend. The boys tried pulling the fox off him. Lovetta quickly joined them.

"Familiars cannot be harmed by a witch!" Lovetta shouted as she began to explain. "One of us has to summon a familiar!"

"*Cunnan cunnan hemming til mec!*" Aldric cast. A mix of glowing red sparks exited his wand and summoned his familiar. It was a fox; his sported red fur. "*Andfeng,*" Aldric commanded his familiar.

The red fox attacked the black one as it listened to its witch's commands. The kids picked up Caden from the ground and began to run out of the forest. Aldric felt a bit unsettled as he left his familiar behind. The wind started to thrash violently, sounding like dying breaths.

They ran until they reached the edge of the forest. Caden could barely stand on his own two feet as he bled out.

"We have to get you to the hospital wing," Lovetta whispered, as her instincts told her to. Something about the silence as they exited the forest felt unnerving.

"I can't run any more," Caden admitted.

The kids all felt the same, as their hearts had never beat so fast. They too needed to catch their breath. The school was within their eyesight.

Luckily, they didn't stumble across any unwanted strangers as they made it to the steps of the school. Before they could pull the doors open, Dr Ace had pushed them apart. Both parties seemed to jump at the appearance of one another.

"What are you guys doing here?" he asked in a hurried voice, trying to cover up the fact that he had just leaped back in fright. He narrowed his dark brown eyes. He squinted as he took note of Caden's injury. He noticed the blood, torn flesh, and bone visible in the tear on his forearm. He rolled his eyes. "Can't you guys just stay out of trouble?"

Caden almost fell backward onto the ground as he passed out, but Ace caught him just in time. He swooped his nephew up as if he were a baby. The three friends stood, shocked. He had just picked up the school athlete as if he were a feather. However, it wasn't too surprising, as Dr Ace was athletic himself. He carried Caden off over to the hospital ward, where his friends followed.

Dr Scaasi had ordered them to stay outside the door until he alerted them further. They stood close to the door that stood ajar.

"I hope Professor Silwhet is okay. I mean, what if the king or Daeva got to him?" Lovetta sighed as she longed towards the school door.

"I mean, if Caden could handle them, I'm sure a professor can," John Jr mentioned.

"True," Lovetta smiled. She had to admit, Caden had finally impressed her.

Lovetta and Aldric, while waiting silently amongst themselves, had begun to yawn profusely.

"If you guys want, you can go home. I'll wait here for Caden," John Jr offered. Too tired to say any words, they settled for shaking their heads.

As the hospital door slowly creaked open, Krum sat up in bed and tried to see who was coming in. The room was too dark to tell. He had known he was in the hospital but felt disoriented as he woke up. Krum wore a hospital gown and fluffy green socks that were supplied to him by a nurse. The bandage on his abdominal wound pulled on his chest hairs as he sat up.

He barely flinched at the stinging pain. The person who entered walked back out.

Krum was in hospital wing B. Wing B had solitaire rooms where long-term patients would stay. He reached for the lamp and pulled down its string, allowing the chamber to fill with light. Despite the pain that would make anyone else bedridden, he slowly dragged his large legs off the bed. Krum sat at its edge, leaning forward, catching his breath. He extended his arms and leaned towards the green armchair where his clothes lay. Krum reached for his beige riding breeches and pulled out his harmonica. Once it was in his grasp, he allowed his bottom to fall back on the bed. With one boost, he threw his legs up onto the bed and laid himself back down.

He lifted the harmonica to his full, pouty lips and began to blow into it. He played the music beautifully despite the pain it caused in his stomach.

Dr Scaasi approached his nephew and his friends with good news on Caden's health. After hearing that Caden would recover, the three decided to head off back into the forest. However, it had taken some persuasion from Lovetta to convince her friends. She needed to see if Gower was all right and tell him about her discovery of the child's poem. She had explained to them that this information would be too risky to write in a letter.

However, before arriving at Gower's, they came across the white door. It now stood open. The only thing that they could see inside was a black mass. John Jr gritted his teeth, as he had feared this would happen. He had dreaded the moment they'd cross paths with the door.

Lovetta ran straight for it. He and Aldric reluctantly followed.

"Can you see anything?" Adric asked, both curious and frightened.

"No — but it looks like it leads down somewhere. There are no stairs, just a drop," Lovetta mused as she leaned her head through. She looked back at her two friends with a wild smile on her face. "I'm going in!"

"What? Are you crazy?" John Jr exploded. "You have no idea where that leads! We can alert Professor Silwhet about it when we get to him."

Lovetta looked over the ledge and immediately jumped backward. A low growling noise came from below. "On second thought," she said as she continued to step away, "maybe we should close the door."

A massive black paw emerged from the darkness. Its long claws dug into the dirt in front of them. The creature's arm was bear-like. However, it looked to be almost five times the size of a typical bear's paw. The three kids ran towards the white door and tried to close it. The creature howled in pain as the door began to drag its arm backward. The arm was strong, and the three kids struggled against it. Their feet slid as the beast fought against the door. John Jr began to dig his heel into the ground. He laid his whole upper body and left cheek against the door to give it all his might. With one last push, they locked it back inside, forcing the creature down. They rested their backs against the door, each heaving a sigh of relief.

"I think we should head back. I think the forest has given us enough warning signs for the night," John Jr breathed.

"No, we have to talk to Gower about the poem! Worst case scenario, the Ministry's mansion isn't too far from here. We can go straight there if we need any help." Lovetta overruled the boy's suggestion. "Okay?"

"Okay." John Jr rolled his head to look at Aldric, who looked as if he was dreading this plan as much as he was.

"Okay, let's go." She began to march off.

Cold, damp air rushed past them. Total darkness was approaching, and the kids' eyes had a hard time adjusting despite the sky's slow change. The moon's dull light sprinkled from behind the leaves above them.

"I can't believe we ran from Gower's to the school." Lovetta began to laugh, as they were finally nearing their teacher's property for the second time.

Suddenly, Aldric and John Jr saw Lovetta leap forward, sprawling herself out on the ground.

"What in Galdorwide are you doing?" Aldric asked, holding in a laugh.

"Help me!" she yelled angrily. She began to shake her fist to reveal a thorny branch that had wrapped around her wrist. It continued to twist around her arm, digging its thorns deeper into her skin. Before the boys had any time to react, they fell onto their backs. Twigs had wrapped around each of their ankles and pulled them forward.

With her free hand, she began to pull at the branch. She didn't care that her fingers started to bleed. She knew that this was a little suffering compared to losing her whole hand. She pulled at the branch with her left fingers as she spun her right hand in the opposite direction. She successfully freed her hand. The vine recoiled back towards its root, which lay beneath a great big tree. Its trunk was armed with thorns. She turned to the boys, who struggled as both their ankles suffered at the tree's tight grip. The branches began to move faster, crawling up around their legs.

She reached into her pale blue cloak pocket and pulled out her wand. She aimed it but was unsure what more to do.

A thinner branch emerged from the ground and sprung itself up and around Aldric's neck. The vine was piercing his neckline with tiny holes.

"What spell do I use?" Lovetta asked in a panic as the boys shouted their screams of fear.

"I can't breathe!" Aldric gasped.

The branch had begun twisting its way up to his chest. She stood to her feet and looked around. She aimed her wand at the tree's root base and said the only spell she believed could be somewhat helpful. "*Ad!*" Blue firebolts exited her wand and rushed towards the origin. It caught fire. The flames raced up towards the tip of the tree and engulfed the branches that wrapped around her friends. The boys could feel the vines loosen their grip as the living plant succumbed to the flames. They continued to wriggle around until the branches finally burst into blue dust. Lovetta wiped the sweat from her forehead and ran to John Jr's side.

"What if we had caught fire too!" Aldric shouted before reaching up to his throat, which continued to bleed out.

Aldric was right. Lovetta had only intended the fire to hit the tree's base and kill off the active branches. She wasn't expecting the whole tree to catch on fire. She allowed her long messy brown hair to fall over her pale face.

"Let's just go to Gower's." John Jr glared at Aldric after taking note of Lovetta's shame. "What the actual spunk butler?" Aldric said in a tremulous voice as he stood.

He turned to Lovetta, who aided John Jr to his feet. They looked to Aldric, who was pale and shaking his head as if he were giving up on life.

"Look." He pointed down the path. The dirt path was getting bombarded by bundles of rocks. All other trails had seemed to disappear.

Rocks continued to pattern along the path. The wind picked up, causing the lake's usual calm trickling sound to turn into something much more hair-raising. The trees along the trail began to slump over, and they barely stood as they arched over the pathway. Each of their hearts did an unpleasant jolt as a dragon approached from the end of the path. *Not again*, they thought.

"You see that too?" Lovetta asked her friends.

The dragging sound of the monster's feet devoured that of the rustling leaves in the wind.

"Yep. Now what?" John Jr moaned.

"I don't know," Lovetta whimpered.

"Look at the size of its wings. It has to be twice the size of the last dragon." Aldric scrunched his face as he studied the creature.

"Do you see that?" Lovetta squinted. She pointed to a block of glowing red light from behind the dragon. It looked to be a lantern floating beside the dragon at the height of its shin.

As the creature continued to approach, the kids decided that their best bet was to run. As they ran, they stumbled across a small cabin that they had never seen before — a brilliant shine of lights emitted from the building, giving the place a welcoming feel. The building was tiny, and it looked only big enough to house two rooms. The pointed tip of the roof had a layer of snow despite the kingdom's currently hot weather. Instead of knocking, they entered. Inside the home was a single rocking chair that sat in front of a lunar-shaped fireplace. A jeweled bronze-colored scarf hung on top of the chair, and a teapot and long spoons dangled above the open fire. Alcohol bottles smothered the surface of a thin table that rested beside the chair. Beside the entrance sat a kitchen table clothed in red. Two chairs sat on either side of it. A tea set and basket lay upon the small table. Light beige floral curtains hung by the building's front window. On the far wall was a massive wooden door.

"Do you think we're safe here?" Lovetta asked as she shut the door behind her.

"Probably not," John Jr began. "But we don't have many other options."

Bored, Aldric began to roam the room until the wooden door piqued a spark of interest in him. He reached for the door's handle, but the homeowner had it locked.

Curious, his friends walked to his side. All three of them tried pulling at the door's handle. The door wouldn't budge, not even with Lovetta's new strength.

"Unlocan," John Jr cast. It was unsuccessful as the door remained firmly in place.

"There has to be a key somewhere," Aldric mused.

The two boys began to look around the house ferociously. Lovetta looked up. She got onto her tiptoes and stretched her tiny arm up to the top of the door's frame. Just as she thought, a key lay upon it.

"Found it!" she declared, bringing it down.

"Where did you find it?" Aldric asked.

"On top of the door frame. That's where I'd hide my keys." She turned to place the glittery bronze key into the lock of the same design.

Before she could place the key in the lock, a terrible crunching sound came from the room. Lovetta jumped backwards.

"Go on, open it! Don't be such a baby." Aldric laughed.

She shook her head in dismay, and she handed Aldric the key before taking another step back. She grabbed hold of John Jr's arm. Without any hesitation, Aldric rammed the key into the lock and twisted it. The door became unhinged. Aldric looked at his friends. A broad smile spread across his face as he took note of their ghostly white faces and wide eyes. He pushed the door open.

Though the door was open, they couldn't see anything. The room was too dark. Aldric stepped his right foot in, and a lantern lit the inside of the room. The sudden light sent his body reeling backwards. Inside the room was a mattress, pressed along the far-right wall. A red and blue plaid blanket was spread on top of the bed messily. Beside the bed sat four Styrofoam cups. These were the only things inside, and the walls were made up of black stones. Lovetta shivered slightly. In the corner opposite the bed, stood a lone rifle.

"Is this the bedroom?" Lovetta asked as her voice trembled.

"Nooo," Aldric replied sarcastically. "The bedroom is the other room with the kitchen table."

Lovetta smiled nervously. The three of them stood at the entrance of the room. They didn't feel welcome any more. Her knees began to vibrate, and she had a bad feeling about the place. She looked to the boys, who also looked uncomfortable. However, they didn't look as distressed as she did. She stepped out of the room, gripping her stomach as she tried to keep its contents inside. The boys followed, shutting the door behind them. Lovetta slumped herself against the left wall that was unoccupied by furniture.

"When can we leave?" Lovetta asked as her chin rested on her knees. She looked up to her friends, her face blank. "Maybe we should go see Gower."

"Merlin!" The boys exaggerated.

"Woman!" Aldric continued. "Are you mad? Hasn't tonight shown us more than enough times that seeing Gower is a terrible idea!"

"The poem's important," she mumbled to herself. "We have to tell Gower about it. There's no way around that. If not today, then tomorrow during daylight." Her body continued to convulse. She looked up to John Jr with desperation.

"Tomorrow." John Jr nodded.

A disgusting smell filled their nostrils; they pulled their arms up to their noses, and their eyes began to water. A crackling sound approached from the right of the building. Lovetta stood to her feet as her eyes caught a glimpse of a silhouette of a man walking by the room's front entrance.

"Go back to the room!" John Jr whispered harshly. "Now!"

Aldric pulled open the door before placing the key back onto the door's frame. The three of them ran in. John Jr took out his wand and drained the ball of light's energy that floated inside the lantern beside the door. The three of them, with no hesitation, jumped onto the bed. They threw the covers over themselves. Lovetta, who lay on the far side from the wall, got a good whiff of the cups; alcohol. A crunch came from beneath her pillow. She reached beneath it with a wince. It felt like a folded paper, but she couldn't tell, as her eyes did not adjust to the darkness.

Lovetta let out a sigh, hoping that it would release the anxiety that had built up in her chest. It didn't. Her lips quivered.

"I'm home!" the man called. His voice was deep yet soft and very soothing, Lovetta found.

They could hear the clatter of bottles coming from the other room. They lay silent, holding their breaths in. They listened to the man gulp down the alcohol. They could hear the man's hand skidding across the top of the door as he struggled to find the key. Alas, he located it on the opposite side that he had placed it. He smiled.

Before they were ready-minded, the man walked in and sat at the side of the bed where Lovetta lay.

"I need to get a new lantern." He leaned forward towards Lovetta. "I knew you would come back, love." He began to caress her face.

CHAPTER 17

"Oh, you!" Bella squinted her eyes. Her face was becoming somewhat demonic.

Ben twitched at the sight. The couple had just separated themselves from the rest of the Ministry. Once they had arrived at the castle, Bella had ordered Ben, now in human form, to go upstairs so that they could talk.

"I thought — never mind. It doesn't matter what I thought." Bella's anger seemed to cease as a new emotion began to wash over her; the loss of hope.

"I know — I know what you thought," Ben began smoothly. "I know I don't seem the type. However, that's the thing. There are no typical types when it comes to werewolves. We're not all nature lovers, like Gower, or menacing, like the werewolves we've dealt with in the past.

"I'm the same me that I always was. Except now, I'll spend my nights swooping around like a bat and the nights of a full moon as a wolf. I'm sorry that none of the signs led to this, but how did you honestly expect me to tell you?"

Bella furrowed her brow. Her face blanched in disbelief. This vampire-werewolf being wasn't her Ben, most certainly not *her* Ben. "You should have told me," Bella cried. "What if you try to kill me? I am made of flesh and blood, the two things monsters like you crave."

"No, Bella, listen to me, I could never hurt you. Much less kill you. Since the great werewolf attack of the year 2004, all of my friends have been werewolves. When Gower transformed, he was shamed and thrown to the woods by everybody because the entire kingdom couldn't live with a wolf living among them. So Olly and I decided to be changed so that our friend wouldn't have to suffer alone. So we could control each other's blood lust. We didn't know about John's wolfism until Olly and Gower and I worked with him at the school."

She broke her eye contact with him. "You comforted your friend who turned into a monster by becoming one yourself? Now how does that make any sense?"

"It makes sense to me," Ben said coolly despite how helpless he was feeling. "I wanted to tell you, but then again, I didn't. I mean, there's no point for you to know since I have it under control. Plus, we could go on our nightly walks because there are potions to free us from our transformations. With all the chaos last night — none of us had taken it. I'm sorry you had to find out this way."

Bella snapped her fingers, causing Ben to levitate. She approached him, her face enraged. "You lied to me — your queen! You're two creatures in one — you're a monster! If my father were ruling, he'd sentence you to death for the risk you bring to our kingdom! You stalk the nights with your sharpened fangs and claws. How can you be a monster and a member of the Ministry when you can barely focus on the current mission!"

"Bella — I'm still the same me," he was able to mutter as he struggled in his frozen heightened position.

"Certainly, you are. Maybe the werewolf part of you, but you're a vampire now too, and who knows what will happen to a creature like you. Galdorwide — hell — no land has ever seen a creature like you before. I can't trust you. For all I know, one night, you'll tear off my head or suck my blood dry."

"Bella — just hear me out, please."

Behind her stood a large mirror, and it revealed Bella's backside. She was wearing one of his favorite dresses. The gown was a crushed velvet, long, dark purple dress. On top of her head, she wore one of her tiaras. The one she wore blended in with her dark hair. It was black and lacy with three points. However, that was the only reflection the mirror showed. He looked to where his appearance would have been. These past few days, his reflection in the mirror had begun to fade, and now it was gone entirely. He officially had the non-existent soul of a vampire. His soul now belonged to the underworld, waiting for him if he ever died.

"No — I'm done hearing you talk. We will head downstairs and act as if everything is fine and focus on the case. After that, we can focus on us — well, whatever 'us' is." Bella turned to face the mirror. She brought her hands to the glass and began to dance her fingers where Ben's reflection body would've been. "Our main focus is to come up with a plan for the forest."

All Ben could think about was how beautiful his queen-to-be looked. Her pale, delicate face contoured with black makeup. She painted her eyelids a smokey grey and kept her lipstick the same — deep red. Soon the powerful queen stood outside of her castle. In her hands, she caressed a sword as she looked at him. Behind her stood the royal graveyard. The closest tombstone read his name. He shook the vision from his head. No matter how angry she was with him, he knew that she couldn't kill him.

He fought against her magic which held him upright in the air, but the magic didn't give. He could only manage to look like a fool with the little wriggling the magic allowed him to do.

"I don't know why you hate me, love. I feel like you'd like me dead." He couldn't get the image out of his head. He hated being a Pure. Pures would get visions during times of vast emotions. Though right now, they were on a path where she would see him dead, he knew that she would cool off soon.

"I don't — I don't hate you," Bella struggled to get the sentence out. Her voice sounded similar to that of a girl saying "I love you" to an ordinary stranger. She began to walk around the mirror, admiring its craftsmanship. The arched mirror, made of gold, would've looked quite breathtaking if it weren't for the thin layer of soot that covered it. "I wouldn't want to see you dead, no matter how ill my feelings toward you are." Again, the words choked out as if they were a lie, but they weren't, she assured herself.

She walked around, returning to the front of the mirror to face Ben.

"I heard you crying the first night that I refused to share a bed with you. At first, I thought it was Olly after being threatened by Krum."

A flicker of embarrassment flashed across his grey face.

"Sometimes, it's nice to see that side of a man. Considering how I have never seen you cry, I took it to heart. However, if you're becoming some emotional wreck and cry and complain as much as a woman, I will not consider you as my king," Bella said as she crossed her arms.

She was never good at giving compliments, and it was always usually followed by criticism and a threat. "I need a king by my side, not a princess. It's already hard having to try and picture a vampire-werewolf as a king."

"You mean to say that you want things to work out between us?" Ben asked, seeing if he had heard correctly.

"Yes; ever since I met you, I wanted you to be at my side forever." She spoke quieter and less professionally than usual. "When I met you, my father had wanted a Scaasi man to be the one to watch over me at all times, but I refused. However, no matter how much I refused, my father believed he knew what was best. He was going to set me up with Zein Scaasi, remember him? You came along with your family to a feast, and you saved me from a woman who tried to kill me. That made my father change his mind. He placed me with you, and ever since, I have been forever grateful.

"I was young, and we were foolish together, but it was a thrill, and you brought happiness into my life. However, now I am a woman, and I know what my kingdom needs, and I'm not quite sure if a vampire-werewolf is what Galdorwide needs right now. I have devoted myself to following the footsteps of my father — keeping in mind the way he would have ruled. Right now, I'm not sure what my father would have done if this had happened to my mother. You have to understand that this will be a hard decision for me." She shivered.

"I understand." Ben's face was sullen. "But I am more powerful now, and we both know that that is something your father would have appreciated. Whether or not I become your king, I still promise to be by your side as long as that's something you'd want. Is that something you'd want?" Ben's voice trailed as he asked the question, as he had been dying to know the answer.

However, the moment it slipped from out of his pale lips, he regretted it. He didn't want to know her answer. He winced. Bella whispered something underneath her breath.

Ben's thoughts raced. All he could think about was being her right hand, watching her fall in love with a regular, powerful witch. He would be forced to sit back, watch the view, and be ordered around like a dog. However, that wasn't the worst possibility. The worst one would be her writing him out of her life entirely as she started one anew, leaving her memory of him behind. Ben fell to his hands and knees as Bella unconsciously released her magic.

To the couple's horror, their conversation was interrupted at a very awkward stance. Ben remained on all fours staring up at his girlfriend. Gabriel had entered the room and immediately swooped Ben up onto his feet. He glared at the queen.

"You okay?" he asked the man, who looked remarkably frail at his side.

Ben looked up to the man who appeared to be concerned for his well-being. "Yes," was the only word he could choke out without shedding a tear.

"As lovely a chat as I assume you two were having, we should consider the case. Angel says she can hear more screams coming from the forest, and Gower is gone. Come downstairs with us, and we can get the night over with, and then you two can work everything out, okay? You have to." Gabriel looked down and smiled at Ben.

The two men exited the room; Bella followed. She walked closely behind them. She breathed in the scent of blood that emitted from Gabriel's clothing, as he had been the first to come to Krum's aid. Ben closed his eyes and stood still, as he could smell it too. He pushed the kind man off him and brought his arm to his nose.

"The true stance of a vampire," Olly said with a cheeky smile.

Ben looked up from the sleeve of his black peacoat. He was pale and frightening. Olly could only imagine the wrath Bella had just unleashed on his friend. He had expected his friend to give a smile at the joke. However, just a scowl was present on his face. His amber eyes flickered as the chandelier light reflected off them.

"Well?" Ben grew impatient as the room stayed quiet upon their entrance. "What do you guys want to talk about?" He no longer felt the drive or courage he once had when it came to the case.

"You know what to do," a woman's disembodied voice whispered. Bella looked around. No one else seemed to have heard it.

Bella grabbed onto her stomach as the room began to spin. She turned around to head for the nearest restroom. Bella leaned her left hand against the wall to keep herself on her feet. She knew whose the voice was. It was her mother's. It was a voice she had never heard so real and so loud for a long time.

"Come back. You know what to say," the voice called after her, as if

the spirit had remained in the living area. She continued to walk away.

Suddenly, the woman appeared before everyone in the room. She was shorter than Bella yet a few inches taller than her youngest daughter, Angel. She was slim with dark brown hair and had eyes that were just as dark. She didn't wear the attire of a queen or any other royal, though she never had. The only time she'd worn a dress longer than her knees was if there was a grand event at the castle. She had grown up a normal girl and had studied to become a doctor; once graduated, the king's father had hired her. Moreover, that's when she fell in love with her daughters' father.

Forever doomed to roam around in the clothes she had died in, she sported grey exercise pants and a matching sweater and beneath it, a purple tank top. Red smears extended from her lips up to each of her cheekbones. It appeared as if her ghost had stitched up the fatal injury that had left her jaw on the floor.

Bella rooted herself to the ground. She had known of her mother's arrival after she heard the gasps of everyone present. Bella couldn't move, frozen in position. Bella didn't want to look at her mother. Especially if she looked just as the intruder had left her. They never did find her killer, but she was determined to find out who it was. Bella slowly turned on the spot after building enough courage.

Bella would have screamed if her mother's jaw remained detached. However, her mother almost looked the way she had remembered her. Elizabeth was just as beautiful as Bella had recalled. The only difference was that she now sported a bit more of a pale tinge on her skin.

"Bella." The ghost of her mother smiled, opening her arms wide. She tried to take a step forward, but she couldn't move.

"It's me." She smiled wider, stretching the stitches on her face. "I'm sorry I didn't appear to you two earlier." She looked at both Angel and Bella.

Angel stepped closer to her mother, reaching her hand to caress her mother's face. "I've been with you girls, in your hearts and minds, I hope you know that." She smiled at her youngest before embracing her. She then looked to Bella, who still hadn't approached any further. "I appear today because I've seen the future of Galdorwide, and I also know how to stop it. That woman you guys saved from the forest — she has the answers. Now, why don't you guys visit her? Oh, and I'd also interview the new man who came to town a few months back — Mark Bisterne."

Bella went to approach her mother but fell forward.

Being the closest to her, Ben and Gabriel were the first to help her onto her feet.

"You guys should go before you join me in this afterlife." She looked at the boys as they lifted her daughter to her feet. "How touching." She didn't seem impressed. She had disappeared before continuing to appear solely to her eldest daughter. "You know, I always admired your courage, Bella. You were brave, just like your father and me. I died to protect you; I hope you know. I never saw the intruder's face, but he was looking for you that night, and he still is. I died for you because I knew that you'd have a better chance of defeating him when you were older, but now I'm not so sure. Maybe I shouldn't have died for you."

She was always like that, putting her best face forward in front of anyone who wasn't a Carter.

"BRANDED IDIOT!" Bella screamed. She bent forward, taking off her heels similar to her favorite except in the color brown.

The shoe went straight through the ghost of her mother. It would have struck Angel's forehead if she hadn't moved out of the way in time. Bella could still see her mother. She wanted to run towards her, but the two men held her back. After losing their grip on her shoulders, they reached for her tiny wrists with their large hands. Their grips tightened. The friction cut her wrists as she struggled against their strength. She was determined to break free. Once the boys had lost their grip on the queen, Elizabeth Carter's ghost disappeared. Bella looked around wildly for her mother's spirit. Calmed with the lack of ghostly presence, Bella looked to her wrists where she could feel her blood pump. She rubbed the wound and looked around the room at the scared faces apologetically.

**

In the darkness, the man lunged at the boys. Unable to watch the man caress Lovetta any further, John Jr had let out a fake cough to get his attention. Once out from beneath the covers, it was as if the man could see him despite the blackened room. He knocked John Jr against the wall.

When John Jr's body fell back onto the mattress, the man got on top of his chest and wrapped his hands around the young boy's neck. John Jr's eyes began to adjust to the light. He could make out the outline of the man's head. A large mane of hair outlined it. Soon his vision began to fade. He couldn't tell if it was his eyes failing to adjust further or if he was slipping out of consciousness.

Lovetta ran to the corner of the room where she could see the shadow of the rifle. She raised it and pointed it to where she could see the man. Her eyes had almost entirely adjusted to the darkness. She shot the man, who then howled in agony. He released the boy" neck and began to scramble around the room on all fours like a rabid animal.

The man raised his hand as Lovetta pointed the gun at him once more. The darkness played a trick on her eyes, as his hand looked rounded, like a paw with claw-like nails.

"Why do you hurt me, love?" She shot once more.

"AAAARG!" The man rolled onto his backside. He reached up to his face where a beard lay. However, she did not remember seeing one when he was looking down at her.

Aldric, who had run to the door, jumped back over to the bed, grabbing hold of John Jr's arm. The man continued to scream in pain. The man's mixture of yelling and shrieking echoed in Lovetta's head. She could feel her head pulsate with each of his screams. It felt as if each of his shouts filled her brain, enlarging it. She thought her head was about to explode, and she could no longer see in front of her. As tears began to stream down her face, she began to wonder if he had cast a curse on her brain. She reached for her head with a grimace on her face.

She felt the man's hand wrench around her waist as she gasped for air as he pulled her to the ground.

A pair of gold eyes glistened above her. The view doubled, or so she thought.

A low growl came from behind the man; it was a wolf. The man released Lovetta and turned to the intruder.

"Run!" A familiar voice came from the wolf, Gower.

She joined the boys at the door and exited the cabin. They waited outside for their teacher. She stared at the building as she quaked in her clothing.

"Who in Galdorwide was that freak?" Aldric asked.

"Shut up, Aldric." Lovetta didn't want to hear any of their voices. The real hero was inside the house, and she feared whether or not he'd be the one to walk out from behind the door's frame.

"Why should I shut up?" Aldric asked, shocked by her random rudeness.

"Relax." John Jr spoke calmly. "Can we just all appreciate we're alive right now?"

"Yeah, sure — but why should I shut up?" Aldric looked back to Lovetta.

"Because you didn't experience a brush of death today as we did." She pointed to herself and John Jr "You jumped up from the bed the minute things got out of hand, and you stood at the door waiting for us to handle the beast on our own. I mean, you act all tough, Aldric, but you're just a disappointment." Lovetta spoke her mind, cutting her friend with her hurtful words.

***

Samantha rubbed her head as the Ministry members surrounded her as she lay in her hospital bed. She swallowed and looked around the room at all the strange faces. Next to her were gifts. They were all written anonymously, but she could tell whom they were from based on the words inside them.

"You seem to have many friends." Bella eyed the bedside table in the solitaire room where a pile of gifts sat.

"Moving on," Ian began. "We're here to speak to you about last night. What happened in the forest, and who injured you so badly?" he asked in a sing-song. It almost sounded scripted.

"Who knows," the woman replied in a soft, sensuous, drawling voice before looking up at the doctor. "The last thing I remember was being at my friend's house. Then I remember being awakened by a vampire's fangs, and that's when you came and helped me." Her response also sounded somewhat scripted, as she had been planning on what to say over the night.

"Do you know a Roman Scaasi?"

She shook her head. "I've heard of the Scaasis but never met one." Her eyes looked at Gabriel, Teddy, Selena, and John. "Well — until last night."

"Okay, and have you ever encountered the spirit of the late king?"

"Why would the king waste his time on someone like me?" She smirked, looking down as she picked at a green thread on the sheet.

"Is there anyone you know who's been out to get you?" Ian asked. Gower burst into the room with three dirty kids.

"Sorry — they needed me." Gower breathed heavily and nodded behind him.

"Junior?" John asked before running to his son and hugging him. "What in Galdorwide happened?" John turned to Gower.

"There was a house," Gower began to explain to his friend. "I had never seen it before. I heard gunshots and screams. I arrived just in time to pull the werewolf off Lovetta."

"Werewolf?" Lovetta asked.

"His glowing eyes and growing hairs gave it away," he said.

"But the moon — he should've been in wolf form, like you."

Gower shook his head. "Not a werewolf like that. That man chose to be who he is, and he can choose when he turns. You're lucky that those werewolves transition the slowest out of all the werewolf breeds. Nonetheless, I was almost too late." He looked to the rest of the Ministry members before walking into the room where the patient sat, confused and intrigued. "I had to kill the man, and I will lead you to the body once we finish our duties here at the hospital."

"Kill?" Lovetta repeated to herself. For some reason, her heart ached at the thought even though she had just tried to kill him herself a few hours before.

"Wait," said the bedridden woman; Dr Morgan had patched up the left side of her neck. "If you're a part of the Ministry — you can get away with murder!" Her smile suggested that if it were true, she'd join the team.

"Anyone can get away with murder if it's self-defense. Therefore — not murder." Gower wriggled his index finger like a correcting father.

"Samantha, we need you to try and remember anything else from last night, even if it may not seem important." Dr Morgan continued to speak with her therapeutically. However, his eyes sent a different message.

She concentrated. "Well — one thing I do remember hearing before my last memory at the house was a man say, 'Death is an adventure.' At first, I thought it was my friend, but it wasn't him when I looked behind me. He was much shorter and wore a mask."

"What type of mask?" Dr Morgan grew intrigued, as he was getting answers from the injured girl.

"A dog, I think. It looked like the head of a German Shepherd. I didn't get a good look, but that's when he grabbed me — that's my last memory."

"And you didn't think that this was important information before?" Bella asked.

"Is it?" Samantha grew defensive. "Is it that imperative? A man in a dog mask narrows down to all the freaks we know that wear dog masks. Oh, wait — no one knows anyone who does that."

Bella squinted.

"Do you know what the man might have wanted?" Dr Morgan hid a smile. He admired the girl's fire.

"Money — maybe."

"Seems like a poor choice of a place to look for money," Bella snapped.

Samantha glared at her queen. "Yeah — you're right." She leaned her head down on the fluffy white pillow. "Witches do have a knack for making the wrong choices."

Bella was, for once, at a loss for words.

Samantha lay down, humming and singing a Heofsij song. "Don't ever laugh as a hearse goes by. For you may be the next to die." She smiled up at the ceiling.

"Is that a threat?" Bella roared.

"Are you Heofsij?" Ben immediately took note of the British song made for children. He longed to revisit London. It had been months since he had stepped foot in his art studio.

She shook her head. "No — I'm a born and raised Viridi girl." Her big brown eyes enlarged as she stated the color of her aura. "But I've been fascinated by the Heofsijs — fragile, like newborns. Enough about last night — let's talk about who's going to stay by my side until that sadistic freak is found and poached."

"Well, we might not resort to killing him, but you are correct. We need to find this man, and let's hope he's related to the awakening of the forest as well. I would suggest Selena and Gabriel watch over you. I would have assigned you Krum, but he is unfortunately in the same state as you," Bella explained.

Selena and Gabriel nodded.

"You two can stay, and if we need your help, we will summon you."

After the Ministry left, John joined the kids out in the hall to discuss different matters on what had happened last night. He also wanted to know what news there had been on their new powers. The kids went on to tell them about the odd cabin with snow on its roof, and the kid's poem. John assured them that they had already known about the poem and took this information very seriously. They then informed John that his nephew would be joining them on the unlocking of magical powers. That's when they also told him that he had occupied a bed in the hospital.

"It does not do to leave out any suspects; for all we know, your mother is right about this Mark Bisterne guy." Ben began trying to persuade Bella as they stood outside.

"Fine, you and Teddy can go interview him. The rest of us will go to the forest and clean up Gower's mess," Bella agreed.

Ben pulled out a piece of paper with Mark's address, pulled out his wand and summoned himself, along with Teddy, to the location. No one had known where Mark resided, so Ben had looked through Galdorwide's logbook held at the castle entrance, where newcomers could become a member of Galdoriwde officially.

"Is this it?" Teddy asked, looking around the empty lot at the edge of the forbidden forest.

"Must be." Ben looked down.

By their feet was a small latch that read, "411". Ben looked at the piece of paper that read, "411 Forestside Lane". Ben knelt and knocked on the steel latch's surface. After a few clashes and bangs from beneath the ground, the lid began to squeak open. A pale face with messy dark hair and blue eyes appeared through the hatch. The man's arm shook. It seemed to be from both the heaviness of the latch and fear of what stood above him.

"Yes?" the man asked in a high-pitched, snide voice.

For a moment, the man's tone made Ben believe that he was mocking them. However, after seeing the man's fear, he knew that it was just the man's natural voice tone.

"I'm Ben Black, and this is Teddy Scaasi. We're members of Galdorwide's Ministry," Ben introduced.

The man's eyes flickered over to Teddy. The tall, slim man with spiky black hair was wearing purple-tinted rectangular glasses. The man's pale face turned a sickly gray; he gulped, and his arm began to quake faster.

"We're here to ask you a few questions; may we come — down?" Ben asked, unsure if he had used the proper term associated with his unique choice of home.

The man pushed the top over and allowed the men to climb down the steep steps. Teddy closed the latch above them. Two bronze gold-trimmed pillars held up the stone ceiling. Inside there was no furniture, just a large space filled with clusters of jewels and money, as well as junk. There were piles of blankets, books, tin containers, plastic buckets, and empty plastic and glass bottles. At the far-right corner of the room was a staircase that led down to a lower level.

"This is your — home?" Teddy asked, appalled.

"Yes, this is his home," Ben said through gritted teeth after taking note of the man's pale face turning red.

Ben focused, allowing his mind to vibrate and numb on a new plane level, allowing him to talk to Teddy telepathically. "*You can't just insult the man that we want answers from.*"

"You've got some nice stuff," Teddy said, in a tone almost believable. "You're plausibly querying why my companion and I are hither."

Ben furrowed his brow. He had never spent time with Teddy but never expected such a vocabulary to come from a man who spent four years of his life in and out of prison.

"We simply wish to ask you a few questions," he continued. "Like, what brings you to Galdorwide; any friends or relatives here?"

"No." The man spoke softly. "But my mother, as well as my father, has a history here. I needed to get away from my home, and this was the only kingdom that felt somewhat familiar."

"May I ask your parents' names?" Ben questioned.

"You may — but may I not answer? They have a rather dark history, and they had run from someone who still resides in Galdorwide. I'd rather them not know who I am or know where my parents are now."

"Okay, you don't have to tell me your parents' names. Where did you come from?" Ben asked gently.

"A kingdom that goes by the name Port," the man answered.

"May we question what yourself was doing yesterday evening, and does yourself have an alibi?" Teddy asked yet another wordy question.

"I was out at the café with a friend, Monica Morgan," Mark explained.

"Monica Morgan — Dr Morgan's wife?" Ben asked.

The man nodded. "Yes; I recently got a job at the school's hospital ward and met both him and his wife. I befriended Monica, but not so much Ian."

"Do you happen to know Roman Scaasi?" Teddy asked.

The man tensed, and his eyes widened. "No. But I have heard of him."

"Has the spirit of Galdorwide's departed king visited yourself?" Teddy questioned.

The man shook his head. "No, sir. And I'm sorry to hear of your leader's tragic death, but I have not seen him or any other ghostly being."

"Have any of the deceased king's fans come to visit yourself?" Teddy asked.

The man shook his head yet again. "No, not that I know of."

"Did you notice anything peculiar or strange last night?"

"Well," Mark began. "My house began to shake every few minutes or so. I thought my house was going to cave in, but it's still standing."

Just as Mark finished explaining the previous night's events, the house began to shake once again. Dirt began to seep through the cracks in the stone ceiling.

"Did you notice any questionable characters, wander into the forest?"

"No." The man shook his head. He stuffed his hands in the pocket of his black sweater. "Is this all you need to know? I'm exhausted."

"Yes, thank you for your time." Ben smiled before exiting with Teddy in tow. They closed the home's hatch beneath them and stood on the neon grass outside of it. "Looks like we still have no lead." Ben sighed. "What was the point of Elizabeth telling us to visit them?"

"You're a gentleman from honesty. Not many are. For all we know, one of them is fibbing. Or both," Teddy said positively, as if his words would encourage the soon-to-be king. "Thus, no matter what they stated, we must continue to keep our minds open."

The two men walked down the road where they knew they would soon arrive at the Morgan residence.

"Yourself seems unusually depressed, Ben. It would be best if you remained proud of yourself and all you've accomplished thus far for this kingdom. So what if we don't possess any leads? We'll develop a plan and stop the forest from becoming awakened."

Ben shrugged.

"Well, Ben, yourself may not stand satisfied with yourself. However, I sure am."

"Thanks." Ben managed a smile as he threw on his shades to protect his eyes from the sunlight's burn. "If only Bella were proud of me. She's sure that my vampirism has distracted me from the case and that it will be all my fault once the king and his followers take over the kingdom."

"You're not considering that you are not yourself, are you?" Teddy asked.

Ben shrugged. "What if I'm not me, and what if that leads the kingdom to fall?"

"Yeah, right — over my dead body." Teddy chuckled.

"Are you sure this is the way to Ian's house?" Ben asked.

Teddy smirked. "I possess faith in yourself. All I request is that you possess the equivalent in me. Come on." Teddy motioned as he walked up to a fortress of wooden panels.

Teddy, with Ben's help, was able to push the wooden gate open. Within the wooden corridor was a row of floating parked broomsticks, all in pastel shades.

"Who do all these brooms belong to?" asked Ben.

"Monica; she's an expensive missus, that one." Teddy shook his head in amazement as they passed through the brooms. "Follow me."

Ben's eyes fell on a pale-yellow broomstick as he continued to walk through the yard. "Are you sure this is the Morgans' property, and you're not taking me somewhere secluded to kill me and steal my broom?"

"I know I told you to stand proud, but I suppose I possess several imperfections of my own, violence being one of them. Although ever since Selena and my babies were born, I've been a reformed man. If I were past Teddy, I'm sure your speculation would've been correct. I got rid of my violent tendencies — well — I preserved some, just in case a fight ever came to me, but I have not started a match in about twenty years or so. Anyways, it's good to be cautious, even if that means you're cautious about me, and we have to be ready for anything. Heck, my nephew Roman is a follower of the shaft butler king." Teddy spoke as they approached the back of the wooden home.

The sun was beginning to set, so Teddy raised his wand and lit up the backyard lanterns with green fire. The lamps lined a wooden dock-like pathway as it trailed above a dark pond with glowing fishes within it. Fairies flew above them. Ben looked to the left, where he could see the blond Monica digging in her garden. Her hair was pulled back and pinned up out of her face, and she wore a loose blue shirt, presumed to be an old shirt of Ian's. She looked around, shocked by the sudden light.

Mark walked down to his home's basement, where he took a seat at a lone desk that doubled as a workspace as well as a kitchen table. Beside him sat a mini-cooler where he kept few alcoholic beverages. Mark gazed off in space as he twirled his glass of frosted blaze. He brought the drink to his lips as he stared at an image that sat on his desk of a red-haired woman who looked to be about forty. Next to her stood a man who seemed to be in his sixties.

A knock came from the latch upstairs. Mark took another sip, finishing the glass and headed back up the stairs.

"I already told you everything I know," Mark said as he reached the top of the stairs. He immediately froze in his tracks. Mark became immobilized, and his rapid heartbeat was the only thing that reminded him that he was still alive.

"Congratulations." A man spoke from behind the shadows of Mark's dark home.

Mark finally mustered the courage to step forward to make sure that what he saw was real.

"You did what I knew you could do, what I told you to do. You lied."

Mark's heart began to flutter unpleasantly, and he took a step back, regretting stepping closer to the monster.

"I'll be back where I belong. Back on top. Everyone thinks I'm not a threat — as if it'd be that simple."

Mark wanted to reply, but he couldn't. His lips didn't budge.

"Tonight, they'll see." The man stalked closer, walking into the lighting of the room supplied by a sole green lantern hanging in the middle of the room. It was the king. "That my reign's only just begun."

Mark gulped, his mouth dry. He had never felt this nervous in his whole lifetime.

"You kids." John shook his head as he stared at his nephew, who had his left arm wrapped up in a cast. "So — curious — curiosity killed the cat, you know. Speaking of curiosity, Caden — I'm curious to know why you invaded the privacy of Aldric and Lovetta and listened in on their conversation."

"I wanted to know the truth." He sat upon his bed, showing little to no emotion despite the pain that shot up his arm.

"The truth about what?"

"I don't know. I guess — everything — I want to know the truth about magic and my family's history. My dad hates to talk about our ancestors, even though their actions have shaped us into who we are today. My father, well — he trained me to fight like a pirate — I'm practically a Heofsij. All the spells I know, I learned at school, and we all know school teaches us a fraction of what there is to know."

John sighed as he placed his head in his hand.

"Why are we hiding who we are? Also, why does my dad never speak of my mom, even though he says he loved her completely and purely?"

John let out another sigh before looking back to Caden. "I'll respect your father's wishes with how much I tell you. I can tell you that your mother died giving birth to your sister, who was stillborn. Your father loved her, you, and your sister, whom they named Annaliese. Your father lost two people at the same time. That's a pain I wish upon no one. Being close to my brother, I felt his pain before even hearing of the news. I had awoken from a deep slumber, and when I stood up, my heart ached. My eyes burned with the pressure of tears that were soon to pour from my eyes. I fell to my hands and knees. I felt everything that your father was feeling at that moment.

"The love I have for my brother connects us, and it connects me with my children, my nephews, and even my close friends. Love is powerful, and not many have the power to love many fully, but your father and I — we do. Love is the greatest feeling, but once the person we love is gone, it cuts a deep hole in our hearts. Your father loves you deeply, but any stories of our past, whether good or bad, are always painful to say. Not from shame or guilt but the hurt that comes when we pull the words out of our mouths. Though your mother is gone, her love still surrounds you and your father. Your father puts on an act, one where he comes off as hateful and greedy, but it's far from the truth. What your father has gone through from childhood to now can only be described as pure agony. That also goes for almost all the Scaasis from our past."

A sudden bang on the door gave Caden time to dry his eyes on his green hospital gown before anyone could see. "Who is it?" he asked once he was sure that his voice would not show any signs that he desperately needed a good cry.

John went to open the door, as the person on the other side struggled against the lock. "Let go!" John shouted. He drew out his wand just in case. "I'm going to open the door."

The twirling of the knob ceased. When he opened the door, he saw a familiar, burly man with a worried face. It was Krum.

He gently pushed past his younger brother. His eyes glistened at the sight of his son, whom he had not seen in two years.

"I knew you were here. I had an aching, pounding pain in my arm every time I passed by this room. It took me forever to get here, since the nurses never got off my back," Krum explained.

Krum embraced his son. Rosie Crimson, a sweet yet strict nurse, walked in. She had short hair gelled to a point on top of her head. Its roots were orange, and its tips were neon pink. She had long lashes that made her eyes droop. Her lipstick was the same color as her hair; her bottom lip was orange, and her top lip was neon pink.

CHAPTER 18

Mark Bisterne gave Mrs Morgan a rundown of his plan. Long before he had finished, he realized how crazy it sounded. It was mad — even for him — the man who lived and breathed crazy. To his surprise, Monica Morgan seemed to agree with the idea.

"This is going to sound weird," she began, "but I think you're right; my husband fears the coming of dragons, but maybe it's just what we need. Dragons used to work alongside humans, and maybe they can stop the king." She shook her head.

"If this sounds good, there's more," Mark said. He explained how the king himself had appeared to him, wanting him to join him and his followers. Mark told her how the king asked him to summon the dragons. The king had said how he was more important than he knew. "The king thinks I'm helping him, but if I summon the dragons, they will be under my control, not the king's. We can take him and his followers down."

"Important, huh?" The blond woman took a sip of her morning caffeine quake. "That's impressive, Mark. It sounds like you're no longer the town weirdo." She smiled.

"I guess, but what's so important about me? Why did the king come to me to summon the dragons?"

"I don't know." Monica shook her head. "But it sounds like they need you, or at least they think they do. I'm glad you're taking advantage of this opportunity. I know how the king can easily brainwash the weak-minded with his lies."

"Good morning, Mum and Mr Bisterne." Mikayla rubbed her eyes as she held onto her favorite teddy bear. She fixed her baby blue nightgown. "Where's daddy?"

"Getting close to dawn," Ian Morgan said as he looked up to the sky that peaked from behind the twisted branches of the forest.

Bella looked up to the sky. "Maybe I should call on Gabriel, John,

288

and Selena." Ben and Teddy had already joined the Ministry on their journey. She grabbed out her wand and placed it on her temple. The tip of her rod emitted a bright purple glow. *John, Selena, Gabriel, summon yourselves to the forest as soon as possible.*

Bella noticed a horde of people in the distance as she returned her wand back under her long purple cloak. Seemingly numbering in the hundreds, people were led by Roman and Daeva. Bella finally knew who the group were — followers of her father, the ghost king. Despite the warm days that frequented Galdorwide's daytime, the night-times grew ever more frigid, as the Ministry's members could see their breath cascading upward in the moonlight.

Far in the distance, Queen Bella had noticed something, a terrifying sight that caused her to question not only her eyes but her sanity as well. Emerging from a fiery flame in the distance, in the center of where Daeva and Roman gathered the followers, the ghostly king himself appeared. He rose from this fire as an eerie silhouette and was embraced by his followers as though he were alive and well.

Bella and the rest of the Ministry noticed that more and more followers joined the group in the forest's distance. Bella, having keen eyesight, observed her father's ghostly chants into their ears, bending them to his influence.

"You, my child, shall become like me. Feel no pain, no sorrow, no heat, no cold, for you are under my wing. I shall protect you from pain, sorrow, heat, and cold." He was transforming them, binding them to him and his powers. With a touch of his hand and repeating those words, he turned the witches' auras black. The queen herself had almost become a follower. However, her father was always interrupted as he began his chants. The crowd looked excited, and the followers were finally coming together. It wouldn't be long now, Bella feared.

Bella reached for her head. "John, Selena, and Gabriel will meet us soon." She looked to the crowd. "Those aren't even all of his followers. This area is like his temple. Like every religion, not everyone goes to the ceremonies, especially the baptisms; this isn't their meeting place. It's a place my father never revealed to me."

The Ministry could only feel agony at the thought of even more followers coming together to support the king. However, Ben was appalled at the idea of a battle between the Ministry's supporters and the king's followers. The whole kingdom — men, women, and children — would be at war.

"Aren't you a little concerned?" Ben questioned his queen.

She gave a puzzled look as if to ask why that was even a question.

"I know that a war between witches is rare, but can you imagine how serious of a battle they are probably planning to bring? They will be out for blood!"

"I don't know what's going to happen," she admitted. "But we are just going to have to trust that we will make it together."

Despite Bella's smile and use of the word "together", Ben wanted to shout at her. It was her father, and she was going to sit back and allow her dad to bring more witches into his army. He stared at her, making her smile widen. A feeling of ease, peace, and well-being washed over him. She was beginning to look like the Bella he had met all those years ago. A deep-seated thought pushed its way to the front of his mind — he wanted a battle, for he would be at her side, fighting with her, for her. Maybe it would bring them closer, he hoped.

He looked back over to the horde of followers. The king squatted as he talked to children, lowering himself to their eye level. Turning his head, he looked up to the sky as a feeling of intensity washed over him. He stood to his feet and smiled. "It is time." Everyone in the opening of the forest cheered. They were more than willing to lay down their lives in service of their king.

The Ministry looked skyward where a blood moon lay immediately above the pit of fire.

The edges of the moon began to churn like a small puddle in the air. As the moon grew more extensive, it evolved into a shape that looked similar to a grand fountain's top. It continued to whirl, and soon the whole sky was a pale red with deep burgundy clouds. The clouds expanded before releasing pools of blood down onto the kingdom, drenching everything in sight in the macabre substance.

Mark entered the forest, his umbrella in, blocking off the thick liquid that fell from the sky. The air around him rippled like the hood of a car on a hot summer's day. It was difficult to see as he trekked further into the forest and to Doryu Edjer's museum. He stalked up the steps and closed the umbrella after reaching the roof's shaded asylum. He walked down into the basement where the king told him the items would be. At first, the basement looked anything but extraordinary. Only crumbled wood and dust matted the floor. However, a door at the very back glistened with a light hue of silver.

His eyes widened with surprise as he pushed the door open. A trove of treasure surrounded him. There was everything from lost artifacts to precious metals. He picked up a handful of rubies and diamonds that he shoved into his black bag. As he turned around to leave, he noticed another item on the king's list: a silver hand mirror. He felt no changes. However, the iris of each of his eyes was now a solid silver.

He walked back up the stairs, clutching his bag as he remembered what the king had said to him. "Take no more than I tell you; dragons do not take a liking to those who steal from them. You shall bring these items into the heart of the forest, pile them among a fire of ambers, cut your hand with a silver blade, and chant this spell."

Mark's heart dropped to his feet, as he could not remember whether or not he had brought the scroll with him. On the rotten museum's porch, he opened his bag and rummaged through it.

Beneath the shiny items, he saw the scripture scrunched beneath them. His heart rose back into position, and its beating returned to its standard rate.

At the edge of the forest, Monica waited. She wrapped her blue sweater tightly around her chest as her umbrella swayed above her in the strong wind. He smiled as he bid her farewell and passed by her. She recoiled in horror after noticing his silver eyes.

The rose-red sky hung around them. Bloody droplets, clots, strings, and streams fell from the sky. The Ministry members huddled tightly between two large trees. They watched the king and his followers as they walked, ran or rode on brooms and motorcycles deeper into the forest as they followed him. Many of the followers wielded wands, bows, knives, glowing swords, and even guns. Soon, they were out of sight. Ben presumed that they were on their way to summon the dragons.

Having to endure the foul-smelling and tasting weather, they continued to walk and keep a close eye from a far distance. They walked up a hill so that they could look down at the king's party. Krum walked up next to Ben as he carried Angela in his hand. He was grinning from ear to ear as blood dripped from his long hair and onto his broad face.

"Isn't this a great day or what?" he asked, looking more sadistic than ever. "I am so glad I joined the Ministry. We are going to kick some major ass tonight, aren't we?" He laughed more confidently than Ben had ever heard him before.

Ben wanted to smile, but he couldn't. He had no doubt that they could handle the dragons, and that was plenty to be excited for, but he couldn't help but think about the damage the king and his followers could do. Bella herself looked worried, as she was thinking the same thing. She couldn't help but feel sorry for her father's followers. He didn't care about them, and in fact, he was leading them straight to their certain deaths. The dragons would be thirsting for revenge after Galdorians had made them extinct on this land. He wasn't a god or even a good leader. He just acted like one. On the inside, he was a monster, and she had thought more people had known, but looking at his mass of followers, she realized that most people were not aware of the king's many horrific atrocities. He was only out for power, and he would sacrifice each one of his devoted followers for just a glimpse of more power at his fingertips.

Krum felt healthy and energized, with none of the fear that his fellow team had. Krum couldn't help but wonder why none of them seemed to be enjoying what they were doing, but he assumed it was because they weren't thrill chasers like him and the rest of the Scaasi family. He also had more experience with the world's dangers, as Krum couldn't recall the number of times that he had had a brush with death. Dragons were something he had never fought before, but he had, however, defeated a Naga, and that was pretty damn close, considering that they were both of serpent species. Krum supposed that he was more experienced than the rest of the Ministry, whose worst creature encounter was the Werewolf Uprising, when his younger brother Lewis was still in high school.

Ben leaned over to Bella, who walked along his left side. "You know, we should do something about your father tonight. You can't let this continue any further. He will be responsible for the death of hundreds under your queenship, and this is something as queen, you cannot allow.

Regardless of him being your father or not."

She didn't look at him as she answered. Her mouth tightened. "It's too late and too risky. Can't you feel his power?" She raised her hand to allow a pool of blood to fill the palm of her hand. "It's a literal tidal wave of death. We will fight him when he comes to fight us, we will prepare, but we can't go after him, because that's what he wants. The king wants *more* blood."

Despite his plea to her, he knew that she was right; this wasn't Galdorwide's typical creature or murderer. They were dealing with the ghost of the king, whose followers treated him like a god. He had hundreds of followers; there was no way for the Ministry to fight them all. Tonight, was history in the making. Trying to stop the king now would be like trying to block a tsunami with a straw wall. They needed to do something to stop him, but what? They needed a plan and fast.

The king and the followers continued to march. The king led the crowd as Daeva and Roman walked on either side of him, like bodyguards. They were approaching the next opening in the forest, the heart of the woods. An arched gate made of steel stood tall and locked up. On the top of the gate, in the arch, was a carving of a heart, similar to those on the doors of the castle's dungeon cells. Bella never did understand its significance to her father's prisoners, but she never questioned it either. Ben furiously tried to think of a plan.

"I'm coming with you!" Monica gripped onto her sweater as she raced towards the man who was about to bring forth the rise of dragons. He noticed that her eyes were silver. She had caught a glimpse of the mirror that peaked from his bag.

They both smiled. If all went as planned, this was going to be fun. He'd be a hero.

By the time they reached the heart of the forest, men, women, and children filled it. All of them were just as anxious as them.

As soon as they entered the gate, a black ribbon wrapped around Monica's wrists. It was so tight that her hands were already turning red from the pressure. Roman appeared beside her, grabbing hold of her arm to keep her from trying to escape as well as doing something stupid.

Everyone knew that she wasn't supposed to be there. The well-respected doctor's model of a wife never dabbled in any dark forces. To her surprise, Roman's face looked sorrowful. She didn't know why — she had never met him personally. It almost seemed as if he were worried about her. The Scaasi man doubted that the king would allow her to live after intruding on the event rudely. If the king were merciful to let her live, she as sure as Mania would not come out of the heart of the forest the same.

She stayed behind with Roman, as the followers made way for Mark to approach the king's fire. He shuffled his bag higher onto his shoulder. He now had the eyes of the king, Daeva, Roman, and the rest of the following fixated intensely on him.

Mark approached the front of the crowd as he stood near the king and Daeva. He looked around at the king's followers and took note of the countless teens and even children — some were still too young to walk. If Mark was going to have the dragons join him, he knew that he would have to make sure that the only victims tonight were those worthy: Daeva and Roman, along with any ill-minded adult members. Mark hesitated, considering the risk but understood that they were bound to the king. If they were to die, at least they'd feel no pain, as he had promised.

A sea of other doubts floated through his mind. Were they here of free will, or could they be like me? What if they were being forced or manipulated, like me? Mark felt his anger rising, and his thoughts only made him want to destroy the king and the plan even more. He was tired of being pushed around and being told what to do. All he needed was luck on his side.

"The time has come!" The grey king shouted loud enough to catch all of his followers' attention, silencing them.

Heat and fear washed through Mark's shaking body as he placed his umbrella down, allowing the blood to cover his dry clothing. The followers pushed one another as they squished to get a good view of what was about to happen. They began to shout incoherently at one another. Those whose eyes met the silver mirror had turned the color of the metal object. The followers started to push, kick, and hit one another. Too many people were in the crowd, with many of them just itching at the chance for a fight. This event couldn't happen without some sort of violence. With a flick of Daeva's hands, she sent the crowd of people back out of the gate, closing it behind them. The only people who remained from the group were Roman and Monica. The crowd had silenced, now focusing in on the spaces between the gate's bars. Monica looked afraid, and Roman — now with silver eyes — looked concerned.

Mark continued to quake in his shoes, and he began to wonder how his body was even managing to remain on his own two feet. The first rays of dawn emerged through the trees' branches, and the bloody rain had ceased.

"I'm so glad you came today," said the king as he looked to the trembling man, who forced a smile.

"Me too," Daeva added. "I'm surprised you didn't collapse at the sight of the king."

The king smiled and looked to his right-hand woman. "Did you have any doubt that I had chosen the wrong man for this mission?"

"No," she said. "I never doubt you, Your Majesty."

"Are you ready?" He looked back to Mark.

"As I'll ever be." He rubbed his hands together as if it would magically stop his nervous trembles.

Mark reached into his bag and grabbed out a single ruby, tossing it atop the glowing embers. Mark then grabbed out a silver pocket knife from his green cloak. He took it in his right hand and began to cut a horizontal line on his left palm. Once the blood had reached his hand's surface, he held it over the fire, allowing one drop to fall upon the ruby. Mark then bent down and grabbed the silver mirror in his left hand, staining its handle with his blood. On his right, he picked up the scroll and read from it as he held the mirror in front of his face. *"Dracan dracan dracon, ic clipung uppan. Nrls fram incer byringes and gegangan a later mec."*

The fire began to rumble and glowed with black energy. Electrical sparks emitted from the flames. They could hear the followers chanting excitedly from behind the gate. The dragons were rising.

Ian watched in horror from the hill as the beast rose from the flames only a few feet from where his wife stood. The crowds cheered as loudly as they could, in awe of the power of their ghostly king, knowing that their faith had been well placed, as he was indeed even more powerful in death than he had been in life. The king began to laugh.

Mark turned the mirror to the dragon. "Follow me, for I am your master!"

"Silly fool!" The king laughed. "The dragons no longer want a master! Witches from Galdorwide wiped them out. They're vengeful, ready to bring justice to the witches of Galdorwide."

"But you brought your followers — were you just going to let the dragons slaughter them?"

"Not my followers," the king began. Mark took note that Daeva had vanished. "My *sacrifices*. Those who wronged me — yet wanted to follow me for my powers."

Roman snapped his fingers, allowing all of the sacrifices back into the heart of the forest before disappearing himself. Mark ran as far as he could from where the dragons had stood, hearing the screams of panic as blood spilled and spattered around him. The first rows of the king's sacrifices had been slain by the bloodthirsty dragons, which had been summoned to do the king's bidding. The followers, now realizing how their former king had tricked them, had decided to fight back against the dragons at all costs. For the longest time, Galdorians believed that the only magic effective against dragons had been that of electricity, so that is what most of the witches had decided to muster for their defense.

To their horror, these new-age dragons were much more powerful than what their ancestors had faced. The electrical spells just repelled off the thick scales of these dragons. The spells' active effects returned towards their casters, sending their bodies into convulsions and causing many young witches to become scorched with burns deep into their skin.

Mark ordered Monica to run as far and as fast as she could, as he was going to remain back, to provide whatever medical treatment he could to his fellow fallen witches who showed even the slightest signs of life. It was the least that Mark felt he could have done, as it was his fault that the dragons had come back, so their blood was on his hands. However, Mark powered on. He was gathering as many disabled witches as he could near the gate, while those former followers began to strike back with various firearms and bladed weapons, all of which seemed to be just as effective as the magic was against the thick scales; useless at best. They quickly became surrounded and overwhelmed by the dragons' devastatingly sharp claws, which seemed just as lethal as their fiery breath.

Adelaide watched in horror as the nightmarish battle took place. A witch armed with a large spear managed to embed the spear deep inside a creature's body. This was the first successful attack on a dragon so far in the battle, and the sight of the dragon's blood had a rally-cry effect on the surrounding witches. "If it bleeds, we can kill it!" Mark heard cheering in support of the attack on the dragon. However, the celebration was short-lived, as the dragon grew enraged at the sight of its blood spilling on the battlefield. Letting out a blood-curdling roar, the dragon inhaled a massive breath as many nearby witches began to scream in fear, as they knew the dragon was about to cast an enormous fireball. Anything within the fireball's range would be immediately burned to a crisp.

The king observed in amazement, with the smile of a small child on Saturnalia morning, as his sacrifices were burned to a crisp by the dragon's fiery breath. Many witches cried out for their king to make the dragon's assault stop, to which he just let out the most resonant laugh — one from the deepest spot in his diaphragm.

Queen Bella expected carnage at the hands of her father, but nothing could have prepared her for the slaughter before her. The Ministry couldn't handle standing idly any more, as the members began rushing down the massive hill to do whatever they could to fight off the dragons and save whatever witches remained. Ian started to assist Mark with providing medical assistance to any witches who showed signs of life. Two things became clear to Ben, Bella, and the rest of the Ministry. One, they were going to need every non-disabled witch to fight the dragons. Two, there were going to be even more severe losses of Galdorians, a battle that would take generations to replace all the families lost.

Adelaide noticed Krum lying on the ground, his body blackened from a close brush of the dragon's fire. He had been the first to make it past the gate, coughing as smoke filled his lungs.

Adelaide rushed to his side. *I'll be sickened if he is hurt more*, she thought to herself as she grabbed hold of his arm and began to help the large man crawl away from the dragons.

"Do you have your gun?" Adelaide asked once they were at a far enough distance from the dragons.

He grabbed hold of his gun with a smile. He lifted it. The fingers on his right hand had been burned black. Adelaide tried not to stare at the crumbling, charcoal-like fingers. She focused her eyes on the three-barreled gun instead. She had never used one before, but she trusted that Krum could handle this — burnt fingers or not. Krum reached into his long black coat pocket and pulled out the items it took for him to reload the gun.

Krum hid behind a rock as he loaded the gun before turning back towards the dragons.

Adelaide followed quickly behind Krum with her wand drawn as he stood up to his feet. Noticing nearby dragons casting fiery breaths, the two members charged fearlessly into the heat of battle. After healing whoever they could, Ian turned to Mark. "I am going home to my wife and daughter."

Mark nodded as he turned direction back into the scene of battle. Returning to battle, Mark had a brilliant idea. *I'll freeze the bastards*, he thought to himself. Raising his want and chanting "*Freosan*," the nearest dragon was frozen solid. Mark began to laugh hysterically at the proof that just a simple freezing spell would render the powerful beast immobile. However, this celebration was cut short when the king quickly teleported to Mark's side. The Ministry members stared intensely at the arrival of the king back on the battlefield.

John, Gabriel, and Selena appeared, joined by the rest of the Ministry members.

"Why did you do that?" Teddy asked. "I grasped that you happened to be moderately insane — but serving this dictator?"

Mark turned away. "I wasn't serving the king," he mumbled.

"Oh, but you were," the king cackled. "I needed you to summon the dragons, and you are the only man in Galdorwide who could — being a descendant of Doryu Edjer and all."

Mark's eyes widened. "That can't be — I come from a poor family."

"Ah — but it is, for Doryu — on your paternal side. He used blood magic on the summoning items so that only someone of his blood could summon them. As you can see, it was a success." The king motioned to the dead bodies that lay around them. With one last laugh, he vanished.

The creatures creaked in position behind Mark. He began to burst into tears.

"I — I didn't know! I wanted to control them and use them against the king and his followers! I didn't know that the dragons would be vengeful. I'm sorry — I thought I was helping." He looked around at all the dead bodies that lay still on the ground alongside the weapons that were of no use to them. He was barely able to breathe as his bitter tears filled the back of his throat. The sky turned pink once more, sending off waves of blood floating like a galaxy above them before finally raining down on them once more.

"These deaths! These deaths were meaningless!" he shrieked to the sky as he fell to his knees.

The nearby frosted dragon erupted free from its icy binding, sending sharp pellets into the crowd. "Stay behind us," Krum shouted as he threw the much smaller Mark behind him. The pirate aimed Angelica right at the heart of the aggressive dragon. However, before Krum could shoot a bullet into the heart of the dragon, the beast raised its massive paw and slashed the chest of the pirate. The pure force of the scratch sent Krum, who was by no means a small man, flying across the battlefield. Upon his landing, his head thumped a large rock, causing him to lose consciousness temporarily.

The commotion of battle and the thought of missing out on a good fight seemed to cause Krum's consciousness to resume rather quickly. However, this did not solve the massive chest wound he had suffered from the dragon's claws. *I can't die*, he thought. *They need me to defeat the dragons. If I die, the kingdom dies. If the kingdom dies, Caden dies. Come on, Krum — you've been through worse. Remember when that unicorn impaled you with its horn? You lived, and it was right in the chest too. Why does everything aim for my chest? First, the unicorn, the manticore, and now the dragon. Krum! Focus! Okay, okay, try to get your vision back. You've got this.*

Soon the black vision was now grey, and he could see the silhouette of Adelaide crying over him, but he couldn't hear her cries or anything, for that matter. Slowly, his hearing came back.

"Don't you dare get up, Krum," John threatened once his eyes met his brother's. His consciousness seemed to be back. "I'll take the gun and use it against the dragons." They were all outside of the gates, away from the dragons.

His brother's voice was stern for once, and Krum obliged, but if it didn't work, if John couldn't kill them — he knew that he would get up and kill those damned creatures. The heaviness in his chest lessened, and Mark flipped the large man over, with the help of John and Gabriel, to heal his head wound. Krum, while the hole in his head began to shrink into its normal position, stretched out his arm and laid it lengthwise for his brother to grab.

Monica, whose arms were still tied, began to run awkwardly, as her arms were behind her back. She ran closer. She seemed more frightened now than when the dragons had started attacking. "Roman and Daeva are coming! They want to finish you guys!" the woman shouted in a craze.

Mark healed Krum enough so that he could sit up. He heard the woman's cries, and his attention immediately went to her. With no pressure in his chest, he decided that he could stand despite Mark's quiet pleas not to. The skin where the rock had split his flesh stung, but that was the least of his concerns.

Monica was soon standing next to them. John walked behind her and began to untie her hands. An expression of relief washed over her face.

"Thanks," she said as the kind man released her from the black ribbon. Burn marks circled her wrists.

"What happened?" Ben asked.

She looked past him and the rest of the Ministry members, only to see the horror of the six remaining dragons prancing over the dead charred bodies of their victims. There had to be at least two hundred Galdorians lying dead.

"Never mind that; defeat the dragons before the Scaasi couple gets here and releases them from these gates."

CHAPTER 19

Krum ran as fast as he could, attacking as many dragons in his sight as he could with his frost energy spells. He was trying to catch up with his brother, John, as he witnessed John shoot Angelica into the heart of a nearby dragon. Krum noticed his brother and his skills with Angelica, thinking that if he ever wanted to leave Galdorwide and become a pirate, he would make a good one. The bullets seemed to have practically no effect on the dragons' thick scales, to everyone's dismay. So Krum decided that it was now up to him to take matters into his own hands. He convinced himself that even with a severely damaged chest, he was to be the one to slay the next dragon.

Before John could even react, a large black tentacle of energy enveloped his body; this caused him to let out a terrifying scream in pain as Gabriel tried desperately to free him. Gabriel realized that this tentacle was electrified and shocked his hand when he tried to free his cousin. Luckily, however, the magic seemed to dispel, as John's screaming stopped as he fell to the floor. As the dragons approached the Ministry members, they cast spells of all kinds to protect their fallen friend. Mark and Gabriel tended to John, but they found it impossible to find a pulse when they looked for one. Mark began to panic, feeling responsible for his death. Without a central source for his injuries, they couldn't decide where to focus their magic. With one last desperate effort, they both cast electricity spells into John's heart, and to their amazement, this caused John to begin stirring once again. The two men cheered in amazement that their friend had been saved. John convulsed before his eyes opened.

Krum took the gun from his brother's hands and reloaded. They had seen him approaching, but he had arrived sooner than they had expected. He aimed at the nearest dragon's heart and shot. The creature's legs immediately collapsed, sending its body forward. Bella moved out of the way so as not to be crushed. Too close for comfort, another dragon dragged down its paw, striking Adelaide's face. She fell to the ground, motionless. Krum wanted to help her but knew that the best thing to do was to stay focused and shoot these boulder-heads down. He reloaded again.

"What was that?" Krum asked Gabriel, who was still caring for his brother.

"I don't know!" he shouted across the field. "It was black magic; maybe Daeva's!"

"Is he okay?"

"I think so! I'll stay with him behind the gates! We have to hurry!"

Gabriel brought John outside the gates where they sat on the blood-covered grass where its neon lights struggled to emit through. He looked pale and as if he were about to pass out. Gabriel had a hand on his back as he noticed his cousin's slow rocking movements.

Ian Morgan approached the two Scaasi men and his wife.

"It's about time you showed up," Gabriel scowled.

Monica frowned at her husband.

"I was looking for you." Ian looked to his wife. "I thought you had left! Where's Mikayla?"

"I went home and brought Mikayla over to the neighbors."

"Well, the evil Scaasi duo was at the house — did a number on me. Tied me up."

"How did you get away?" Monica asked worriedly.

"They headed for here, and I was able to unbind my hands."

"I'm sorry," John mumbled out weakly. "I'm sorry my brother hurt you."

"It's not your fault." His frown turned into a smile.

Mark approached and opened the gate. "Krum isn't having much luck," he explained. "Mark, you brought the dragons here. Maybe you're the one who can defeat them," Monica suggested.

"Now there's an idea," John said as he struggled to stand to his feet. Gabriel followed him, keeping his helping hand on his back.

A wave of weariness came over Mark. The world around him began to spin, and he fell to the ground.

"Mark!" Ian shouted as he ran over to the man. He knelt beside him. Monica followed.

"What's wrong?" she asked.

Mark was conscious but didn't have the energy to answer her. John, too, fell onto his knees. Ian looked back and forth between the two men, panic in his eyes. "I," he took a deep breath before continuing, "I think it's the Scaasi couple," Ian said in a calm, hushed voice. "I think they're draining their energy."

Mark couldn't move his head to look at the man. Instead, he was able to roll his eyes so that he could see him. Ian, concerned, listened to the battlefield where he saw Krum hold his chest wound with his left hand as he shot at the beast with his right. Krum looked as if he could barely manage to stand, but he remained on his feet.

"They're draining their main threats first," Ian said. "But I'm pretty sure we will be affected soon." He looked to Monica.

"What do we do?" she asked.

"You — you don't do anything. You go to Mikayla, and I'll take care of this." He closed his eyes and furrowed his brow in concentration.

Nothing happened at first, then suddenly, a transparent green blast of waves circled the doctor. Mark felt his energy returning slowly.

Ian's brow furrowed profoundly. He balled his hands into fists and stood up, concentrating intensely. Ian entered through the gate as he rejuvenated his energy that they had tried to drain from him. Daeva and Roman froze the five remaining dragons — their spell would only hold so long. The couple, as well as the rest of the Ministry, looked to Ian, confused. The couple looked shocked, as if they weren't expecting Ian to be a threat. They appeared small as they lost their confidence. Daeva's menacing, dark makeup, black dress, and matching neck ornament looked like a little costume, as she no longer gave off an ominous vibe.

No matter how scared and small they appeared, the Scaasi couple were still dangerous. Daeva was first to snap out of her shock. She gave the doctor a venomous glare. "Clever attempt, listening to a child's prophecy, but you're going to need much more than a Heofsij weapon to kill these dragons. These are ancient creatures, and they won't be destroyed easily."

John sat up slowly and rose to his feet.

"We took some of them down." Ian motioned to the few dead beasts that stretched along the field.

Mark, too, stood to his feet. Both John and Mark pushed the gate open. Gabriel followed the two men, keeping a close eye on them to ensure they would not fall once again. They weren't back to their full strength yet, but they were getting stronger by the minute. Adelaide, who had been struck by one of the dragons, began to stir awake. With the help of Arthur, she stood to her feet.

The confusion left Roman's face as a sly smile replaced it. He turned to face his brother, John, who approached, now standing beside Ian.

Mark let the tip of his wand and the top of the scroll slip out of his green cloak pocket. He began to mumble the summoning spell in reverse. "Mec laterea a gegangan and byringes incer fram nrls. Uppan clipung ic, dracon dracon —" as he read, but before he could finish, Roman lunged towards him.

Roman successfully caused Mark to drop his wand, causing the reversal spell to end.

Yanking Mark's rod around and casting *"Nescius"*, a mix of grey and black magic hit Mark, rendering him unconscious.

"Quicksand!" Daeva aimed her wand at Mark. Her spell hit the forest floor, but nothing happened.

"The forest is awake. It won't listen to any command that is not its own," Dorothy said in a sassy tone with her arms crossed. *"Electra,"* she cast, as a constant rose rush of spikes exited her want, striking Daeva directly.

The magic zapped her, sending her onto her back. She sat up and looked up at her husband. She wasn't back to her full strength, so Roman helped her up onto her feet. Dorothy stood, her eyes sealed shut as she awaited the wrath of the Scaasi's husband.

He didn't do anything at first. Instead, he looked out at the battlefield and took note of how many followers — friends — he had lost.

"See what you've done?" John asked his brother, who had once been his favorite.

"Yes, I do." Roman softly spoke as he turned his eyes onto his younger brother, who was now quite a few inches taller than him. "I've won, we've won, and we will continue to win."

"You've won nothing," Bella hissed.

Roman looked to the queen and smiled as his hazel eyes stared into hers. *"Cunnan cunnan hemming til mec!"*

Bella stole her eyes away from him. She looked to the man's side, and there was a snarling fox. Before they had any time to process what was happening, the animal sunk its sharp claws into Mark's neck. Mark awoke from his unconsciousness and gritted his teeth as his body began to jerk with pain. The fox kept its massive paw on the man's neck before lifting its sharp teeth over to the man's eyes, where it would gnaw until it ate the eyes whole. Mark shrieked in agony. As the fox released its paw, blood poured from where the animal's nails had pierced through his skin. Mark reached up to the animal, who still chewed at his eyes, trying to push it off him, but he was unable to reach. He turned to Monica with an unreadable look before his breathing and struggling stopped. Monica collapsed to her knees. John shot forward towards the Scaasi couple, who had spent Mark's dying moments laughing.

"*Levitate!*" A simple blue glowing beam exited John's wand and struck Roman, lifting him high into the air.

"*Nescius!*" A black intertwining duo of waves shot out of Daeva's wand, striking John in the chest, rendering him unconscious. John's magic had been halted and returned Roman to his feet. Daeva grinned. "What a fool. Before we leave with these darling dragons, I need one more thing." She looked to Krum. "I need to kill you — as a sacrifice to our Lord Delanie."

"A sacrifice?" Krum asked with a smirk, unfazed by her comment. "To the king? He isn't a god, you know."

"Oh, but he will be. Once there is enough blood shed in his name, he will return with more power than ever."

Krum looked to Roman, who avoided eye contact. "What do you mean, he will return?" Bella asked.

"Those who've died today, they've released their powers. Your father, the king, absorbs those powers. Soon he will be back to normal and eventually even better and stronger than ever."

Krum took a step forward, his arms open.

John and Gabriel stepped in front of Krum to protect him.

"This is gonna be fun." Daeva wielded her wand. She bared her sharp, cold and hungry teeth before approaching Krum.

John and Gabriel began to shoot at Daeva with all the spells they could think of at that moment. A barrier of black electrical energy appeared around her. The electricity crackled from the impact of their charms. Roman's wand was aimed at his wife, protecting her. Magic wasn't going to work; sure, they could've just attacked Roman, but no, the Scaasi men wanted to make things fun. Plus, they'd always wanted to beat the shit out of their brother's crazy wife. Krum summoned his handy boarding ax before stuffing his wand into his pocket. He handed both John and Gabriel two knives which he had pulled out from one of his many coat pockets. Krum rushed towards the woman, who had once been on Galdorwide High's cheerleading team over thirty years ago.

Daeva laughed as the three Scaasi men approached her. She opened her arms as if she were greeting their attack. John aimed his knife at her heart, while Krum's weapon met her throat. John was reluctant to push his blade any further, while Krum had no problem pulling his ax up over his shoulder and bringing it down with a swift swing. The knife went right through her as if she were a ghost, and not even a slight scratch marked her body.

John and Krum tried to back up out of her reach, but she was too fast; she reached for both of their throats. She held them tight. "I'm done wasting my energy on you pathetic Ministry members." Then, as if they were ragdolls, she threw them to the ground.

The two men flew six feet before falling hard onto the ground. John felt a rib crack as he landed on the hard dirt surface which lay beneath the bloody mud. The pain stunned him, but he tried to stand to his feet. His body contradicted this idea. All he could do was push himself onto his hands and knees as Daeva and Roman turned to face the frozen beasts.

Bella and Ben stepped in front of the dragons, unsure of what plan they had to stop them.

John and Krum admired the couple's bravery, but they feared that trying to stall the Scaasi couple further would only get them killed.

"Run!" John called to the royal couple as well as to the rest of the Ministry members. "Run!"

If they had heard him, they gave no sign. They only stood and watched with wide eyes as the couple approached the dragons further. When Daeva and Roman reached the brave couple, they regarded them for a moment. Daeva's lips curled.

"I can't believe your father ruled — just to have you as his replacement." Daeva sighed.

Then, before Ben and Bella could react, Roman and Daeva raised their arms. Grey and black electrical sparks exited their fingers and shot Ben and Bella in the middle of their eyes. Roman and Daeva then moved their arms as if pushing the couple out of their way, sending the couple to the ground. Their bodies convulsed before becoming stiff. John didn't know if his friends were dead or just stunned but, right then, his main concern was the dragons. Now, nothing stood before the Scaasi couple and the beasts.

No way in Galdorwide was John going to let his brother and his sister-in-law bring on the end of the kingdom. He pushed himself onto his feet before staggering towards the couple. He struggled as he fought against the dizziness in his head and the pain in his body. The ground was littered with discarded wands and weapons; John knew that none of them would work on the Scaasi couple, not now when they had their defense in full force. Then again, he didn't want to kill them. He just wanted the dragons to disappear.

"Krum!" he shouted. "Your gun! While the dragons are frozen!"

Krum, who had been enjoying his quiet time, lifted his head and looked to his brother. After processing John's shouts, Krum reached into his pocket. The Scaasi couple didn't seem to notice the brothers scheming. Daeva pointed her wand at the closest dragon's belly.

"I thank you, you kind, kind beasts, for bringing chaos to this kingdom." Daeva tenderly spoke, as if she were talking to an old friend. "The death you bring — will give our lord the everlasting life he deserves. It is the king who will outlast us all, for he will become immortal — a god."

The Ministry shook their heads in terror as tears dripped from the corners of their eyes.

"Please, don't," Gabriel, who had followed them, whispered. For once in his life, he felt hopeless.

For a very brief moment, it looked as if Daeva had considered his kind and fearful request. However, she then said, "I must fulfill my destiny."

John quickly snuck up on Roman, punching him and knocking him to the ground as the two men got into a wrestling match. Gabriel grabbed hold of Daeva's arm and twisted it severely into a position where he almost broke it. With the couple rendered immobile, Krum was free to deal with the remaining dragons, all of which were frozen solid and easy kills for the pirate. "All this fighting, for the end to be this easy? What a waste of a worthy opponent." He laughed to himself as he slowly shot each of the remaining dragons. Each shot shattered the dragon into hundreds of icy-looking pieces.

"Looks like the end of time has been put on hold," Krum said slyly.

The girls in the Ministry had their weeping heads in their hands. Krum looked around and saw the bodies of men, women, and children who had died for the king to live life once more.

Frustrated, the Scassi couple vanished once no more dragons stood.

"Too bad we couldn't stop it sooner," Bella said through cries.

"Yeah," Krum said. "The real concern is — he did this all to gain the powers of those he sacrificed. He won't be just a harmless ghost any more."

CHAPTER 20

They looked around at all the dead bodies. Ian noticed that he recognized many, as some were his patients. John took note that almost eleven of them had been some of his graduate students. Teddy and Ben looked down at Mark. Their hearts ached for the man who thought he was helping. Bella joined them, realizing that she had seen him before all of the chaos. She remembered him walking into the café and assuming that he was just another freak. She felt terrible for making this assumption without getting to know him. He did try his best to help the Ministry and the kingdom fight against the king and his dragons.

Bella held a meeting where she would announce the deaths and allow those with missing persons in the family to view the bodies and identify any of the deceased. For those who identified the dead, Bella asked the family members to bring pictures of the deceased to the castle so that she could host a memorial and display the images.

Angel was sitting in the castle's kitchen, staring at all the images that had been turned in. She held back tears as one was just a young boy, with blond hair and big brown eyes. He reminded her of Thomas.

"The sleeping spell finally worked." Ben walked in holding a glass of dark ale. "Bella's asleep."

Angel's eyes stayed fixated on the picture of the young boy. Ben took note and placed his drink on the table beside her. Before he could speak, he was interrupted, as they heard tiny, fast footsteps pat down along the staircase and into the hallway and to the kitchen.

Thomas waddled in as he gripped a piece of paper tightly to his chest. He walked straight to Angel. "I want to sleep in my old bed."

Ben picked up his drink. "Tommy, what have you got there? Hmm?" Ben sat down on the kitchen chair beside Angel to be closer to Thomas's eye level. "What you got there? Let me see." Ben reached for Thomas's tiny arm that lay beneath his soft green pajama shirt. He pulled Thomas closer. "Can I see?" He took the paper out of the child's hands.

He looked at the paper and saw that it was an image taken from the table. It was a picture of Mark.

"Oh, ain't this a nice picture? Did you ever meet this man?" Ben asked the child with a smile.

Thomas took the picture back from the soon-to-be prince's hands. He shook his head. "I want to keep this picture and carry it around with me. I know how to bring him back."

"Tommy," Ben objected sternly. "Things don't work like that."

"I can — I swear it." A tear began to stream down the right side of the young boy's face. "I can bring them all back — then people won't be so sad. I can."

Ben sighed.

"All I need is this picture and a favorite object of theirs."

"Tommy." Angel finally spoke.

By her tone of voice, Thomas knew that she didn't believe him. He began to wail. He dropped the picture, ran out of the room, through the hallway and back upstairs. They could still hear his purposefully dramatic cries from the kitchen.

Ben looked to Angel. "Angel, look after your little boy. He's got a heart of gold. He's going to need you around this dark time."

The boy continued to cry loudly. Angel stared blankly. Not knowing what else to say, Ben stood up, leaving Angel alone to brood.

Angels sang. Their voices echoed throughout Galdorwide's memorial field. The priest had just finished prayers and was now allowing family members to say a few words. The guests stood in front of and on either side of the priest, extending to the field entrance.

The five Scaasi brothers stood along the left side of the priest. As much as they wanted to pay attention to the families' joy-filled stories about those who had passed, they couldn't focus, not after Lewis took note of a mysterious woman who stood in the front row across from the priest. She held a black umbrella and wore a black hat and glasses that hid her eyes. The woman also wore an elegant floor-length black dress. She was short in stature and had long, flowy red hair and pale skin.

Lewis had nudged John, who nudged Krum, who nudged Roman, who nudged Ace. They all thought the same. It couldn't be, because the woman she reminded them of looked as they had remembered. She

seemed to be in her upper thirties, around the age the woman she reminded them of had died. It couldn't be her; she would've been in her early seventies by now, but still — they couldn't take their eyes off her.

When the ceremony was over, and the people began to disperse, they remained standing, staring at the woman, who then approached them. They looked down at the tiny woman, who lifted her black-gloved hand to remove her glasses, revealing emerald green eyes. "Hello, boys."

"Mom?" the grown men asked the young woman.

CPSIA information can be obtained
at www.ICGtesting.com
Printed in the USA
LVHW101907160922
728572LV00004B/226

9 781800 742727